She's on First

Barbara Gregorich

This is a work of fiction. Any resemblance to actual people, places or events is purely coincidental.

This book was published in hardback in 1987 by Contemporary Books, Chicago, Illinois. It was published in paperback in 1988 by PaperJacks of Ontario, Canada, and New York, USA.

Cover photo by Laura Wulf
Cover design by Robin Koontz

Gregorich, Barbara
She's on First
Philbar Books

For Phil

Note to the Reader

This novel takes place during the 1970s. It is, with one difference, a reprint of the novel which I published in 1987. That difference is a small scene in Chapter 3. This scene was in my original manuscript, but my editor didn't want the scene in the novel, so in 1987 I removed it. I am now including it.

1   The Scout

Timothy Michael Curry, known to baseball statistics as T. M. Curry and to his old teammates as Curry Powder, or just plain Powder, sat on the barren bleachers and wiped the sweat off his neck. Curry muttered to himself, questioning the sanity of his presence in this little Pennsylvania town, watching a college baseball game that not even the college punks bothered to see. The team favored to win the college World Series played right here – here, in Pennsylvania, not in California, Arizona, Florida, or any of those other places that reeked of what was chic and trendy. It was probably in California, thought Curry, that baseball players began wearing gold chains around their neck, for chrissake. It wasn't being in Pennsylvania that made him question his sanity. No, he'd rather be here than on the West Coast. It wasn't watching a practically unattended college baseball game that made him question his sanity. He had watched, with pleasure, many a barely attended baseball game. No, what made him question his sanity was that he was here against his wishes, about to bring never-dying disgrace to the greatest game on earth, and it was all the fault of that goddamn Al Mowerinski. And it wasn't the first time that Al had put him in such a position, either.

The first time, though, he had had a choice. This time there was no choice. No, that was technically wrong, Curry realized, correcting his view in midthought much as he would have corrected a catch in midstride. There was a choice – if he didn't mind losing his job. This meant, to T. M. Curry's practical mind, that there was no choice. T. M. Curry was no dummy. Big Al was the owner and president of the Chicago Eagles, Curry only the scout.

The first time. He remembered it all too vividly, even though ten years had already passed. He and Big Al had been off the baseball field for five, maybe six, years. Al had plunged into business, but Curry knew only one life, and that was baseball. He had served the Eagles well as a player and in short time had become one of their scouts. Unlike many a scout, he didn't request a move to California. A scout out there could practically pick them off the avocado trees. But Curry preferred helping the players of his native Midwest, even though it meant he had to travel six or seven states to do it.

He had never been what you would call close with Big Al, not after Al's rookie year. But they had shared that easy camaraderie of men who had practiced and played and showered and shaved together, men who had gotten drunk together and fought together and thought they knew each other. So when Al had invited him to Pittsburgh that summer ten years ago, he had thought Al wanted to . . . well, let bygones be bygones. He had accepted. That summer – only now did Curry think of it as "the first time," never dreaming back then that there would ever be a second time.

So Curry had gone to visit Big Al, partly because they had played baseball together, and partly because he, Curry, had been curious. When their big league careers had ended, Al had returned to his native Pittsburgh with a vengeance. "You can stick around and be a scout for the rest of your life, Curry," he had said, "but Big Al has *big plans.*"

Big Al's big plans – going into the lawn mower business! – had looked like peanuts to T. M. Curry. And yet Curry had heard through the grapevine that the business had made Al a fortune. *Mower Down With Mowerinski.* Billboards sprouted all over Pittsburgh (hell, all over Chicago, too) like an early spring explosion of dandelions. Right up there on the billboards Big Al stood in a smooth, lush outfield, one hand on a Mowerinski Mower. Only a dumb Pollack would be lucky enough to make a fortune selling lawnmowers, especially with that stupid slogan. Why hadn't the big jerk gone into the sausage business like a good Pollack? Then maybe he wouldn't have made a mint and T. M. Curry wouldn't be sitting here, about to betray baseball.

Not even bothering to show him the business, Big Al had shown him around Pittsburgh. Then they had gathered some tackle, hopped into a car, and taken off for fishing country. Even now Curry remembered those two weeks of fishing. Beautiful. And they had topped it off by returning to Pittsburgh to watch a doubleheader.

And then, the day before Curry had been scheduled to fly back to Chicago, Big Al had asked, "Curry, do you know what Freedom looks like?"

"Red, white, and blue," he had replied.

"Not this Freedom. Come on, let's go."

"Where?"

"To Freedom. A perfect way to end the trip. One more baseball game – and a little scouting."

So Curry had leaned back in the car as Big Al drove them through the city. They passed the confluence of the Allegheny and Monongahela. The Ohio turned northwest and so did Al, naming the towns they sped through: Ambridge, Aliquippa, then Baden and Conway. *Fort Pitt, That's It,* declared a faded and forgotten billboard. Thirsty, Curry opened the cooler and pulled out the beer they had brought, opening one for Al, too.

On the Allegheny Plateau, they followed the river through the small towns that lay between the steel cities of Pittsburgh and Youngstown. The towns looked peaceful and undisturbed. Well, Curry had thought, it wasn't the most exciting way to end a vacation, but, what the hell, it was at least relaxing.

Big Al had stopped before the river turned west to flow to the Mississippi. "Here we are."

"Here? Here where? Where the hell we gonna see a ball game in this place, Al?"

Today, sitting on the bleachers watching the college game, Curry again wiped the sweat off his neck with a handkerchief. Scouts did not sit in the bleachers. They sat behind the screen, usually in small flocks, some of them with radar guns, all of them with notebooks. Curry sat in the bleachers because he did not want to be seen or noticed. Not for this job: no thank you. Frowning at the baseball action below, he folded the white cotton square neatly and put it into his sport coat, which was likewise folded neatly on the bleachers beside him. A tall, muscular man who had played third base by meeting the ball with his body and forcing it down, even now he carried no excess weight for his age. His once blondish-reddish hair, which, along with his temper, had earned him his nickname, was now graying. The temper wasn't.

His hair was cut somewhat shorter than was fashionable, but not so short that it was out of style. Curry consciously trod that thin line, priding himself on his ability to blend in. Besides, he thought, rubbing his hand lightly over his hair, the cut did him justice. He considered himself a handsome man and was not wrong in that judgment. As he stared at the reality of the game before his eyes, he thought back to Big Al's invitation of ten years ago. He, T. M. Curry, had been set up – set up then for what he had to do now.

They had seen a baseball game all right. Al had found a Little League game (or something like it), had driven up behind left center field and parked the car. The two of them left the car and leaned on the chest-high chain-link fence, the sun sparkling off the World Series rings they both wore.

A green chalk scoreboard had informed them that it was the bottom of the first and scoreless. Al passed a flask of Four Roses to Curry.

The team on the field had worn gray and green uniforms, tattered but recognizable. Freedom Fighters had been stitched across the front in cursive script. Offhandedly pointing a thumb at the center fielder's uniform, Big Al had asked, "Good name, huh?"

"Damn good."

The batter popped a fly ball to right field. Easy out. The first two pitches to the next batter hit the ground in front of the plate. Curry winced. Fans, probably parents and other assorted relatives, had filled two short bleachers along first and third. Half had applauded the bouncing ball. The other half had screamed at the pitcher, telling him he ought to be taken out. The next two pitches were strikes. Chatter filled the infield and drifted back to Curry and Al. "Atta boy, Jimmy." "Good work."

"Keep it up, Jimbo." "Easy out, Jimmy, easy out." "Swings like a rusty gate." "Won't even see it coming."

The batter connected. A hard grounder. A symphony of clanging cowbells and screeching whistles filled the air. Saved by the shortstop, out at first. "Nice play." Sipping from the flask, Curry gave the shortstop his due. Not so half the fans, who shouted at the umpire who made the call, threatening to end his life.

A strikeout retired the side. The other team took the field, their red and gray uniforms identifying them in block letters as the Warriors.

The Fighters at bat performed an exercise in basic math: three up and three down. In the bottom of the second inning, the first Warrior batter hit a home run. 1-0. The Fighter coach strolled out to talk to his pitcher. "Leave him in," somebody shouted. "Take him out, coach – your son's a bum!" somebody answered. "Send him to the Peewees!" Spitting tobacco juice behind the mound, the coach talked to his son. Then, empty of saliva and advice, he strolled back to the bench.

Curry observed that the next Warrior batter was the biggest of the bunch. An Al Mowerinski of the Little League, he must have been an old twelve, playing out his last summer, dwarfing the others, who looked like average ten-year-olds. The big kid took two balls and one strike, then smashed a line drive that caromed off the left field fence. The miniature Warrior giant made it to second base. Could have made it to third if he'd been a hustler, Curry informed Al.

Again the Fighter coach sauntered out to talk to his pitcher. Meanwhile, another pitcher began warming up outside the fence. The pitcher on the mound appeared nervous but struck out the next batter. The chatter in the field picked up again. One down, two to go. 1-0. One on base. The batter nipped the ball and it dribbled away from the plate, toward the pitcher. *"Fair ball!"* shouted the umpire. Flinging off his mask, the fledgling catcher ran awkwardly toward the ball. At the same time, the pitcher snapped to attention, running toward the ball and scooping it up.

"First!" shouted the shortstop. *"First base! First-first-first!"* The pitcher, his back to the field, turned and fired the ball to third. Too late. Now the Warriors had runners on first and third.

"Should have listened," said Curry, shaking his head at the circus of small-town kids' baseball. What amazed him was that every now and then a scout, tipped off by a network of bird dogs (men who acted as scouts for the scouts), actually found a good player in these places. Now these Warriors, Curry thought, had one good player, the big third baseman who had clouted the line drive. The kid modeled himself on the power hitters, though. That's what every kid wanted to be. Every big kid, too. Some of them could never be broken out of going for the big one. Like Big Al: he had always gone for the big one. So he had been a home run hitter. So what? So that's what the fans paid to see. That's what gave men like Al bigger salaries than men like Curry. The real *hitter*, the guy who choked the bat a little, didn't go for the long one, placed his hits – he was more important to the club, any club, than the 40-home-runs-a-season power hitter. Curry reflected with pride that National League statistics showed that he had a higher batting average than Big Al Mowerinski. And Curry hadn't been a show-off, either. Many was the time, Curry suspected, that Al had *deliberately* let two strikes go by, waving them aside as if they were nothing, hushing the booing crowd that was ready to kill the umpire, and then swatting the next pitch into the stands.

The crowds had loved it.

Swallowing more of the whiskey, Curry passed the flask to Al and appraised the Fighters. Two good players, the shortstop and the first baseman. Both quick on their feet, quick to think. Speed was the first thing a scout looked for. Speed couldn't be taught. You had it, or you didn't. Show me a good fielder, thought Curry, and I'll make him a good hitter. Show me a good fielder with speed, and I'll make him a great fielder. Could either of these two hit? He knew a lot of shortstops who couldn't. Too small, some would say, but that wasn't it. Anybody could hit, thought Curry, if he knew how. Or learned how. A small player could use his speed, his quickness. Of course this shortstop was tall and skinny, the tallest Fighter player on the field. Maybe they had him playing the wrong position. And the first baseman, he was average-sized, maybe smaller. Curry retrieved the flask from Al.

The infield shifted to the left for the next batter, who hit a high fly to left field. It was caught, but the runner on third tagged up and scored; the runner on first advanced. The fans screamed their pleasure or dismay, depending on which team they supported.

Two out, runner on second. 2-0. The coach took out the pitcher and put in another. The one who had been taken out hung his head. Not even coaches' sons could afford to lose.

"Play ball!" yelled the ump.

A strikeout quickly retired the side. The Warriors took the field for the top of the third, their spirits lifted by their 2-0 lead. The Fighters' first baseman stepped up to the plate, eyed a fast pitch, and drove it over the center-field fence for a clean home run. The Fighters cheered: 2-1 and no outs. The shortstop came up next. A low, fast pitch. Crack! Another home run, this one over the left-field fence. Curry made a grab for it, knowing even as he did that it was out of reach. Score tied.

He was enjoying himself. Yeah, it was sloppy, it was awkward, it lacked *finesse*. It was just a bunch of kids, for chrissake. But it had pizzazz. It was baseball – sport, where skill and chance met and one or the other won. Yeah, thought Curry, that was what he loved about baseball. There was skill, no denying that. Let some of those big football players see how hard it was to hit a little ball coming at you nearly a hundred miles an hour. With a rounded stick, that's all. Just you and the pitcher, face to face, each of you fighting to make a part of the plate your own. Baseball was the American game because it was equality, that's what it was. Curry swallowed more whiskey.

Now these other sports, they had no equality. You take football. Your average American couldn't be a football player. He wasn't big and beefy enough. Wasn't stupid enough, either, Curry thought. Then you take basketball. Today there was no equality in basketball. What chance did the average American have against seven-foot-tall black giants?

Those other sports – hockey, soccer – they weren't American. Let the commies play hockey and the hunkies and guineas play soccer. Baseball was *American*. It was a game of equality. So mused T. M. Curry as he sipped his Four Roses, offering Big Al his thoughts along with the whiskey.

The little guy and the big guy stood an equal chance in baseball. The big bruisers, like Big Al, were power hitters, getting all they could out of their brawn and muscle. Then there were the tough guys like himself. Curry reminded himself again that he had been a better (though less spectacular) hitter than Al. And there were the little guys. Yeah, they could hit, too. And what they lacked in power they made up for in quickness. They were all equal in the batter's box.

Flustered, the Warrior pitcher walked two in a row. His coach came out and patted him on the shoulder, trying to give him some confidence. The next batter struck out. One out. Two on base. 2-2. What they needed was a bunt, Curry informed Al.

A bunt is what they got. Out at first, but now the runners were on second and third. The next Fighter batter hit a ground ball toward the second baseman, who picked it up, fumbled it, then picked it up again and threw it hastily to first, his best bet. But the throw was high; the first baseman missed it and the runner continued to second. A run scored, making the score 3-2. The Fighter runner who could make it 4-2 threatened, but he retreated to third under the shouts of his coach.

The Freedom Fighters were now winning. Two on, second and third, two out. Out came the Warrior coach to talk to his pitcher. The infield huddled around him, soaking up his wisdom, shuffling under his anger. The next batter was the Fighters' second baseman, a shrimp of a boy whose uniform was so big that he had the pants' waistband rolled over and folded over his belt, which Curry surmised was under all that cloth somewhere. The shirt sleeves, short on the other players, came below his elbows. He looked to be eight, maybe, but he must have been ten. Curry watched. The shrimp caught a piece of the ball, popping it up high, from where it came down without effort into the first baseman's glove, retiring the side.

The sun beat down on the players in their old flannel uniforms. Curry looked at the outfielders nearest him, noticing the dark sweat marks on their uniforms, noticing their wet and clinging hair. They were tired and hot, their reflexes slowing rapidly. From now on it would be a matter of which side weakened less. Sometimes victory depended not on being better, but on surviving – holding in there until the other side tired. An unwillingness to accept defeat, that's what made winners.

Curry chattered as Al watched the game silently. In the bottom of the third, the Fighters' second pitcher was already tiring under the heat. He walked one batter, then another. Two on, no outs. The tobacco-chewing coach ambled out again, talking to this pitcher while a third was warming up outside the fence. The shortstop talked to the shrimp, who played second. The third baseman played close to the bag. The shortstop moved close to second, opening up a bigger hole than Curry thought was safe.

"Come on, Kevin." "Let's go, double play." "Make him hit it, Kev, come on, boy, atta way to go." Kevin pitched a fast ball. *Crack*! A low hopper, hard down the middle. A backhanded grab by the shortstop, who tagged the runner heading for third, pivoted, and fired the ball to second. The shrimp on the bag caught it and threw the ball as hard as he could to first. Out! *A triple play!*

Curry couldn't believe it. He guffawed, poking Big Al in the ribs. "Did you see that?" He was laughing so hard the tears came to his eyes. "My god, I can't believe it. A triple play!"

"For chrissake, not so loud, Curry," cautioned Al. "Don't make the other side feel worse than they do."

But Curry was beyond recall. The whiskey inside him played the event back to him better than instant replay could have. A triple play, a triple play. From short to second to first. A kids' game with a triple play. His laughter (or perhaps the whiskey) toppled him, sending him sliding down to the ground, his curled fingertips holding the chain-link fence. It was so wonderful, baseball, so beautiful.

Al lifted him off the ground, but not even Al could stop the laughter.

Curry brushed off Al's hand and staggered to his feet, holding on to the links. These dumb Pollacks were all alike, no glory in their souls. Oh, if only some of his Irish buddies had been here to see this! Wait till he told them; just wait.

Brushing the dried grass off his clothes and hanging himself over the fence for better support, Curry felt his mirth subside to chuckles. The witnessing of a triple play called for another drink, so he helped himself. The top of the fourth was over with before he stopped chuckling.

"Game warms up the scouting blood, doesn't it?" asked Al.

"I don't know about me blood," answered Curry in a thick brogue, "but me soul's nice and warm, if you know what I mean."

"Yeah, I'd say that first baseman would warm any scout's blood. Sure an' you'll be givin' the lad a lookin' over, professional like, you might say," Al brogued right back at him.

"Ah, sure an' it's not the first baseman I'm interested in, good as the laddie is. It's the shortstop I would talk to first."

"The shortstop!" exclaimed Al, his eyebrows up. "But the first baseman's a better player, don't you think?"

"Ah, Al, you stick to the lawn mowers and let me stick to the scouting," advised Curry, waving the flask around. Shaking it, he held it to his ear. It sounded empty. Curry peered in: not a drop left. Sure an' it was a shame.

"Oh, there's no denying the shortstop's good," admitted Al. "But between the two, wouldn't you say the first baseman is better? Not as big, but stronger and quicker."

"Stronger, maybe. Just as quick, no! Ain't you got eyes? Can't you see? The shortstop is quicker, quicker on his feet, quick to think. A thinker, that shortstop. More important, *heart,*" lectured Curry, waving his forefinger around and poking it in the place where he supposed Big Al's heart to be. "You just leave the scouting to old Curry Powder."

"You can't see heart."

"Ah, if I could, though, I'd be rolling in clover." He let out a sigh. "No, I have to try to see it. Have to guess. 'N I'm not a bad guesser either, don't let anybody fool you." Curry belched and straightened against the fence. Again he waggled his finger at Al. "Now this shortstop could be a big leaguer. Not *will* be, I'm saying. *Could be.* Might be if he wants to be, if he has a good coach, a good scout, the proper conditions. You stick to your lawn mowers and I'll stick to my scouting. I'll check out this kid after the game."

"You're the scout," Al relented with a shrug.

The Fighters were still ahead, 3-2. Al started to say something about the Fighter first baseman, but Curry waved away his comments. Ducking back into the car for a beer, he brought one out for Al, too. Ugh. Warm. He spit out the first mouthful, but then adjusted and sipped the rest slowly.

By the time Curry had finished two warm beers, it was the bottom of the sixth (the last inning in kids' play), and the score hadn't changed. The Fighters were still leading, 3-2. Just hold on now, thought Curry, who found himself rooting for the Fighters. Just hold on. Don't let the others score and you'll be home okay. You'll win – just hold on. The pitcher walked the first batter, bringing up the Warrior who had hit the home run. The Fighter coach yanked his pitcher and put in the one who had been warming up outside the fence. The new pitcher was wild, not soothed by the raw voices of the screaming fans. He threw two balls, then hit the batter with the third. No outs, two on base. Curry believed he knew how the Fighters felt. Tired. Too tired to score, knowing that your only chance is to keep the other side from scoring, but maybe too tired to do even that. "Come on, Freedom Fighters!" he urged loudly. The batter hit a sharp line drive to the first baseman, who caught it just in time. Nobody advanced. One out, two on. Last chance for the Warriors. Last chance for the Fighters, too.

Al elbowed him, nodding toward the first baseman, approving the play. Curry ignored him. Come on, shortstop, he rooted silently. It was tense, tight. He could practically see the pitcher sweating up there. Up came that big kid, that old twelve. The base runners had big leadoffs. The pitcher wasted some energy throwing the ball to first, then second, trying to pick them off. He just doesn't want to throw to the big one, thought Curry. He didn't blame the kid. He'd never want to be a relief pitcher, brought in at the last minute to stand or fall on half an inning of play, no sirree.

Finally the pitcher mustered up strength and threw to the big one. *Smack!* A hard hit, deep into center. Curry stifled a silly desire to leap over the fence and help the fielder. But the kid didn't need help. He caught it, grabbed it from his glove, and threw it hard to second. Not in time, though, to keep that runner from tagging up and reaching third. But in time to keep the one on first from reaching second. Should have thrown ahead of the runner. Should have had a cutoff man ready for the ball. Should have, should have. Curry felt the sweat on his palms as he gripped the top rail of the fence. Two out. Two on, third and first. "Come on, Fighters!" he cheered, waving his hand and sloshing beer onto the playing field.

The pitcher hurled the ball. Ball one. He got the ball back, wiped it off, looked around, and threw another pitch. Strike one. One-and-one the count. Come on, kid, come on. The pitcher stared at the winning run on first, then went through the motions and threw again. Ball two! Two-and-one the count. Again the pitcher caught the ball, wiped it off, and stared at the catcher. He threw. Ball three. It looked bad. Curry informed Al that it looked bad. Al nodded. It was the best way to win, coming from behind in the bottom of the ninth (sixth, in this case). The worst way to lose. Hold on, thought Curry, hold on. Ball four. Curry sighed. The runner on first advanced. Bases loaded, two out. Curry wanted another beer, but he didn't want to take his eyes off the game.

Up stepped the new batter. Wiped his hands in the dirt, on his pants, on the bat. Took his time getting into the batter's box. Hell of a situation to be in, Curry knew. This was it: he would score a run or lose the game. In came the pitch. A swing! A high fly to the infield! Who would get it? "Mine!" shouted the shrimp. "Mine!" He circled under the ball, shading his eyes for a second.

The ball fell on his head. His cap, already too large, fell over his eyes. Frantically he circled around, searching for the ball. The pitcher, shortstop, and first baseman ran for the white sphere. The Warrior runners, who had seemed breathlessly suspended on the bags, reminding Curry of the mobiles he used to hang above his children's cribs, now sprang to life and raced around the diamond. The runner on third made it home easily. 3-3. The runner on second raced for home full speed, head down, arms whipping at his sides. He had nothing to lose, all to gain. Trip, why don't you? thought Curry, already seeing the loss. Scooping up the ball, the shortstop hurled it to the catcher.

Too late.

The game was over, 4-3. The Warriors cheered wildly, clapping each other on the back, jumping up and down. Some Fighter fans booed the shrimp, who still stood where he had been circling the ball. Suddenly he started to cry. Curry was embarrassed. Baseball players, no matter how young, did not cry. The shortstop put his arms around the shrimp's shoulders, patted him on the back, and picked up the now discarded green cap. The first baseman, too, went to console the shrimp. Then came the catcher. The pitcher walked to the bench: he had problems of his own. The coach started to put away the bats, slamming them together. Then he, too, went out to the shrimp, put his arm around the kid's head, and guided him back to the bench.

Curry slammed a fist against the fence. He liked to win. Winning was what it was all about. His team – the team he had chosen to side with – had not won. Getting another beer from the car, he opened it, tasted it, then emptied it over the fence.

"Too bad," said Al, watching the Fighters.

Curry recovered. He had a job to do, didn't he? "Come on," he said, leading the way around the fence and toward the gate, where the players were stuffing their equipment – bats, balls, gloves, helmets, masks, kneepads – into a large bag. They reminded him of a group of ants, clearing the field of debris after a battle.

"You know, I think you're right about which one's the better player," said Al.

"Course I'm right." He wasn't a scout for nothing, no sirree. "Hey, there," he hailed convivially to the shortstop, who was just coming out of the gate with the first baseman and the shrimp. "That was a good game you played there. Too bad you had to lose. We were rooting for you all the way."

"Yeah," replied the kids in unison.

Curry hitched his thumbs through his belt loops and swayed back on his heels, surveying the three players. "You like baseball?" he asked for starters.

"*Yeah!*" The shortstop replied as if there couldn't be any other answer.

The first baseman shrugged. "Football is better. I'm gonna be a football player when I grow up. Lindy can't, though, 'cause girls can't play football."

Curry felt funny. He was sure the kid meant somebody else. Kids talked like that, as if you knew their brother, sister, best friend, dog, and cat. "Who's Lindy?" he asked, holding his breath.

"Me," said the shortstop.

"You're a girl?" asked Curry, already taking off the kid's hat and looking at her. Now he could see it. A girl. Goddamn it! Curry could see that and more. He could see Big Al grinning. Goddamn it again! T. M. Curry didn't like being played for a fool. The goddamn Pollack, *he had known it all along!*

"What's your name?" Al leaned over and asked her.

"Linda Sunshine." Then, as if responding to a parental reminder, "Sir."

"Well, you're very lucky, Linda Sunshine. This man is Timothy Michael Curry, and he's a baseball scout for the Chicago Eagles."

Curry watched as she looked up at him. *So?* her face seemed to say.

"Mr. Curry was telling me that he thought you were the best player he saw today. If he's a good scout, he's going to report that to the Chicago Eagles. He's going to keep an eye on you, Linda, and if you keep playing baseball someday he might sign you to play for the Chicago Eagles."

"Honest?" she asked, looking at Al, then back at Curry.

"Ah, girls can't play real baseball," said the first baseman. "You're just fooling." He laughed.

The shrimp laughed, too.

Curry saw the girl staring at him, waiting. Two eyebrows, straight and black, gave her small face an intense, solemn expression. The dark eyes stared at him without blinking, waiting.

Big Al poked him in the ribs. "Come on, Curry – didn't you say she was the best player on the field? The kid's waiting to hear what you have to say, Scout."

"Ah, yeah. Yeah." Suddenly he didn't feel so good. His stomach was very upset, and it was all because of Al. "Yeah. It's too bad," he muttered.

"Whaddya mean, too bad?" demanded Al.

Curry glowered at Al. He wanted to hit Al Mowerinski, topple him, make him look ridiculous. Instead, he took a breath through clenched teeth. He wasn't going to play games with this dumb, clever lawn mower salesman. "Too bad she's a girl. She'll never play hardball, and you know it as well as I do." Even as he said it, Curry felt strangely guilty letting her hear it. He turned to her, leaning down so that his face was almost on her level. Her nose wrinkled upward; she took a step back. "You don't want to play baseball when you grow up, do you? You want to be like all the other little girls, don't you? I have four little girls, and none of them wants to play baseball."

The wide dark eyes continued to stare at him. "Uh-uh," she answered. "I *do* want to play baseball!"

"But you're a *girl!*" exclaimed the first baseman. "Who

ever heard of a girl signing a contract!"

"That's no reason," she argued back, dragging the toe of her shoe across the dirt.

"Ah, sh–" Curry started to exclaim. Straightening, he waved a hand at the kids. "Forget it," he said, walking away.

Behind him, he heard Al. "Don't pay any attention to him. You keep playing baseball. Just keep playing the best you can, and someday you will be a baseball player."

Curry waited at the fence, by the car. "Ya know," he said to Al, "you've got a piss-poor sense of humor. That wasn't a bit funny. Not a bit."

"That had nothing to do with humor, Curry. Nothing."

Al was stone-cold sober. Jesus Christ, why couldn't he be drunk? Jesus Christ, a sober Pollack was worse than a drunk one!

Big Al stood between him and the car. "You call yourself a scout, do you? You call yourself a scout, then you can't even talk baseball to the best player in the field."

"You're fulla shit, you dumb Pollack! Talk baseball, my ass. I don't believe in wastin' my breath, like some people I know. Whaddya wanna lie to that kid for? What's the matter with you, anyway? Christ, it's bad enough she's on the *Little* League team!"

"I didn't lie to her, you thickheaded mi– jerk. I'm talking about baseball future. Why shouldn't she play if she's good enough?"

"She shouldn't because she can't. Not in the majors. She's a *female*, for chrissake." Curry looked hard at Al. "It's an old argument, Al. I thought you had forgotten it."

"I'll never forget, Curry."

"Dropped it, then: not forgotten." Curry held out an

unsteady hand to support his argument. "Women can't do it. They can't."

"Doesn't anything ever change you?" asked Al.

Curry ignored the question. "Naw, you aren't serious. You can't be. Just your idea of a joke. Well, I'm not in the mood for jokes now, Al. Come on, let's get back to the city. I drank too much." He started for the car.

Big Al blocked his way. "I told you before, Curry, I'm not joking. That kid is good enough for you to have a bird dog keep an eye on her. That's what you'd do if you had any balls." He spit out the last word, sneering at Curry.

"That's what I'd do if *she* had any balls." He should have let it go there and walked around Al to the car. But he couldn't let it go. "Even if they *could* play in the majors – which they can't – what would happen to the game, huh? We'd have pantyhose and lipstick in the locker room. We don't need twats in baseball, Al."

Big Al's fist (it must have been a fist, though it felt like a hundred-mile-an-hour fastball) slammed into his jaw. As Curry's knees gave under him, he felt himself propelled backward before he hit the ground.

Staggering to his feet, fists clenched, Curry was about to hurl himself at Al. But in an instant, his brain, reeling as it was, took over and informed him that Big Al had five inches and forty pounds on him, all of it housed on a frame that would have done justice to the Merchandise Mart.

"Come on, you bastard, come on," Al coaxed, his arms held out at his sides in clear contempt.

Oh, yeah, he wanted to. But he couldn't take on Al after drinking in the sun all afternoon. Nobody in the big leagues had ever beaten Big Al anyway. The reverse, however, was not true: there were plenty who had been beaten by Big Al. He, Timothy Michael Curry, wasn't going to be one of them.

"Naw." Curry waved his hand as if to say that this was beneath him. "I don't want to fight you, Al. You're welcome to your ideas." He walked around Al and opened the car door. "Me and the rest of the world, we're wrong and you're right."

Al snorted, dismissing the sarcasm. Before Curry had even collapsed into the front seat, Al was at the wheel. Turning the key with a grip that nearly snapped it in two, he started the car in a fury, pulling away with a squeal of wheels, huge tire tread marks testifying to his anger. It was not a silent anger. All the way back to Pittsburgh Curry had to put up with righteous lecturing. He had to listen to Al bellow at him about equality, democracy, and fair chance – and even worse crap about women and discrimination. Curry kept telling him to shove it and shut up, but that didn't stop Al from bellowing louder.

He took his suitcase from Al's and left without a word. It would be a cold day in hell before he saw that bastard again. One side of his face was swollen and getting worse. He'd have to call in sick a couple of days when he got back to Chicago, until the swelling went down. Goddamn Pollack. Goddamn lawn mower salesman. He'd fix him, but good. Wait till he spread the word, in a casual sort of way, that Al Mowerinski wanted broads in baseball – right there in the big leagues.

Ten years ago he hadn't known that Al Mowerinski was going to make enough dough to actually *buy* the Eagles – buy a major league *baseball team,* mind you. Had he known, he might have become a scout for some other team. But Al had bought the Eagles just two years ago, and by that time it was too late to change. Curry pondered his situation, realizing that the truth was that he had chosen not to leave. Once an Eagle, always an Eagle. Which is why he was here today, at this dumpy Pennsylvania college, watching this goddamn baseball game. Which is why he was about to do something truly terrible.

Although T. M. Curry was not one to forget an injury, he had been polite to Al and had gone about his business. Al would find nothing to complain about, not the way Curry was doing his job. Wasn't he one of the best scouts in the business? Okay, then, just let him go about his business.

And he had, without any problems. Al had even promised (and delivered) big bonuses. There had been $15,000 the first year for that pitcher, Merle Isemonger. Lenny Black, the manager, had been beside himself with joy; you couldn't shut him up about the kid. There had been $10,000 the next season for that Mexican kid. He was in the minors now but looked like a sure thing.

This season, though – this season was the catch. This was what Al had been leading up to. Curry knew it. He knew it, but he still couldn't accept it.

Last week Al had called him into the office.

"I've got some scouting for you in Pennsylvania," Al had said, skipping preliminaries. "The Liberty Bells."

Curry had settled into a chair, thinking the whole time. Pennsylvania. Liberty Bells. What was it about them that caused the fluttering in his chest?

"They're going to the college World Series," said Al, watching him. "Take my word for it."

"Who've they got?" asked Curry, unable to associate the school with any top player.

Al had stared at him for a moment. "I want you there the

end of this week and all of next," he replied, ignoring Curry's question. "Take a look at the shortstop. I want a full report on her."

Even when the word was said, Curry couldn't believe it. It was from the past, a joke. It couldn't be for real. *"Her?"* His mouth was dry as he finally understood the reason for the fluttering feeling: the Liberty Bells played with a girl on the team.

"Yes, her. I'm glad your hearing's still accurate."

Curry stood up and stared at Al. Turning, he walked to the water cooler and, with fingers shaking, got himself a cup of water. "You want me to go to a college game and tell you how a *female shortstop* plays? C'mon, Al. What good will that do?" He tried to sound nonchalant but was sure he hadn't succeeded.

"I'm not going to argue with you, Curry. Your job is to scout the players. I'm telling you to check this one out and give me a full report. And I don't want a word of this to get out to *anybody*. Understand?"

"Oh, I understand that. I understand why you don't want a word of it to get out." Curry moved back to the chair. "Only thing is, why do you want to do it at all, Al? That's what I don't understand. Why do you want to waste my time and your money for a joke?"

Big Al's hands, resting on the desktop, twitched. "I told you once before it isn't a joke. You're going out there for one reason only – to fill out a scouting report on the shortstop. I'll take care of the rest." Then he added, "Based on your report, of course."

"You want to sign a woman to play in the big leagues? She'll never make it to the minors. You're out of your mind."

Al, out of his mind or not, appeared unperturbed. "You're

behind the times. I want more people at the gate, understand? She'll be a big draw."

Curry took a deep breath, not believing Al's reasons for a minute. It was the past Al was interested in, not the future. "Then have another scout do it, Al. Don't do this to me. I can't do it. Hell, I *won't* do it! Think of what it would do to the team, for chrissake. Nobody's going to play with a broad on the team."

"Watch it," Al warned, pointing a hairy finger at him.

If Al was serious, he was crazy. Crazy. Curry didn't want to be anywhere around when the shit hit the fan.

"You're the one who's going," Al ordered, biting off the end of a cigar. He put it in his mouth and puffed away, trying to get it lit. "Tell me how she plays. Got that? *How she plays,* not the color of her eyes, the length of her hair, or the fact that she's a woman. Just give me the facts."

"Um-hmm. Suppose I tell you she's a two on a scale of eight? Dead bat, swiss cheese for a glove, and afraid of her own shadow – what're you gonna do then, fire me?"

Al waved his hand. "Just fill out the fucking report."

Curry rose from his chair, slammed a fist into his hand, and paced the office. Okay. Okay, he'd go. He'd fill out the fucking report. He had gotten to the door when it hit him, propelling him in an arc, a semicircle that took him straight back to Big Al's desk. "Wait! Just a minute. Just wait a minute." He leaned over the desk, his face inches from Al's.

"You're going to draft her. You're going to draft her no matter what I say. *And then you're going to say I was the one who recommended her!*" Rage overwhelmed him; his hand clenched the desk, the weight of his body pressing on it. "I'll be the laughingstock of the game! I won't have a friend left! My name will be *shit*! Nothing doing, Al – nothing doing!" Curry walked toward the door. "Get yourself another scout."

He was in the doorway when Al's voice caught him. Just three words: "Ten thousand dollars."

T. M. Curry stopped. "What?"

"Ten thousand dollars. That'll be your raise."

"You're serious," whispered Curry in awe. Closing the door, he walked back to the desk and stared at Al. He licked his lips to wet them, so that he could speak. "Ten thousand? A raise of ten thousand dollars?"

Al, his cigar lit by now, puffed and nodded his head.

Shit, thought Curry. A puff and a nod were no answer at all. "What do I have to do – give her an eight on the scale?" he asked contemptuously.

"You give her what you think she deserves on the scale, Curry. You go there, you watch, and you fill out the fucking report."

"Why?"

"Because I want something to draw the crowds. I explained that already."

Curry shook his head, negating the explanation. "I mean why ten thousand? Why ten thousand when you could get somebody else to do it for nothing, just for his job? Pennsylvania's not even my territory, Al. Why me? Why the money?"

Blowing a puff of smoke into the air, Al followed its drift and dissipation. Then he looked at Curry. "Let's say it's for . . . old time's sake."

Curry swallowed hard, looking away, his mouth dry again. He thought hard, ignoring Al's remark. He could scout her and still disagree with the whole idea. He was just following orders, that's all. She probably wasn't good enough, anyway. Maybe they'd have to lower the scale to rate her. Maybe she wouldn't sign. Maybe somebody else would draft her. All Al was telling him was to go there and look her over. Again Curry crossed over to the fountain of bottled water that stood against one wall. The water was ice-cold. Crushing the pointed paper cup, he tossed it into the basket. "Yeah. Okay. I'll go there and fill out the fucking report, for chrissake."

T. M. Curry was no dummy. He knew who she would be. The mimeographed roster merely confirmed what he had known: SS – Sunshine, Linda. Sitting on the barren bleachers, he watched the Liberty Bells take another game from still another opponent. Liberty Bells. Dingdong Bells is what they were, playing with a woman on the team. Not just on the team, but at short! Curry shook his head, transferring his anger to the players, blaming them for playing something less than baseball. There weren't nine men out there. There were eight men and a woman. Whatever they were playing, it wasn't the same game he had played. His had been played by men.

He had followed his orders and followed the baseball team. Four away games, four home. The coach had recognized him, so he had told the coach that he was just here on vacation, visiting old friends, and thought he would look the team over for a few days. Relaxation only, no business. Sure, it wasn't business at all for a scout to look at a championship baseball team. The coach had just grinned. Eventually, Curry asked, casually, how and why a woman was on the team.

"Pressure. The school."

"Too bad."

"No," answered the coach. "Not really. Oh, I was against it at first. Completely. Said I'd quit if they forced me to put her on the team."

"Yeah? What happened?"

The coach shrugged. "They made me put her on the team, I didn't quit. It was too late in the season then to get another job. I guess the college was more or less forced to do it, you know? Somebody in the administration said alumni donations depended on it – on equality, they said."

"How long ago was that?"

"Four years. This is her fourth season. Made it on as a freshman. Hey, listen, I've got no complaints about her. She's a good player, good as they come. One of the best I've ever coached, I'd have to say. Never missed a practice. No grumbling, no wisecracks. A steady, serious player."

Curry sat there watching her. Whenever the team took the field, he could always spot her. It wasn't the long braid her hair was in, even. Braids on a baseball team, for chrissake! It was the ass. That's what he looked for. Why did she have to look so goddamn good in uniform? He wondered what the other players thought. Especially the left fielder. What a view *he* had.

Curry watched her. She was leaning forward, balanced on her toes, following the pitch. He had seen enough, to tell the truth. One game had been enough. He stayed all eight, hoping for mistakes, an injury, something. Nothing. She did nothing that he could use against her. All a ball player had to be able to do was hit the ball, throw the ball, field the ball, and run. That's all. Curry snorted at the thought of how few could do those four things well. Linda Sunshine could do them well. If she'd had balls, he'd have given her a seven. If he'd had balls, he'd have given her a two. On his scouting report he gave her a five, which was considered average major league quality.

Big Al was the last person he wanted to talk to, so he sent him a telegram. Like the old days. GOOD FIELD. GOOD HIT. SHE'LL NEVER MAKE IT.

Al telephoned to tell Curry that telegrams were behind the times. Al also told him to bring her to Chicago for a talk.

Curry would carry out his orders, but he would not be responsible for what happened to her. Or to Al, for that matter. It would be a disaster. She'd never make it, and Al wouldn't have a decent player left on the Eagles. Nobody would play for him. Nobody.

2   On Deck

Sprinting up the rooming house steps two at a time in her baseball spikes, Linda opened the door to her room, slammed it shut behind her, and without interrupting her momentum jumped upward, touching the ceiling with the palm of her right hand. She wanted to scream her joy and disbelief to somebody. She grabbed the telephone and dialed home to tell her parents about Timothy Michael Curry and her flight to Chicago. Fleetingly, she remembered that it was almost finals week; she shouldn't have clattered up the stairs while others might be studying.

All guilty feelings were lost when her mother answered the phone: Linda blurted out the news, her words tumbling out in excitement. It wasn't until she found herself repeating, "Isn't it wonderful?" for the fourth or fifth time that she realized her mother was listening in uncharacteristic silence.

"Hey, Mom?"

"What?"

"Don't you think this is fantastic news?! Don't you think Al Mowerinksi might want me to play baseball, huh? Don't you think that's why he's asking me there?" Linda twirled on one foot as she spoke, wrapping the telephone cord around herself in her excitement.

There was a pause on the other end of the line. "I don't know," replied her mother. "Maybe he wants to see you for some other reason."

"Oh, *Mom*, he doesn't! He doesn't want to talk to me about history or literature or even the Liberty Bells. He wants to talk to me about baseball," she asserted euphorically.

"Don't be disappointed if he doesn't sign you, Lindy. The chances are he won't, you know."

Linda felt a slight stab of disappointment. Her mother was probably right: no owner was going to sign a woman to play baseball. But she didn't want to believe that. "Maybe he will, though. Wouldn't that be wonderful?!!"

"It won't be like college."

What kind of answer was that? She had no time to think about it. She said goodbye, replaced the receiver, and untangled the cord, wondering why her mother didn't seem excited.

Wow! The Chicago Eagles! She jumped again, slapping a palm against the ceiling, landed with her feet apart, pivoted, and pantomimed a throw to first. Then she glanced at the clock on her desk: she would have to hurry to make tonight's flight from Pittsburgh.

Unlacing her spikes, she tied them together and tossed them over her desk chair, then kicked the chair closer to the open window. Reminding herself to close the window before she left, she hurried into the bathroom, stripped off her soggy, sticky uniform, and threw it into the laundry bag. Unbraiding her hair, she shook it loose, stepped into the cold tub, adjusted the water to warm, put in the plug, and lay back, her head and back pressed against the cool of the tub, her long legs crossed and resting against the wall at a comfortable angle just above the faucet. The mixture of cool and warm felt good, and she stretched and arched against it. The water, which had already started to wet her hair, reached the back of her neck, tickling her. Tilting her head back, she moved it sideways in the water. Sliding up a few inches, she rested her head on the tub's inclined back, moving her feet lower down on the wall. Moving her left foot to the hot water faucet, she grasped it with her toes and increased the hot water a fraction. Her foot tested the temperature, found it satisfactory, and went back to the wall. She sighed. No bath felt as good as a bath after a game. A shower would have felt even better, but she had no shower in the rooming house. Or, for that matter, in the baseball locker room: she'd have had to shower in the women's facilities, three buildings away from the field.

She waited until the water covered her waist and shoulders, then the bodies of water on her left and right met between her breasts. Holding up an arm, she examined it from fingertip to shoulder, lightly flexing a muscle. Sometimes she wondered if she would be playing baseball if her anatomy were different. What if she had short arms and legs, for example? Could she make the throw to first? Tipping her head back into the water, she believed she could, under any conditions. She could play baseball no matter what the circumstances.

Linda had always had a feeling that if the sex barrier in baseball – the major league sex barrier, not the school sex barrier – was going to be broken, she would be the one to break it. She had told that to her father once, after she had made the college baseball team. "Isn't that a bit conceited?" he had asked jokingly. "No!" she had protested half indignantly, half laughingly. "It's not conceited, Dad, because there *are* no other women college baseball players. We've played other teams across the country, practically, and I haven't seen another woman." Her father, suddenly serious, had nodded his head. "So it's you or nobody."

Let it be me, not nobody. After today's game, the scout had called to her, introducing himself as Timothy Michael Curry. She had offered her hand and, after a brief hesitation, he had shaken it. Then he had told her he was a scout for the Chicago Eagles. Immediately Linda had straightened and almost stopped breathing. In her four years of college playing, not a single major league scout had ever introduced himself to her. Timothy Michael Curry had made small talk until everybody else was off the field, then he had asked her to come to Chicago to meet the owner of the Eagles. That was when the thought flashed through her head – was it all a joke, a cruel joke? But as quickly as the thought came, she had dismissed it. And what had made her dismiss it was that this scout didn't *like* what he was doing. Somehow, she had always felt that if it happened, that's how it would be – the people who asked her to play wouldn't really want her to play. And then, quite seriously, Timothy Michael Curry had told her to mention this to nobody.

Linda sat up suddenly in the tub. She had told her mother – and her mother would of course tell her father, and they would tell her younger brother and sister. Frowning briefly, Linda slid back into the water. She had to assume that family was exempt from the instruction to tell nobody.

Why had her mother reacted that way? No sound of joy, of surprise, no sense of . . . no indication that this was a good thing. If, unbelievably, Linda would actually play baseball in the major leagues . . . if that actually happened, she owed it to her mother more than to anybody else. Linda couldn't remember back to the first time she had picked up a baseball bat. For all other sports she had vivid memories of her introduction to the rules of the game – basketball sure, track especially, volleyball, swimming, field hockey. But not baseball. Maybe, in the jargon of sports writers, she was born with a bat in her hand and the smell of glove leather in her nostrils.

One spring weekend, when Linda had been eight years old, she had asked: "Mom, why can't I play baseball on the Freedom Fighters, just like everybody else?" Her mother had started to reply, had stopped and stared at her, and then had said, "No reason at all. There's no reason at all why you can't play baseball if you want to." Then she had picked up the phone and called the head of the local Little League. It took all spring and half the summer, but her mother forced the Freedom Fighters to allow Linda to try out for the team.

Whatever athletic ability she had, Linda believed came from her family. She recognized the irony in this since she, her younger brother, and her even younger sister were all adopted. And yet they all excelled in sports. So it was not entirely biological, her ability, but a result of nurturing – nurturing by her mother especially, who had always encouraged Linda to participate in organized sports. *Particularly* baseball. After Linda started playing in the Little League, her mother told her long ago she had been a fan of the AAGBL, the All-American Girls Baseball League. Women once played professional baseball, her mother told her. Linda listened, thought about it, and presumed to correct her mother. "You mean softball, Mom." Her mother snapped back, "No, I mean baseball." Wolfing down cookies and milk, Linda had argued, "But I never heard of 'em, Mom. Did they play with Stan Musial or

Frank Robinson? Or Mickey Mantle? They didn't play with Hank Aaron or Ted Williams, I know they didn't. I never heard of 'em." Her mother sighed. "They didn't play with men, Lindy – they had their own baseball league." Linda scoffed, "Then it wasn't baseball, Mom. If they didn't play with baseball players, they didn't play baseball."

"Ouch!" Linda had dug the shampoo brush too deeply into her scalp. She was taking too much time thinking, anyway. Hurriedly, she finished scrubbing her scalp. The water had drained out of the tub. Sliding up to the faucet, she crossed her legs Indian style. Under the heavy gush of water she rinsed her hair. Stepping out of the tub, she dried her hair with a towel, then wrapped another towel around it while she packed some clothes quickly. In thirty more minutes she was dressed, wet hair braided tightly, suitcase in hand.

Balancing her suitcase on the top of her head, Linda walked quietly down the stairs, remembering the time when her mother was probably sorry that Linda loved baseball. It was because of Linda's high school coach, who had wanted her to train in track for possible Olympic competition. At the age of thirteen she had reached a height of five-nine. Full of energy, she could run for hours. And she loved running. Almost as much as she loved baseball. At first Linda had been excited about track. But then the coach had explained what Olympic training meant. It meant giving up baseball. And so she said no.

The coach tried to change her mind for weeks afterwards, talking about gold medals and serving her country, about fame, visiting Europe, Mexico, Japan. Nothing swayed Linda.

One day the coach must have called her mother, for when Linda came home from school, her mother sat her down at the kitchen table to talk about life. "Mom! I've been menstruating for two years! I know all about it!" she had replied in typical teenaged embarrassment. But that wasn't what her mother meant by life. Her mother talked about opportunity and making the best choice and Linda's chances of excelling in running. Linda listened, hearing what her mother wasn't saying. Her mother wasn't saying that girls could never play professional baseball. Linda recognized even then that her mother would never say that outright. It would be a betrayal of something. Linda listened, then answered that she would not give up baseball.

Her father tried talking to her next. Same results.

"What is it that's so different about baseball?" he had demanded.

Linda had shrugged. "I don't know. It feels good. I like the running. I like the hitting. I like the fielding. I like them all together, Dad. They aren't together like that in anything else."

Although she made the track team in both high school and college, she didn't train for the Olympics. Her coaches didn't take her seriously as a runner because she wouldn't give up everything else for running. She made the baseball team in both high school and college. But baseball was not an Olympic sport. So Linda had dreamed about the majors. And now, today, the Eagle scout showed up.

"You can have a drink for all I care," said Timothy Michael Curry, motioning to the stewardess.

"No thanks," answered Linda, wondering whether this was a test. She watched as he ordered scotch, opened the little bottle with a twist, and poured it into his plastic tumbler.

"This is probably illegal," he said after a large swallow of the scotch.

Linda, sitting in her seat at an angle so that she could see and talk to Timothy Michael Curry, was uncomfortable – not physically, but psychologically. Since take-off, the scout had talked and talked – but always to a point straight in front of him, not once turning to look at her. "You mean they can't sell it on the plane?" she asked.

Swiftly, he glanced at her. She recognized the look as one of exasperation.

"What's illegal," he said, still looking at her, "is talking to you. You can't talk to a ballplayer before –" He stared at her, then trained his eyes toward the front of the plane again. "There's a rule against women playing professional baseball."

"Actually, that's not true," she blurted out.

Her reward was a slow, slow turning of Curry's head toward her and a boring of his eyes into her own. "What did you say?" he demanded.

She cleared her throat. "It's not true that there's a rule against women playing professional baseball. The –" She stopped as the scout held up his hand just inches from her face.

"The equal opportunity law – amendment, rule, guide, title, whatever the fuck it is – excuse my language – does not apply to major league baseball. It's fucking up high school and college sports, but it does *not* apply to professional sports." He swallowed the rest of the scotch and angrily ordered two more.

Linda realized that he was referring to Title 9, the recent public law that prohibited sex discrimination in any institution of higher learning receiving federal financial assistance. "I don't mean Title 9!" Indignantly, she moved in the confines of the airline seat. She was getting angry. "Listen, I'm not playing baseball because some law made them take me on the team. I'm playing baseball because I *want* to, and because I'm good enough to make the team, that's why."

Curry, his tumbler halfway to his mouth, jerked forward, sloshing scotch over the pull-down tray and over his pants. "Jesus!" He wiped his pants with a napkin, then pulled at the crease.

"There's no rule against women playing in the major leagues. The 1952 ruling only forbids women from playing in the *minor* leagues."

"Who told you that?" he demanded. "You weren't even *born* in 1952!"

"My mother told me."

Curry twisted the cap off another little bottle of scotch, dropped the cap on the tray, and poured the scotch down his throat. "You can tell your mother that the rule will apply to the majors, too, if I have anything to say about it. It'll apply *especially* to the Eagles."

"If you're so much against me, why are you sitting here with me?" she demanded angrily.

Linda could tell by the way the question seemed to startle him that he knew what she meant – and that he didn't like her asking the question. He stared straight ahead and after several seconds she thought he was simply going to ignore her. But then he turned and looked at her. "I'm paying for me sins," he said in a brogue.

Turning away from her, he pulled a newspaper out of his briefcase and began to open it.

Linda, feeling dismissed and confused, twisted in her seat so that she faced away from Timothy Michael Curry.

When she looked his way again, he was reading the front section of his newspaper. She was so angry she didn't want to speak to him. But she realized that if she wanted to play baseball she had to deal with him – with him and hundreds like him. Clearing her throat, she asked for the sports section. With a heavy sigh, he separated it from the rest of the paper and handed it to her.

Okay, she told herself, forget this scout for the time being and read about baseball. She opened the sports section. The first thing that caught her eye was the headline, "Eagles Need Heart" The byline read "Neal Vanderlin." The photo that ran with the column pictured a man who could have written for the college paper: he looked young, confident, healthy. Gentle, though: not arrogant. Neal Vanderlin: had she heard of him before? No matter, she'd better pay attention to what he had to say about the Eagles.

As Linda read, the antagonism with Curry left her. Vanderlin was talking baseball, and talking it good. The new Chicago Eagles under Al Mowerinski were, he said, a body that wasn't completely built yet. *Great – Al Mowerinkski's building a team!* Wally Szczpanozowski, the team's center fielder and slugger, was swinging wildly at any ball that looked round and white. Since all balls coming into the plate looked round and white, Zowski was doing a lot of swinging and hitting a lot of air. *Oh-oh. Was Zowski really that bad? Or did Vanderlin have a grudge against the Eagles?* Vanderlin complimented Harland Abilene, the young catcher just up from the minors, who showed he could take the pain, blocking dirt curves with his body. *Good.* It's too bad, Vanderlin pointed out, that the Eagles had so many pitchers who threw curves in the dirt. *Ouch!* Lacey Griffin, the third baseman, would be one of the all-time greats, as would Frank Laughing, the second baseman. *All right – a strong infield.* But Zack Weiss, the aging utility man who played shortstop for the Eagles, was not the person to cover the hole – he had already waved goodbye to an entire family reunion of Spaldings as they sped by him on their way to left field. *Jesus! What was with this Vanderlin?* Merle Isemonger, he wrote, was a big, strong pitcher who threw mighty hard. Once he could think mighty hard, he'd be what the Eagles needed to win. In short, concluded Vanderlin, the Eagles had a lot of body parts, but were missing a heart and a head.

Linda sat up. She looked at the photo of Vanderlin again. Had she thought he looked college? Had she thought he looked gentle? The photo lied. Either Vanderlin was waging a vendetta against every player on the Eagles, or, she supposed, this was the price you paid for playing in the majors. Making the majors meant more than batting, fielding, and base running: it meant becoming the butt of sportswriters. It meant having every error you made magnified and teletyped across the country.

Linda read the column twice, then stared out the window, thinking. She stole a glance at Timothy Michael Curry, who continued to ignore her. What was the sense of worrying about errors and sportswriters? The worry was just part of the wishful thinking: chances were that Al Mowerinski wouldn't sign her. Who was she kidding but herself, believing she could be a major leaguer?

In Eagle Stadium in the city of the Big Shoulders – Sandburg's tall, bold slugger set vivid against the little soft cities – a secretary, a black-haired, black-eyed symbol of efficiency, turned a knob and silently slipped through the temporary opening of an oak door, telling Ms. Sunshine that she would notify Mr. Mowerinski of her presence. Linda remained standing, gazing at the framed photographs hanging on the wall, photographs of the Chicago Eagles from the past – the 1940s and '50s, she judged.

Silently the secretary reappeared, announcing, "Mr. Mowerinski will see you now," then standing aside. The narrow band through which the secretary had gone and come now loomed open before Linda, wider than the hole between short and third. Her palms were moist and her throat was dry as she walked through the doorway and into the office.

Behind the desk was a big man. A very big man. Momentarily, Linda stood still in awe. The stories about Big Al Mowerinski had failed to convey the enormity of the legend. He stood up as she approached, extending his hand to her across the desk. In its grasp, she felt as if she were a child of four again, holding on to her father's hand, her entire hand wrapped around one of his fingers. She realized that even her thumb was lost inside the warm hand of Al Mowerinski. Under the conditions, she couldn't even give a proper handshake. Now he would think she couldn't play baseball. For what seemed like a long time, they stared at one another. Linda felt out of her element, a sandlot player in the presence of a professional. Why he was silent she didn't know. Maybe he was already regretting having spent the airfare.

"Sit down, Linda, sit down." His voice was deep, not unpleasant. "You don't mind if I call you Linda?"

"No. Sir." He must have called the others by their first names.

"Good." He appraised her. "You wonder why you're here, right?"

She nodded.

He stared at her intently, holding her dark eyes with his

equally dark ones. "Why do you think you're here?"

She blinked, then clasped her hands together and clamped them between her knees. "Well, uh . . . I hope I'm here because you want me to play baseball for you."

He nodded, studying her. "If I told you that I wanted you to play baseball for the Eagles, to be the first woman baseball player in the big leagues, what would you do?"

"I'd do my best," she answered without hesitation. "I'd do the best I can. I could do it, I know I could."

Ignoring her enthusiasm, he asked, "What do you know about the Eagles?"

That was easy. She told him they were in fourth place now, had finished fourth last year and the year before that. They had some great looking new players – Harland Abilene, for example. Lacey Griffin was probably the best third baseman in the National League, and Frank Laughing the best second baseman. She stopped short of telling him the Eagles needed a shortstop. Al Mowerinski knew that far better than she did.

"The Eagles haven't won a pennant in fifteen years," he said when she had finished. "What they need is to believe in themselves."

"Yes, sir."

"Call me Al."

"Okay."

He smiled at her. "Okay. Okay, who?"

"Okay . . . Al."

He nodded in approval. "What kind of reception do you think you'd get?" he asked.

"What do you mean?"

He studied her. "I mean what kind of response do you think you'll get from the other players – the manager, the coaches, the fans?"

Her heart was racing so fast she thought she couldn't breathe. He was actually discussing it with her, discussing it as if . . . as if it would happen. She clasped her hands together: the palms were sweaty. What had he asked? Response. What kind of response did she think she would get. Pulling her lower lip in, working her teeth against it, she thought about how to answer. "Well," she started off slowly, "I guess I'd have a lot of problems. Like Jackie Robinson did." She glanced at him quickly, hoping it didn't sound conceited. She considered it further. "More than he did."

Al Mowerinski nodded. "Are you prepared for it?"

"Yes! No! I mean, I am if I have to be." She wanted to play baseball, not be prepared to tolerate bigots.

His voice increased in volume, as if he weren't satisfied with her reply. "Are you prepared for hatred from your teammates, bad calls from the umps, and catcalls from the fans? Are you ready to be spiked in plays at second base, hit by the pitcher, and ignored by the manager?" Rising from his chair, he walked around his desk toward her. "What'll you do when the press is against you, when the players on your own team saw your bat in half, put your uniform down the crapper, and make life miserable for you? Do you *really* want to play baseball?" he demanded.

"Yes! I do! I will. I'll play baseball," she answered. "I'm playing with men now."

"You're playing in *college*," he replied, as if correcting her. "In the majors, they'll say you can't play. They'll say you hurt the team."

"I *won't* hurt the team," she protested. "I'll be the best baseball player I can be. I'm as good as any other player you can draft out of college. Maybe I'll make it, maybe not. But I want to try." That wasn't quite right. Linda swallowed hard. "I can cover short, I know I can."

His eyes hadn't left her since she had walked into the room. She was not used to being stared at so hard. She fidgeted under the intensity of his gaze, unable to decipher it. Did he think she could do it? Would he sign her up? She watched him walk back to his desk, sit down, and light up a cigar. Still watching her.

Puffs of smoke rolled out of his mouth. "What if," he asked, puffing, "what if I told you the same thing Branch Rickey told Robinson the first year?"

Linda nodded, gazing at the little balls of smoke, as elusive and ephemeral as screwballs. "Lay back, you mean?"

Something like a smile touched the corners of his mouth. "Lay back," he repeated. "What if I told you that no matter what they did to you, I wanted you to lay back?"

She scratched her head, realized it was a nervous habit, stopped, clamped her hands between her knees again, and bit her lower lip while she considered the situation. "I think that would be the wrong advice."

The lifting of his eyebrows called for her to explain. She rubbed her moist palms together. "Rickey's advice was wrong. He told Jackie Robinson to be a good Negro, to turn the other cheek, to give a soft answer, and other things like that. No matter what abuse he got, he was supposed to smile. That was frustrating, according to Robinson. Then, later, Rickey told him to be himself. Talk back if he wanted to. Shout. Slide with his spikes up." She looked at Al Mowerinski. "I guess Rickey thought if Robinson was himself from the start, the other players would never accept him, or would make things worse for him." She hesitated, wondering how far to go. There was no coach to stop her, so she rounded the bag. "That's racism. Blacks shouldn't have to live up to anybody's image of proper behavior for them. Don't tell me Lacey Griffin turns the other cheek – not with all the fights he's had. I won't turn the other cheek, either. I'll be, well, calm – but I won't be meek."

Al Mowerinski remained silent.

Linda thought the game was over. Forfeit.

"You want to be like them?"

"Who?"

"The other players."

She laughed, his question driving away nervousness. "No! I mean, Yes! I don't want to throw temper tantrums or start fistfights. I just want to play baseball."

They stared at one another.

She could stand it no longer. "Are you going to give me a chance?" she asked, holding her breath, her leg muscles tense.

He waved his hand as if dismissing the question. "We'll choose you in the draft."

She let out her pent-up breath, relaxing visibly. She thought she saw a look of, what was it – surprise? – on his face, then again the tugging of a smile, maybe, at the corners of his mouth. "Why are you doing this?" she asked before she realized the question had even formed in her mind. "You don't have to meet . . . some sort of quota, do you?"

Al Mowerinski shook his head.

Linda sighed in relief. She wanted to be chosen because she could play baseball. "Nobody else is thinking of women in baseball," she mused out loud. "Why are you?" And then she felt as if it were none of her business. Maybe it was best not to know the motives, only the results. She wouldn't like it if he viewed her as some sort of "noble experiment."

"History," he answered slowly. "Let's say I'm doing it for history. Let's say I'll be remembered, if nothing else."

"Oh." History. She realized she had wanted him to tell her that she was a good player, that the team needed her. In the awkward silence that followed, she stared out the window, aware that Al Mowerinski was still looking at her.

The sound of his hand slapping the desk brought her attention back to him. "Let's get down to baseball. You'll be in the minors for a while – until you can prove you deserve to be moved up. It won't be easy. I want the green rubbed off before you get here. You're no good to us until you're scuffed. Understand?"

"Yes." She was perfectly aware of what he meant. Shiny white baseballs were "scuffed" (rubbed with mud) to remove their gloss. Without the superfine grit, the balls were too slick to handle well. Scuffing, an almost invisible process, made the ball grippable without changing its natural flight, as scarring would have done.

"There's more to it than that," he continued. "Use the minors to *learn*, for god's sake. They don't teach you in college what you'll have to learn to make it to the majors. Look. Listen. Watch. Analyze. *Learn*."

"Yes, sir," she answered automatically, nodding. Then, seeing the look on his face, "Al, I mean."

"Good."

And then the interview was over and Al Mowerinski ushered her out the door and gave her a tour of Chicago, leaving her little time to wonder whether this was standard procedure for all new ball players.

Seeing the Loop turned out to be similar to being caught

in a rundown between first and second, with the players driving cars at her from both directions. Al Mowerinski drove like a power hitter, boldly, seeming to move the cars in front of him with his sheer brawn and baritone voice, forcefully flowing in and out of traffic (ignoring Linda's white-knuckled grip on the seat edge) while pointing out the Sears Tower, Marshall Field's, the Merchandise Mart, the Standard Oil Building, the recently opened Water Tower Place, the John Hancock, until she couldn't keep them straight in her mind, awed less by the giant buildings than by the giant man beside her, unable to believe that she would be living here, playing here. Not releasing her grip on the seat edge, she twisted to look out the window. Chicago. She tried to imagine herself coming back to this city, living here, playing here. But maybe like countless others, she would never make it out of the minors.

Al Mowerinski announced that he was taking her to lunch, but that lunch would not be in Chicago because he didn't want to be seen with her until she was officially drafted. "What I'm doing – meeting you – isn't strictly legal. But the commissioner will have more to worry about than the fact that I met you, believe me!"

On the drive he kept asking her questions, throwing them in like a pitcher who thought you weren't ready, hoping to put one across without working for it. The questions were all about her, ranging from what she did when she was a kid to why she liked baseball. "You're twenty, aren't you?" he asked.

"Yes."

"Height?" he asked, looking her over.

"Five-ten."

"Good," he chuckled. "You won't be the shortest player in baseball! Weight?"

"One-thirty-two."

"Umm. You could gain a few pounds." He looked her over again, then added, as an afterthought, "We're heading north."

North of the city the landscape included lakes and trees and pastures full of horses. It also included a restaurant that served a hearty lunch.

"What will your parents think of this?" he asked while ordering champagne.

Linda wondered what the waitress thought he meant by "this." What *would* her parents think? A day ago, she would have answered that they would think it wonderful. Now? "They'll ... well, I think they'll be for it."

The champagne came and Al Mowerinski raised his glass. Linda followed suit. "To the World Series," he said.

"To the World Series!" she laughed, clicking her glass against his. "It's just a week away."

Al, who had his champagne glass to his lips, stopped and stared at her. He shook his head, brought his glass back into the air, and motioned with his finger that she should do likewise. "Not the college World Series," he admonished.

Oh god, she felt foolish.

"To the World Series!" he toasted a second time.

Sipping her champagne, Linda vowed to put college baseball out of her mind for the duration of lunch. Throughout lunch, almost as if he were trying to get all the scuffing done here and now, Al Mowerinski warned her of all the problems she would face, first in the minors and then, if she survived, in the majors. By her second glass of champagne, all the problems seemed insignificant. By her third, she didn't understand what Al was talking about. He took her champagne glass away and made her eat her steak, baked potato, lots of bread and butter, and ordered her to drink three cups of black coffee.

On the drive back, Linda slumped in the seat while Al told her about himself, his teenage years during the Depression, the war years, his career in baseball. His stories intrigued her. She tried to imagine playing some form of streetball in Pittsburgh, wondering whether the bases were uphill or downhill from home. He talked about making margarine during the war, squeezing the color into it from a tube, something about the butter lobby, then how the club took him out to his first expensive restaurant and the thing that impressed him most was the real butter. He laughed about it.

He didn't laugh when he told her about his last year for the Eagles. He sounded bitter, criticizing the way ball clubs treated their players when they were through with them.

"But you were good," Linda said. "Couldn't you have become a manager?"

Another booming laugh escaped him, as if he were enjoying a joke. "Thanks, Sunshine." He stroked her hair. She moved her head away, embarrassed. "What for?" he asked, not noticing. "Is that any more secure than being a player? Managers get traded, hired, fired, just like the players."

"How did you get to own the Eagles, then?" she asked, curious.

"Design. And hard work. I knew what I wanted. And I got it."

"How?"

"Went back to Pittsburgh, started a business. Actually, took over and expanded my father's business. I put a lot of work into it. And imagination. I had something to look forward to. It grew. Of course, it helped to have a name to advertise with, and I guess you could say I had that." He turned to look at her. "Is there a Mowerinski Mower in your family?"

Linda couldn't help but laugh. "That's a slogan?"

"No. I was asking you."

"Oh. Yeah. It's the only kind we buy."

He nodded, satisfied.

"So – what did you think of Al Mowerinski?"

Linda, eating peanut butter cookies and drinking milk, looked across the table at her mother. "I like him."

"Why?" asked her mother.

Linda thought about it a moment. "Because he likes baseball. Because he knows so much about it. And because he's giving me a chance."

"What about the scout? Does he want to give you a chance, too?"

"Well . . . not exactly. No." She stared at her mother. "I think he thought I could play, but he didn't want me to play, you know? I don't think it was his idea at all."

"You mean Al Mowerinski made him do it," her father supplied.

"Yeah, I guess so." She frowned, unhappy with the direction of the conversation. She had been sitting there, eating cookies and drinking milk, puzzling over the fact that Al Mowerinski had made it all seem so . . . so *easy*. In her daydreams she had never envisioned it like that, not that easy. She just wished Curry had been more encouraging. She *knew* she could fill the hole between second and third. Couldn't he see that she was the one? She had to be the one.

As if reading her thoughts, her father spoke. "You'd better get used to that, Lindy. Even if the owner is all for you, you know you're going to run into a lot of people who aren't, don't you?"

"He's going to be typical of what you'll meet, Lindy." Her mother paused. "You're sure you want to do this?" asked her mother, looking not at Linda but at her father, who was likewise eating cookies and drinking milk.

Linda picked up a crumb and placed it on her tongue. She tried to chew it, but there wasn't enough of it. Should she have another cookie? Ignoring her own doubts, she felt annoyance that her mother wasn't enthusiastic. This was it – the big time. Professional baseball. Better than the Olympics. "Sure. I'm sure," she answered, taking one more cookie. She preferred the kind that had big chocolate kisses in the center: these did not.

"It's going to be hard on you," her mother said. "It's going to be a lot harder than college baseball."

"Sure, sure, Mom, I know. It's the majors."

"That's not what she means," said her father, pushing his empty glass away and folding his arms across his chest. "She doesn't want you to have to put up with . . . what she thinks you're going to face."

"Like what?" Linda asked in irritation. Did they think she was a kid? She was twenty years old. She'd been playing baseball for twelve years. And why weren't they encouraging her? Didn't they think she had worries about it?

Her father answered. "What about that woman reporter in the men's locker room? You know the one. They – " he hesitated, then continued angrily – "pissed on her. We don't want you to have to face that, Lindy."

"You're so young," her mother offered. "Maybe you should go to graduate school first. You could get hurt."

Linda toyed with the cookie crumbs, smashing them

under her finger. "I haven't gotten hurt so far."

Her father uncrossed his arms and pointed a finger at her. "You haven't played with men yet, either. One of them blocks you at the plate and you're liable to end up in the hospital."

Men. There it was: men. By implication, inference, or outright statement it came down to men. Men would not like her as a teammate. Men would ridicule her. Men would threaten her. Men would injure her. It was as if they were monsters descended upon the world of what should be. She had never looked upon men as alien human beings. She could not begin now, and could only hope that the worst predictions would not come true. She sighed. "You think I haven't thought of those things? I have! Don't worry. I can handle it."

The three of them sat in silence, thinking.

"You're so young," her mother repeated.

"That's okay. I'll get scuffed."

3　Bush League

Sitting on the Chicksaw Bluff above the Mississippi, Memphis was terribly hot and horribly humid. At the base of Beale Street, Linda stood gazing at the river, a travel brochure folded in her back pocket. The brochure told her that Memphis was the home of the blues. It did not mention the Memphis Arrows, class AA baseball team. Minor league teams came and went. The Memphis Arrows of today might be the Springfield Shooters of tomorrow. Not a very auspicious place to begin a baseball career, all things considered. Better than single-A, though.

Pulling at the neckline of her green tank top, she fanned it back and forth, trying to relieve the stickiness that clung to her skin. Abruptly, she turned and walked back to her car. The Memphis stadium was in the fairgrounds and easy to find – so easy that she had found it the previous night.

As she parked her car near the stadium, Linda glanced at her watch and hurried. Approaching the stadium entrance, she stopped. Reporters. Photographers. Television crews. All waiting for someone – she hoped it wasn't her. Once they saw her they swooped toward her, talking at once, flashbulbs popping, video cameras running. Fighting a sudden urge to say she wasn't Linda Sunshine (it would never work – who else would be carrying a pair of spare baseball spikes?), she took a deep breath. Be calm. Be polite. *You're going to have to face reporters from now on – if you're lucky!*

"How does it feel to be the first woman baseball player?" "Do you think you'll make it?" "Why do you think you were chosen?" "Are the big leagues ready for you?" "What kind of response do you think you'll get?" "What about the fans?" "The other players?" "What does your manager think?" And on and on.

"Wonderful. Yes. I don't know." She disliked reporters. Once, watching television, she had heard a reporter ask a starving person if it hurt to be hungry. To her, the question portrayed the level of insensitivity, lack of understanding, and invasion of privacy that the news media excelled in. Now she was the center of their questions, the focus of their humming, shuffling, whirring, and flashing. Finally, she brushed past them. "I have to get on the field."

A strong grip on her arm drew her back. Affronted, she turned to see who was trying to stop her.

"Are you going to shower with the other players?"

The tall thin man asking the question held a notebook in his hand. Linda sensed his hostility. *Yes. We'll invite the umpires and even the sports reporters to join us, Jerk.* "That has nothing to do with my playing baseball."

"It's what my readers are interested in."

"Bullshit, Sengal. It's what *you're* interested in." The man who spoke stepped between her and the thin reporter and began walking toward the field. Linda stared back a moment at Sengal, then ahead at the other reporter. She was chagrined. It looked as if she were being rescued. That she definitely didn't need. Nevertheless, she headed toward the field.

He stopped until she was even with him, then matched his pace to hers. He looked familiar.

"It's a reporter's job not just to report the news, but to elevate and direct the readers' interests. Sengal doesn't elevate: he sinks to the nearest prurient level."

They reached the stadium gate. Linda saw the uniformed players standing around on the field. Her heart raced. *The minors. Almost the real thing.* She took a deep breath, then took a step forward.

"I saw you in the college World Series," the reporter said.

She had momentarily forgotten about him. She looked at him, acknowledging his presence. *Why does he look familiar?*

"You were outstanding. Al Mowerinski said the Liberty Bells couldn't have won without you. Look, it'll just take three minutes, maybe four – I'd like to ask you about the ruling on women in baseball."

Linda wondered whether he really did think she played outstanding baseball or whether he was just saying it to get an interview. "Okay," she relented. "Shoot."

His initial questions were phrased in such a way that he supplied her with information about the past, but Linda noticed that when her answers indicated she knew about the ruling he stopped providing the information and asked more pointed questions. "Yesterday the baseball commissioner ruled that he would hold the rule in abeyance for the summer and reassess it when the season ends. What do you think of that?"

"Well, naturally I'm glad to be playing, but I don't like the thought that somebody could decide that I can't play just by making a ruling. If I earn my place on the team, I belong.

Forget the exclusionary rules and rulings. Let women be signed to play just like black men were signed to play – on the basis of ability. I think the commissioner should strike the rule against women from the books. He says he's the commissioner of all of baseball and has to act in the best interests of baseball. Well, I'm part of baseball, and it's in my best interests not to be excluded because I'm a woman." Linda readjusted her baseball shoes on her shoulder as she watched the reporter take notes.

He glanced at his watch. "I'd better let you go," he said. "Thanks for taking the time to talk to me." He reached into his sport coat and pulled out a business card. "Neal Vanderlin. I hope to see you playing for the Eagles."

Horrified, Linda stared at him, then at his card. This was the guy who wrote that the Eagles were a body that needed a heart and a head. Oh, my god. What would he say about her and the Memphis Arrows – that they were undergoing a sex change operation? *Nice going. Can't you find out who you're talking to before you open your mouth?*

He was looking at her strangely. "Take it," he said. "It won't hurt you."

She took the card, turned, and walked into the stadium.

A ring of uniformed players stood around the edges of the field. They had been staring at her, but turned away as she drew closer. She looked them over quickly. Nobody she knew from college ball. Damn, it would have helped to know somebody. Taking a deep breath, she walked up to one of the players. Number 41. "Hi," she said. "Where's the manager?"

Number 41 bobbed his head a fraction of an inch toward the third base dugout. Not friendly. But not bad. "Thanks," she said, already walking in the direction of the dugout.

Walking toward her was a short man with an enormously

round belly. His feet splayed outward and his fat jiggled sideways. Linda studied him as he walked.

He stopped before her abruptly, two inches shorter and a yard wider, blocking her way. "Who the hell do you think you are?" he demanded in a squeaky voice. "You're gonna be sorry you made this mistake, girlie. Sorry."

Momentarily taken aback, she didn't know what to say. Being warned about her reception and being confronted by it were two different things.

"Who are you?" she demanded, dreading the answer.

"I'm the manager, girlie."

This is definitely not college. "Look," she said,"I'm here to play baseball, so skip the welcome and tell me what to do." She stared at him with what she hoped was a sufficiently belligerent expression.

"Get this and get it straight, Sunbeam –"

"Sunshine."

"I said get this and get it straight, Sunbeam. This is a man's game. When I get through with you, you're gonna go home cryin', forever grateful that you and baseball have parted ways." The manager's nose twitched as he talked; he rubbed the tip of it with a finger. "How those assholes in the front office ever got bamboozled into drafting you, I don't know. But I'm gonna break you – hear?"

Anger flushed inside her, warming her skin. "You'll break your balls before you break me," she said quietly, her own words surprising her. "I'm here to play baseball, not to be broken. Now where's my uniform?"

His face turned red, then worked its way to purple. "It's in the clubhouse, smartass." He looked at his watch. "You have seven minutes."

Watching him depart, Linda suddenly became aware of the silence on the field. Everybody – players, coaches, grounds crew, even people in the stands – was staring at her. Oh, god. What a beginning. *What happened to calm? What happened to patient?* She'd have to watch her temper. Maybe she should have handled it differently. Too late now. She looked at the other players, still standing around the edge of the field. They looked away.

With what she hoped was dignity, she walked into the dugout, through a tunnel, and into a locker room. She looked around. No unclaimed uniforms. The orange lockers were labeled with strips of masking tape, each strip printed with a felt-tipped pen. Long lines of names were crossed out on each locker, testimony to the constant shuffling of players down to class A and up to triple-A. She walked along the row of lockers. And then she saw the uniform, on the window ledge.

Unfolding the pants quickly, she held them up, inspecting them. They looked a bit large, but they'd have to do. Kicking off her shoes, she pulled off her tank top and slipped out of her jeans. She rejected the uniform undershirt: it must be ninety-five degrees out there already. No sports bra included. She should have brought one. Slipping on the shirt, she pulled on the sanitaries and the socks, then the pants. Grabbing her spikes, she turned around and sat on a bench.

Peripheral vision warned her of somebody's presence. Her head jerked up. A player was standing in the doorway.

"You forgot your cup," he said. "Regulation. All players must wear cups." He tapped his own under his uniform.

Linda bent down to lace her shoes, her face hidden. She wondered how long he'd been standing there.

"You also forgot your bra."

The whole time. Definitely not college.

"Don't tell me that's regulation, too?" She stood, straightened her uniform, looked down at herself, and made for the door. "I know Porkfat needs one, but I'm surprised about the rest of the team."

He moved aside to let her pass. "Porkfat? Porkfat. I take it you mean our illustrious manager. I'll let him know you think so." He shook his head from side to side. "And he speaks so highly of you."

She wondered if he had been there on orders of the manager or as a scout for the rest of the team. Or maybe on his own. She wasn't going to ask. Walking out, they saw the team lined up in formation for calisthenics.

"My name, by the way," he announced, doffing his hat in mock gallantry, "is Jack Doyle, center field."

"Linda Sunshine."

Porkfat began them with jumping jacks. Linda wasn't surprised to see that he didn't perform the exercises himself. "Hey, Jack Doyle center field," she asked between breaths, "what's the manager's name?"

Doyle put a hand to one side of his mouth as a shield. "Porkfat," he whispered loudly.

She laughed easily. Maybe Doyle would be all right. "No, no, I don't mean his marketing label, I mean his name."

"*You there, Sunbeam! Faster!*" Porkfat singled her out.

"Barr," answered Doyle. "J. F. Barr. Known as the biggest asshole in these parts, bar none."

"*Doyle!* Save the sweet talk. Faster! Faster!"

The team moved in surprising precision. *Slap, clap, slap, clap, slap, clap.* For what seemed forever she heard only the sounds of bare hands on thighs, hands meeting in air. Barr circled the group, which was organized into four loose rows. Then he stationed himself behind the last row, where he could watch them unobserved.

Jesus, she thought, what's with the jumping jacks?

"I think he lost count," whispered Doyle as if reading her mind.

In the center rows three or four players stopped and looked around, puzzled.

"Did I say stop?" shouted Barr from behind.

The players looked at one another, then started again. To her right, one player slowed down perceptibly. Then another. They didn't seem to be in as good shape as college players.

"I've got it," said Doyle.

"What?"

"I think this is for you."

She smiled. Barr was in for a surprise if he thought this would break her. She looked forward to what he would try with the wind sprints. A whistle shrilled in her ear. The half-hearted slapping sounds ceased as everybody stopped.

"All right. Sit-ups. Let's move it, boys. Three, four, let's go! Don't stand there like a buncha pussies."

They lay on their backs, hands cupped behind their heads. The grass felt good to her, the coolest place on the field. The manager's stomach cast a shadow that covered both Linda and Jack Doyle.

He drove them relentlessly. If he kept up the pace, they would be in no shape to play tonight. A dull throbbing filled her left side. Doing sit-ups too fast. She slowed down a fraction.

"Faster, college hotshot, faster. Keep up with the men, or out you go."

"You show me," she grunted.

"You watch your goddamn mouth around here, girlie!"
The shadow moved closer, heavy and menacing.

"Hey, Barr, for god's sake, it's hard enough doing these
things the way it is. With you standing there I feel like the
Hindenburg is coming down on me." Doyle glared at the
manager.

A few players in the front row turned around to witness
what was up. "Thomas, turn around and do your fuckin'
exercises!" Barr shouted. To Linda he growled, "Think you
helped win the college World Series, don't you, Sunbeam? Why
couldn't we have gotten one of the *real* ball players from your
team, huh?"

She sensed him move away. The light returned. Out of the
corner of her eye she saw him walk to the front. The players
must simply love him, she thought. Her side ached. She tried to
think of each sit-up as one more defeat for Barr.

Next came the leg-overs. "You move like a buncha old
ladies. Show me you have some *balls*! You gonna let them turn
this into a ladies' game? We gonna play hardball or not, huh?
We gonna let them turn this into a game of softball, is that it?"

Doyle spoke between breaths. "The only thing soft around
here," he said as, lying on his back, he swung his right leg
across to his left hand, "is Barr's head. I think," he continued,
now swinging his left leg to his right hand, "it's even too soft
for softball. Mushball, maybe."

"What in the world is mushball?"

"Soft softball."

"Thomas, if you can't do the fuckin' exercises, go sit on
the bench!" Thomas went.

Barr blew the whistle furiously. "Push-ups!"

Again his shadow fell over her, as if he knew her weakness. Push-ups were the single hardest exercise for her. Linda looked around as she lowered herself to the ground. Down. Up. Down. Up. If it was true that baseball players weren't the greatest of physical specimens, she would be saved from embarrassment. She figured she could do thirty easily. Fifty not so easily. After that?

"Gee, coach," grimaced Jack Doyle after thirty, "I don't think I can keep it up."

"*Man-a-ger,* Doyle, *manager!* I'm not your fuckin' coach, how many times I hafta tell you that?"

Stepping forward, Barr kicked the back of Linda's foot, hard. She fell on her face, the taste of blood filling her mouth. Her tongue, exploring, found the cut. Angry, she glared at Barr over her shoulder. "Watch where you put your hooves!" She got back on her toes and continued the push-ups, wondering how else to respond. If she jumped up and punched Porkfat in the snout just because he tripped her, it would look like she was coming out of left field. She just wasn't sure how to handle it.

The whistle sounded sweet. As if possessing one giant breath, the players whooshed in unison and sat on the ground. It no longer seemed cool to Linda.

After a few minutes, Barr divided them up: wind sprints, pitching, batting practice, fielding. He pulled her and two others to the side. "Okay, Sunbeam, these here men are my two slowest sprinters. I'm gonna time the three of you from home to first. I expect you to do at least as good as they do. If not, you're gonna practice till you get it, hear?"

"There's nothing wrong with my hearing." She looked at the two men, one about her age, the other about forty. They looked back but said nothing.

Barr, holding the stopwatch, had the men run first. He wheezed loudly, as if it were his legs pumping and stretching, trying to get to the bag.

"Okay, Sunbeam, you go."

She went. One foot hit the bag perfectly. She turned around and trotted back. Barr was looking at the stopwatch with squinted eyes. "Once more," he said, waving her toward the plate. "Something's wrong with this here watch."

"Not bad," the older of the two players remarked after her second sprint.

"Thanks."

"Okay, Sunbeam, let's see what you can do with the stick."

She did all right with the stick, too. By the time practice ended, she felt a lot better. *I can do it! . . . if I survive.*

While the rest of the players ambled to the locker room, Linda confronted Barr, who couldn't waddle away fast enough. "Where's my shower and locker room?" she asked.

He smirked. "Same place as the rest of the club. You're just one of the boys."

"Fine with me." She started toward the clubhouse.

"Sunbeam! Stop! You just stop, girlie!"

Turning, Linda faced Barr, who was huffing, trying to catch up to her long stride.

"You stay outta there!" he screamed.

"Then where do I shower?" she asked calmly.

"You want the Arrows to build a new shower, just for *you*? For one person?" He laughed.

"I don't care if it's old or new. I want a shower."

He pointed a finger at her. "Stay away from my boys, Sunbeam. That's the one rule you better obey on this team. You go *near* the men's showers and you're off the team." He walked away, hitching up his pants.

She was about to shout after him when she noticed the reporter . . . what was his name? – Sengal. There he was, in the dugout tunnel, scribbling notes. "What are you doing here?" she asked in irritation.

"Me? I'm local – I cover the Arrows."

Great, just great.

Jack Doyle jogged up to her and handed her her Levis, tank top, underclothes, and street shoes. "You forgot these."

"Thanks."

"I was waiting for you to come in and get them."

"Not today." She turned and walked toward the first base dugout, in search of the visitors' showers.

Linda sat on the bench and watched the Arrows win that night's game. Her parents, who had driven down from Pennsylvania, sat in the stands and watched an AA game that she didn't play in. Of the team, only Jack Doyle talked to her. Barr talked at her. "See that hit, Sunbeam? You couldn't do that. That's why you're not in there."

Couldn't do it? The pitcher had a nowhere curve that hung in there like a tetherball. Even so, Walchek had barely managed to hit it past the infield. "Put me in and find out."

"No way, Sunbeam. Why don't you make it easier on us all and go home now?"

Tuesday, Wednesday, and Thursday night the Arrows played Arkansas at home, dropping all three. This put the Arrows in fourth place in the league's Eastern Division. Not bad, except that there were only four teams *in* the Eastern

Division.

Each night, chin in hand, Linda sat on the bench and watched the errors. Aiken, the Arrow shortstop, must be on his way down to class A. He was hitting .198. She could hit better than that. Barr wasn't going to keep her out. Not the whole season.

Thursday night's loss over, the team boarded a bus and headed south to El Paso, where a day game was scheduled for Saturday, a doubleheader for Sunday, and night games for Monday and Tuesday. The minor league schedule consisted of daily games, many of them doubleheaders. "No time off at all," she had complained to her parents, showing them the schedule card. Her father had said, "Look at the bright side – at least you'll get to play baseball every day." *Play baseball every day. Fat chance. Sit on the bench every day is more like it.*

Sitting alone on the bus, she began to sort through the various sports pages until she found one that carried Neal Vanderlin's column. When she found the column she was looking for, she let out her breath in relief. He hadn't twisted her words or used her to criticize the Eagles. Thank god. She pushed the papers aside and tried to read a book, drifting in and out of sleep. In front of her Aiken was talking to Thomas. "Tits like you wouldn't believe. Enough tit to last a lifetime. I mean a *lifetime*, boy!" Linda didn't understand what any woman would see in Aiken, a .198 hitter who played short with glue on his shoes. She wondered if Thomas believed the story or if it was part of masculine rites to accept such stories without question. "I was in tit heaven," Aiken added, in case Thomas missed the point. If Aiken's batting wasn't enough of a clue to his character, she decided, his language was.

Behind her Vincenti was snoring and Doyle, half asleep,

was grumbling. Country-western music filtered forward from the back of the bus; the strong backbeat of rock throbbed backward from the front. Across the aisle Walchek was arguing with Crowder about the three losses. "What we needs is some hitting, man, some hitting," Crowder answered to whatever Walchek had aid. "This whole team batting at .201. Can't make winners out of that. What we needs is some hitting, man, some hitting."

"I mean, was she a good fuck or was she a good fuck?" Aiken grew louder. "Man, these southern chicks, they're something else. This one come up from New Orleans. I think she's got some colored blood in her. Man, when those broads got that colored blood in them, they're hot to trot."

Linda sensed, rather than saw, Crowder stiffen. She wondered if he was going to do anything, or if he, too, would let it alone. Probably let it alone. Like her, he probably let 999 remarks out of every 1,000 go by. Somewhere along the way she drifted into sleep.

Something wet awakened her. Drugged with sleep, she couldn't quite place it. Uncomfortable. Wet. Blob. She squirmed against the seat, adjusting, compensating. Jumping awake, she grabbed her neck. *Yech!* Reaching a hand down the back of her shirt, she removed it: a plug of slobbery chewing tobacco. Goddamn it! If she knew who had done it, she'd have hurled it down his throat. Even thought it was pitch dark, the middle of the night, she knew that somebody was staring at her. Well, if they expected her to scream, they were in for a long wait. She got out of her seat, disposed of the chewing tobacco, washed up, and returned – checking out the seat just to make sure nobody had put something on it while she had been gone. It was a long time before she fell back into sleep.

She jumped awake, blinking. Something had moved in the seat beside her. Bright sunlight. Flat land. A metallic taste in her mouth. Sengal, traveling with the team, had seated himself next to her. "Read last night's edition?" he asked, showing her a Memphis paper.

She rubbed her eyes. "Yeah," she answered, stretching.

"Well?"

"It's not a bad paper." She knew what he meant.

"I mean the sports section."

"I'll bet you mean the baseball articles."

"Yeah."

She shrugged. "The reporters don't seem too interested in my ability to play baseball."

"What do you mean? That's all they talked about." Sengal lit a cigarette. The smoke drifted toward her.

She leaned closer to the window. "No, they didn't. They said a woman on the team would turn the interest of men from baseball to sex. Everyone knows baseball players never think of sex. It's a shame to introduce them to the subject."

"Welllll . . .." he leered, drawing out the word as if it were an answer. But after two cigarettes and ten minutes of trying to make conversation with her, Sengal left.

In El Paso, the bus took them directly to the field – no time to check into the hotel first. There was only time to unload the bus, change into uniform (Linda had to do that in a public women's room), and practice.

Afterward, in the dugout, Barr read the lineup. She was in it! Linda was elated: she had thought it would take weeks, *months*, before Barr put her in the lineup.

"I want everyone to know," Barr announced to the players, "that I'm starting Sunbeam because I've been ordered to. *Ordered* to!" He looked at them sorrowfully, his jowls drooping. "That's not the way the game's played, boys. A manager shouldn't have anybody tellin' him what to do."

"You can always quit in protest," Doyle said in mock sympathy.

"Doyle, shut the fuck up when I'm talking." Barr looked over the team. "Boys, I just want you to know I'm on your side. But a man in my position ain't got no choice."

Nobody replied. Linda, leaning against the dugout wall, watched the show, excited about the chance to play, but nervous, too.

Then he told her she was playing left field.

"But that's not my position."

"I got one question for you, Sunbeam."

It was going to be sarcastic.

"Who's manager around here, huh?"

Left field consisted of brown grass, with rampant weeds just outside the chalk line. Linda patrolled her area, looking for holes, stones, or other possible problems. In the weeds a rusty can lay on its side. She kicked it far out of the area, then took her position. She watched the batter, only half-hearing the bilingual shouting. Lots of boos and catcalls. Some cheers.

"Hey, cutie! That isn't where the cheerleaders stand, honey! How about moving over to the sidelines where you belong?"

She spotted the heckler in the left-field bleachers. A real winner.

One clothesliner, a low-hit line drive, came her way in the second inning. "That's a line drive, cutie! Try to catch it with that thing on your hand, babydoll!" It was hard to see the ball in the evening light, but she fielded it adequately. Aiken, at short, already had one error. She pounded her glove in frustration.

Barr had her ninth in the lineup, a position she hadn't occupied since her first college game. Her turn to bat came in the third inning. The eighth batter, Vincenti, walked. She stepped into the batter's box. The noise of the crowd increased. A few hot dog wrappers and paper cups were thrown on the field. Those that came close to the plate the umpire swept away. "No, no, cutie! Don't stand there! That's where the hitters stand!" It sounded like the heckler from the bleachers. What was he doing – following her around the field?

Then the pitcher called time. He wanted to talk to his manager. The manager sauntered out to the mound. The catcher joined them. Their voices carried to where Linda was standing outside the batter's box.

"I don't want to pitch to no fuckin' broad!"

"I know how you feel, champ, but there's nothing we can do about it."

"Why isn't there? You mean we're going to have to put up with this shit?" The pitcher was pumping his arms up and down, pacing the mound.

Linda leaned on her bat and listened.

"Look, champ, just put three aspirins down the middle and you'll strike her out. She's not gonna make it, anyway, and at least you'll get a strikeout. Hell, if they want to *give* you a strikeout, take it! Atta babe." The manager patted the pitcher on the back.

If you want to tell me what you're pitching, that's fine with me, babe. The three troglodytes seemed satisfied: the manager left, the catcher returned. Taking her stance in the batter's box, she wondered if the loud words were a trick – or would she get a fastball down the center?

It was no trick. Right down the middle. She swung early, catching only a piece of it. The ball flew off into the stands, provoking more crowd noise. Would the foul make the pitcher reconsider? She wished she had really connected with it. Anything but a strikeout. Rubbing her hands on her uniform, she took her stance and watched the stretch, looking at the release point, where the ball would appear out of the pitcher's hand. It came hurling at her down an invisible tunnel, a beautiful white blur, a tiny sphere whose direction she could reverse. Another fastball. It would have been a strike, but she hit it solidly this time, into the alley between center and right, bringing in Vincenti and collecting a double. A hit and an RBI. Strike her out? *Not so easy, babe.*

That brought the Arrows to the top of the batting order. She wasn't left dying on second. Crowder hit her in, and Doyle hit Crowder in, making it 3-0 before the inning was over.

The Arrows won, 3-0. Hands were slapped all around. Almost all around: only Doyle slapped Linda's, then followed the men to the locker room. Again there was no place for her to shower. And this time she couldn't go to the visitors' dugout: the Arrows *were* the visitors. So she sat on the step of the bus, waiting for the team. Her hair was wet with sweat and dirt. Her socks and sanitaries looked as if she had been dragged across the infield by the grounds crew. Her uniform was covered with dust. If she didn't watch it, she thought, the players were going to call her Pigpen. She lifted her damp shirt, pulled it out of her pants, and fanned it. She squinted at the setting sun. The temperature must be a hundred degrees.

A woman and man walked by, glanced at her, stopped, and looked again. "Nice game," they said. "You were good."

"Thanks!"

She felt five degrees cooler already.

At the hotel, Barr grabbed her shoulder, pulling her aside. He placed a roll of money in her hands. "Go find yourself a hotel room."

"Huh?" She stared at the damp money.

"You can't stay here, so go find yourself a hotel room." He turned away.

Linda grabbed his shoulder and tried to turn him around. God, he was heavy. "What are you talking about? Why can't I stay here? *Hotels* don't practice sex discrimination."

"You can't stay here, Sunbeam, because I say you can't. Now git."

She was hot, dirty, tired, and thirsty, far too impatient to try to unravel his particular problem. Walking up to the desk, she asked for a room.

Barr came after her. Some of the other players stood around, watching. Sengal sat in a corner, staring, probably taking notes for some "human interest" article.

"I'm ordering you to stay in another hotel!" he screamed at her.

"I'm a member of the team and I'm staying with the team."

Barr became avuncular. "Look, Sunbeam," he leered, hooking his fat thumbs into his belt, "it's common knowledge what men and women do when they're together in the same hotel. Now, it's my job to see to it that my boys get the proper rest. My rules are, no women in the hotel rooms, understand?"

"One room for three nights," she said to the clerk, shoving the money across the counter.

"Don't do it, Sunbeam! I won't have no woman undermining the morals and health of my team!" He was hissing this at her while circling around her, his ridiculously little feet almost bouncing on the floor.

He was a flake. An honest-to-god minor league flake. Hadn't she read somewhere that some football coach made his players sleep in a motel the night before a home game so that they wouldn't "drain their energy in sex"? Maybe Barr had a brother in football.

She took the room key from the clerk and turned, bumping into the still-circling manager. "Look, Barr, it would be impossible for me to undermine the morals of this club. But if you want to stay up and guard their doors all night, suit yourself." She grabbed her bag and walked off toward the elevator.

"You'll regret this!" he shouted, pointing the index fingers of both hands at her.

She laughed. Couldn't he see how ridiculous he looked?

"My room or yours?" asked Jack Doyle in a loud voice as he entered the elevator with her, winking.

"Why not both?" she replied, loud enough for Barr to hear.

Jack followed her off the elevator and to her room, standing behind her as she put the key in the lock. He kissed her ear; she dropped the bag she had been holding, turning around to face him.

"You winked," she accused. "It was a joke. For Porkfat."

"Sure," he said, dropping his bag and putting a hand against the door, his arm blocking her. "Let's spend the night making love. That'll really get him angry. Might melt a few pounds off his gut. Why not?" He moved his face close to kiss her.

She moved aside. "Nice try," she said, "but still an error."

"I thought you liked me," he said.

Linda laughed.

"What's so funny?"

"Gimme a break, Doyle – what a line!"

Jack Doyle pulled at his lower lip. "It's worked before."

"With who? The catcher? Pitcher? Third baseman?"

He drew back. "Hey! That's not funny."

Linda stooped down and picked up her bundle of clothes. "Sure it is. Don't be so sensitive, Jack Doyle center field."

He bent to pick up his gear. "I'm in Room 405," he whispered, blowing a kiss in her direction.

"Sleep well."

In her room, showered at last, she wrote a letter, read, watched some television and, finally, went to bed. She wondered whether Jack Doyle was in his room. She wondered whether his roommate was in the room with him. It would be nice to have a roommate. She wondered what would happen if she knocked on their door, walked in, sat down to talk: talk baseball, talk reporters, talk music, talk politics, talk people. Just talk, like fellow workers talked on the job. *They're probably out drinking and talking sex with Aiken.*

Why not? Doyle had asked. The question irritated her, not simply because it demanded a reason when a simple No should have been sufficient answer, but because the complexity of why-nots in this situation confused her. She had confronted it only briefly in college. What if she liked the second baseman and made love to him? Then the third baseman would say, "I see you're making love to my friend the second baseman. Why not me?" And then what if she broke up with the second baseman? Would the other players view her as property to be passed around? – as if belonging to a man was a natural state of being? She had carefully avoided getting involved with the other players.

It hadn't been difficult. In college, baseball was not king. Baseball was not even a princeling. The players were not thrown together constantly as they would have been had they been football players. And there had been David, a student in one of her literature classes. But a philosophy major, she had learned. That was all right – philosophy was about as far away as you could get from baseball. They had become lovers . . . for all of three months. The putout had come in the spring, when David had requested that she not play baseball. She had laughed. He had insisted. "Why?" she had demanded. Because, he informed her, she was "too intelligent" to spend her life playing a game. She had shrugged and asked him what was philosophy but a game. "It's a mind game, David, but it's a game. It's not as if you're going to be a biologist curing diseases – that's *not* a game." He had pursed his lips and replied that philosophy was superior to baseball. Linda laughed and skipped down the campus paths. "Come on, David. It's spring. Let's not argue." Then, impishly, she added, "Spring means baseball – everybody knows that."

They made it to David's apartment, and to bed. Later, David brought up the argument again, asking her to give up baseball. "Why?" she had demanded again. Because, he informed her sternly, she could injure her reproductive organs. This time she had laughed derisively. David had sat up in bed, his hairy mesomorphic body (so unphilosopher-like, she used to think) wrapped in sheets, a sheet corner thrown over his shoulder: Socrates lecturing. "I want a large family," he had informed her. Family? Who had said anything about marriage? About children? Linda had been indignant. Then he had ridiculed baseball. She retaliated by ridiculing Berkeley and

Hume and the tree on the deserted island. "At least when somebody hits a homer, baseball fans *hear* it, David! They don't need a philosopher to explain it to them." The argument had continued, and at some point he had said, "Linda, I know I'm right. You can't refute that!" She had picked up her clothes from the floor, gathered them in her arms, and kicked the bed. "Thus I refute it!" she had shouted. Her foot had hurt for a week afterward.

Rolling over, she faced the ceiling, seeing shadowy shapes by the cracks of light that came in under the door. In college she had had other social activities – classes, the dorm, the rooming house, friends. It would not be so easy here. Just her and twenty-four men. More if you counted Barr, the coaches, and the reporters, which she didn't. They would be spending almost all of their time together. She sighed and rolled over again and finally fell asleep.

Sunday afternoon she was still batting ninth, but playing shortstop. The guardian of morals never announced why he took her out of left field. "Bust your butts," he advised the Arrows. "Bust your butts out there."

Linda scraped the toe of her shoe across the infield dirt. Hard, dry clay. She had never seen an infield quite like this: holes everywhere, and, where there weren't holes, pebbles. "What is this, prairie dog heaven?" she asked the second baseman. "Fuckin' boulder heaven," he answered, throwing a stone off the field.

The first El Paso batter singled to left. The second hit a hard ball that bounded away from her. Linda twisted, reversed her field, and caught it on the bounce, throwing to second. From second to first in time for the double. More boos from the crowd. And more cheers.

When she came up to bat in the third inning, the score was 0-0. Just like Saturday's game. As she waited, she estimated the crowd at maybe a thousand. Somehow, she had expected more, even though she heard the loudspeaker announcement that this was one of the largest crowds in El Paso minor league history.

At bat, she was less nervous than on the previous night. With two hits and one RBI, she had the credentials to strike out. Not that they, her teammates, would look at it that way. Then she told herself to stop thinking "they" and "them." *We're all on the same team.*

The catcher began to talk at her. "Hey! You're no kind of hitter. Hey, you don't belong here. Hey, my mom hits better than you."

"Your mom probably hits better than you, too," she muttered.

"Stick it to her ear!" somebody yelled. The sound, she could swear, came from her own dugout. *Love that team solidarity.* The first pitch went sailing over her head as she ducked. Applause from the stands reached her ears. *Okay, you scared me. Now throw to me.* The next pitch was a fast one, low and outside: her favorite. She slapped it into right field for a single.

Just as he had done yesterday, Ulysses S. Crowder drove her in. Jack Doyle drove him in, and the Arrows scored three runs in the third.

Back in the dugout, Barr started in on her. "Who the hell told you to swing at the first pitch, Sunbeam?"

"What do you mean?"

"I mean, where the hell did anybody ever tell you a ball player swings at the first pitch? You know something about that pitcher we don't, huh? You maybe batted against him before, huh?"

"You didn't tell me to take the pitch. It was good, so I swung. Besides, it was the second pitch. The first one went over my head."

"It was good, so you swung. Listen to the genius, boys."

Linda stared out at the infield, watching Jack Doyle on third base. He winked at her. Linda shook her head. Jack, for all his friendliness, couldn't see her as just another teammate. You don't wink at teammates. Next thing you know, he'd be blowing her kisses.

"Now listen up, Sunbeam. That's not the way it's done. You *never* swing at the first pitch. You take it, hear?" Barr spit tobacco juice out toward the field. It landed on the steps. "You know why, Sunbeam?"

She considered the question, the trap. Surely he wasn't going to say that it wore out the pitcher. "No," she conceded.

"I didn't think so." He spit again, tobacco juice dribbling out of the corner of his mouth. He wiped it away with the back of his hand. "Wears out the pitcher, Sunbeam."

"But what if it's a strike?"

"What if it's a strike, she asks." Barr looked at the rest of the players as if she were hopeless. "If it's a strike, it *still* wears out the pitcher."

Walchek was at the plate, the count 2 and 1.

"He's gonna get his pitch now, just watch and see," cheered Thomas. "He's gonna give it a ride. Come on, babe, let's go."

Linda watched Walchek, who got a fastball down the center but fouled it off into the stands. She looked at Doyle on third. Jack was still a long, long way from home. He needed somebody to bring him in.

It wasn't Walchek. The Arrows retired, with Doyle left on base. She grabbed his glove on her way out of the dugout, tucking it under her arm while she slipped her hand into her glove.

"*Aaaa!*" Something wet and slippery was in her glove. She dumped it out. Chewing tobacco again. Linda threw Jack's glove to him, wiping her hand on her pants.

"Here." He pulled out a handkerchief.

She wiped out the inside of the glove. "Thanks, Raleigh. I owe you a clean handkerchief."

The Arrows took both games of the Sunday doubleheader, 8-5 and 1-0. Monday night Barr moved her to eighth in the batting order, explaining that it was traditional for the pitcher to bat last. She was one for three that night. More importantly, she drove in the winning run. That win pulled the team out of the basement and into third place.

Linda was happy. She was batting .400 for the series and had three RBIs. The team was out of last place. Jack Doyle was friendly. A few others were neutral. It all added up to progress, didn't it?

Not for Barr. He didn't play her Tuesday night.

"Why?" she demanded.

Barr looked at her. He spit tobacco juice, just missing her. It was all the answer she got.

Aiken, playing short, struck out, lowering his batting average even further. Then he made an error that put an El Paso runner on second. The next batter singled, driving in the run and putting El Paso ahead 1-0.

"Aiken can't pick it," muttered Barr. "He doesn't keep his head down. Christ, can't he *look* at the fuckin' ball?"

"Play me," said Linda.

"When I want your advice, I'll ask for it, Sunbeam."

The El Paso half of the inning over, the Arrows came into the dugout.

"Shit! It wasn't my fault I missed that ball!" Aiken threw his glove against the dugout wall. "It hit a fuckin' hole and bounced outta my reach. Damn it, I can pick it as good as anybody." He glared at Linda, as if daring her to refute it. "The infield's a fuckin' mess."

By the bottom of the seventh, the score was 5-1, El Paso. Crowder paced the dugout. "We need some *hits,*" he repeated, "some *hits.*" Just as Aiken was about to step out of the dugout for the on deck circle, Crowder stopped his pacing and stood over Barr. "Come on, Skip," he said softly. "We need some hits."

"What the fuck you talkin' about, Crowder? And get outta my way. I can't see through you."

"It's bad luck to break up a winning lineup," Crowder pleaded. "Don't mess with success. We need some *hits.*"

"Then get out there and hit."

Linda saw Crowder glance at her sideways, then turn quickly back to Barr. "I mean," he persisted, "we need us somebody who can start a rally."

"What the hell is this 'we need us' business, Crowder? You the manager, huh? You got somebody specific in mind, huh?"

Crowder studied his spikes. Linda studied him. Barr chewed his tobacco. The others looked away. Barr spat past Crowder. Aiken selected a bat and entered the on-deck circle. Crowder stood there a moment longer, then sat down.

Batting with the same skill he displayed at short, Aiken looked at a fastball for strike one, looked at a curve for strike two, looked at two balls, and went down swinging on a high, outside pitch. Storming into the dugout, he hurled his batting helmet against the wall, sending players ducking. Still holding his bat, Aiken began pounding it against the dugout steps. When his bat broke, he savagely kicked the halves up the steps and onto the field. Turning, he ran back into the dugout and began pulling bats out of the bat rack, hurling them left and right. Players jumped out of his way, several of them taking shelter in the tunnel. Everybody watched. Nobody tried to stop Aiken's temper tantrum. Exhausted, Aiken threw himself on the bench. The other players returned.

Linda stared at Barr and realized that he was not going to put her in. She studied the dugout steps, counting the tobacco stains on them. She had read once about a minor league player who had only one arm. He had managed to make a career out of baseball – even made it briefly to the majors, if she remembered correctly. Probably wasn't even booed or hissed at because he had one arm. She had two good arms, too good legs, good hitting, and excellent fielding, yet she knew that Barr, and probably the team, too, would have sooner tolerated a no-armed pitcher who kicked the ball to the plate than her.

A thatch of red hair and freckles appeared about two inches from her face, intruding on her thoughts. "Hey, Sunshine," said Doyle, "game's over. Time to go."

"Oh, sorry." She got up. The others were already leaving.

"What a terrific rally! We came back and beat them 7-5 in the top of the ninth!"

Startled, she stepped back, then got the joke. "How bad was it?"

"Six to one."

Linda followed Aiken into the bus. After he had chosen a seat, she took hers. Far from Aiken. The reasons for sitting far from Aiken kept increasing. *By the time we reach Memphis, one of us will be sitting in a rumble seat.* From El Paso the bus took them north into the panhandle, where they had a three-night stand in Amarillo. The rest of the team made plans to go out on the town when they arrived. Nobody invited her to go along. She felt a pang of loneliness, then pushed it away. *You knew it would be rough.*

On one of the bus's infrequent stops, Sengal barely made it back in time to reboard. Amid the hoots, he came panting back to her seat. "Mind if we chat?" he asked, breathless.

His notebook was nowhere in sight. That, she suspected, was when reporters were most dangerous. "You chat, I'll listen."

Sengal pulled out a cigarette and lit it.

The smoke drifted her way. She waved it away with a hand. Too bad the bus driver hadn't left without him.

"Tell me – what are you doing in baseball?"

Linda waved away the smoke. "I thought I'd enjoy the fresh air."

Sengal switched the cigarette to his other hand. "Good way to meet men, don't you think?"

Turning in her seat, Linda stared at him. "What do you mean by that?" she demanded.

"You know," grinned Sengal. "All those hot young studs. The odds are entirely in your favor. You can have any one you choose."

"I'm here to play baseball, Sengal. Try to get that through your thick newsman's head."

"Not from what I see."

"If you don't see me playing baseball, you need glasses."

Sengal exhaled more smoke her way, then leaned closer. "I've seen Doyle coming out of your room," he whispered.

"Bullshit!" she answered loudly. "You know you haven't. Where do you get off?

"Language, language," he admonished, leering. "Methinks the lady doth protest too much."

"Get out!"

"Now wait –"

"Leave me alone," she said through clenched teeth. "Just get out of here – and take your goddamn cigarettes with you."

From the front of the bus a voice told them to keep it down.

"Touchy about it, huh?" asked Sengal.

She glared at him. "Leave, Sengal. I don't want to 'chat' with you."

Doyle leaned over from the seat in front of her. "Hey, newsboy, fuck off." He motioned with his thumb toward the front of the bus.

Sengal blew smoke in his face and left.

"Jesus, Sunshine, don't you know better than to talk to that jerk?" asked Doyle.

Linda ignored the question. Slouching against the window, she placed one cowboy-boot-encased leg on the top of the back of Doyle's seat, then crossed her other leg over it. There were a few advantages to sitting alone. She pulled a cowboy hat over her eyes and closed off the world. Sengal was a worm. He was trying to get his kicks either by talking about sex or by imagining her making it with the whole team, or . . . or . . . or what if Sengal, with his nose for rotten news, was merely tracking down a rumor?

Anybody on the team could have started the rumor about her and Doyle. Doyle's winks were cause enough to start rumors. Hell, Doyle's winks were probably *meant* to start rumors. She blew her breath out under the brim of the hat. She wouldn't put it past Jack Doyle to lie outright. She could just hear him in the locker room. "Hey, guys – guess which shortstop I laid last night." The friendliest guy on the team had his own reasons for being friendly, damn him.

Somewhere in the middle of Texas she fell asleep, mixing dreams of Sengal, Doyle, baseball, and buses. Once she opened her eyes and thought she saw an enormous billboard sign that advertised FREE TEXAS BEEF DINNER. Must have been a dream. She tried to uncross her legs but couldn't. Groggily, she tried to sit up. *Ummph!* Her feet came down with a thud. Somebody had tied her feet together with rope. *Better than tobacco any day.* Twisting into a more comfortable position, she went back to sleep, leaving the rope around her boots. *Don't let them know it bothers you.* When the bus rounded a cloverleaf somewhere near Lubbock, she saw the billboard again. "FREE 72-OZ. STEAK if this dinner is eaten in one hour." She laughed.

Doyle and Crowder stretched, partially stood, and turned around. "It wasn't funny," Crowder said.

"What wasn't?"

"The game."

"I was laughing at the billboard."

"She was laughing at the billboard," Doyle repeated to Crowder. They rolled their eyes, shook their heads, and slid back into their seats.

The bus pulled up to a hotel that looked like the one they

had left in El Paso. Walchek got out of his seat, stretched, scratched himself under the arms and in the groin, yawned several times, and announced, "All right, you boneheads, all out for Armadillo!"

"*Amarillo!*" the team shouted back in unison.

"That's what I said – *Armadillo!*" shouted Walchek, grabbing his bag and running into the hotel, shouting, "Charge!"

Barr didn't give her any trouble about the hotel room this time. Jack Doyle asked, "What are we waiting for, Sunshine?" and parted with "Let me know when."

Uniformed, her cleats clicking on the cement floor of the tunnel, Linda came running into the dugout.

"This is horseshit!" shouted Thomas angrily.

"Real horseshit!" Aiken, kicking the bench, agreed.

"A mess, a real fuckin' mess." Barr hitched up his pants and spit tobacco juice out of the dugout, toward home plate.

"One was bad enough."

"*You!*" argued Vincenti, pointing a finger at Linda. "You started it. Fuck it all anyway!"

"Yep," agreed Barr, spitting more tobacco juice. "I knew this would happen. It's a matter of principle, boys. A matter of principle."

Linda looked around in confusion for a clue. Why the increased animosity?

Doyle winked at her. "Look toward home plate and you shall see what ails these mighty warriors."

"Shut up, Doyle," intoned Barr.

Linda stuck her head out of the dugout and looked. So what was wrong with home plate? Did somebody lop off a corner, changing the pentagon into a square? No, it was there, looking no worse than most home plates. A bit more cockeyed, maybe, but – the umpire! The umpire had long blonde hair tied in a pony tail. *The umpire was a woman!*

Pressing her lips together to keep from smiling, Linda turned back into the dugout, found a seat in the corner, and grabbed a baseball, turning it in her hand and studying it. She counted the stitches. If she didn't do something, she'd laugh so hard that Barr would send her to the showers. The nonexistent showers.

Linda batted seventh that night. Progress again. When she got to the plate, she heard the crowd behind the screen.

"Now there's two of them! Hey, umpire sweetie – don't change your mind! Hey, shortstop sweetie – this isn't ladies' day. That was last week!"

The Arrows won the first and lost the second, during which Barr was ejected by the umpire. Naturally Barr blamed the second loss on the umpire. "She robbed us, boys. Robbed us. See what's happenin' to the game?"

They won the third game, the Friday night one, by one run, Jack Doyle's top-of-the-eighth homer, which brought in Linda and Crowder to tie the score and Jack to win. Doyle was so happy that he grabbed Linda, whirled her around, and told her they would celebrate. The other players snickered. Barr told Doyle he was heading for a big fat fine. Linda knew everyone was getting the wrong idea. But it was good to have a friend.

She was sitting on the bus steps when Doyle and Crowder walked up, dressed in white pants and unbuttoned silk shirts. Doyle wore four gold chains around his neck, Crowder one. Linda looked at them and shook her head. "They shouldn't allow baseball players to wear necklaces. What's the world coming to?"

"Tch, tch," said Crowder, ignoring the remark and rubbing the sleeve of her uniform between his thumb and forefinger. "Lady doesn't know how to dress."

Doyle nodded. "Think maybe it's the latest fashion?"

"Nah. Too cheap. If it was fashion, it would be silk, man, silk."

Doyle grabbed one of her arms, Crowder the other, leading her back to the field. Doyle held her bundle of clothes.

"Hey! Where're we going?"

"We're going to treat you to a steak dinner," answered Jack.

"But we should treat you. You hit the home run. *Where* are we going?!"

"Shh!" he warned. "Nobody's going to pay for my steak, I'm getting it for free. Keep quiet."

They tiptoed into the dugout, down the tunnel, and past the visiting team's showers. When they reached a dark doorway, Jack pushed her through, turning on the light as he did so.

"Take your shower and be quick. We don't want to miss the bus."

Standing under the running water, she realized she must be in the umpires' shower room. The dark room smelled of stale water. Green slime covered the wooden shower boards. The stadium owners must not have liked the umpires. She wondered if the players' shower room was like this. Maybe she wasn't missing much. Hurriedly, she toweled dry, put her wet hair into a Dutch braid (for celebration – only an English braid held through a game), and pulled on her clothes.

"Where the hell did you change, girlie?" growled Barr

when he saw her on the bus.

"Behind second base."

When the bus stopped, Jack put an arm around Linda and an arm around Crowder and marched them off to the Big Texan Steak Ranch.

"My treat," he announced. "Order up, hear?" He imitated Barr.

"But—"

"Don't question the man when he says his treat," interrupted Crowder. "He intends to pay for only two dinners, not three."

"I intend," said Jack, "to get my dinner free. Also my drinks."

"The Eagles are playing in Texas tonight," Ulysses told her.

"I know. I heard Zack Weiss is on the injured list. Think they'll call somebody up from the Iowa team?" she asked.

"If they do," announced Jack, leaning across the table, his face inches from Ulysses and Linda's, "I hope they call me up to Iowa."

"You!" snorted Ulysses. "Shit, you ain't a shortstop, man!"

"So?" asked Jack, sinking back into his seat. "I'm the best man around."

"So, shit, man," explained Ulysses, enumerating his points on his fingertips. "First off, Weiss plays short, see? So it stands to reason they're gonna call up a shortstop from the triple-A team, see? Lucky dog, whoever he be, going to the bigs, man, the bigs! Then, see," continued Ulysses, ticking off the points, "they'll have to call up a shortstop from the double-A – that's us, dig? – to play in triple-A. And shit, Jack, you ain't a shortstop. Dig?"

"They're going to call me, of course," said Linda. "I can see it now – today the doubles, tomorrow the triples, and then . . . the homers!" She lifted her beer in a toast, clicking her glass against the others.

"You! Shit, Linda, I hate to break it to you," Ulysses said, patting her on the shoulder, "but you're just a double-A nobody."

"U! That's the nicest thing anybody's said to me all season." Patting Ulysses' cheek, she wiped a mock tear away from her eye.

"Don't call me U, you. That name's nowhere. You can call me Ulysses – short for Ulysses S."

"You can call me anytime," said Jack.

"I'll call you when I get to the majors – you can come visit me," retorted Linda.

"Hey!" Jack finished his beer and ordered another round. "I'll get there before you do, Sunbeam. I was called up to the triples for three weeks last year."

"What was it like?" Linda and Ulysses asked in unison.

Jack waved a hand in the air. "Not bad. Better than this dump, I'll tell you that."

Linda looked at Jack. She liked him. He was friendly, funny, and a good ball player. She liked him, but she didn't trust him. No way.

Ulysses and Linda got high, drinking, laughing, joking. Celebrating. Jack got loaded.

"If you don't stop drinking, man, you ain't gonna have *any* of that 72-ounce cow," warned Ulysses.

"You have to pay for it if you don't finish it within an hour of the time it comes," warned Linda, who had studied the details of the offer.

"Hour, hell!" belched Jack. "We've only got forty-five minutes before we have to catch the bus!"

He finished it, then had ice cream for dessert. Ulysses had to help him wedge his wallet out of his back pocket. They ran back to the bus, Linda and Ulysses dragging Doyle between them. "Ohhhh!" he groaned. "Stop it, stop, you're killing me." In the bus, he collapsed and fell into a deep, snoring sleep.

"Has Doyle been to the steak house?" Walchek asked her, leaning across the aisle.

"Yeah. I think he ate too much."

"Not Doyle. He does this every time we come to Armadillo."

In Memphis, the press was waiting. Sengal, who had been with the team, walked over to stand with the reporters. "How's the pace?" one of them asked Linda. "Do you feel tired?"

Her bones ached, her eyes felt full of sand, her spine felt as if it had been curved on a bench for twenty years, and she longed for just nine or ten hours of deep sleep. "I feel fine," she answered. "The pace is fine."

"How are the other players treating you, Linda? Are you getting along with them?"

"Sure." *I think they're beginning to recognize that I'm human, the same species as they are. I can even have dinner with them now and then, if they're in a good mood.*

"I'd like to do a human interest story for the women's pages," said another reporter. "How about tomorrow?"

Human interest. Why not baseball? "Call me then." She could think of an excuse by then.

When the alarm went off the next morning, Linda dragged

herself out of bed and opened the Arrows' schedule card. A game every day from now until September 3. *Two* games on many of the days. She groaned, dropped the schedule, and stumbled into the shower. The hot water helped, but not much. She realized she had misjudged the other players. Perhaps she was in better shape to do calisthenics and wind sprints, but they were in better shape to play baseball every night, ride a bus through the outlands of Texas, go out drinking, and then go out and do it over again. *Specificity, it's called.*

At practice, Barr heaved a gray sack of mail at her, ordering her to get it out of the clubhouse. Back in her room, she dumped the letters on the bed and spent the hours between practice and the game reading them, first sorting them into two piles: "For" and "Against." The "For" pile had maybe 200 letters in it, the "Against," 800. In the "Against," some called her anti-American, commie, pinko, red, harlot, strumpet, whore, dike, lesbian. A few even threatened rape. They didn't call it that, but that's what they meant. Angry, she threw all the hate mail in the wastebasket, then put the wastebasket outside her door. She didn't want the letters in her room. The people who wrote them were crazy.

The people who wrote the "For" letters weren't all that sane, either. One person wanted to be commissioned to write her life's story - at twenty! Another informed her she was wasting her time playing with men: she should be playing softball with her sisters, who would give her love and encouragement, and she, in turn could help raise softball out of the second-class citizenship it had been forced into by the male chauvinist pig establishment. One letter was from a coven of witches in Oklahoma, promising to hex her opponents. Another explained that sports played with balls were sports invented by men to oppress women. Women should have nothing to do with such sports. Especially sports played with balls *and* bats. It concluded by wishing her a good season. Several letters came from nearby women's groups, asking her to speak at meetings. There were even a few invitations to speak at college campuses. It felt good to know that some people out there supported her. Her favorite letters were from kids. These all expressed enthusiastic support. "Hang in there," one girl urged her.

She hung in there. The Memphis fans were not particularly friendly, but she had faced boos before, even in college, and knew that most of them would die out. There were cheers, too, sometimes louder than the boos. According to the local sports page, the attendance in Memphis had doubled since she joined the team. She wondered whether Al Mowerinski knew and whether he would be happy. She thought about him sometimes, remembering the big, big man outside the Little League game so many years ago, the man who had told her to keep playing baseball if that's what she wanted to do. It had been him, hadn't it? It had to be. He had to be the one.

By the end of July, when the rest of the team was hot, tired, and aching, Linda had toughened. Her bones no longer ached, and she no longer felt blurry-eyed or weary. Only the heat got to her, leaving her damp and limp. They were playing games in 98-degree heat and worse humidity. Yet they kept winning. By the end of July the Arrows were in second place, threatening to catch Little Rock.

In the first week of August, they played out of their division, beating Alexandria two games out of three, moving up on Little Rock. Then Little Rock lost to Amarillo, moving the Arrows to within 3-1/2 games of first place. They went down to the wire with Little Rock, one game out of first place the last week, the final series of the season coming up. In Little Rock.

She hated Little Rock. The dugouts had no roofs and the drinking water tasted awful. In August, Little Rock was hot, dry, and dusty. The hoarse, primal screaming, the threats and obscenities shouted at her seemed worse than elsewhere, even though they probably weren't. Every time the Arrows were in Little Rock she had a tight knot in her stomach.

The knot did no harm. Her playing in the last three games was beautiful to watch: graceful catches, perfect throws, clutch hitting. From the Arrows' bench she heard something she hadn't heard all season: cheers for her plays. Winners and losers certainly behaved differently. The Arrows swept the series and won the divisional title, leaving the Little Rock crowd silent at last. A specter from the future had visited them and would not go away.

From Little Rock the Arrows' bus went directly to Midland for the league championship battle. They won one and lost one at Midland, then came home. Memphis had never won a divisional title.

The Memphis crowds, hungry for victory, were not disappointed. The Arrows won the series and the title, driving the home crowds crazy. Thomas, who hadn't hit a ball past the pitcher all season, bounced one over the first baseman's head to drive in the winning run. Thomas was carried off the field by his teammates, and his picture was splashed all over the sports section.

Linda's parents, sister, and brother had come to Memphis for the final games, just like they had for the opening games. What a difference, though. The morning after the victory, they were all having breakfast together in the motel coffee shop when Jack Doyle and Ulysses S. Crowder came up to the table. Linda introduced them.

"We just came to say good-bye," said Crowder, grinning. "You were a good luck charm."

"Next season," said Doyle, making sure she caught the intent of his words.

When Jack and Ulysses left, Linda caught her mother staring at her. "Do you like him – that Doyle?" asked her mother.

"Sure," Linda answered easily. "I like him. But I don't trust him."

"Does that make a difference?"

"All the difference in the world."

Pouring more coffee, her mother exchanged glances with her father. They must think I'm blind, thought Linda.

"I wouldn't want you getting involved with a ball player," her mother added.

"Mom – I *am* a ballplayer!"

In February, Linda reported to the team's spring training camp in Arizona. It felt good – natural and normal – to return to baseball after a few months relaxing at her parents' house. It felt almost as good to have her own shower, conspicuously new, conspicuously labeled, SHOWERS WOMEN. The shower wasn't the only change: Jack Doyle had been traded to New York. As a result, he wasn't in Arizona with the Cactus League teams, but in Florida with the Grapefruit League. Ulysses S. Crowder was there, and he and Linda slapped hands in greeting. "We're going to Iowa," Ulysses told her. "Wait and see."

Ulysses was right. The two of them were sent up to the class AAA Iowa Pioneers.

If Memphis had been baptism by fire, then Iowa was the reward. The fans made her feel at home, comfortable and relaxed. Possibly because of their warmth, her hitting, which she feared would be cramped by the cold Iowa spring, started with a single, a double, then a triple.

"Where's the homer?" asked Ulysses.

"It's coming," she promised.

She felt at home in the land of corn, soybeans, hogs, and John Deere factories. The hostility against women in baseball was still there, but it wasn't as blatant as it had been in Memphis -- probably because she had survived a year in the minors.

Fischer, "Call-Me-Fish," the manager of the Pioneers, was cut higher off the hog than Porkfat. "Okay, Moonshine, show us what you can do."

"Sunshine."

"Like I said, Moonshine, show us what you can do."

Whenever she got a hit, Fish would wait until she returned to the bench, then begin. "Where'd you get that godawful batting stance?"

"I always stand like that."

"I don't care if you always stand like that, that's no way to stand. Too deep in the box. Get closer to the plate so you can hit those curves." Unwrapping three sticks of gum, he folded each before stuffing it into his mouth. "Annowdath."

"What?"

Chomp, chomp. Chew. "I said, another thing. Be sure to swing at the first strike. Never let a good pitch go by."

At first she thought Fischer was just like Barr, but when she followed his advice, she realized he wasn't. He had her smashing pitches all over the field. Then he helped improve her double play. "Hit 'em between the eyes, Moonshine! That's right, go on – throw it at their fuckin' eyes! Now listen, Moonshine, those runners are going to come in high on you, trying to take you out of the double play. You throw that ball high, make them come in low, see, that way you can get the double play." Then he gave her light weights to work out with. "Just the hands, Moonshine. You work on your hands, your wrists, 'cause you're a hitter. That's right, light weights, lots of repetitions. Here – here's how."

The Pioneers had been second place finishers in the division for more years than they wanted to remember. This year they grabbed first and never gave it up. They lost the league championship after a series of close, hard-fought games, but when Linda got back to her locker room, she found Al Mowerinski waiting for her. "You're scuffed," he said. "Not let's show the Eagles what a good shortstop looks like."

4   At Bat

The *Chicago Sun Vindicator* broke the news by splashing Neal Vanderlin's column across its front page the evening before opening day.

Eagles Threaten Strike If Sunshine Plays

The Chicago Eagles, unable to win, place, or show for the last four years, appear ready to move out of their perennial fourth place slot – and gallop off the track, across the infield, and out of the park, all before the season even begins.

Something pretty awful must be causing this sudden bolt. Is there a fire in the starting gate? A snake in the stable? Nothing like it, pal. The panic is reaction to one human being: Linda Sunshine by name, female by sex, major leaguer by ability. Rumor is strong that the team (or, more correctly, the male members of the team) will strike tomorrow if manager Lenny Black puts Sunshine in the lineup.

Big Al Mowerinski, trying to spur his fourth-place steed toward victory, has had the ungrateful beast kick and buck at the notion of equality. The unruly animal does not want to enter the 20th century. Mowerinski is learning that his horse has many parts, and the part with some horse sense isn't nearly so large as the part of the horse that swats flies.

While Mowerinski spurs the beast, perhaps dismounting and

pulling at the reins, perhaps kicking it from behind, keep in mind that this is an owner *taking a historic step forward. It is the players who are balking – looking and sounding more like hardheaded cousins to the horse than like the thoroughbreds they are supposed to be.*

Instead of being proud that a former baseball player (a former member of the Chicago Eagles, a member of the Eagles' last world championship team) has taken the lead in the struggle for equality, a lead that surpasses Branch Rickey's hiring of Jackie Robinson, the male players on the Eagles are acting like children, throwing a temper tantrum over a childish privilege (keeping baseball for the boys) that has been taken away from them.

Not all of the male members of the Eagles are talking strike. Second baseman Frank Laughing and utility man Zack Weiss would never stoop so low. They realize they have nothing to fear – and all to gain – from a good Eagle shortstop. Others on the team are acting more like nags fit for the glue factory than like champions ready for a challenge.

The season will go on. It will go on with or without the players who are acting like the wrong end of the horse. And it will go on with Linda Sunshine playing baseball.

Sunshine is one of the top three or four rookies in baseball, and, if the players' "strike" is swatted across its rear end with a whip as it should be, I predict she will develop into one of the top shortstops of all time. In Memphis Sunshine batted .319 and had only two fielding errors in a ten-week season of 85 games. This is more than creditable, it is downright impressive. In Iowa her statistics improved: she batted .324, scored 86 runs (four of them homers), and had 70 RBIs. Read those statistics again, and you'll realize that the Eagle players who want Sunshine off the team are not concerned with winning their baseball games. Their first, dominant, and in this case blinding concern is asserting their own prejudice, privilege, and ignorance.

If Lenny Black were any kind of manager, he would turn this strike around. But in my presense, he listened to the hate-filled shouts of Merle Isemonger and certain other team members and said nothing. Could it be that Black is paying homage to the wrong end of the horse?

Baseball fans can put a stop to this kind of backwardness by showing Sunshine they support her right to play baseball – by showing the strike "leaders" they will not tolerate this attack on the game of baseball, where all players are created equal.

Linda read the column twice while preparing salad, garlic bread, sausage, sauce, and mostaccioli in her new apartment, loading up on carbohydrates for the long season ahead. Not bad. Vanderlin's column was not bad. She read it a third time, then cut it out and dropped it into a wicker basket on top of her desk.

The wrong end of the horse. A good way of putting it. Vanderlin had touched on all the right points. All, she thought, spearing a mouthful of greens on her fork and crunching them in her mouth, except one. Tokenism. Not tokenism in that she was the only woman in baseball: that, she hoped, would change. But tokenism in another, equally pernicious, way. She had been playing ball with the whole horse, front and back, for the last two months down in the Southwest, and she thought she understood both ends of the horse. The front end (Frank and Zack, for example) probably thought it very strange to be playing with a woman. But they accepted it. ("You're just a rookie, as far as I'm concerned," Frank had told her down in Arizona.) The middle (Harland Abilene, for example) would go along with whichever end of the horse dominated. The hind end (Merle Isemonger, Lacey Griffen and Bobby Knuff, for starters) would buck and kick for all it was worth to prevent her from playing baseball. *Especially* to prevent her from playing shortstop.

That was the one point Vanderlin hadn't touched on. Shortstop was the key infield position. The shortstop told the second baseman (and not the other way around) who would cover the bag. The shortstop talked to the third baseman and pitcher, keeping them alert. In short, the shortstop gave the infield orders. It was bad enough for players like Isemonger that she was on the field: it was heresy that she played shortstop. In the exhibit games, where she played short, she would talk to Griffen, the third baseman, and he would send hostile stares her way, stares that said "I Don't Take Orders From Women." Knuff, the first baseman, acted as if every throw she made to him was tainted, reeking of Essence-of-Woman or something. Yeah, she thought, angrily tearing a piece of garlic bread off the loaf, it was nothing new. She had heard it all before, and not just in the minors. When she had worked summers to earn college money she had heard it – heard it in the cardboard box factory, heard it in the steel mills, heard it in the bookstore: I'll work with women, but I'll quit before I take orders from them. *Quit, then, you bastards. I'll welcome someone else in your place.*

After dinner Linda walked down the eight flights of stairs to the back door and out to the beach. The night was already dark; the beach held only a few hardy dog walkers. Shivering in the cold and damp, she turned back to the front of the building, then walked up Sheridan Road. At a drugstore, she bought two more copies of the *Sun Vindicator* so that she could send Vanderlin's column home.

No sense in walking up eight flights – she didn't need the exercise tonight. A man stared at her as she stepped into the elevator. She looked up from her papers. A strange sensation came over her, as if she had been there before. Was it *déjà vu?* She felt she was in a dream, from which she would awaken any second.

Suddenly he pointed a finger at her. "You're Linda Sunshine."

"That's me," she smiled, sensing from his tone that he wasn't hostile. She punched the button for the eighth floor.

"It took me a second to recognize you. You got your hair cut."

Grinning, she ran her fingers through what was left of her hair. "Manager's orders. I had it all cut off this morning. At least, it seems like it was all cut off."

"Did Black really order you to cut it off?" he asked in amazement.

She nodded. The door finally closed. She knew him. She knew she knew him: she just couldn't place him. He was leaning against the elevator railing as casually as if they were chatting over the outfield fence.

He shook his head. "I suppose he'll want you to wear a cup next."

Linda laughed. "I've been issued one already. The same thing happened in Memphis." She hesitated, then said, "I'm sorry – have we met?"

Pulling away from the wall, he thrust out his hand. "Neal Vanderlin. Columnist for the *Sun Vindicator.* We met in Memphis. I asked you about the baseball commissioner's ruling."

How embarrassing. Why hadn't she recognized him? "I'm sorry," she said, shaking his hand. "I remember." She laughed nervously. "I spent two years in the minors, and the rule is still in abeyance, not rescinded." Then, to make amends, she added, "I was just reading your column." Suddenly she realized he was aware of that – he had been staring at the two copies of the paper. *Great move, Linda. At least he doesn't know about the third copy up in your apartment.* "I'm sorry I didn't recognize you," she repeated, feeling as if she were babbling nonsense. What was the matter with the elevator? It was so slow she could have scored an inside- the-park home run.

"No problem. Those newspaper photos never do us justice anyway. First day on the job, they take a mug shot of you, photoengrave it, and you're forever imprinted on a block of wood that's kicked around the composing room. The makeup men play soccer with it on the day shift and hockey on the night. Just in case there's any resemblance left by the time the paper goes to bed, the pressmen scar the plate right across your eyes." He underscored the latter remark by making a slicing gesture with his fingers across his eyes.

The door opened. Linda stepped forward eagerly. Vanderlin placed his hand across the rubber bumper. "Do you live here?"

"Uh. Yeah."

"Wow! I can't believe it! All the buildings in the city of Chicago, and you move into this one. Fantastic."

"Uh. Yeah." Of all the dumb moves to make, this was the dumbest – moving into a building with a sports reporter. Come next March, she'd move elsewhere, that was for sure.

Linda awoke to a cold, gray April morning. This was it, she realized with a start. She turned on the radio, dialing to find the news. Turning up the volume, she stepped into the shower, still listening. Would there be a strike? No, please no, she thought. It would be too . . . humiliating. The news came as she stepped out of the shower. She listened, towel in hand, not even daring to dry herself. *Come on, come on, get to the sports.*

"In sports today, the game will go on. There will be no baseball strike as threatened by the players. The Chicago Eagles will play their opening-day game against California today. Good luck to the Eagles."

Whooshing a sigh of relief, Linda toweled dry, then dressed slowly. She wasn't due at the ballpark until 11:00, and she didn't want to arrive conspicuously early. Pulling on a jacket and scarf, she trotted down the stairs and out to the corner drugstore to buy a paper. Brrr! It must be below freezing, she thought, hurrying back. She took the stairs up to her apartment, then made breakfast and read the paper.

This was it. Today was the day. Just two years ago she had been a college student. Today she was a major league baseball player. Shaking her head in awe, she puzzled over it. It had been hard, yes: she had had to put up with more animosity than she could swing a bat at. But it had also been . . . not hard. That was it: it had been easy. Nervously jabbing a piece of toast into her egg yoke, she stared out the window, the toast halfway to her mouth. Why had it seemed so easy? Did it mean she was better than she gave herself credit for? Or did it mean she was riding for a fall? Pushing aside her unfinished breakfast, she glanced at the clock. 10:15. She gathered her jacket and scarf, got into her car and took Lake Shore Drive south.

At Eagle Stadium, the opening-day crowds were already in line, the vendors already hawking their wares. Linda drove up to the players' parking lot, where an attendant would park her car. "Thanks," she told him, trying to determine whether he was for her or against her from the look on his face. Couldn't tell. Down the tiled, sanitized corridor, past the clubhouse door, past the field manager's office, to the very end of the hall she walked. On her left was a new door. She pushed it open and walked into her own "clubhouse" – a locker room and shower room. No lettering on the door, though. She wondered why. Didn't Al Mowerinski know what it should say? Or did he think it was for her protection? Wooden pegs on the wall for her clothes, built-in shelving with partitions for shoes, gloves, and whatnot. Two three-legged stools, two chairs, a couch. To the left was a shower (just one) divided from the lounge by a tiled partition. On a shelf in front of a mirror was every imaginable deodorant, hair spray, foot spray, and talcum powder known to humanity, all provided by the Eagles.

Walking around her room, Linda took it all in. It had everything – everything except teammates. With a sigh, she sat down at a table and pulled her basket of mail toward her. Wow! It looked like ten times the mail she had received in Memphis and Iowa. There was a small package on top. Hand lettered, neatly wrapped with strapping tape. What was it? Not high enough to be a baseball. Not big enough to be a book. She shook it. Something inside slid heavily from side to side. Looking around, she found a pair of scissors and cut off a side of the package, tipping it toward the table. A dead rat fell out.

Jumping back, Linda turned over her chair and tripped backwards across it, falling on top of it to the floor. Adrenaline coursed through her system; her stomach lurched. Her wrist hurt where she had come down heavily on it, trying to break her fall.

Feeling her heart pound furiously, she stood, pulling the chair upright. Rubbing her wrist, she stared at the package, not wanting to touch it. No return address. The stench was awful.

She looked around for something to dispose of the rat with. Grabbing a can of hairspray in one hand and the mailing box in the other, she held the box just alongside the table, then pushed the rat off the table and into the box with the hairspray can. Then she dropped the box into a wastebasket and put the wastebasket outside her locker room. With soap and hot water, she washed first the table, then the edge of the hairspray can. Finally, she sprayed scented deodorant all over the room. Flopping into a chair, she realized she was close to tears. Biting down on her lips, she squeezed her eyes shut. *No. Don't cry. Not on your first day. Not because of hatred. Don't let them drive you out.*

Jimmy Clayton, the equipment manager, knocked and came in, carrying a tray of pre-game munchies: bananas, pears, apples, oranges, doughnuts, pastries, and a pot of hot coffee. "Everything okay with the equipment?" he asked. "Uniforms? Shoes? Helmets? Sunglasses?"

Linda stood. *Try to look natural.* "Great. Everything looks terrific, thanks. And, Jimmy – you don't have to knock. Just walk right in, okay?"

"Can I get you anything else?" he asked, setting the tray on a table. "Pop, hot dog, taco, Italian beef, potato chips? We've even got some brownies over in the . . .. Uh, I think they're not all eaten yet. I can try to get you some if you want."

She shook her head and thanked him for asking. Maybe after the game, but not right now. She doubted she could eat even later. Maybe if she had teammates all around her it would be different.

Jimmy left and she started to undress.

Another knock. Busy place. "Come in," she called as she bent forward, pulling her sweater off. She began to unbutton her shirt.

Frank Laughing pushed the swinging door open, saw her, and stopped. "Oh. Uh."

"Frank, don't knock, okay? Just walk in. I'm going to be walking into your room all season long, and I'm not going to knock." She smiled at him. "Anyway, thanks for coming, whatever you want. I'm kind of nervous."

"Ah, what rookie isn't?" He was staring everywhere but at her.

Linda straightened, about to remove her shirt, then realized that Frank wasn't ready for this yet. "What did you want?"

"It's not for me, but some of the guys could use some extra comps, and I said I'd see if you had any. I mean, I know you're not from Chicago and don't know anybody here, so I thought maybe you might have a couple of extra for today's game? I know it's late notice, but . . . well."

Comps, the complimentary tickets that each player received for each game, were always exchanging hands between those who needed them and those who didn't. Linda would have given hers to her parents and anybody they chose to bring along, but since the Eagles would play Pittsburgh *in* Pittsburgh next week, her parents decided to see her play then. "But," her mother had suggested, "we have friends in Chicago; maybe they'd like tickets to opening day." Linda had said fine, her mother had called the friends, the friends had called Linda, and Linda had given away all her comps for opening day.

"Sorry, Frank. I gave them to friends of my parents. But I have four left for tomorrow's game – I'll be glad to give them to whoever needs them."

"Terrific. I'll let everybody know." Frank hurried away.

A few minutes later, Linda was fully dressed. She looked at herself in the full-length mirror. Green baseball spikes, white socks, green stirrup socks, gray pants with brown and green trim, green jersey, gray shirt with brown and green trim and the number 18 on back, green baseball cap. She smiled at herself in the mirror, then laughed. An Eagle uniform! She was a baseball player. Frowning, she noticed that one pant leg came farther below her knee than the other. Bending, she adjusted it, then inspected herself in the mirror again. Not bad. Everything she could see looked good. And the things she couldn't see (like the layer of long underwear) were even more necessary than what was visible. Turning, she walked out the door to the field.

The next ninety minutes were warm-ups. Pickup. Hot potato. BP – which today consisted of five swings at whatever came from the pitcher, then two bunts and two hit-and-runs. If the batting coach felt like it, it included a squeeze bunt. Today he did not. Then fielding. Toss it around. Bobby Knuff and Lacey Griffen avoided throwing to her; Frank Laughing didn't.

By 12:45, the Eagles had finished practice and returned to the clubhouse, letting California take the field. Game time was 1:15.

T. M. Curry, not on the road scouting, for that would have meant missing an opening-day game, sat in his usual seat in the Eagles' block, talking to Collette, one of his daughters, and her husband, Jeff. Curry was glad his son-in-law loved baseball. Collette did, too, of course, but then she was a Curry, and baseball was in her blood.

"Curry Powder." Al Mowerinski took a seat next to Curry. "Collette, Jeff." He shook hands with both of them.

"Al, this is going to be quite a game," Jeff offered. "Just think, we're watching history."

Collette agreed. "I think it's just wonderful! I'll bet she

does real well, too. Don't you think so, Dad?"

Curry settled into his seat better. "I want to see the Eagles win."

"They'll win," said Al. "They won in Memphis and they won in Iowa because of her."

"You mean they won *despite* her!" snapped Curry.

"*Because* of her, Curry."

"Despite her."

"Hey, hey!" kidded Jeff. "Can't we agree that they won *with* her, huh? That sounds fair to me."

Curry glared at his son-in-law. It was different for him: he wasn't a ball player; he didn't know how difficult it was to win. No, Jeff sat back and enjoyed watching, praised when things went right, grumbled and criticized when they went wrong. He didn't know how hard it was to get everything right – to keep up the skills, to prevent what they called "mental lapses," to concentrate, concentrate, concentrate on every pitch, every play. It was difficult enough to do that with nine good men. Now . . . well, if the Eagles won now, they would do it despite their shortstop.

Jeff leaned across Curry to speak to Al. "I'm surprised that Lenny Black is playing her."

"Yeah," said Collette, continuing his thought, "the papers make him seem one-hundred percent against it."

"You can't believe everything you read in the papers," replied Al, smiling.

Smiling! Curry was incensed. He knew why Big Al was smiling – because he had *ordered* Black to play Sunshine at short, that's why! Yeah, you couldn't believe everything you read in the papers, but in this case the papers were right. Lenny was against it, one-hundred percent against it. It would serve Al right if Lenny Black quit in protest. Only thing was, thought Curry, again shifting in his chair, there was no way Lenny would quit. Leastwise, not while Merle Isemonger was on the Eagles. Curry knew the truth about Lenny – not just the truth about his two mistresses, one on each coast, for chrissake, while he was a married man with a family. No, Curry knew that Merle Isemonger was Lenny Black's bastard son. Maybe nobody except he, T. M. Curry, knew it. And Lenny, of course. It had been suspicious the way Black had insisted on having Merle Isemonger. Curry had found out, by accident, that when it looked like New York was going to get Isemonger, Black had made secret probes to see if he could work for New York.

That was what got Curry thinking. T. M. Curry was no dummy. A manager doesn't quit managing to follow a player around, for chrissake! So Curry did a little scouting on his own. He checked out Merle Isemonger. Isemonger was his mother's name. The kid was raised by her out in Los Angeles. Curry went to talk to her. She didn't *say* Lenny was the boy's father, but Curry was no dummy. Somebody had sent money to put Merle through school. Somebody had sent money to give Merle everything he wanted. Then Curry had talked to some of the boys who had played in the California League with Lenny about twenty-five years ago, and they told him enough. Curry smiled to himself as he thought of his scouting job. It was a good thing to know. You never knew when you might need this kind of information. Not that Curry had anything against fathers getting their sons into baseball. Hell, no – today baseball was a lucrative business, and more and more sons were following in their fathers' footsteps. What Curry objected to was . . . well, the secret nature of the thing. And Black doing something illegal like talking to New York without getting permission from the Eagles. Black was a devious, underhanded bastard. Probably why he was manager – they didn't call managing the underworld of baseball for nothing, no sir.

"Hey, let's go Eagles! Look at that action out there!" rooted Jeff. "Hey, Al, look at number 18 – she's really digging them out. Not bad!"

Curry frowned at Jeff, but only halfheartedly. A few more minutes and the game would begin. T. M. Curry felt the old excitement rise in him.

The dugout temperature gauge read thirty-six degrees. Thank god for double-layered underwear and uniform jerseys, thought Linda, huddled on the bench, peering out at what she could see of the stands. Homemade banners proliferated. LET THE SUNSHINE IN read one in the left-field stands. YOU ARE MY SUNSHINE read a sign down the first baseline. WE LOVE LINDA battled for a spot next to SUNSHINE GO HOME and SS = SOFTBALL FOR SUNSHINE. BASEBALL IS A MANS' GAME proclaimed the biggest, draped over the center field fence. Can't punctuate, she thought. Can't think. FACE IT WITH A GRIN. Was that a "for," or an "against"?

"And now, ladies and gentlemen – the Chicago *Eagles!*"

Hearing the public address broadcast, the unsmiling players left the dugout one by one as their names were called. She heard her name announced and jogged out to the lineup, getting a better look at the crowd. At first the sound washed over her in a wave: it was the loudest sound she had ever heard. There must be 50,000 people out there. As she stood in the lineup, she began to separate the wave of sound into decipherable parts. She heard cheers. She also heard loud, prolonged boos. Her hands were cold and sweaty.

"Keep on your toes, kid. Head down. Look that ball into your glove."

"Thanks, Zack." Trotting out to her position, Linda watched Zack Weiss take left field. Up until this year, Zack had played shortstop. Actually, he had told her down in Arizona, he had played every position in the game, starting out as a pitcher more than twenty years ago. He had gotten the nickname Wacky Zacky when, apparently bored by pitching one day, he fired three pitches in a row, three seconds apart, across the plate, the feat being performed with three different baseballs (two had been hidden in his ill-fitting uniform in specially sewn inside pockets). The last two of the three pitches had been fired across the plate as the astounded batter was recovering from his swing. Not long after, Zack had been converted from a pitcher into a catcher, a most unusual conversion. When his knees gave out there, he became a first baseman. Zack claimed to have worked his way around the infield in proper order, and then to the outfield. Now he was playing out what he said was his last year, waiting for retirement.

Isemonger kicked at the dirt in front of the rubber, digging a hole. The first California batter stepped into the box. Harland Abilene, the catcher, signaled. One finger: fastball. "Hum, hum!" chattered Linda, conveying to Lacey Griffen that the pitch would be a fastball. She signaled to Zack in left field. Icehead took his windup and hurled the ball. The batter swung, missing. Icehead's delivery left him twisted toward first base, his back parallel to the ground, his right knee touching earth. Not the best fielding pitcher in the world, but, Jesus, he has speed, thought Linda. According to the Eagles' program,

Isemonger stood 6′3″ and weighed 228 pounds. His height, weight, and the speed of his pitches made him a formidable opponent. She knew: whenever he threw batting practice, Icehead made a special point of pitching her tight, coming in so close she had to move back from the plate quickly. Harland signaled. Two fingers: curve. Linda leaned forward, on her toes, her glove ready. "Easy, easy," she conveyed to Griffen. Icehead's curve was outside. One and one the count.

Icehead was the ringleader against her, she knew that. He never saw her without making a comment. "Is that Little Miss Sunshine herself?" he would ask. Or, "Why that must Lyndon Sunshine, the girl who wants to be a man." Or, "Hey, I didn't know you needed tits to play shortstop. Is that some kind of new regulation?" She wondered where he had gotten his baseball nickname, but she didn't want to ask. "Icehead" seemed extremely appropriate.

Isemonger struck out the first California batter. The second batter lined a single to right. Knuff jumped for it but had no chance. One on, one out. That brought up Prosan. Harland signaled a curve, but Isemonger shook it off. Harland signaled curve again and Isemonger, glaring at him, nodded. The pitch broke, and Prosan missed it. Prosan fouled the next two pitches into the stands. Nothing and two the count. Prosan had to protect the plate now; Icehead was way ahead of him.

Crack! She was already moving. The ball was sailing in a high arc down the left-field line, just behind third base. *"Mine!"* she called. It was the shortstop's ball. She caught it just short of the stands and threw it to Frank at second.

"Hey, Sunshine – way to go!"

"Lucky catch!"

"Hey, lady – go home!"

Trotting back to her position at short, Linda suppressed a grin of happiness. It had been a routine catch, but she had made it. Her first major league putout! She flashed two fingers to the infield, indicating two outs. Griffen scowled at her.

Waving his bat around his head as if it were an ax and the ball a tree to be felled, the third California batter limbered up, removed the doughnut from his bat, and finally stepped into the box. Icehead threw a fastball and the batter connected. Frank Laughing fielded it on the hop and threw to first. Three up, three down.

Griffen doubled to start the Eagles' half of the inning, advanced to third on Zack's sacrifice fly, and scored on Harland's single. 1-0. The crowd roared. Frank Laughing, batting cleanup, hit a homer, making the score 3-0. What a way to begin the season. The crowd stood in ovation, screaming and clapping. The twenty-foot-tall wooden Eagle atop the scoreboard released the rag doll gripped in its talons. The doll (dressed like a California player for this series) fell into the bleacher crowd. Whoever got the doll and turned it in to the box office would get two free game tickets, plus a free ball and bat. Kids and adults alike scrambled for the stuffed toy. Zowski struck out, and Bobby Knuff popped out, ending the bottom of the first.

The top of the second passed without a California run. Bottom of the second and she would be the third batter. *Be calm. Look at the pitch. Don't let him whiff you.* Ulysses, batting seventh, led off the second inning. He was walked. A reprieve. More than a reprieve, she thought, because whatever he did his next time up would be just that, his next time up. He hadn't struck out. *Anything but a strikeout, anything.* From the on-deck circle, she watched Isemonger at the plate. Black was insulting her by letting the pitcher bat ahead of her. The count was one and two. The next pitch came in; he was caught looking.

The boos began when she stepped out of the dugout, grew louder as she walked to the plate, and reached full volume as she settled into the batter's box. Cups, hot dog wrappers, candy wrappers, popcorn, cardboard megaphones – all came flying out on the field, a cornucopia of garbage. The umpire called time, telling the grounds crew to clear the field. Linda looked into the California dugout. The players were smiling. They love it, she thought. She looked at the crowd and listened to the boos. A sharp stab of disappointment filled her: she had expected the major league crowds to be better than this.

A steady, undying sound, the booing gave no sign of ceasing. It drowned out the cheering. Debris accumulated in the home plate area as fast as the grounds crew could sweep it up. Then the bleacher fans joined in, causing the grounds crew to run to the outfield. The April wind lifted the hot dog wrappers to the upper deck; they fluttered down slowly, gracefully drifting this way and that until they landed on the field with the other flotsam and jetsam of civilization.

Standing well outside the batter's box, Linda wiped her hands on her pants. The pitcher threw some easy balls to the catcher to keep warm. They were bound to run out of trash sooner or later. The home plate ump walked over to the Eagles' dugout and spoke to Lenny Black. Black charged out of the dugout in a fast, bowlegged roll, following the ump back to the plate, shouting. The umpire had warned him the Eagles would forfeit, 9-0, if the home crowd's behavior delayed the game much longer. Turning, the ump bumped chests with Black, warning him to back off or be ejected. A wonderful opening game. Soon, Linda realized with a start, it would dawn on

Black that he could pull her out. *No! I want to play!*

"It's stopped," she said to the umpire, pointing to the dwindling amount of fluttering paper. The ump pulled down his mask with one hand, brushed Black aside with the other, and shouted: *"Plaaaay baaaallll!"*

This, then, was it.

"A little chin music there, Ned." "Stick it to her ear, Ace." "Hey, Ned, she's a big pussy, she can't hit. Ha, ha, ha." The calls came from the California dugout. Supposedly a cry of "stick it to his ear" meant ejection from the game. Supposedly.

She dug in and waited for the pitch. *It'll be a strike. It'll be right across the plate and I'll hit it.* It came straight at her, shoulder high, missing her only because she threw herself backward into the dirt. More boos from the crowd. Against the pitcher? Or against her? She picked herself up, dusted herself off, and dug back in.

"Hey, Sunshine," advised the catcher, "get out while you can. Nobody'll blame you if you leave now. They can still send in a pinch hitter for you."

Considerate of him. She concentrated on the pitcher, ignoring whatever else the catcher was mumbling as he tried to distract her. The ball came spinning at her and was by her before she could blink. A strike. One and one the count. As contrasted to the pitching in the minors, the pitching in the majors was . . . awesome. *It's in another league. Ha. Come on, concentrate. If they can throw it, I can hit it.*

Behind her she heard the soft shuffling sound of the catcher's feet, sensed him settle into place and lift his glove. She watched the pitcher intently. *It'll be a strike. Coming right at me. I'm waiting for a fastball, low and on the outside corner. That's my pitch. Here it comes.* Focusing on the release point, she saw the white blur appear above the pitcher's shoulder, coming out of his hand. *Almost here, it's a fastball, hit it!* She hammered it through to left for a single, advancing Ulysses to second.

"This must be lady's day," said the first baseman when she had settled in at first.

It was all Linda could do to keep her feet planted firmly on the bag: she wanted to jump up and down. A hit! A hit! Put that in your record books, she thought happily. Suddenly she noticed the first-base coach. Oops. Time to take a lead from first. She stepped out, her eye on the pitcher, who ignored her.

Griffen singled to right. Ulysses scored, and Linda took third with a bent-leg slide. The coach at third clapped his hands and nodded his head. Zack hit into a double play, and the inning ended. Eagles ahead, 4-0.

California alternated runs with outs in the top of the fourth, scoring two. The score stood 4-2, California up, two outs, runners on first and second. Harland signaled for a change of pace. The batter connected; the ball hooked crazily down the left-field line. Another shortstop play. "Mine!" She made the catch with ease and turned to throw to Griffen. Something soft and wet hit her in the neck. Startled, she looked toward the stands, brushing something (an egg?) away from her neck. The egg was followed by something even more dumbfounding: the runner on second started toward third. Incredible! Linda fired the ball to Griffen at third.

The runner was out by a country mile, and the Eagles were safely out of the California half of the inning. Frank jogged in behind her. "You should have seen your face when Saunders started toward third. What was that, an egg?"

"Yeah. I think there was more egg on Saunders's face than

mine. He was crazy." She wiped her neck with her hand, then sniffed the hand. "I'll probably smell like a rotten egg before the game's over."

Isemonger, coddled in his heavy jacket, stood in front of her, blocking her line of vision. *Talk about bad eggs and they all appear.*

"That ball wasn't yours," he said.

"The ball I caught? What do you mean?"

"I mean the one you called for, you dumb broad! That was Zack's ball. Leave it alone."

"Don't call me a broad," she said evenly. "The word is *woman*." Isemonger glared at her. She considered calling him a dumb prick, but thought better of it. "I judged it as my ball." She turned, deciding to ignore Icehead.

"Hey! Look at me when I talk to you, Sunshine!"

"I'm looking through you, Isemonger."

"Sit down." Zack's hand on Isemonger's shoulder turned him around. "It was her ball. Why don't you just pitch and leave the fielding to us, huh? Just like you always do."

"You talking about my fielding?!" demanded Icehead. "There's nothing wrong with my fielding. You check my statistics. I can field as well as any pitcher." Icehead paced the dugout, returning to where Zack sat. "Fuck off, Weiss. You're too old to be playing this game anyway." Isemonger did not forget personal injuries or insults, however wildly imagined they might be.

"I'll be here long after you're gone, Icehead."

"You're fulla shit." Isemonger sat in a corner and huddled inside his jacket, changing his hand warmer from palm to palm. Black stood in front of him, facing Zack Weiss. Zack sneered before he sat down. Tension sat in the dugout, a twenty-sixth player, biggest one on the team.

In the top of the eighth, California loaded the bases, one out. Saunders, the batter, hit a hard liner that Linda leaped for, trapping it in her glove. Then, just as she touched ground, taking a step to throw, she tripped over her own feet, fell, and dropped the ball. The runner on third scored, making it 4-3. The runners on second and first advanced, and the batter made it to first, all before she could recover and throw the ball somewhere. Wildly, she looked around. Nowhere to throw. Bases loaded. Holding the ball a second longer, making certain she was in control and the runners weren't going to advance, she threw to Isemonger. Catching it, he spit in her direction. "Error," flashed the scoreboard. The boos were deafening.

"There goes the pennant!" yelled a heckler.

The next California batter met the ball totally by accident, surprising himself and Harland. "Fair ball!" shouted the ump as the ball dribbled toward Isemonger. Griffen ran toward home to cover the plate as Linda ran to third and Harland ran out to get the ball. Icehead came to his senses a second too late, picked up the ball, and fired home. Too late. Score tied, 4-4. Griffen, walking back to third, glared at Linda. She looked away, guilty. It was her error that had started the mess. She felt terrible. As she leaned forward, waiting for the next pitch, she could feel her thighs tremble, her arms shake with nervousness.

The Eagles got out of the inning when the next California batter flied out to deep center. In the dugout, Linda sat on the bench silently. Nobody spoke. Nobody scored, either. They went into the top of the ninth tied 4-4 with California, their arch rivals. Black put in a reliever for Isemonger. They came out of it okay, with California failing to score. But the Eagles likewise failed to score. The game went into extra innings.

Then the rain started, a cold, stinging drizzle. Griffen simply glared at her as they took the field for the top of the tenth. Linda, her head hanging, took her position.

In the bottom of the twelfth, the Eagles finally scored on a single by Zack that brought in Ulysses. The crowd, damp and cold, nonetheless roared its approval. The players walked off the field to the showers.

Linda sat on a hard-backed chair in her locker room, arms resting on her knees. She hadn't bothered to remove her wet clothes and didn't even feel their coldness against her skin. Some big-league debut. Her error had all but lost the game. It had certainly caused the game to go into extra innings. She had wanted to be so good out there, wanted to contribute, to help the Eagles win -- all she had done was make 50,000 people sit through three extra innings of freezing rain.

The door swung open. Jumping up from her chair, she turned her back to the door, wiping a hand across her eyes. She took a ragged breath, walked to her locker, and fumbled at the buttons of her uniform shirt.

"Come on in," she motioned to Vanderlin.

He stood there in the doorway, staring at her. Then he stepped forward, letting the swinging door go behind him. "Hey," he said, "you won. You're supposed to look at least a little bit happy."

"I am." She thought her voice sounded awful. "I'm a little bit happy. I mean, I'm happy we won."

"Good." Throwing his coat over one of the chairs, he walked over to the table and inspected the food. "Umm. Looks better than what we get in the press dining room."

Pulling her shirt out of her pants, letting it hang over her belt, Linda walked over to the table and inspected the food. "Help yourself. I'm not hungry." She had her voice under control now. "Anyway, there's enough to feed the whole infield here."

"Thanks." He walked around the table, inspecting the food. "You *must* be hungry. You were out there nearly four hours. Look." He grabbed a plate and pointed to the food. "Ribs . . . bread . . . baked potato . . . hmmm, no hot soup."

"I'm not." Linda sat and watched him pile food on his plate.

Sitting down across from her, Vanderlin balanced his plate on his knees. "Everybody makes errors, Linda."

She whirled away, staring at the walls.

"I think you were impressive."

She turned swiftly, to see if he was being sarcastic. He sat there, munching on a rib, looking totally unsarcastic.

"Two hits out of five at-bats. Great fielding."

"*Not* great fielding! Tell the *truth*. I'm not some . . . some . . . some . . .." She stood, glaring at him. "Jesus, it was awful. I feel so *stupid*, so *dumb!*" She paced to the door, then around the food table, her hands in the back pockets of her pants. "I can just see it now, some sports writer somewhere is going to say I'm starting the season on an eighty-five-error pace."

Licking sauce off his fingers, Vanderlin returned a now-meatless rib bone to his plate. "Actually, I checked. It's closer to ninety."

Linda stared at him, speechless. Still staring, she backed into a chair and sat down.

"C'mon, Linda – I'm not going to write that, for god's

sake! I'm a columnist, not a reporter. When I give facts, I put them in the big picture. In the big picture, you're terrific." He paused, speared a piece of potato on his fork, paused in midair, and continued. "You're lucky you didn't pull a real boner, like booting the ball. Or throwing to the wrong base. Or colliding with the runner. You're a rookie – rookies make mistakes."

He was making her feel worse, as if she were some childish superstar who had to be cajoled out of a bad mood. But he was making her feel a lot better than he was making her feel worse. The Eagles hadn't lost – they'd won. She was afraid Black wouldn't play her tomorrow, but she'd have to deal with that herself. She smiled at him. "Thanks."

He pointed at the food. "This means you aren't eating with the other players. That doesn't seem right to me."

Linda snorted in derision. "I guess they get off on eating naked or something."

"Yeah," he said, looking at her, "some of them do. Eat naked, I mean. I don't know whether they get off on it or not." Placing his empty plate on one of the empty stools, he cleared his throat. "Are you going out to dinner with any of the players?"

"No. Nobody invited me."

"Well, they're probably all going home. After a day game, everybody leaves fast."

"Yeah. Probably."

Vanderlin stood. "I have a story deadline in an hour."

"Oh, sorry." Linda stood.

He laughed, and she gave him a questioning look.

"You're the first ballplayer who has ever said 'Sorry' to me. It's not your fault."

"Okay. Happy, not sorry," she smiled.

"Would you go out to dinner with me?"

She was so surprised she didn't reply. Dinner? With a reporter? She didn't know. It wasn't off limits, was it? No, it couldn't be. Reporters were everywhere – on the team bus, the team plane, the hotels, the dining rooms.

Vanderlin continued hurriedly. "You need some hot soup. I know a great restaurant in Greek Town. I can be back here in an hour – seventy minutes, I promise."

Linda grinned and motioned at the food on the table. "How can you eat in the press dining room, eat here, and still be hungry?"

"This is just sort of an appetizer," he assured her. "A warm-up."

Removing her shirt, Linda balled it up and flipped it into the laundry basket. She stood in front of the food table and looked over the spread, unbuttoning her jersey as she did so. "I guess I can have a few appetizers, too."

"Uh, yeah," he mumbled, watching her.

"First I'll strip down," she said, removing her jersey and flinging it into the laundry basket, "then I'll eat." She kicked off her shoes and pulled off her pants. Standing there in her long underwear and socks, she looked at Neal, then burst out laughing at the look on his face. She was enjoying her joke tremendously. He had made her feel good. "Yes. I'd like to go to dinner with you. Thanks for asking."

"I'll meet you here in a little over an hour?" he asked.

"Great."

She waited for him to leave so that she could shower. He stood there looking at her. Hadn't he ever seen thermal underwear before? "Good-bye, Neal. See you soon."

He backed out of the swinging doors.

Linda stretched, took off the rest of her clothes, and stepped into a hot, hot shower. She felt hungry.

She was just stretching luxuriously, yawning, when the phone rang.

"Linda, this is Al. I'm calling a meeting in my office. Ten o'clock today. Be there. Those boneheads say they're going out on strike unless you're barred from playing."

She swallowed. Her stomach felt as if she had swallowed a ton of air.

"Don't worry," he said. "They don't stand a chance."

When she walked into Al Mowerinski's office, Frank Laughing, Harland Abilene, Charlie Kovack, and Zack Weiss were already there. Al Mowerinski was not. She looked at the four players. Harland was leaning up against the center wall, facing Al's desk. Kovack was with him. They looked away as she entered. Frank and Zack were leaning against the wall farthest from the door. Linda walked over to join them, aware that the sides were lining up.

Lacey Griffen, Ulysses S. Crowder, Merle Isemonger, and Bobby Knuff swaggered in. Griffen, Icehead, and Knuff lined up along the wall directly across from Frank, Zack, and Linda. Like soldiers ready for battle. Linda looked at Ulysses, but he avoided meeting her eyes. Instead, he walked over to the "neutral" wall, greeted Harland, and began joking nervously with him. Linda, hurt and disappointed in Ulysses, watched Griffen frown at Ulysses' back.

"This is gonna be good, betcha," said Zack, nodding his head at the row of three. "Betcha there's no strike, either."

"What strike? What you talking about, man?" asked

Griffen.

"Don't believe everything you read in the papers," added Knuff.

"Yeah, especially in that shithead Vanderlin's column!" Isemonger glared at Zack.

"The only reason we're here, Icehead, is because of your bonehead play. You, Knuff, and Griffen." Zack stabbed his finger at each of the three across the room from him. "What you're doing is bush, strictly bush."

"Fuck you, old man," Icehead laughed, looking around at his companions for approval. "You're too old and dumb to be on this team anyway."

"Only reason we're here," Knuff snapped, never even glancing at Linda, "is because of *her*. She doesn't belong here."

"Don't blame this on me, Knuff. This is all your idea," she retorted angrily.

"Shut up, you dumb dyke, shut up!" screamed Isemonger. "Go get laid; then you wouldn't be here."

"You first. Another five seconds and I think you'll come in your pants."

Isemonger blanched while Frank looked at her calmly and Zack swallowed so hard she could hear it. Then four things happened simultaneously – Isemonger started for her, she straightened from where she had been leaning against the wall and moved forward on the balls of her feet, Zack moved in front of her, and Wally Szczpanozowski walked in, followed by several reporters and their accompanying photographers. The motion stopped, creating a tableau.

"Shit!" grumbled a photographer, snapping away. "Missed something good, I can tell."

The players backed off to their respective walls while the

reporters looked for advantageous positions and the photographers for interesting angles. Isemonger's lips twitched. His eyes settled on Vanderlin, who had been part of the group that followed Zowski in.

"Hey, you! Vanderlin! You think you can get away with calling me a horse's ass?" Isemonger flexed his neck belligerently.

Neal, standing in the middle of the room, scratched his chin. "Well," he drawled, "they censored what I really think of you and settled for my calling you a horse's ass, so I guess I can get away with it."

The remark knocked Icehead off his tether: he started for Vanderlin, who lost no time in shortening the distance between them. As the flashbulbs popped, Wally Szczpanozowski, standing in the middle of the room, grabbed Isemonger from behind while Zack jumped at Vanderlin and pulled him back.

"You're on her side because you want an easy piece of ass!" shouted Isemonger.

Vanderlin broke free of Zack's grasp and jumped Isemonger, who was still being held by Zowski. Zowski, transferring his grasp on Icehead to one hand, held Vanderlin away with the other, then looked about in confusion, wondering what to do with his two problems.

"Did you get that?" an angry television reporter asked her camerawoman.

"No! The damn meeting was supposed to start at ten!"

"Shit!"

Linda avoided looking at Neal. She wished he hadn't reacted to Icehead's remark. At the same time, she wished he had connected a fist to Icehead's jaw.

Hector Gutierrez walked in, looking confused. Knuff

reached out and pulled Hector into line. That was too much for Linda. She walked across the room and spoke to Hector in halting Spanish, asking him if he was going to stand with them against her. Hector looked at them – Isemonger, Knuff, and Griffen. Hector looked at her. Hector looked at Frank and Zack. Hector shook his head and walked across the room with her, making it four against three. Linda looked pointedly at Ulysses, who looked away.

The favorable odds didn't last long. By ten o'clock, the team was, if not assembled, at least all in the room, along with the coaches, trainers, traveling secretary, business manager, scouts, and PR director – and the reporters. Most of the team took the safe center position, with Harland and Kovack. Of the remaining team members, Linda counted far more along Isemonger's wall than along hers. Lenny Black, the manager, stood close to Isemonger, his star pitcher.

Al Mowerinski stepped into his office from a private entrance at ten on the dot. The room went silent. Linda focused on Al, watching him intently.

"What's the problem?" His challenge was addressed to the players along Icehead's wall. The only response he got was a symphony of mumbling and shuffling.

"Lenny. What's the problem?" demanded Al brusquely.

Linda looked away from Al to Lenny Black, the manager.

"The boys are afraid, Al. They're afraid they'll lose games like last night's because she'll make errors like the one she made. It's too much of a handicap, having to play with a woman on the team."

Al walked to his desk and stood in front of it, arms crossed, facing the room. "Okay. Every player who's never made an error, step forward."

Nobody stepped anywhere.

"That's not the point," shouted Icehead.

"What is the point?" demanded Al.

"She's a *woman!*"

"That's biology, not baseball."

"Fuck it! They're one and the same!"

Linda realized that Icehead would flunk biology.

Al walked behind his desk, pulled a wire-bound book out of its center drawer, and dropped it on the desktop. Examining a pen, he adjusted it in his writing hand. Then he opened the book, which everyone had already deduced was a business-sized checkbook. He looked over the room. Several players shifted uncomfortably under his gaze. "I called this meeting," he said softly, "because of the report of a strike tonight." He paused, glancing briefly and dispassionately toward the wall where Isemonger stood. "I guess," Al continued, "I haven't made my position on the question of discrimination clear enough." Again he paused. Then his voice boomed out at its natural level: "*I won't tolerate it!* Anybody who doesn't want to play with Sunshine on the team can leave. Don't bother with a strike, because I'll smash it before it ever gets to the playing field, understand? If you don't want to play with a woman on the team, fine. Everyone's got an inalienable right to stupidity. Step right up, and I'll write you a check for your year's salary. You can spend the season fishing if you're too cowardly to play baseball. When your contract's up, maybe some other team will want you." Flashbulbs popped; reporters scribbled furiously.

"Come on, Knuff." Al wiggled his finger in a beckoning motion to Bobby Knuff. "Step up here and get your $64,000. Two years from now, somebody else can sign you. *Somebody else can sign the whole bunch of you,*" he suddenly roared, "if you're too cowardly to play for the Eagles!"

"You can't do that," replied Knuff.

"I can do a hell of a lot of things, Knuff. I can send you back down to the minors – way down. I can take you to court. I can break you in two. Just try me."

Knuff was silent.

"Come on, show some balls!" Al stepped around the desk and headed toward Knuff, who started to back toward the door ever so slightly.

Zack Weiss ran forward and grabbed Al by the arm. "Al!"

Big Al flicked Zack's arm away and returned to his desk. Facing Icehead's lineup, Al shook his head. "Gutless," he muttered. "Gutless."

Linda watched him in awe. An uncomfortable silence filled the room. Al turned toward the reporters. "You can see there won't be any strike," he said. "The game tonight – all the games – will go on."

Lenny Black, his shoulders ramrod straight, stepped forward. "Al, I should be the one handling this. You're interfering with my job." As he spoke, he looked at the reporters.

Neal Vanderlin laughed. Black glowered at him.

"Your job?!" bellowed Al. "Your fault is more like it, Lenny," he continued, striding across to the manager and jabbing a giant-sized finger into the air about two inches from Lenny Black's face. "Your boy is one of the ringleaders of this. If you were any sort of manager, you'd be handling these players, not kissing their asses."

Black flushed crimson, turned on his heel, and walked out.

Al moved back to his desk. "Okay, enough. It's over with. If you want to play baseball, you walk out that door and tonight you play baseball. If you don't want to play, you just step up here and collect your money. Okay, okay," he waved out the reporters, "it's over. You got your story, now you can go."

Linda dallied, curious to see whether any player would collect. No. Damn. She wished Icehead, at least, would take the money and run. In the hallway, she hastened to catch up with Frank and Zack.

"How you holding up?" asked Zack.

"Okay."

"Good. Only 161 more games to go."

5 Balk

In the shaded Los Angeles press box, Neal Vanderlin sat with his elbows on a table, head in hands. Before him was a blank sheet of yellow newsprint, behind him a telex. Running his left hand through his hair, he smoothed down his mustache with his right hand, then picked up a pen. He sighed. Beginnings were always difficult.

The *Sun Vindicator* reporters and sports columnists rotated Eagle road trips; this one, from San Diego to Los Angeles to San Francisco to Texas, was Neal's. A long road trip, the longest of the season. Thirteen days, to be exact. Smiling, Neal thought of how Isemonger (as superstitious as he was arrogant) must be reacting. Enough procrastination. He cracked his knuckles, splayed his fingers, then began his rough draft, jotting down sentences here, isolated words there. He would compose the final column on the telex, sending it directly to the *Sun Vindicator.*

LA, May 1 – April has ended and the spring showers have ceased. Was that a good beginning? Stop worrying, he admonished himself. His pencil had the right idea: it was already scribbling out the next sentences. *Somewhere the showers are gentle, somewhere the days are bright. Not so in Chicago, where the mighty Eagles have . . . what? . . . settled into fourth place. Yes, as surely as spring rain settles into the earth, so the Eagles settle into their perennial position.*

But it doesn't have to be that way. Of course it didn't. The Eagles had played twenty games so far, winning only eight of them – a .400 winning percentage. California, in first place, had a .620 winning percentage. Everybody knew what was wrong, but only a columnist would say it. The regular reporters wouldn't, and Thwardz, Neal's boss, didn't even want Neal to say it. "Get off the soapbox," he had said over the phone. "Stop using those big words – discrimination, prejudice, sexism. Talk about baseball, Neal, my boy."

To put the matter succinctly, the Eagles are stuck in fourth and sinking fast because Sunshine is stuck in left field whenever the team takes to the road. What about Zack Weiss? *Weiss, who should be used as the outstanding utility man he is, should not be at short.* Zack was forty years old. He was a better-than-adequate pinch hitter, but he had no business being played at short, a position he hadn't filled adequately for the past three years. Neal snorted, drumming his fingers on the table and wondering how to say it. He paced the press box. Zack wasn't asking to play short: but in playing it, he was giving it all he had.

The responsibility lay with Black, and if fingers had to point anywhere, they had to point there. The manager was ultimately responsible for fitting the best person to the best job. Neal didn't know why Black was platooning (if that was even the right word for it) Zack and Linda between short and left. You didn't platoon players whose skills varied so greatly. No. You gave the position to the better player.

Staring out the press-box window, legs wide apart, hands clasped behind his neck, Neal focused on second base, thinking about what words to use. If Black kept it up, the Eagles wouldn't even make fourth place by season's end.

Any baseball fan would understand why Black was balking. Excepting the uniqueness of the catcher's position, shortstop was the key infield position. Strong down the middle, as the saying went. If a team wasn't, it could kiss too many balls good-bye as they whizzed through the hole. The shortstop conveyed signals to the outfield. Talked to the pitcher. One of the two pivot players at second. Necessary for the double play. The cutoff on plays to left. Backed up third when necessary. Neal gave a desk chair a spin and mounted it backward. Black couldn't bring himself to give a woman that responsibility.

Scribbling furiously, Neal covered two more sheets of the yellow paper. *The Eagles' infield should be filled with Sunshine and Laughing. But a Black shadow has fallen over the infield. Indeed, over the entire team. It is the shadow of ignorance and prejudice.* He chewed on his index finger a moment, wondering if perhaps he were laying it on a bit too thick. Well, let Thwardz (old Thwack-n-Thwart, as Neal had dubbed him) worry about that.

In this baseball battle, the hero is named Sunshine and the villain is named Black. It is a battle between a rookie (let us call her the Rookie of Baseball Future) and a busher (let us call him the Busher of Baseball Past).

The problem is, the busher is the manager, a master of chiaroscuro. The rookie should be playing the position of shortstop, where she positively scintillates. But the busher has taken the tenebrous position that she will never play shortstop because . . . because she is a woman, and as all bushers know, this is a crime worse than losing.

Black knows. He has already chosen what he considers the lesser crime.

One is a rookie for only a season. It is the tragedy of our national pastime that one can be a busher forever.

Lining up his three sheets of paper, Neal jogged them into line. He wondered whether Thwardz would ask him to point the finger away from Lenny Black. It was a standing rule in the newspaper business that the boss would not let reporters attack the interests of the baseball barons, football monarchs, and hockey magnates who owned teams. Attacking their lackeys was sometimes permissible. Thoreau had been so right about those hacking away at the branches of evil. Neal laughed, doubting that his comments about Lenny Black would upset Al Mowerinski. No, they would upset Thwack-n-Thwart more than they would upset Al, for to talk about Lenny Black was only the beginning. What caused a Lenny Black? What could be done about the Lenny Blacks? The newspapers, Neal had learned rather quickly, didn't want to get down to the basic causes (let alone solutions) of what they called "social issues." If he wrote a column saying that Linda was deeply wounded every time she heard a discriminatory remark (she'd be dead by now), that she went out and cheered herself up by buying new clothes (he'd never seen her in anything resembling new clothes, he realized), that she was a great cook (could baseball players cook?), and that she liked all her teammates (ha!) and hoped they would in time accept her – if he wrote that crap, Thwack-n-Thwart would love it. Call it a "human interest" story.

But if he wrote the truth about baseball, Thwack would tell him to get off the soapbox. "People don't wanna read that stuff," he would say. "This is the sports page, you lunkhead!" Neal sighed.

May 2 found the Eagles in San Francisco and Neal in the ballpark, watching practice. The May wind bit sharply. Neal hunched his shoulders, kept his hands in his pockets, and put his feet on the rail in front of him. He felt especially lonesome on the road trips, despite the presence of fellow reporters. The vast majority of humankind must feel lonesome. They must, he figured, because there were so few people one could . . . share with. People needed somebody. A friend, a partner. Someone you looked forward to seeing all the time, someone you wanted to be with, someone whom you respected, someone you desired.

He thought about her all the time. Lying in bed at night, he had to resist the urge to run down four flights of stairs and knock on her door. Sitting in the office, he stared at the green letters on his terminal screen and saw her crouched in the infield. Standing in the ballpark watching practice, he imagined slowly taking her clothes off. He could imagine that for long periods of time, wondering what she looked like naked, whether her breasts were as round as they seemed to be when outlined by a sweater, wondering what her midriff looked like. Was it as long as it seemed? Would he see the outline of her ribs? He imagined coming into her locker room while she, naked, stretched to reach for her clothes on the peg. She would turn around to see who was there. Then she would drop her clothes and face him, arms at her side, waiting. Her pubic hair would be dark, much darker than her hair, as black perhaps as her eyebrows.

It was wishful thinking; it could never be. She was known throughout the country. He wrote articles that people wrapped fish in. She was lying on the grass in right field, doing calisthenics. The dark green and brown Eagles jacket brought out the different colors in her brown hair. He watched her start the wind sprints. It wasn't just that he didn't know how she would respond (that he didn't even know if *she* needed someone). It wasn't just that she was a baseball player and he had never made love to a baseball player before. It was what journalism courses would call a "conflict of interests." Thwardz had hinted as much, waving one of his black grease pencils at Neal: "Are you fuckin' this what's-her-name, Sunshine?" Neal had slammed a fist into his terminal keyboard, sending the machine into green contortions as he stood to face Thwardz. "Okay, okay," Thwardz replied, thrusting the grease pencil behind his ear, waving both hands, palms up, to calm him. "No harm meant. I just mentioned it." Neal glared at him until he left, then sat back down at the terminal and tried to decipher the damage he had done. Later, Thwardz came back and sat on Neal's desktop. "Now, Neal, don't get upset. I take it you were telling me 'No.'"

"That isn't all I was telling you."

"Okay, okay. I get the point. I was crude."

Neal didn't bother to reply, and Thwardz looked at him with concern. "We've got to talk this out, Neal," he said, then rushed on: "You're emotionally involved. You write about her too much."

"No, I don't. I don't mention her in every column, do I?"

"No. But . . . you're too *interested* in her. Where does your interest end and your detachment begin?"

"I write a column, Thwardz, not a play-by-play account.

Readers expect to hear my opinions."

"You want to be taken off the Eagles for a while? You can cover the fights, football's coming up, horse racing?"

Neal had looked at him in astonishment. "You think I've lost my objectivity?"

"Not yet. I'm trying to prevent something we might all regret."

"Don't say anything you'll regret." That had been Frank Laughing's parting admonition to Linda when Neal had taken her to the Greek restaurant. First Neal had violated every traffic law in the city getting back to the *Sun Vindicator.* Then he pounded the keys off his keyboard getting out his story. Running down to the parking lot, he had sped to the stadium. It was all he could do to walk calmly down the dugout and into her locker room – to find her and Laughing, both in their street clothes, analyzing California's strengths and weaknesses. Neal had immediately thought: *She's going to break our date: she's going out with Frank.* But Linda had smiled, looked at her watch, and said, "Sixty-four minutes. Not bad for a day's work."

"Thirty-five minutes of work." He went along with her kidding. "The rest was driving time."

Frank had stared at him. "We missed you in the locker room, Neal."

Neal had laughed. "That's a first! You *missed* me?"

"In a manner of speaking."

"Hey," said Linda. "I'm starving. Let's go."

"Don't say anything you'll regret," Frank warned.

Sitting in one of the empty box seats near the visitors' dugout, Neal thought his situation was ironic. The editors were concerned that the reporters would get too close to the players and lose their objectivity. The players were concerned that the reporters weren't one of them and couldn't, therefore, be trusted to cover up whatever it was the players wanted covered up that day, week, or season. And Linda didn't trust him. Not that she had told him that. Not that dinner had been anything but great. They had talked about common things, telling each other about themselves. They had talked baseball and reporting and movies and books and food. It hadn't *seemed* that they were avoiding talking about anything in particular. But he could tell that she didn't trust him: he could tell by the way she looked at him. She was always so guarded. The expression on her face always said, "Is he going to report this?"

Neal wasn't about to begin every conversation by assuring Linda (or anybody) that he would or would not report it, that it was "on" or "off" the record. He wasn't two separate people, one of whom could be told things "on the record," the other of whom could be told things "off the record." He was a whole human being. She would have to figure out that she could trust him. If she stopped to think about it, she would realize that no reporter traveling with the club reported one-tenth of what he saw.

Zack came out of the dugout, saw him, waved, and headed up to batting practice. Griffen jogged into the dugout to drop off his jacket. "Well, well, if it isn't that reporter from the *Sunshine Vindicator*," he gibed. Not bad: Neal smiled to himself in appreciation. He waved a hand at Griffen, motioning him back. Griffen turned and looked at him. "Yeah?"

"Hey, Griff. Why do you let a jerk like Isemonger lead you around?"

Griffen bristled. "Nobody leads me, Vanderlin. Isemonger and I are on the same side."

"How do you figure that? I don't think Icehead's on

anybody's side but his own. He's not on the team's side."

"The enemy of my enemy is my friend," replied Griffen, turning to go. He spun back around, pointing a finger at Neal. "And the friend of my enemy is my enemy."

Neal, unintimidated, watched Griffen trot back to practice. Out in right field the players had paired off, helping each other stretch. Linda lay on her back, legs up, while Frank pushed her toes inward. Neal heard her laugh, a giggling, bubbling sound. Frank's deeper laughter reached him. Part Ottawa Indian, Frank had come directly from his Kansas home to the Eagles eight years ago. The players, thinking equality was achieved by imposing a nickname on everyone, started calling Frank "Chief." They stopped it quickly enough after Frank flattened a few of them against the clubhouse walls. Neal remembered the stories. That had been his rookie year, too. Frank and Linda brushed themselves off and walked toward him. Would she notice him?

She looked toward him, as if to scrutinize the person watching daily practice. Smiling widely, she turned and walked toward him. Frank waved, then continued on his way toward the plate.

"Hi. What are you doing here?" she asked, removing her cap and brushing an arm across her forehead.

"Practicing."

"Practicing what?"

"Practicing watching. I thought that if I ever tired of reporting I could become a baseball scout."

"Listen," she said, "I'll talk to my manager about it."

Just then the manager himself stepped out of the dugout and, without an apparent glance at either of them, announced, "Batting practice." Spitting tobacco juice precariously close to both of them, he continued his bowlegged walk toward the batting screen.

"Gotta hustle," she murmured, waving as she left.

Neal's eyes turned toward the cage just in time to see Frank swat one out of the park. The cage was a clutter of bats and hitters, the hitters crowded around three or four at a time, waiting to take their turns.

He enjoyed watching her bat. She had a sweet swing. A born hitter. And hitters were born, he thought, not made. Which was to say, if you weren't a hitter by the time you were six or seven, forget it. But Linda was going to get more brushbacks, more walks, and more all-around bad pitches than the average rookie. What would that do to her average? – to say nothing of her morale.

Black stopped the pitcher and called for Isemonger. Neal tensed. What was he going to pull? Black wanted to drive her out of the game, and Isemonger was cooperating for all he was worth. Batting practice was semicasual, but there was nothing casual about the way Icehead grabbed the ball from the box behind him, nothing casual about his windup. It was the brushback, beanball, "purpose pitch," and Linda fell backward into the dirt. "Asshole!" growled Neal. "You're a goddamn asshole, Isemonger!" he shouted. Icehead looked over, then gave him the finger. Linda was up and dusting herself off.

His next pitch was a fastball. A crack and a ping rang out almost simultaneously: the pitching screen swayed as both ball and bat hit it. Isemonger jumped back, a natural reflex. Linda stood and looked at him, letting him know the bat "slipping" out of her hands was deliberate. Oh-oh. Neal looked at Black to see what he would do. Nothing. The bastard. Isemonger grabbed another ball from the box behind him. Zack grabbed

Linda's elbow and pulled her away. She argued, stepping back to the plate. Zack pulled her back again. She pushed him away again and stepped up to the plate.

Neal held his breath.

Icehead threw four more pitches, and Linda hit the dirt four more times. Neal let out his breath and rubbed his moist palms against his pants. So much for batting practice. So much for objectivity.

Linda knocked on Zack's door and was relieved when she found him in his room. "You've got to help me, Zack."

"I'd love to, kid, but my wife is here, and I'm getting too old to handle more than one at a time."

"Funny, Zack, funny." Linda brushed by him and walked into his room. "Hi, Rachel, how're you?" she asked Rachel Weiss.

"I'm fine, Linda. Just ignore Zack." Rachel pointed to a chair. "Have a seat."

Linda pulled out a chair and sat in it, knees drawn up, feet on the seat of the chair. "I don't know how to play left field. I'm doing it all wrong. It's so different, Zack. You know more about it than I do. Can you help me? Tell me what to do. Give me some hints. I've got to do a good job, help the team."

"Umm," grunted Zack, scratching his face and sitting on the bed. "Well, it's different from short, that's for sure."

"The glove feels like a bushel basket. I can't get used to playing so shallow. I keep wanting to back up, but then the hits might fall in front of me. And the lights – god, I can hardly see the ball sometimes! I don't know how you do it, Zack, playing all those positions."

"Variety is the spice of life." Zack winked at Rachel, who told him to be serious. "Okay, okay." He turned back to Linda. "Why are you playing shallow?"

"I . . . I don't know. I mean, they told me to. Mack, the coach, told me to. And I asked Ulysses. Left field was his position in Iowa. He said more balls drop in front of the outfielder than behind."

"Maybe," said Zack. "Maybe a good left fielder – an experienced one, I mean – can afford to play shallow because he'll know how to run back, be able to account for the lights, and not give a damn about meeting a fence face to face. But you're not familiar with the position. So I think you're better off playing deep. That way, you'll get a better look at the ball. A better angle."

"Play deep," Linda summed up. "Okay. I'll try. What else?" she asked eagerly.

"You're having trouble with balls hit by lefties."

"Yeah, I noticed that. Why?"

"You've been overrunning them, not remembering that they can hook back on you." Zack bounced off the bed and walked to the balcony. "You've got to watch the line drives, too. They're the hardest, in some ways. Just turn your back on 'em and run to where you think they'll be, then try to spot them when you turn around."

"I don't know," she said, hanging her head. "I'm trying, I'm doing the best I can. I just don't know if left field is for me."

"It's not."

Linda looked up in surprise.

Zack laughed. "Of course it's not for you. Your position is short."

Linda stood. "I can't get used to the switching. Back and

forth, back and forth. Short to left, left to short. Can you?"

"Nope. Call Mack," advised Zack. "Tell him to hit you a couple of hundred balls out there. Try to judge 'em like I told you."

"Okay, I will."

There was an awkward silence: had she overstayed her welcome? Slowly, she rose to leave.

"Don't go yet," said Rachel.

"Okay." Linda returned to her chair, realizing she had sounded awfully eager to stay.

"We're going out to dinner after the game with Frank and Keena. Frank suggested that we ask you if you'd like to come."

Yes! Yes! I get so tired of asking for a table for one. "I'd love to," she answered, keeping a rein on her runaway enthusiasm. Out of the corner of her eye, she checked Zack: had Frank really asked, or was Rachel making this up out of kindness? As far as she could tell, Zack reacted as if it were true. "Do you and Keena travel to a lot of the away games?" she asked Rachel out of curiosity.

"Not as many as we'd like to. We come to Frisco once a year, though."

"They love to shop. Frank and I have to put a limit on their spending," complained Zack good-naturedly.

Eventually, Linda had to leave: she wanted to get in some extra practice before tonight's game. "Thanks, Zack. Bye, Rachel."

Zack walked her to the door and let her out. She backed out, and, standing in the hallway, said, "Thanks again, Zack."

"They all say that," he replied, closing the door.

She turned, shaking her head, and saw Neal standing in the hallway, looking at her. "Hi, Neal." She felt herself about to explain why she was in Zack's room, then stopped before she began. Why did she feel she had to explain to him? What was she afraid of – that he would hint at something that wasn't true? Like Sengal had in Memphis? No, she thought. Neal wouldn't start rumors like the one about her and Jack Doyle.

"There's that look on your face again," he said.

Huh? "What look?"

"The look that says that you think that I think you were in there having an orgy with Zack and maybe the whole infield – the look that says you wonder whether I'm going to report it."

Linda swallowed guiltily, not knowing what to say. She realized not only that he could read her thoughts, but, more importantly, that she had hurt his feelings. "You're right," she answered at last. "I did think that – in a sort of confused way. I'm sorry."

"Okay. Apology accepted. Are you going somewhere?"

"To the ballpark to shag balls, if I can get Mack to hit them to me."

They walked down the hall toward the elevators.

"Look, I'm sorry I sounded so hard," explained Neal. "I know it's rough on you. I know you want to be accepted as just another baseball player."

"I don't want to be treated special," she replied. "I just want to be here because I can play baseball *well* enough to be here."

"I know. And you can. There shouldn't be any doubt about it."

She was staring at the elevators, but she was studying Neal in her peripheral vision. He looked and sounded sincere. He wasn't putting her on. She realized she was smiling happily, glanced up guiltily, and saw Neal grinning at her. She grinned back and pushed the elevator button.

The evening of May 2 was damp and foggy; the press box was probably the only warm seat in the ballpark. At the end of two coffees and two hot chocolates, one hot dog and two hamburgers, Chicago was leading San Francisco 4-3, bottom of the seventh. Frisco had one out, two on base. Doug Rooks was pitching for the Eagles. Garfield, the Frisco shortstop, was at bat. Neal thought that Rooks came in with a beautiful change of pace, but Garfield wasn't fooled. Smacking the ball, Garfield raced to first as his line drive raced to deep left. Linda raced after it, her back to the plate, glanced once behind her, slipped suddenly, recovered, then lost it after all as a gust of wind seemed to puff it just out of reach. The ball bounced off the fence, but she recovered quickly and threw to Zack, who had moved into left center to become the relay man, while Frank Laughing had left second and moved between Zack and third base to back up the catch. The tying run had scored from third. Zack caught the ball, faked a throw to home to drive back the winning run, then burned the ball down to Bobby Knuff (now covering second) to tag the sliding Garfield, who had hesitated at first. Zack's throw was high: Knuff leaped straight up to get it, but it kissed the webbing of his glove and skimmed off into the huge hole in right field. Wally Szczpanozowski was pounding in after it like a steamroller attacking an egg, but Hector Gutierrez got to it first.

The winning run scored easily. Neal snapped the pencil he had been holding. The third base coach waved Garfield in as Hector scooped up the ball and pegged it to Abilene at the plate. It came in like a bullet, without even a hop, and Harland put the tag on the sliding Garfield. Out!

Thank goodness for that, thought Neal. At least Garfield didn't get an inside-the-park homer. Shit! He hated to see errors like that. Rooks, with a 3-0 record this season, took the ball with disgust written over his face in boldfaced caps. He was 3-1 when the game ended.

When the series ended three days later, Isemonger, Hannibal, and Kovack had also added losses to their records, and the Eagles had sunk to sixth place in the division standings. Neal pointed out in his column that Zack had five errors in four games and Linda had two errors – errors that had contributed to the Eagles' losses. He concluded that Weiss and Sunshine should be playing their home positions, not the ones Black gave them on the road.

And then, sitting in the hotel lobby, waiting for the team bus, Neal saw Al Mowerinski stride through the lobby and out the door. Neal jumped up and chased after Al. What was he doing here? Did he have a story? "Later," Al replied. Then he seemed to relent. "You'll figure it out," he said, giving Neal a half-smile. He waved and, not so much hailing as commanding a cab, stepped in and disappeared.

Nobody spoke to Neal as he boarded the Houston-bound team plane. People who used the word *error* in print were not popular. In the plane he sat in an aisle seat several rows behind Knuff, who was drowning his sorrows (hell, the whole team's sorrows, the way Knuff was going) in drink. Across the aisle sat Zack Weiss, brooding. "I'm talking to you, Vanderlin," announced Zack, "as long as you don't talk about the last six games." Staring vacantly forward, thinking about Al

Mowerinski's trip to San Francisco, and wondering whether Linda would talk to him at all, Neal noticed her leaning into the aisle from her seat, looking back at him. Then she got out of her seat and walked toward him. She was wearing gray trousers, a short-sleeved white shirt, and a turquoise pendant. He was sure he could see the dark outline of her nipples moving against the white shirt.

"Mind if I sit there?" she asked, pointing to the empty seat beside him.

Mind? She couldn't be serious. "Of course not." He stood up to let her by. Her perfume was musky.

"Actually," she said, "Frank just told me you were on the plane."

"Oh?"

"I hope that doesn't sound like I don't want to talk to you."

"I trust in your ability to avoid members of the fourth estate when you want to," he answered, surprised that she had sought him out. Those who had *error* coupled with their name in print seldom looked you up for a friendly chat.

"They're impossible to avoid," commented Zack from across the aisle. "You may as well get used to that, Sunshine."

Linda squeezed by Neal, muttering, "Wonderful series, wasn't it?"

Neal began to wonder whether Linda had read his column. She must have. "That breeze is so tricky you need a wind sock on your glove."

"Oh, that. Actually, I lost it in the fog. No," she said, slumping down into the seat, "poor joke. I just couldn't handle it well enough. I didn't mean my errors – I meant the whole rotten thing. Poor Zack. Poor Frank. Poor Knuff. Poor everybody. Even Icehead probably can't sleep at night."

"Serves him right," grumbled Neal.

"We have terrific players on the team. We have the talent, ability, and potential to win the pennant." Her fist clenched on the arm rest. "But instead of flying free, we're shackled and chained."

He stared at her. "Would you mind if I used that in a column?"

"What?"

"You know – Eagles, flying free, shackled and chained?"

She blushed. "Sure. Go ahead."

Zack leaned over and said to Neal, "If you're looking for what to say, I can tell you what to say. I have a few choice words reserved for Black. Wanna hear 'em?"

"Can I print them?" Neal asked.

A snort was the only answer he received. Neal turned back to Linda, who was still slumped in her seat. He looked down at the top of her head. "Hey. Don't *ever* worry about Isemonger losing sleep. The guy's a bastard – a creeping, crawling caveman. The only good thing he can do is throw hard. But to not coin a phrase, if his arm and his brain ever had a contest, the arm would win. Hands down."

"I know," she answered. "It wouldn't be a fair contest, though, because his brain would be unarmed."

Neal tried to put an expression of distaste on his face, but she was already laughing. He couldn't resist: he joined her laughter, hoping it served as catharsis.

"I like talking to you," he told her, lowering his voice so that Zack wouldn't overhear.

She stopped laughing. "I like talking to you, too."

"You're not like the others," he said. Then, correcting himself: "Well, you don't tell me everything you're thinking, but what you do tell me is straightforward. And you don't take the reporting of every error personally.

"You know," Linda mused, "I used to imagine that the worst thing that could happen to me in baseball was having what I did reported in the papers."

"And?"

"Hmm?" She seemed lost in thought. "Oh, it's not so bad, compared to the alternatives."

"Which are?" he asked in curiosity.

"Which are, number one, that I had no errors to report because I wasn't playing baseball; and, number two, that the press didn't have the freedom to report them."

Neal scratched his chin, then kidded her. "Still a typical baseball player, I see."

"What do you mean?"

"You put freedom of the press second on your list."

"Second on the list only, not necessarily in importance," she rallied. "I wasn't ranking them."

"Well, I guess you're not like the others. Baseball players are a hard lot to talk to. Sometimes I feel I have a love-hate relationship with them," he admitted.

"Why?"

"Lots of reasons. Most of them are spoiled. They're treated like superstars all their lives now that baseball is getting to be a big money business. They have it made in high school and college, and when they make it to the majors they look down on people who aren't members of their exclusive little club."

"Like reporters, you mean?" she asked.

"Reporters, especially. They treat us like aliens. They want us to glorify their good plays and bury their bad. They want it both ways, and life's not like that." Neal studied her. "You're different, though."

"Because I realize you can't have it both ways?"

"Because you don't walk with a swagger. You don't chew tobacco, either."

Linda laughed. "I don't advertise shaving cream or razors, either. Hey, did you know that a razor company asked me –" She stopped.

Trust. Again, thought Neal. She could discuss errors with him, but she held a lot back. Christ, why couldn't she just talk to him? Why was there this barrier between them?

Her hand was on his arm. "A razor company asked me to do an ad for them – did you know that?"

He looked down at her hand. She had large, strong-looking hands with long fingers – the hands of a good infielder. He liked the warmth of her hand on his shoulder. "No. A spoof?"

"No! They wanted me to shave my legs and advertise their razor."

Zack, getting up, leaned across their seat. "She refused," he told Neal. "Dumb. I think she shoulda done it. I think she should do ads for chewing tobacco, too. And underarm deodorant. Athlete's foot. Maybe even jock itch. She's a purist, Neal. Watch out for her. She won't do it because she loves baseball so much."

"Well, I think I'd feel like an idiot – it would be so embarrassing!" Linda protested. "And I *do* love baseball," she told Zack.

"Everyone loves baseball," hiccuped Zack, departing in the direction of the washroom.

"Ever since I can remember," Linda told Neal, "I've

wanted to be a baseball player." Her finger poked his arm. "Do
you know that I used to read all the sports magazines when I
was a kid, like in fourth, fifth, sixth grade? Junior high, too. But
my friends – girls, that is – didn't. They thought I was *weird*. I
couldn't read their magazines, all that stuff about setting your
hair and what makeup to wear and how to act on a date – yuk!
But I wouldn't let them see me reading the sports stuff. I'd hide
it inside another magazine or book." She looked at him for a
moment. "It wasn't just the girls. Boys, too – *they* thought I was
weird because I read sports magazines and played baseball."

"I don't think anybody's weird who wants to play
baseball." She was actually opening up to him. He didn't want
it to stop. She was actually touching him. He didn't want that to
stop, either. "What do you like best about it?"

"Everything! The way it all fits together. You know – that
the ball doesn't score, people do. That the team *with* the ball
can't score, the team *without* the ball can. That there's no time
limit. That the diamonds and fields and fences all fit together,
and the runner's speed and the fielder's speed and the speed of
the ball in flight – I feel silly saying all this, Neal."

"You don't sound silly."

Zack returned. "Harland's on his way," he announced.
Almost like a warning.

Neal looked up; there stood Harland Abilene – tow-
haired, well built, good-looking. A soft-spoken Texan, Harland
seldom had much to say. This time he had volumes to speak.
"Linda," he said, "I think you should come back and sit with the
club."

Neal saw the astonishment on her face.

"I'd like to buy you a drink. We can go to the lounge."

Linda frowned slightly. "Well, thanks, Har. Sure. That's

great. I'll meet you there later, okay? I'm talking to Neal right now."

"I know." Harland straightened his arms at his sides and stared at Neal. "Look, Vanderlin, I don't have anything against you. I mean, as far as I'm concerned, you're an okay guy. But you aren't helping Linda any by what you write. And I don't think you're helping her like this, either."

Neal started to reply, but Linda leaned across him, cutting him off. "I came back here to talk to Neal," she told Harland. "And who put this idea in your head, anyway?"

"Nobody. I can think by myself," Harland replied.

"I didn't mean it that way," she said quickly. "I meant that the problem with me and the club has nothing to do with me and Neal. It doesn't matter if he exists or not as far as the problems are concerned."

Thanks a lot, thought Neal.

"I only want to help you," explained Harland.

Still leaning across Neal, Linda touched Harland's hand. "I know that, Har." She withdrew her hand. Neal thought that Harland started to go after it, but maybe it was an illusion. "But I wish you wouldn't think Neal is hurting me, because he's not. He's just a columnist expressing his opinions." She ducked her head and grinned at Neal.

Harland frowned. "I think he should write about some other team or some other game for a while."

Linda drew back into her seat and smiled. "A good reporter goes where the news is, Har. Sort of like a good catcher goes where the pitch is."

"How about going out to dinner with me after the game tonight?" asked Harland suddenly, ignoring Neal, who felt awkward and uncomfortable in the middle of this. He felt angry, too. He looked at Linda sideways and noticed that her face was red.

"Uh, thanks, Har – why don't we talk about it later, okay?"

"That means No," Harland complained.

"No, it doesn't."

"Then it means Yes?"

Again she waved her hand, this time in mock dismissal. "Oh, Harland. It means we'll go out to dinner sometime."

Still frowning, Harland jerked his head in Neal's direction. "You aren't going out with him, are you?" There was enough belligerence in the question to fuel Neal's mounting anger.

"Harland – don't crowd me." Her tone was a fastball down the middle. There was no quarreling with it.

Recognizing a strikeout, Harland left, promising to see Linda later, not even looking at Neal.

"That was embarrassing," sighed Linda.

Neal said nothing.

She poked an elbow into his arm. "Reporters – excuse me, columnists – have it rough, don't they? Now Harland's against you, too."

"Only because he thinks I'm blocking the plate." Neal loosened his tie.

"What do you mean?"

"He was trying to score."

She backed off from him noticeably, raised her eyebrows. *"Score?* Are we getting back to puns? The only score I'm interested in is the one at the end of nine innings."

"Sorry." Why had he said that? Now she was angry, damn it.

"You should be. I'm not a run in a game. I'm not a plate, either."

"Right. You're not. I'm sorry." Neal was embarrassed.

Linda punched him lightly on the arm and settled into her seat, staring ahead.

Neal wondered whether she would go to dinner with Harland tonight. He would never have expected that Harland Abilene would be interested in her. Maybe he wasn't. Maybe he just wanted to keep her away from Neal. No. That didn't seem likely. With a jolt, Neal realized that it raised his opinion of Abilene considerably. He almost wished him luck. Almost. Now he couldn't ask her out to dinner tonight: it would look terrible. Damn! With a sidelong glance at Linda, he wondered if she could be interested in Harland. Neal thought they didn't have much in common. She was quick, serious, yet full of humor. Abilene was slow. Sincere, hardworking. Definitely independent if he liked Linda. No sense of humor at all. Neal looked at her. There was a slight furrow in her brow. Her cheeks were sucked in. "Wondering what to order for dinner?" he asked.

All he got from her was a noncommittal "Umm."

"Listen," he offered, "I'd be willing to come along as chaperon."

A slow, sensual smile spread across her face. "No, thanks," she replied. "I never did want to be an umpire."

Tuesday morning Neal settled down to a Texas-sized breakfast at the restaurant across the street from the club's hotel. He had asked for a booth in a far corner. When he ate alone, Neal enjoyed observing people, thinking of himself not as an eavesdropper, but as a student of human nature.

Zack entered and sat at the back counter, near Neal.

Spotting Neal, he nodded. A waitress handed Zack a menu, placing ice water in front of him. "Mornin'," she drawled. "What'll ya'll have?"

"Do you have eggs benedict?" asked Zack.

"Just what's on the menu. Never heard of eggs benedict."

Zack studied the menu. "Can you make eggs benedict if I tell you how?"

"Don't know. Have to ask the cook."

Zack leaned over the counter earnestly. "Ask him if he can split and toast an English muffin, cover each half with ham, top it with a poached egg, and put hollandaise sauce on that."

"What kind of sauce?" she asked skeptically.

"Hollandaise. Holland-days."

The waitress left and Neal shook his head. "Hey, Zack, you know you're not going to get eggs benedict."

"Never can tell, Vanderlin. Never can tell."

"You can tell. They're going to hold the hollandaise sauce, and then you know what you're going to have? An egg and ham sandwich on an English muffin. You could save yourself a lot of trouble by heading straight for McDonald's."

"We'll see," said Zack.

Harland Abilene came in, looked around, and sat down beside Zack. If he saw Neal, he didn't indicate it.

Neal's breakfast arrived: sausage, hash browns, two eggs over easy, biscuits, juice, and coffee. He would have to do a lot of swimming this afternoon to work the calories off. As he ate, he watched the comings and goings of Zack's waitress.

"I brought you what he made," she said, setting a plate in front of Zack. "It don't have that sauce on it."

Zack grumbled while Harland ordered scrambled eggs with biscuits and gravy on the side. Zack informed him that civilized people didn't eat biscuits and gravy ever, let alone for breakfast. Harland informed Zack that he didn't care what Zack ate, as long as it wasn't that raw fish he had had for breakfast in San Francisco. Neal chuckled as Harland further noted, with surprise, that he didn't know they served Egg McMuffins in the restaurant, or he might have had a couple.

The door swung open and Linda walked in with Hector Gutierrez. Neal watched them wait to be seated at a booth. She was speaking Spanish slowly, supplementing her words with hand motions. Hector was listening and nodding his head, grinning from ear to ear, interrupting with his rapid Spanish. Ah Hector, truly the bravest of the Trojans.

Harland had stopped drinking his coffee and was watching Linda and Hector enter a booth. Neal wondered what Harland's face looked like right now. Harland, now Hector. Damn it, he thought. Damn it. They'd never taught him about this in journalism classes.

"What's she doing with him?" Harland asked Zack. "He can't even speak English."

Zack turned sideways to look at Harland. "I can't imagine," he answered. "'Specially since I hear he eats chili peppers for breakfast."

"I don't understand. She could have had breakfast with me."

Or me, thought Neal. Sipping at his second cup of coffee, he determined not to look at Linda and Hector. He folded a newspaper open. Out of the corner of his eye, he saw Zack rise off the stool, fumble in his pocket for some change, pause, then sit back down again. Sensing something, Neal looked up. Lenny Black and his East Coast mistress had just walked in and been seated at a booth near Linda and Hector. Ignoring his newspaper, Neal wondered what caused Zack's pause.

"Oh-oh," said Zack.

"Whazza madder?" asked Harland through a mouthful of biscuits and gravy.

"Who is that woman with Lenny?"

This time it was Harland who turned sideways to stare at Zack. "You wacky or something, Zacky? You know damn well who that is. It's what's-her-name, the one from New York."

"Trudie."

"Yeah, Trudie," agreed Harland, returning to his food. "So whazza problem?" he mumbled, filling up again.

"You are a native of the vast Texas soil, Harland. Tell me – is Texas on the East Coast or the West Coast?"

Again Harland stared at Zack. "I think you been eatin' too many of those raw fish, Zacky. Texas ain't on neither coast. Texas is on the Gulf Coast." Harland scraped up the rest of his food and crossed his knife and fork on the plate.

"Well, then," proclaimed Zack, "Texas is where East and West shall meet. Kipling said that."

"You're wacky, Zacky. I don't know what you're talking about."

But Neal sensed now what Zack was foreshadowing, sensed it an instant before the swinging door opened and Eve what-was-her-name walked in, looked around, spotted Lenny, and, smiling, walked toward his booth.

"Holy Jesus Christ Almighty!" breathed Harland in awe.

Neal could not see Lenny's face: that was what he regretted most of all. He saw West Coast smile at Lenny, then look at the woman with him. Then she seemed to be listening, so Lenny must have been talking. Neal glanced at Linda and Hector, who were oblivious to it all. West Coast slid in beside

Lenny and kissed him on the cheek. Oh-oh, thought Neal. Oh-oh.

Harland, Zack, and Neal sat perfectly still, staring without the slightest embarrassment. West Coast couldn't have been sitting there longer than three minutes when it happened. Jumping up, East Coast hurled her omelet in Lenny's face. Not content with that, she picked up her cup and sloshed coffee in West Coast's face. "You dirty cheating two-timing bastard!" They had no trouble hearing her.

Neal looked at Linda, who had turned around at the noise, then wished he had a camera so he could show her someday what she looked like. Her eyebrows were lost in her hair; her eyes were round with amazement; her mouth was open. She clutched a spoon in her right hand, hand and spoon suspended in midair. Hector, too, stared at the scene, but he appeared to show little surprise, simply shrugging his shoulders.

Now it was West Coast's turn. She stood, grabbed Lenny's breakfast, and threw it in his face. Then she reached across the table and started tearing at East Coast's clothes. East Coast's blouse tore open, exposing a see-through bra.

"Not bad," murmured Zack.

"Holy Jesus Christ Almighty," breathed Harland.

"Now listen, stop it!" shouted Lenny. "Stop it, I can explain." When East Coast lunged across the table and started pulling West Coast's hair, West Coast shrieked. Lenny tried to pull them apart.

The combined efforts of East, West, and Lenny scattered the remaining dishes and cups on the floor, overturned the table, and knocked over one of the booth seats, which in turn knocked the customer behind it into his grits. Linda and Hector slid farther back into their booth, away from the rhubarb. Two waitresses, a busboy, and the cashier rushed over to intervene. By the time it was over, East Coast had lost her blouse, West Coast had lost her wig, and Lenny – Lenny had just lost. East and West huffed off. Lenny stayed to settle up.

"Well," said Zack to nobody in particular, "as the manager always says, breakfast is the most important meal of the day."

"Holy Jesus Christ Almighty," repeated Harland as he followed Zack.

Linda and Hector scrambled out of their booth. The four ball players walked by their manager without a word. Neal swallowed his cold coffee, picked up his paper, left a tip, and paid his bill. The things he saw, heard, and concluded while covering baseball would fill a small encyclopedia of scandal. In reporting, as in baseball, more went on than was visible.

The meeting of East and West was not the most exciting event of the day. In Tuesday night's game Linda was put in as shortstop and Ulysses Crowder took left field. Zack didn't play until the ninth inning, when he went to bat for the pitcher, driving in the run that won the game. Linda drove in one of the other runs, Hector one, and Frank Laughing two. Up in the press box, Neal was jubilant. The Eagles looked royal tonight. He would have liked to think that his newspaper column determined the change. He didn't kid himself, though. It was what Al Mowerinski ordered, not what Neal Vanderlin wrote, that put Linda at short and Ulysses in left.

Wednesday's game was one of the season's two twilight doubleheaders. Neal nodded in satisfaction as the Eagles trotted out to the field. Linda was at short again, Ulysses in left. Neal studied the lineup. Griffen, Gutierrez, Abilene, Laughing,

Szczpanozowski, Knuff, Sunshine, Crowder, and Don Hannibal, starting pitcher. He saw no reason why the Eagles couldn't reverse their losses with a team like this one.

A Texas twanger sang "The Star-Spangled Banner" and the game began. Griffen hit a screamer to short left center. The opposing center fielder came flying in for it, but the ball dropped just short of his out-stretched glove and the scoreboard credited Griffen with a hit. Gutierrez laid down a beautiful sacrifice bunt that advanced Griff to second. Harland was hit with a pitch, and Frank Laughing was walked. Bases loaded.

As Szczpanozowski twitched himself into place in the batter's box, Neal wondered why they didn't assign Zow a number to fit his back – four digits, at least. The count was two and two. Okay, Zow, he thought, this one's going to be an inside fastball. Protect the plate. Zowski, who must have had rabbit ears, did more than protect the plate. He belted the fastball over the center-field fence. Four-zilch. The Eagles were really flying tonight.

In the press room, everyone turned around to watch the instant replay on the monitor, then turned to reality to watch Bobby Knuff at bat. Knuff, his bat poised like a giant exclamation mark above his shoulders, pounded the baseball for an easy double. Way to go. Neal began to hum a reggae number, "Pressure Drop."

"Hey, Vanderlin!" One of the Texas newspapermen came over to Neal and draped an arm around his shoulder. "Your sweetheart's gonna hit into a double, and there goes the inning."

"The inning's already a wipeout for you, Futch. What's the matter, don't you want to see a woman come to bat in your stadium?"

"She can come to bat in my bedroom, Vanderlin, but not

in the stadium. Don't you hold anything sacred?" Futch pulled up a chair and straddled it. "Okay, here comes your Sunshine. Let's see what she does. Don't get me wrong, Vanderlin, I'm not saying I'm against women. Maybe she can bat .280. That ain't bad. The thing is, can she hit in the clutch? I don't think so. Not a woman."

The first pitch jammed her. She started to swing but checked herself in time. Ball one. She started to swing at the second pitch, low and away, but checked herself again. Ball two. She was a fine hitter, aggressive but controlled. Good hitters were aggressive, ready to swing at every pitch. They had to think that each pitch was going to be a strike and they were going to hit it. Go after everything, Neal thought, but stop yourself before you swing at something outside the strike zone. *Don't* swing at any pitch outside the strike zone – that's what the last of the .400 hitters had to say. Do it, and you'll let the pitcher know he can make you go after balls instead of strikes. Do it, and you help the pitcher out in the count. Do it, and inevitably you lose knowledge of your own strike zone, thereby weakening all your future responses to that ball coming at you. *Make it be there, Linda. Make it be there.*

"Didn't you hear me?" asked Futch.

"Huh? Oh, sorry. What did you say?"

"I said, either she's too scared to swing or she's waiting for a good one."

Now the intelligent hitter would be ready for the fast one down the middle. Now, the count at two balls and no strikes, the odds were with the batter. The pitcher couldn't work the corners of the plate – too easy to throw a ball. The pitcher had to get it over the dish now to protect himself. Jensen was pitching, so the chances were even greater that it would be the hummer. *Be ready, Linda, be ready.* Might be the curve, though. Pitchers could think what the hitters were thinking. If Jensen was thinking, he would think she expected the hard fast one, so he might throw her a breaking ball. On the other hand, if Jensen was *really* thinking, he might think she expected him to think that she expected the hard fast one, so she was really expecting the curve. On the other hand . . .. No, it was getting too complicated. Neal didn't understand how anybody could consider baseball boring.

Unfortunately for Jensen, all the thinking synchronized into a fastball that Linda hit over the left-field fence. Jumping up, Neal knocked over his chair. "Fantastic! Did you see that, Futch, did you see that?" When he settled down, embarrassed at the stares and grins he was receiving, he couldn't help asking: "Is that what they call a double play in Texas?"

"I'll be damned," replied Futch. "How in the hell could she hit a home run? Where'd she get the strength?"

Neal laughed, knowing that anybody could. It was all a matter of physics. Assuming the speed of Jensen's fastball was, say, 90 miles an hour, and the speed of Linda's bat at the point of contact was, say, 70 miles an hour, then the ball would travel off the bat at more than 120 miles per hour – in the opposite direction. The maximum distance such a ball could travel was nearly 500 feet. Therefore, it should be no surprise that she hit the ball more than the 385 feet from home plate to the left-field fence.

Futch tapped him on the shoulder, pointing to the plate. Bobby Knuff – Knuff! – was waiting for her. He held out his hand; she slapped it, giving him hers to slap back. No traditional pat on the ass, Neal noticed.

He turned around to watch the replay. The slow motion

showed the ease and follow-through of her swing. She jumped on the plate with both feet, smiling and saying something to Knuff. Neal thought it was "I can't believe it! I can't believe it!"

Six-nothing, top of the first, and only one out. The Texas manager strode out of the dugout, and Jensen went to the showers.

Hammering Texas for 16 hits and 11 runs, the Eagles won the first game. Neal felt terrific. The Eagles were flying now. This was what they should look like. He hoped they'd take the doubleheader.

The second game of the doubleheader is, as the saying goes, a whole new ball game. In reality, as well as in the hearts of the home team fans, the Texans could not recoup their losses, but they could at least break even by winning the second game. The Eagles, however, having won the first game, didn't want the second any less, and Neal knew that Isemonger, going into the game 3-2, was hyped up for the win.

In the whole new ball game, the bottom of the fifth came and went just as the previous innings had: scoreless. Knuff led off the top of the sixth. The first pitch was a ball, low and inside. The second was a curve not good enough for Knuff. Not good enough for the ump, either, and now the pitcher was in trouble. Neal watched as he came across with a slider that fooled Knuff. Two and one the count. Stepping out of the box, Knuff pulled with one hand at his protective cup, wiped both hands on his pants while holding the bat between his legs, stepped back into the box, and glared at the pitcher, who tried to catch him with an outside curve. But Knuff wasn't biting. Three and one the count.

This one has to be good, thought Neal. It was, and Knuff sent it for a ride over the fence. 1-0, Eagles. He watched Knuff trot around the bases. Linda, who had been in the on-deck circle, reached out to slap his hand as he went by. Knuff actually smiled. It must have been the home run. The home run, like Knuff, was a contradictory thing. A team hit and a personal hit. A team hit because it scored at least one run with no chance of an out. There was no defense against a home run, the perfect hit that eliminated any possibility of a play by the opposing team. A personal hit because most baseball owners, and most fans, wanted the home runs. That's what they paid for. And that's where the contradiction came in. The player who always swung from the heels for the fences, who went for the glory, was not a team player. He was interested in his own aggrandizement, his own glory. If the team lost a game because he struck out while swinging for the fences, the go-for-the-fences player never saw it that way. He never saw that the team might lose because he couldn't place a hit. That was the contradiction of the home run, the pure hit that wasn't so pure. But Knuff, Neal reflected, giving the first baseman his due, wasn't the kind of player who swung for the fences at the expense of the team.

In the bottom of the seventh the score still stood 1-0, Eagles. The power of the Texas lineup was coming to bat. TNT: Thayer, Noy, and Teeter. "First you're hit by the TNT, then you're left in tatters," chortled Futch, referring to Tatterman, who batted cleanup.

Thayer led off with a sharp single to right field. Noy, a left-handed hitter, laid down a bunt that rolled toward Isemonger. It should have been a sacrifice bunt, but Merle, one of the poorest-fielding pitchers in the league, pulled a boner.

Running up on the ball, he bent to scoop it into his glove. The webbing of his glove skimmed the ball forward, back toward the plate. By the time Harland captured it, glaring at first and third, Noy was safe on first and Thayer was retreating to second. Neal groaned aloud.

Chuckling, Futch patted him on the back. "First you get the TNT, then you're left in tatters. You win some, you lose some. That's the way it goes, Neal, my boy."

"Yeah? We'll see."

Two on, no outs. Neal assessed the situation for Isemonger, who looked as if he were melting in the heat. Come on, Icehead, bear down. Maybe old Black should amble on out there and pull him. Nothing wrong in going seven innings and then getting some relief. At the plate, Teeter was poised to hit. Come on, rooted Neal. Put Teeter down, and you've nipped the fuse. Isemonger shook off four signs in a row. Harland went out to the mound. A lot of gesturing and head shaking took place. Harland went back to the plate. Icehead nodded.

The pitch. Inside. Ball one. Again the war between Abilene and Isemonger took place in silence. No. No. No. Yes. The Monger stretched and delivered the ball. High and inside, and Teeter fell back, avoiding it. Ball two. Teeter picked himself up, dusted himself off, and glared at the man on the mound. As if in answer, Isemonger spit tobacco juice, threw off more signs, and once again tried to put the ball across the plate. Or was he trying to put it through Teeter's skull? Neal winced at the closeness of the brushback. Why the hell wasn't the pitch banned? He didn't understand where players came up with the cold nerve it took to face the pitch, time after time.

If Teeter had cold nerves, they were gone now. Scrambling up from the dirt, he started toward the mound.

Fortunately, he was restrained by the umpire and soothed by Tatterman, the on-deck player. Teeter shouted something to Icehead, who spit in his direction. Flinging down his bat, Teeter again started toward the mound. The scene repeated itself, umpire and Tatterman jumping to Icehead's rescue. Sometimes Neal felt that in the case of a purpose pitch time should be called so that the batter could go to the mound with a purpose fist. Or a purpose bat. Now Teeter started arguing with the ump, probably telling him that Icehead should be warned. The Texas manager joined the fracas, shoving Teeter aside and taking his place with the ump.

When all the dust settled, the count was still 3 and 0. Icehead fired in his next pitch, a wild one that got away from Harland, who turned in circles looking for it. Isemonger came in to cover home, and Harland retrieved the ball in time to prevent Thayer from even contemplating a run for the plate.

"Oh, ho!" yelled Futch. "The ducks are on the pond now, Neal, my boy!"

Neal put his head in his hands and stared down at the table. No outs. Bases loaded. Drunk as could be. He peeked out of the webbing of his fingers toward the Eagles' dugout. Nothing. He peeked at the television screen. Nothing. Lenny Black was not going to take Isemonger out. He was not even going out to *talk* to him! Neal shook his head. He wished that Black would treat Icehead as just another pitcher.

TNT had done its business, and now Tatterman, a right-handed batter with plenty of power, stepped up. His hitting left the ball, if nothing else, in tatters. The first pitch was a hummer that Tatterman nearly wrung himself out at but missed. Strike one. Thayer stood in foul territory with a more-than-decent-sized lead. Neal caught himself wishing that Icehead were the

kind of pitcher who would try to perfect a pickoff play. Fire the
ball to Griffen and catch the player leading off third by
surprise.

True to form, however, Isemonger acted as if he didn't
have a team behind him. The pitch was inside, meant to jam the
batter, but Tatterman came around on it quickly. The ball
cracked sharply off his bat for a hard hit toward left center.
That's it, thought Neal. There goes the game. But as fast as the
gloom expressed itself, it disappeared with a jolt. Linda leaped
high into the air, stabbed at the ball with her outstretched glove,
and – caught it! She landed with a jarring thud from the height
she had reached, legs apart, falling into a squat and nearly
toppling. Recovering her balance, she snapped the ball to
Griffen at third. In time to catch Thayer! Two outs! Eagles still
led, 1-0! Neal pounded Futch on the back. "Did you see that?!"
he cried. "Did you see that?! That was fan-*tas*-tic!"

"Aw, it was luck," mumbled Futch. "Thayer shouldn't
have been so far off the bag. Lucky, that's all."

"Oh, come on, Futch, give a little!"

Turning toward the screen, they watched the slow-motion
replay. She was stretched to the limit as she caught the ball.
The slow motion showed the jarring bounce of her body as her
feet hit the dirt, the nearly imperceptible readjustment of her
shoulders, elbows, and thighs as she fought to keep her balance,
and the simultaneous (or so it seemed) snap of her arm as she
assessed the situation at third and delivered the ball to the
already-stretched-for-it Griffen. It was beautiful. Neal looked
sideways at Futch and saw him smiling at the second replay.
Neal grinned.

It was the kind of play that could take the heart out of the
offense. Anybody in the situation that Texas had just been in –

bases loaded, no outs, bottom of the seventh, tired pitcher – would have been counting his chickens before they were hatched. Now the eggs were broken. Not all of the eggs, but enough to cause dismay. Texas, though, had to look at the situation one play at a time. There were still two on, one in scoring position. Drive in the man on second, and the score is tied. Drive in both runners, and Texas leads.

Lawrence, the fifth Texas batter, was Zowski's counterpart. Center fielder, Texas style. Neal watched Griffen stand close to third. Knuff stepped back several paces. Linda and Frank played deep on the dirt, watching both second and the batter. Zowski, Gutierrez, and Crowder were holding up the fences.

Neal studied the close-up of Isemonger on the monitor to see some human emotion: relief, joy, confidence, worry. Nothing. Just those two beady eyes staring at the catcher's signals. Neal turned back to the game in time to realize that the Monger's physical fatigue was nothing compared to his mental wipeout. He threw Lawrence a big, fat curve that hung in there like a tetherball.

Lawrence didn't catch it squarely, but he caught it hard enough and fast enough for the crack of his bat to resound through the stadium. The bat went flying down the first baseline. Knuff twisted out of its path; Lawrence lumbered after it. The ball, a hard grounder, took a high leap on the skin. Griffen made a beautiful stab for it, but it was already on a course over his head as he landed with air in his glove. Linda was backing him up, racing into shallow left on a course intersecting the flight of the ball. She made a desperate attempt, leaping through the air toward the ball.

"My god!" yelled Futch, nearly shattering Neal's eardrum.

"She caught it! Did you see that?!"

In the seconds that had transpired, Lawrence was about to land one of his shoebox feet on first base, Teeter was already at second, eyeing third, and Noy, glancing over his shoulder, had stopped at third, then decided to try for home while the third base coach exhibited a bad case of indecision. Knuff had hurried to the cutoff position between Harland and Griffen while Hector had run in from right to cover first base. Isemonger, who was supposed to back up home plate, stood on the mound. Linda jumped to her feet and threw the ball to Knuff, who wrenched it out of its flight and fired it to Harland, who smothered it in his mitt and slammed it into the speeding body of Noy.

"Y'er out!" shouted the umpire as two pairs of eyes and two expectant faces asked him to confirm opposite realities. Noy jumped up, flung down his cap, and asserted his version of reality.   Griffen, Sunshine, Laughing, Knuff, and Abilene converged near the visitors' dugout, patting one another on the back as they disappeared inside.

The seedling lead was protected all the way: the Eagles won, 1-0, their third victory in a row.

Down in the locker room, Harland looked solemn. "Sixth and seventh," he answered in response to Neal's question. "The crucial inning was the sixth and the seventh. Sixth when Bobby hit the home run, because that was the winning run. Seventh when we stopped the Texas rally."

Neal jotted down notes as he listened. He talked to Harland, Knuff, and Ulysses, then looked around for Griffen and Isemonger. They were in the training room – off limits to reporters.

Leaning against the wall, Neal studied his notes. He also

listened to the talk that drifted his way from the training room.

"I'm getting tired of hearing it, Icehead. Let's just enjoy the win," said Griffen.

"Enjoy the win!" Isemonger mimicked. "How the fuck can we enjoy the win with her on the team? You know what's going to happen at the end of the season, don't you?"

"We're going to win the World Series?"

"Don't be funny. At the end of the season, the commissioner is going to rule on whether or not women can play baseball. This is an experiment, see, and we can't let it be a good one."

"You *sayin'* we should lose, Icehead?"

"I'm saying we can't afford to let her stay. If she makes it, there will be more like her. You open the door to one, and they'll all come in."

"Watch it!" warned Griffen angrily.

"Watch what?"

"You don't know what you just said, do you?" demanded Griffen.

"What'd I say? What's gotten into you, anyway?"

"I'm getting tired of hearing about it," snapped Griffen, walking out of the training room. If he saw Neal standing against the wall, he didn't acknowledge it.

Neal parked the car across the street from the apartment building. Although it was mid-May, the evening was cool, made cooler by a wind off Lake Michigan. The gray twilight was touched with mist, giving a shimmer to car headlights. Just as they were about to cross the street, Linda shouted, pointing. "A kitten," she exclaimed, already running into the busy road.

"Watch out!" he shouted after her, starting into the street. But she had already bent, scooped something off the road, and dashed to the other side. Juggling a bag of groceries, Neal followed. "I thought you were a goner." His voice held relief.

She held the kitten cupped to her chest. "It's a miracle it wasn't killed." She stroked it. "It couldn't be more than six weeks old. Look at how little it is."

They entered the shelter of the building and took the elevator to her floor. One hand holding the kitten, she fumbled in her jacket with the other for her keys. The kitten, a dark gray ball of matted hair, meowed.

Opening the door, she flicked on the lights with an elbow and showed Neal where to put the groceries. She shrugged off her jacket and sat cross-legged on the floor, putting the kitten between her legs. "Look, Neal. It's all covered with tar."

Squatting, he examined it, touching a finger to the dirty, matted fur. He sniffed. "That's oil. From the highway, probably." He picked up the kitten and held it close to his face, examining it for injuries. "Its toenails are all worn away. Looks like it was running on the highway for a long time."

"I'm going to clean it up," she said.

"I can warm up some milk while you're doing that."

"Okay. I'll start dinner as soon as I clean up Homer."

He smiled. "Homer? Think he's going to go over the fences every night?"

"If he does, he'll have an odyssey to tell."

He groaned. "That's so bad I'll start dinner myself, just to fortify myself against your puns."

As Linda kneeled over the tub, washing the newly named Homer, Neal scrubbed the potatoes and put them in the oven, put together a quick salad, and wandered around the apartment.

He studied the bookshelf. *Moby Dick. The Blithedale Romance. All About Baseball. The Summer Game. All the King's Men. The Science of Hitting. Absalom, Absalom!* There was no order at all to her bookshelf.

"Did you major in literature?" he asked her over his shoulder.

"Yes."

"I didn't know that."

"Ah ha! Did you think I majored in baseball? I'll bet you think my degree says: 'Sunshine. Shortstop. Five-feet-ten. One-hundred-thirty-five pounds. Hair, brown. Eyes, brown. Bats right, throws right.'"

"You mean it doesn't?" he asked mockingly, still studying the bookshelf. He wandered over to a small desk in the corner of the living room. On the desk was a framed photograph of Linda, her parents, brother, and sister. Hanging above it was a poster of Eagle Stadium. Spotting a date book on the desk, Neal flipped through it. January: a lot of engagements. Dinners . . . movies . . . basketball games . . . concerts. February: more of the same. But that was back in Pennsylvania. He flipped to March, when she was in Arizona, and saw Zack and Frank's names a couple of times. Compared to January and February, though, March was a wasteland. April was even worse. He stared at opening day. She had written in "Dinner, Vanderlin." Things were pretty lonely when you had to write in your dates retroactively. He admired her, though: it took a lot of determination to stick it out.

Closing the date book, he walked back to the bookshelf. He picked the exercise putty and started working it.

"Hey, Neal, there's some wine in the bottom cabinet, left of the sink."

"I don't think Homer needs wine to revive him." Neal stood in the bathroom door, leaning on the doorjamb. "Is this what they call batting cleanup?"

She twisted her head and looked at him from under her shoulder, making a face. "The wine is for us, not Homer."

"In that case, I'll pour." He found the corkscrew and the wineglasses, poured them three-quarters full, gave Linda hers, and wandered back into the living room. He went through the record albums. They also had no apparent order. Linda Ronstadt. Jimmy Cliff. The Grateful Dead. Fleetwood Mac. Taj Mahal. Bob Dylan. Hank Williams, Junior. Van Morrison. He selected an Emmylou Harris album, put it on, and sipped the wine. The room, exactly like his own in design, was cheerful with bright yellows, warm with browns and blues.

Emerging from the bathroom, Linda wiped a hand across her forehead. The now-clean Homer bounded out in front of her, toward Neal. Surprising how such a little kitten could sound so loud when its feet hit the floor. Homer began chewing around the soles of Neal's shoes. Bending, he scooped up the still-damp kitten and placed it on his lap, stroking it. "The milk is on the stove."

Linda brought a bowl of milk, and Neal placed Homer next to it. The kitten needed no further guidance.

"I'll make a salad and put on the steaks," she said.

"I made a salad already. An infield special."

She laughed. "It's got dirt in it?"

"No. Lots of greens."

She sipped her wine as she moved around the kitchen counters. Strands of damp hair clung to her face. Neal left Homer to his milk and walked over to the kitchen. Her back was to him. Standing this close to her, he noted again how tall and slim she was. He could sense the muscles just beneath her blue rib-knit shirt. She turned; he watched the slight shift and bounce of her breasts as she worked. He put his wineglass on the counter. Why not? The most she could do was say no. It would be embarrassing. But this was intolerable. "Linda."

She looked up at him. He saw her eyes widen as she interpreted what he wanted. They stood there a moment as if a live ball was suspended in flight. Then Neal moved forward and, bending, kissed her. He tasted the sweet residue of wine and felt the softness of her mouth. Her kiss was hesitant, her mouth closed. But unresisting. With the tip of his tongue he began to part her lips. And then he stopped, kissed the corner of her mouth, and straightened.

"Let me help with the dinner," he said.

She looked down at something, then up at him. "Sure. It's almost ready."

Damn it, he thought the next day, sitting at his desk, studying the green computer screen in front of him. Damn it. He had balked. He wanted it all – he wanted to call the pitches, fire them across the plate, and control the runner on first. He wanted her, and he wanted to cover the Eagles. He wanted to love Linda and to be a good reporter. After last night, he believed she . . . well, she liked him, didn't she? He could be coming out of left field, but he didn't think so. So what was the problem? Why had he balked? It came back to the question of trust. Trust. He was afraid that, if he loved Linda, he wouldn't say what he should say if and when the time ever came to criticize her in print. It was himself he didn't trust.

6   Hit and Run

Big Al squeezed himself into a seat far above the first baseline, sitting in the shadow of the second-tier seats, sheltered from the warm June sun. Someday, he thought, he would get decent-sized seats in Eagle Stadium, seats into which a large person could fit with comfort, not feel like an adult relegated to sitting in child-sized furniture.

The high walls of the stadium cut off all the traffic noise. In the soft quiet Al listened for the familiar click of spikes on concrete – the sound that would foretell the sudden emergence of the players from the dugout. From where he sat, he could see directly into the home dugout. He was too far back to hear the click, but he listened for it anyway, listened for it as he had listened to it when he had been a player. He had loved coming into the big league stadiums in the morning sun, loved the silence, the dew just disappearing from the grass, the peacefulness of an empty arena.

They came trickling out of the dugout. Frank, Linda, Charlie Kovack. Zack, Griffen, Zowski. The Eagles. Chicago's Eagles. Al's Eagles. Well, technically speaking, the bank's Eagles, since it was the bank that had financed his purchase of the team. But his Eagles in name and spirit, for he had built the team, slowly and carefully.

That was not, however, how his fellow baseball owners viewed it. Not the way many players viewed it, either. No. They would not say "built." "Destroyed," perhaps. "Jeopardized." Of course, the bank wouldn't say "destroyed" or "jeopardized," not the way the attendance figures were climbing. The bank was very, very happy with the paid attendance figures. Since Linda became part of the team on opening day, attendance figures had been on an upward diagonal, "heading," as one bank loan official put it, "for the moon."

Reaching into a shirt pocket, Al pulled out a cigar. Selecting a wooden kitchen match out of the same pocket, he scraped it along the concrete and lit the cigar. For the first several puffs he concentrated solely on the taste, aroma, and warmth of the rolled tobacco. When he glanced up, the rest of the team had entered the field, a few jogging, some walking.

This first day of June the Eagles had played a total of forty-nine games, winning thirty and dropping nineteen. A .612 winning percentage put them in third place in the division standings. Last year that percentage would have put the team in first place, but this year an exciting race was shaping up in the division. The Eagles were only one game out of second place. But, as Curry had said to him just yesterday, "We've got the winningest Eagle team in fifteen years, and we're still five games behind goddamn California, Al!" Five games out of first, true. But, as Al had replied, "We're in third place and moving up, Curry. Moving up." Al believed this with every ounce of baseball wisdom in his body. Moving up ever since that series in Texas last month, when he told Lenny Black that Linda would be the shortstop. Al smiled. Yes, he was his own

general manager, and a good thing, too. What good would it do
to have the power to hire her, then not have the power to allow
her to play? Big Al was not stupid.

He puffed his cigar and lazily rolled the smoke out of his
mouth, first in two streams like a dragon, then in little puffs of
O-o-O-O. The team was filled with enthusiasm. A hope. Hope
that had not been there the previous seasons. It was more than
that, though. The team was part of the future, a new world, just
as the Brooklyn Dodgers of 1947 had been. He thought about
the Dodgers, who had won the National League pennant in
1941. But not in '42, '43, '44, '45, or '46. And then, in 1947, a black
man named Jackie Robinson played the Dodger infield and
wielded a Dodger bat. The Dodgers won the pennant that year
– and in '49, '52, and '53. As far as Al was concerned, the
Dodgers won *because* of Jackie Robinson – not just because
Robinson was Hall of Fame caliber, but because when
Robinson stepped out on the infield dirt the whole Dodger team
stepped into the future, the better world. And it was that way
with the Eagles, too – whether they recognized it or not.

Al knew it wasn't right of him to override Black. But then
a manager with any balls would have played Linda – would
have played her or would have quit when ordered to play her.
He exhaled a cloud of smoke. Black was mean and petty-
minded; his vision couldn't even recognize a team, let alone
build one. Al should have fired him two years ago. Now he was
stuck with him, at least for the season.

Maybe Black wouldn't be so bad if it weren't for
Isemonger, he thought, watching the star pitcher stroll out to
the bullpen. Black reminded Al of some parents he had known
when he was a schoolboy, parents who would come into school
and defend their child no matter what he did. The kids, Al

reflected, usually turned out to be bullies and brats, unreliable and lacking in self-confidence. Children were like fledglings. They had to be allowed to fly free.

Down at the bullpen, Black was talking to the pitching coach. Zack was at the plate, throwing small grounders to the infielders, who practically surrounded the plate. They picked them up, threw them in, and moved back a step. It went on like that until the four infielders were in their positions, limbered and loosened. To one side of the plate Gillespy, the hitting coach, batted fungoes to the outfield. Al tracked the ball easily against the green and brown of the stadium. When he had first purchased Eagle Stadium, it had been painted many gaudy colors: yellow, orange, lavender, blue, green. He had put a lot of money into repairing the old Eagles' nest. That's what it had been to him, too. A nest. A place where he had been nurtured and trained, a place where he had brought back his triumphs to warm applause.

Gillespy switched his attention from the outfield to the infield, which got down to serious business. Grinding out the stub of his cigar on the risers, Al watched as Linda took a long sideways hop to stop a ball from going down the hole to center. Sliding her foot along second, she threw the ball to Knuff.

Range – that lateral movement from side to side – was crucial for an infielder. Most especially crucial for the shortstop, who had to have quick reflexes in an unnatural or at best awkward direction. It was instinctive to jump forward, even to turn and run backward. But it was that reaching out laterally, instinctively moving laterally, that made a first-rate shortstop. Al thought that Linda had that range. Closing his eyes, he pictured it: the classic shortstop maneuver, lunging to the right, stabbing a hot grounder backhanded, and making the long throw to first. "Going into the hole," it was called. Today artificial turf threatened the play. On good old natural grass, you could plant your feet firmly and give yourself the anchorage from which to make the throw. On turf, you couldn't plant your feet. That was the crucial difference between grass and plastic: one held you, the other let you slip on by. The throw to first became risky – your feet slid out from under you, and you might end up throwing into the stands. But the good shortstops came up with an answer to the problem – throw the ball to first on a long, hard hop. Previously unorthodox, now effective. Al opened his eyes. He had seen her do just that on artificial turf. In other stadiums, of course. He had had grass put back into Eagle Stadium when he bought the team. Yes. She could adjust. She was a natural.

Squeezing himself out of the little green wooden-slatted seat, Al walked back to his office, thinking. There was no reason – no *good* reason – why the Eagles couldn't win the pennant this year.

Linda sat in the home dugout, watching the Philadelphia players warm up. Philadelphia was the second-place team in the division, one lone game ahead of the Eagles. We can catch them, she thought. We will catch them, the way we're playing. And after them, California. She felt a shiver of excitement thinking about the pennant race.

"Hey, Linda."

She looked up. Zowski, who hadn't done more than grunt at her all season, was talking to her. "Yeah?"

"Do you have a nickname?"

Oh-oh, she thought. Trouble. "No."

"You should," said Zowski. "Doesn't anybody ever call you anything besides Linda? Or Sunshine?"

Zow sounded okay. That is, he sounded like Zow. Maybe it wasn't trouble. "When I was a kid they used to call me Lindy." She watched as Zowski frowned, thinking about it.

"It's not right," said Knuff. "There's only one Lindy. Lucky Lindy. You know," he explained to the puzzled Zowski, "Lindbergh. The pilot." He waved his hands in plane-like motions in front of Zowski. "The pilot! Charles Lindbergh! *The Spirit of St. Louis!*" Knuff stared into Zowski's eyes, looking for a glimmer. "Aw, forget it! The name's not right for her. Hey, U.S., what did you call her down in the minors?"

Linda looked around the dugout uncomfortably. Black was standing in a corner, looking out at the field. Isemonger was at the water fountain. Out of the corner of her eye she watched him crush his Styrofoam cup and throw it into the wastebasket.

"Mostly Sunshine," answered Ulysses.

"Mostly's a strange name." Knuff scratched his head, considering the moniker. "No, it's just not right."

Harland draped an arm across her shoulder. "Let me call you Darlin', Darlin'."

Linda patted him on the cheek. "No, Darlin', that's too familiar. But you can call me Sweetheart anytime."

Frank, examining the bats, hooted. "She's got you there, Harland!"

"Ah, Linda, come on," pleaded Harland. "I can't call you that."

A sweetheart was a player whose steady hitting, fielding, and morale building year after year won the respect of fellow players. Nobody was about to call her Sweetheart.

"Why not call her Linda?" suggested Zack, looking for a place to sit.

"I like calling her Sunshine," Frank offered as he checked his bats.

"What about Sunny?" asked Zowski.

"For cryin' out loud! She's not a Sunny," pleaded Zack. "Look at her! Sunny, my ass! "

Isemonger strutted to where Linda, Zowski, Knuff, and Harland were sitting. "Why not call her Easy – as in Easy Lay."

"Shut up, Icehead," ordered Harland.

"You have some sort of sexual hang-up, Icehead?" Linda asked angrily.

"Not me, baby – I don't go around fucking the sports reporters to get better coverage." He leaned close to her. "I hear you make it with anybody."

"Shut up!" warned Harland.

"Then you're nobody, Icehead, 'cause there's no way I'll ever make it with you!"

"Yeah?" sneered Isemonger. "You're just dyin' to."

Harland jumped off the bench and pushed Isemonger, who stumbled backward a step.

"Hold it! Hold it!" Lacey Griffen, coming from the other side of the dugout, stepped between the pitcher and catcher. "Calm down," he told Harland. "Knock it off, Icehead."

"You, too?!" demanded Isemonger, pushing Griffen away. "Don't tell me she's making it with you, too? Christ, there's *nothing* she won't do!"

Reaching forward, Isemonger tried to grab Linda's shirt and pull her off the bench. He was turned around by an angry Griffen, who shouted, "What'd you say?! What'd you say?!"

Ignoring the fact that Griffen was grappling with him,

Isemonger continued his verbal assault on Linda." You'd even do it with Griffen and Crowder, wouldn't you?" he sneered contemptuously.

The dugout grew quiet in an implosion of silence that lasted for a fraction of a second. Then pandemonium prevailed as, jumping up, Linda shouted, "You're slime, Icebrain! You're scum!" Shoving at Isemonger, she became entangled with Griffen, who had just thrown a punch at Icehead's jaw. The punch resulted in a toppled Iceblock. It also resulted in Black's racing down to pull at Griffen. "You're dead!" Isemonger shouted at Griffen as he righted himself, backed up the dugout steps, and then hurled himself at Griffen, knocking him into the bench and then jumping on him. Linda jumped on Isemonger. Players pulled at them, but their own momentum was dominant. They scrambled upright, Isemonger in the middle, Linda and Griffen surrounding him, all clutching and hitting. "Get out of my way, Sunshine!" shouted Griffen. "No!" she grunted, feeling something hard clip her face. The trio somehow scuffled up the dugout steps, where it tripped, rolling into the dirt and grass in full sight of the home crowd. The strong arms of Frank, Zack, Knuff, Zowski, Harland, and Ulysses broke them up and pushed them individually back into the dugout.

Big Al had finished his tour of the crowded stadium, had taken in the lifeblood of the friendly, jostling crowd, the smell of the hot dogs, tacos, beer, popcorn, and peanuts, the sounds of the organist playing the clever, rousing songs, the ticket sellers at work, the turnstiles turning, the smell of the bars where the news, radio, and television crews had their pregame warm-up.

Up in the press box, his last stop, Al spotted Neal Vanderlin, his head bent down, writing at a table. He walked over and dropped a hand on Vanderlin's shoulder.

Vanderlin looked up. "Hi, Al. How's it going?"

"Great. I think we're gonna take 'em tonight. There's–" He stopped, staring down at the Eagles' dugout. Three Eagle players were fighting, rolling in the dirt! What the hell was going on?

By the time Al got to the dugout, nobody was fighting anybody. Nobody was talking to anybody, either. Demanding to know just what was going on, Al (and his rage) filled the dugout. Nobody said a word. Al paced the dugout, examining the players. Linda: split lip, dirt all over her face, uniform a mess. Isemonger: bloody nose, puffy eye. Griffen: split lip, cut hand.

Pointing at the tunnel entrance, Al, barely suppressing his rage, spoke to Linda. "Get into that tunnel." He pointed at Griffen. "You, too." Finally, he pointed at Isemonger. "And you."

They gave him sullen stares. But they walked into the tunnel.

Al followed. Behind him, he sensed the rest of the team crowding around the entrance. Good. No right-field camera could possibly see through all those players. He turned his attention to the three belligerents. "Okay, what happened?"

Griffen stared at the opposite wall. Linda studied her shoes. Isemonger looked at Al and sneered. Al repeated the question. The proverbial cat that got tongues must have had a feast in the dugout.

The cat was no match for Al Mowerinski. "You. Isemonger. Did you hit her?" he demanded.

Isemonger, red in the face and red in the neck, exploded. *"No!* She hit me! She's crazy!"

Al stared at Isemonger in astonishment, then stepped back and stared at Linda. "Is that true?" he asked unbelievingly. Was she going to lie to him? And if she did, would he be able to recognize it? Just what the hell was going on here?

Linda looked him square in the eyes. "I didn't hit him. I shoved him." She lifted her chin. "Then I tried to hit him."

Al ran a large hand through his hair, wondering how many more hairs were turning gray at this very moment. "Why? Why did you shove him?"

"He's been looking for trouble all season." She stared at the same tunnel wall that Griffen was glowering at.

"He's been looking–" he said, starting to repeat her statement, then, realizing it wasn't an answer of any kind, he exploded. *"Answer my question!"* he bellowed, sending a few of the players around the entrance back a pace.

She looked at him. "He . . . " She swallowed, looked away, returned her gaze. ". . . made a sexist and racist remark."

"He made a racist remark!" roared Griffen angrily. "Same thing every white man's afraid of."

Linda grabbed Griffen's sleeve. "I *said* racist," she said to him. "I said sexist and racist." She turned to Al. "There's no way he's going to drive me out."

Al stepped back. "Hold it. Just hold it." He looked at Linda. He looked at Isemonger. He looked at Griffen. He ran his hands through his hair again. "Let me get this straight. You shoved Isemonger because he made a sexist and racist remark?"

"Yes. He's been looking for trouble–"

"I know, I know," roared Al, finishing her remark, "–all season." He turned in a circle, bringing himself again face to face with the trio. He looked at Griffen. "What did he say?"

Instead of answering, Griffen jumped Isemonger, beginning the scuffle anew. Al ended it anew, swinging two clenched fists like an ax between the two timberheads, roaring his anger. With one hand he pressed Isemonger against the tunnel wall; with the other he pressed Griffen. If Linda gave him any trouble, he was going to kick her down the tunnel. "Frank, come here."

Laughing stepped out of the crowd and into the tunnel. Al let go of Griffen. "Here," he said, motioning a hand at Linda and Griffen. "Walk these two down to the clubhouse and back. Calm them down. Get them out on that infield in five minutes." Al turned toward the crowd in the dugout. "Artie – go with Laughing and fix their goddamn cuts. Do what you can to make them look like baseball players."

Frank walked off between Griffen and Linda, talking sense to them both. Artie followed closely, medical supplies in hand.

"Can you pitch?" Al demanded of Isemonger.

"Yeah – no thanks to that bitch. I told you that–"

Al's hand around Isemonger's throat squeezed off the rest of the sentence. He waited until Icehead clearly understood that tonight was not the night for this kind of talk. Out of the corner of his eye, he saw Black break out of the crowd of players and elbow his way forward. One look from Al stopped him in his tracks.

"Harland, come here," ordered Al, releasing his hold on Isemonger.

Harland stepped out of the dugout and into the tunnel. Al pointed a finger at the pitcher. "Calm him down. Get him out there and warm him up." He let go of Isemonger and turned to look at Laughing, Griffen, Sunshine, and the trainer walking down the tunnel. He turned back in time to see Harland punch Isemonger in the stomach.

For a moment Al stood there with his mouth open. Then he stepped between the pitcher and catcher, pressing Isemonger to one wall, Abilene to the other. Al breathed heavily, too furious for words. This fury conveyed itself to the pitcher and catcher, for when Al trusted himself enough to let them go, they straightened their shoulders and, without a look at one another, pressed through the crowd, out of the dugout, and into the playing field.

By the time Al had walked to his office for a double shot of scotch, then walked to his seat, Philadelphia had been retired from the top of the first, Griffen had stepped to bat in the bottom of the first and walloped a homer over the right-field upper deck, Gutierrez had popped out, Abilene had tripled, and Laughing had struck out. Zowski hit a line drive back to the pitcher, and that ended the bottom of the first, Eagles leading 1-0.

In the top of the second, the Philadelphia shortstop got a leg hit. Now was the time for a bunt. Or the hit and run, in which the batter tried to hit behind the already-running runner. The Philly runner headed for second, the batter swung, and the ball sailed into right, where it caromed off the wall. Hector had difficulty with it and the runner scored, making it a 1-1 ball game. Isemonger showed everybody behind him he took it personally by kicking the mound and throwing the resin bag. Al watched as Icehead battled not only Philadelphia, not only the players behind him, but the other half of the battery as well.

Every signal that Harland gave, Icehead shook off. This must have wearied the Philadelphia batters, for the side was retired without further runs.

Knuff led off the Eagle half of the second with a single, and Linda stepped up to bat. Al, trying to calm himself, lit a cigar. Seventh was not a bad place to bat her, he thought. Seventh or second, to take maximum advantage of her speed and hitting. Inhaling, he reflected, perhaps with some regret, that he couldn't control everything on the team. He would have liked to manage, sure. But he had made a different choice, had promised himself something different twenty-two years ago.

Al felt a tenseness every time he saw her at the plate. She wasn't just some other ball player. He felt as if he were up there with her. He could almost sense her thinking as she stood there. The Philly infield was playing close – just one small part of the give-and-take of baseball. If you were a good runner, the infield played a shade closer to take away your advantage of speed. That, in turn, made it easier for you to hit the ball over their heads and get on base anyway. Linda laid down a bunt along the third baseline. Knuff sprinted to second, his helmet flying off as Linda raced to first. Safe at second, out at first. Nice sacrifice. Crowder stepped to the plate. At least Ulysses hadn't been part of the fight. Al wondered what the hell he, Al, was going to do about the fight.

On the surface, things had looked, if not good, at least like they were holding together as the Eagles moved toward second place. Al now realized that only the drive itself was holding them together. Centrifugal force. He remembered being a kid, carrying buckets of water to help his father, who was mixing mortar. Al would swing the half-full bucket in a large arc over his head, down again to his knees, up, down, his arm spinning 'round like a windmill's. The water would stay in the bucket – until he slowed down. Then, if he couldn't stop the slowing bucket fast enough in an upright position, the water would come pouring down on top of him. So would his father, who needed the water. The Eagles reminded him of that. What was holding them in the bucket (despite the sloshing) was the speed and direction in which they were moving. Any slowdown could cause a downpour. Crowder hit a hard grounder that the second baseman booted. Crowder was out anyway, Knuff safe at third. Isemonger stepped up, and Al sensed the exodus to the refreshment stands. The inning ended with Icehead's strikeout.

In the top of the fifth Philadelphia scored, taking a 2-1 lead. Isemonger kicked more mound and threw more resin. The next Philly batter singled. Al watched Linda and Frank shield their mouths with their gloves, signaling which of them would take second on a double play. Frank moved two steps toward second. Isemonger threw the ball. The batter connected, but the hard hopper was stopped in flight by Laughing, who tagged the bag and, twisting, threw to first. Double play. The fans cheered lustily. Al, in no mood to cheer or smile, at least permitted himself the thought that he had a damn good team, a team that could take the pennant. He knew it could be done. He was here to see to it that nothing stood in the way.

The next Philly batter hit a hard grounder that tore a divot out of the infield, then scooted along the ground like a torpedo toward the shortstop. Linda charged the ball, smothered it in her glove, scooped it out, and threw to Knuff. From where he sat, Al could see the dirt that she scooped out of her glove with the ball: a small cloud of it seemed to float around her and lazily drift back down to the infield. The runner was out, the inning over.

Al stood and stretched. It was not the seventh inning, but Al stretched when he felt like it. The play reminded him of the photograph. He had wanted one to have, not on his desk, not in his office where he hung the team's pictures, but at home, where he could look at her when he wanted to and where he could feel the unexpected delight of catching sight of the picture when he was thinking of other things. Al could have had any of hundreds of pictures of her, but he chose this one. The photo showed her throwing the ball to first. Infield dirt was pouring out of her gloved hand in a small stream. An aura of infield dust surrounded the ball. The sun glinted off the minute particles of dirt and dust, making them sparkle. The effect was that of looking at a shortstop through a mist, a mixture of sunlight and dirt. You couldn't even tell, until you looked closely, who the shortstop was. After he chose the photo, he became aware that it was symbolic to him. The more he thought about it, the more he realized it expressed his philosophy. You had to sparkle through the dirt.

The Eagles tried to sparkle through the dirt but didn't succeed. Philadelphia took the game, 3-2. There was no such thing as an undefeated baseball team – not in a 162-game season – so Al didn't exactly feel the spinning water come pouring down with this loss. But he felt the threat of it over his head. A baseball team would get nowhere when it wasn't a team – when the players were more concerned with their own problems than with the team's problems.

Stalking toward the clubhouse after the loss, Al shoved people aside. The swinging door vibrated on its hinges as he flicked it out of his path, stunning the players (in various stages of dress or undress) into momentary silence. Al ordered all reporters out of the clubhouse. Then he ordered Gillespy to get

Linda into the clubhouse on the double for a meeting. He glared as a few of the naked players, wrapping towels around themselves, grumbled. Gillespy came in with Linda, who was dressed only in a large towel. Al ordered everybody to pull up a bench.

And then he told them, in tones loud and clear, how the game was played. He ended by fining Abilene $500 (check to be made out to his favorite charity) for punching Isemonger; Sunshine and Griffen $500 each for scuffling with Isemonger; Isemonger $1,000 for his racist remark and an additional $1,000 for his sexist remark.

Al waited for somebody to say something. But nobody, not even Lenny Black, said anything. Al turned and walked out of the clubhouse. He heard somebody (it sounded like Griffen) asking Linda if he could borrow her towel to cry on.

Driving home to his North Side apartment, Al wondered whether he had done the right thing. He thought of Amanda and tried not to. Sometimes he could will himself not to think of her. Tonight, he felt, wasn't going to be one of those times.

At home he poured himself a J & B on the rocks and sank into his favorite chair with a sigh. Elevating his feet to the coffee table, he took a long swallow of the scotch. The drink told him he wasn't going to win. He was going to think of Amanda tonight. He was going to get drunk and think of Amanda.

He had not always had alcohol. He had not always had Amanda. But when he had joined the Eagles at the age of eighteen, he had been introduced to a whole new world. The players delighted in taking a rookie and teaching him how to drink, fight, and screw. Not necessarily in that order, as someone once said.

Picking up the bottle from the floor, he poured himself another drink. Maybe it was a mistake. Maybe the dissension on the team was so great that it couldn't work. "No!" he shouted aloud. It *would* work. Goddamn it, he didn't lay his best plans just to have them balked at and defeated by a bunch of boneheads. No. His plans weren't going to be ruined. The Eagles now had the finest team in baseball, and he, Al Mowerinski, was responsible for it. The Eagles would win the pennant, he was sure of it. Luck, as Papa Branch Rickey had said, is the residue of design.

Linda was tough. Strong and sure. She would make it without any scars. Well, he reminded himself, without any scars worse than a split lip or two. Clinking a few ice cubes from the tray into his glass, Al topped off his drink. He understood how Linda must have felt. He would have done the same thing. He would have done more. Yeah, he would have beaten somebody like Isemonger to a bloody pulp. But it wouldn't have done Amanda any good at all. The thought, passing through his brain in such a form, like a distilled lesson from history, made him suddenly sad, turning down the corners of his mouth and emphasizing the wrinkles around his eyes.

In 1945, young Albert Mowerinski, just turned eighteen, had joined the Chicago Eagles. Al knew he was a good ball player. He also knew that, had it not been for the war shortage of ball players, he wouldn't have made it straight from high school into the majors. A big, raw-boned kid, he had weighed thirty-five pounds under what was later his mature playing weight. Just a skinny kid from Pittsburgh, wide-eyed and in awe of most everything. But he was so well meaning, so honest and open, and hit so damned well that the older players immediately took him under their wing – even after that first game.

Playing center field, Al had been nervous – and slightly paranoid. Every time one of the opposing players blasted a ball in his direction, he had felt they were testing him, looking for a weak spot. But nerves (and skill) had carried him through as he snagged liners and pulled down well-hit fly balls. He had been doing okay (he had had, as today's college-graduated ball players would say, "credibility"). And then, in the bottom of the eighth, with the winning run on second, Red Scanlan hit a long fly ball to short center. Al had circled under it but had misjudged it. The ball dropped. He had looked around in panic but couldn't find it. By the time the Eagles' right fielder had pounded into center, scooped up the ball, and thrown to second to hold Scanlan, the winning run had crossed the plate. Al would never forget the sound of the loudspeaker informing the crowd that Mowerinski got an error on the play. Worse than that, the Eagles lost the game.

Despite this start, Al's initiation had been more friendly than not. The older players had taught him how to eat lobster in Boston (back in the days when Boston had a National League team), rare steak in Chicago, shrimp in New York, and lamb chops in St. Louis. To say nothing of the drinking, he thought, pouring himself another.

They didn't teach him anything about love. That he learned by himself.

It was his first year in the majors that he met her. Al sighed into his drink, remembering that it was Curry who was responsible for his meeting Amanda. Timothy Michael Curry, just a couple of years older than Albert Mowerinski, had the idea that changed his life.

"Hey, kid," said Curry that warm May day, "let's hop the South Shore to Hammond."

"What for?" asked Al, pacing the apartment he shared with the Eagles' third baseman.

"Come on," laughed Curry. "We'll find out when we get there. There's nothing to do here anyway."

Well, it didn't make sense to Al. If there was nothing to do in Chicago, there was nothing to do anywhere. But, he liked the golden-haired Irishman, it was an off day, and so, why not?

Curry, the clever fox, knew just where they were going. A ballpark. A ballpark with a difference.

"Hey! Those are *girls* out there!" cried Al in astonishment as he and Curry walked toward the empty bleachers. The field was full of girls playing . . . playing what? It didn't look like softball. But then, it didn't look like baseball, either.

"C'mon, c'mon," urged Curry, pulling at Al, laughing at his astonishment.

"What is it? Who are they?"

"Kid, where you been? Don't you read the papers? Those are the Hammond Chicks." Curry pulled Al toward the bleachers. "Boy-oh-boy, ain't they gorgeous?!" he chortled, slapping Al on the back.

Al sat on the bleachers, mesmerized. He remembered: he had heard the players talking about girl baseball players. Something about the war and Phil Wrigley and Branch Rickey starting an all-girls baseball team.

The surprise wore off; Al started grinning. Curry grinned back; they started to chuckle. The chuckling turned into loud laughter and enthusiastic back slapping. Al watched the girls, in their short skirts and knee socks, warming up. He was excited by the bare legs and bare arms, the firm thighs, all that female flesh in motion. He was excited by how good they were.

It was the little redheaded pitcher who held his attention. Al couldn't keep his eyes off her. She couldn't have been more than sixteen years old, not more than five-feet-three-inches tall. All curly red hair sticking out from under her cap, all chunky round curves. She was throwing the ball in there so fast he could barely see it. "Jesus, Curry, will you look at that pitcher! Think you could hit her?"

"Hey," exclaimed Curry, only half-laughing, "keep away from the pitcher! I had my eyes on her first." Poking Al in the ribs with an elbow, he added, "You can take the other eight, kid, but leave the redhead to T. M. Curry!"

Frowning, Al turned back to watch the pitching and hitting. Just as he adjusted to the windup and pitch, just as he was able to figure out that the dimensions of the field were some bastardization between softball and baseball, the manager called for a switch. The curly redhead tossed the ball to an incoming pitcher, and (to Al's astonishment) the infield shifted so that the redhead was playing shortstop.

She was fantastic at short.

Curry poked him in the ribs again. "Hey, kid, don't you wish Rocko could play short when he wasn't pitching?"

"Hm? Oh, yeah. Yeah," mumbled Al, his mind elsewhere. He had a hard-on that felt like it was going to bust through his pants. He barely noticed one of the players detach herself from the sidelines and wander over their way.

"Hello," she greeted. "What do you think of the Hammond Chicks?"

She was an older woman, near forty probably. Definitely not one of the players, Al realized. Maybe a coach. She had a sharp, narrow face, dark hair pulled back severely into a bun. She wore no cap.

"Great, m'am," answered Curry. "Just great."

The woman smiled, nodding her head as if accepting the obvious. "You're T. M. Curry, aren't you?" she asked him.

"Yes, m'am," replied Curry, getting to his feet belatedly. Al rose, too. "This here's Al Mowerinski. He's a rookie this year."

The woman again nodded, as if approving of them. "Yes, I believe I've seen you play," she said to Al. "My name is Donna Gattler."

"Uh, are you the manager, m'am?" asked Curry politely.

"Certainly not," she replied with a sniff. "The manager is a man. I'm the girls' chaperon."

Al laughed, then caught the disapproving look she cast at him and tried to turn it into a cough. He failed: it came out a snort through his nose. He looked down at his feet and tried to squeeze his large, raw-boned hands into the too-small pockets of his suit pants. A lock of his dark hair fell in his face, completing the misery and embarrassment he felt. He ran one hand through his hair and shuffled his feet.

"Chaperon?" queried Curry, his politeness contrasting with Al's gaucheness, making Al felt like a busher.

"Yes, indeed, Mr. Curry. Every team in the Girls' League has a manager, a business manager, and a chaperon." She straightened her ramrod back even more so (if that was possible) with pride. "We don't want anybody to get the wrong idea about our girls. They're good, decent young ladies from decent homes," she said, looking directly at Al with something akin to a warning. "They are playing ball to entertain the public and to earn money to attend college. At our training camp in

Pascagoula our young ladies practice playing ball all day. And in the evening, they attend finishing school. They are taught posture, etiquette, and homemaking skills."

Curry coughed discreetly. "That sounds very nice, m'am. Don't you think so, Al?"

"Uh, that seems like an awful lot. Don't they get tired?"

Curry frowned at him, and Al realized he had said the wrong thing.

But Gattler gave him a wispy smile. "Certainly not. Haven't you heard the expression 'A woman's work is never done'? Each of these girls is going to make some man a fine wife one day. You never heard of a decent wife getting tired, did you?"

Al thought of his Irish mother, who went to an early grave last year, lines of overwork and fatigue covering her face and hands, and said nothing.

"Sounds like you have an important job," said Curry.

This time the thin smile was quite open. "Yes, indeed, Mr. Curry. One of the chaperon's most important jobs is to approve the social contacts our girls have. No girl may go out with anybody without the chaperon's approval."

Al felt his mouth slack open. Shooting a quick glance at Curry, he saw surprise there, too.

"Well, I'm sure that's a fine policy, m'am," said Curry. "And what might you as a chaperon think of your girls going out with baseball players? Eagles baseball players, of course," he said with a small bow.

Al stared at Curry in amazement. What recovery the Irishman had! Al hadn't inherited any of the Irish charm. What he got from his mother was love and single-mindedness of purpose. But when it came to charm, he would always be

Polish in any situation.

"Well, Mr. Curry," said the old battleax with a superior sniff, "we generally do not approve of our girls associating with baseball players." Having let her point sink in, she then continued. "*You*, however, seem like a nicely mannered young man."

Al could feel her disapproving eye glance at him.

Curry caught it, too, and put an arm around Al's shoulder. "Now, Mrs. Gattler, don't get the wrong impression about Al, here. He's a nice kid. Kind of unpolished, you know? After all, he's only eighteen, and this is his first year in the majors. But I assure you he's a gentleman."

Good old Curry, thought Al, a warm spot filling his heart. He flashed a smile at the old battleax, hoping she'd believe that a ball player could be a gentleman (never believing it for a moment himself).

The battleax smiled back thinly. "Well, if you would like to meet some of our girls after practice, I'm sure they would be thrilled to meet some real ball players."

"Thank you, m'am. It will be our pleasure." Curry gave his semibow again. Then, when the battleax had gone, he turned to Al. "Whoo-ee!" he whistled, slapping Al on the back. "Whoo-ee, girls, here we come! And don't forget, kid – the redhead's mine."

It didn't turn out that way, though. Amanda had been shy and hard to meet. The other girls had to practically drag her over to the bleachers to meet the two young men. Once she learned they were Eagles, though, she had to be dragged away. What were the Eagles' chances, she wanted to know? What was the matter with Rocko's pitching this year? When were they going to get a decent shortstop to make the double play? Didn't they have anybody in the minors?

Amanda. She had just turned sixteen that spring, her freshness, energy, and enthusiasm rivaling that of the season. The rest of the team loved her. They should have loved her: when the season ended, she was the league's best player – .926 fielding, 34 double plays, 261 putouts, and a .290 batting average (the league's highest). For six years thereafter Amanda Quitman led the Girls' League in everything, her batting average climbing to .366. Nobody could touch her when it came to playing the peculiar game.

What's it feel like to be a rookie? she had asked Al. How much do you get paid? How much batting practice do you take every day? Whenever Al started to answer, Curry stepped in and answered for him. The other girls smiled: they must have been used to Amanda's getting all the attention. When the manager clapped his hands for them, the others drifted away and Al had one second alone with her. He blurted it out, asking if she would like to go to a movie with him that evening.

Curry exploded. They nearly came to blows then and there. But Amanda stomped her foot and ordered them to stop: she would go to the movie with both of them.

"No!" they shouted in unison.

It was either both of them or neither, she replied. She didn't think they should fight. It wouldn't be good for the team.

So they both took her out to the movie. Gattler beamed her approval – whether at the team unity or the fact that the intentions of neither man could succeed, they didn't know.

He and Amanda – and Curry – didn't see too much of each other, what with the Chicks traveling through Michigan, Wisconsin, Indiana, and Illinois and the Eagles on road trips all over the eastern half of the states. When the Chicks were in

Hammond, though, and the Eagles in Chicago, you could count
on the trio doing the town. After a while, Curry and Al even
joked about it. It seemed as if neither of them would get
anywhere.

The winter of '45-'46, Al got to see very little of Amanda.
He had to return to Pittsburgh to work, helping his father in the
lawn mower shop, for $50 a week. Curry, too, had to work in
order to live from the end of one season to the beginning of the
next. Curry sold men's suits in a Chicago store. Amanda went
back to the small Ohio farm where her grandparents, who had
raised her, lived.

When the '46 season came, Al, Amanda, and Curry were
still going out as a trio. Even though each man asked her to go
out alone with him, she refused.

"Why not?" demanded Al, impatient.

"Why can't we all be friends?"

"Because we can't, Amanda," Curry would answer. "It
doesn't work that way."

It didn't work that way. Something, sooner or later, would
have broken them apart. As it turned out, it was baseball:
baseball, which had brought them together, intervened and
broke them apart.

Amanda was the star of the Girls' League, no doubt about
it. The manager encouraged a fast-pitching, hard-hitting,
running game, and Amanda took to it like horsehide took to
string and cork. There was speculation of getting women into
the major leagues. Major league scouts came to Hammond to
look at the Chicks. "If she was a boy, I'd give $60,000 for her,"
said a New York scout of Amanda.

Curry reported the remark to her, saying, "Don't let it go
to your head, Mandy. He's just talking for the press, giving

them a story."

"What do you mean? I could play in the majors," she replied, tossing her red curls defiantly.

"Ah, *c'mon,* Mandy!" Curry guffawed. "Baseball is a man's game! What you're playing now isn't baseball. It can't be. It looks fast, but it isn't."

Amanda's lower lip quivered. Al stepped in. "Hey, c'mon, Curry, lay off. Mandy's a better player than some of the guys on the club, for pete's sake! And how do you know? They just might take a woman in the majors. I hear they might put Negroes in. They've got one playing in Montreal already. Maybe this scouting is for real." Personally, Al doubted they would ever take women into the major leagues, but that wasn't the fault of women, was it?

Something (perhaps the knowledge that Al and Amanda took the question seriously) riled Curry like little else Al had seen. All through May, all through June, all through the hot days of July, whenever they were together, Curry would behave like a bench jockey, riding Amanda about women in the major leagues. It was one of the few questions that the Irishman could not, would not, joke about. It was one of the few questions that Amanda would not, could not, joke about.

At the end of July it exploded.

Curry had just made some particularly cutting remark. What it was Al, couldn't even remember.

"That does it, Curry! Get out! I never want to see you again." Mandy had jumped up off the dining stool as if she were the one who was going to get out. "If you can't respect me, I don't want to know you!"

Curry was shocked. Embarrassed. "Mandy, what do you mean? I respect you. What the hell are you talking about?"

"No you don't, you don't!" she shouted, pointing at him. "I hate your attitude. I can't stand it. I can't stand *you!*"

Curry's face grew red. He stood, jingling in his pockets for change. "C'mon, Al, let's go." He threw a handful of change on the counter and started for the door.

Al sat on his stool and looked at Amanda. "I'm not coming," he said to Curry.

The look that Curry gave him would have chopped a bat to splinters.

Well, what did he expect? thought Al.

Later, in the locker room, Al tried to make amends. "Jesus, Curry – why did you say those things to her?"

"Don't talk to me, you Judas."

"C'mon, Curry, don't be like that. It had to be one of us, sooner or later."

"You!" shouted his teammate, turning on him and pointing a finger. "You wanted it to work out like this! This is your fault!"

"Aw, fuck it, Curry!" Al threw down his shirt and stalked off to the showers. Curry followed him. Al lathered up. "If you wanted her, Curry, why did you keep telling her she was a second-rate player?"

"I *didn't* tell her she was second-rate, you dumb Pollack," spewed Curry through a face full of soap. "I said she was the best woman player there was. Chrissake, what does she want?" he demanded, waving a bar of soap in Al's face.

"Skip it, Curry, just skip it." Al stormed off to dry himself.

Curry asked for (and got) a new roommate on Eagle road trips. He also got engaged in a month and married in a year. A year later, he was a father for the first time. By the end of four more years, Curry had four daughters.

All of which should have given Al a clear field with Amanda. But somebody (Al always believed it was Curry) called old Gattler to report that Al Mowerinski had a wild reputation. Old Gattler agreed and forbade his visits. So Al would sneak into Hammond and wait in the dark outside the girls' boarding house. He would watch and wait and soon hear a window open, then the stealthy scraping of shoes against metal as Mandy climbed out her window and down the drainspout and then dropped to the ground.

They became lovers. Immediately thereafter, Al said they should get married. Never – absolutely never – would he have expected Mandy to refuse. But refuse she did.

"But *why?*" he had demanded. "Why don't you want to get married?"

"If I get married, I can't play ball. You know that, Al. They wouldn't let me. And you wouldn't want me to, would you?" She had sat on the bed, studying him.

"Christ, Mandy – you know I want you to play ball. Why wouldn't I?"

"Suppose our schedules keep us apart. Suppose we get to see each other once a month. How would you feel then?"

Al had been about to protest that it wouldn't make any difference to him – but he realized that it would. He would expect Mandy to be there when he came home. There was no denying it: with marriage, his expectations of her would change. The knowledge left him silent.

In 1947, Jackie Robinson made the Dodger lineup. Maybe women would be next, Al said, still looking for a way to make Mandy happy – still looking for a way they could be happy together. The scouts still came around; the Girls' League was still written up; Mandy was still the darling of all the fans. But the wind wasn't blowing out of the stadium, helping the hitters. It was blowing into the plate, against women. Attendance at the Girls' League games began to dwindle. Then the army was demilitarized, and the men came back, and the women who had been working in the factories were pushed out.

"The Girls' League will be next," Mandy predicted.

"It won't be," he assured her, stroking her thick red hair, patting the bouncy curls.

The Girls' League lingered. In the majors, rumors circulated that the scouts were looking for a girl pitcher. The rumors reached the Girls' League. The scouts didn't.

In 1954, the Girls' League folded. Amanda halfheartedly went looking for another job. "Can you type?" they asked.

"Mandy," Al implored, "I'm sorry it's over, but . . . but now we can get married."

"It was a trap," she said.

"What was?"

"The girls' baseball thing. It looked like a fast, hard-played game. But it was an optical illusion. It was a setup. We had different field dimensions, a different ball, all to fool the public. To fool us, too. We never had a chance."

"What do you mean?" he asked.

She laughed bitterly. "I hit .340, .342, year after year – tops in the league, right? Then that jerk of a baseball scout comes along and tells me I can't be considered as a shortstop in the majors because I'm not hitting a *real* baseball. I'm hitting a deader ball, see? So I tell him, 'Well, if I'm hitting .340 with a dead ball, what do you think I'll bat with a live one?' 'No soap,' he says. 'You wouldn't be able to hit a live one.' It was a setup, Al. They gave us a *deader ball* to play with and said they did it out of consideration for our sex. But that wasn't why. It was a setup all the way, to keep us from playing the real thing. I accepted their rules. I never had a chance, Al, never," she cried. Curled up in a wing chair, feet tucked under her, her head reclined against the chair's embracing arm, she looked forlorn. Al knelt in front of her and kissed her tears away. There was nothing he could do.

It was nearly 1:30 A.M. when, down in her locker room, Linda finished eating, showering, and dressing.. The Eagles had taken the second, third, and fourth games from Philadelphia, moving into second place. But it hadn't been easy. Tonight's game had gone fifteen innings and ended well after midnight. The team was jubilant but exhausted as it trudged back to the locker rooms. "Good save, Charlie." "California, here we come." "Your batting average went up five points this game, Sunshine." "Hey, Griff, don't forget you owe me some comps." "My wife is going to be pissed, my getting home this late. Thank god I can prove where I was!"

After showering, Linda talked to the rapidly speaking reporters, all of whom asked the same question: Think you'll catch California? Their pencils flying (probably writing the answers in advance, she thought), they hurried away to their stories. She missed Neal: his questions never sounded as if he knew the answers in advance. He had gone to the races to interview some jockey and look some racehorse in the mouth. The waiting food tasted as if it had been waiting far too long, but she was too hungry to go out and get something else.

The rustle of paper caused her to look up from her food. What had she heard? Looking around, she tried to place the sound. There . . . on the floor. Somebody had slipped a folded note under her door. What was it? she wondered, slowly getting up and walking to the door. Some fan wanting a rendezvous? A notice for home-delivery pizza? Bending, she picked up the paper. Slowly she walked back to her chair, unfolding the note with one hand.

Eagle stationery. "See me in my office after tonight's game. Al."

Oh, man, thought Linda, falling into her chair, is he crazy? She glanced at her watch: nearly 2:00. What did he want? She picked up the sandwich she had built out of various cold cuts and bit into it. *Oh my god!* She nearly choked on the food. "See me in my office." Oh, god – that's what they told you in the minors when they were sending you down. Or trading you. She hadn't been hitting well all week – but tonight she had hit her stride again. Was he sending her down just because she had whiffed a few times? Dropping the sandwich, she ran out of the locker room, down the darkened tunnel, into the stadium, up the stairs, and, finally, to Al's office.

The windows of the outer office were dark. Linda hesitated. Had he left? She tried the reception room door. It opened. "Hello?" she shouted. "Al?" Nobody answered. No shard of light came from under the door to his office. Linda knocked on the door, then, when there was no answer, tried the doorknob.

The door to Al's office opened, only to reveal a darkened interior. She shrugged her shoulders and was turning to go when she sensed somebody behind her. As she started to turn around, a violent push knocked her off her feet and into the office. "Ow!" she cried, banging against something in the dark, tripping and falling to the floor.

The lights blinded her at first, then she saw Isemonger

standing there, his back to the office door. First came her fury. "What the hell is this, Icebrain?! Is this your idea of some sick joke?!" she demanded, scrambling to her feet.

And then she saw him reach behind himself and lock the door. Fear flooded through her, centering in her stomach.

"No joke, Sunshine. Nobody gets away with calling me the names you called me."

"Me?!" she demanded indignantly. "You're the one who's spent the season name calling!"

"Remember 'slime'? Remember 'scum'?" Isemonger moved forward. "You didn't think you could get away with that, did you?" he asked in a low voice.

Stepping backward, Linda glanced around the office quickly, looking for a way out. "You've called me names all season. You should be able to take a few in return."

"Nobody calls me names. Nobody."

"Well I did, and I'm not sorry for it!" she retorted angrily. "There's nothing you can do about it. Learn to live with it," she advised, trying to brush by him.

Grabbing her arm, he flung her back toward Al's desk. "Nobody calls me names. You're going to get what's coming to you."

She watched as Isemonger made a fist out of his right hand, rubbing it into his left hand. "You had Harland to protect you. Even Griffen," he sneered.

Linda laughed out of nervousness and disbelief. "Are you threatening to beat me up, Icebrain? Don't be ridiculous."

"Yes!" he shouted, smacking his fist into his open hand. "You're going to get what's coming to you, what comes to anybody who calls me names."

She backed up, but bumped into Al's desk as Icehead

advanced toward her. "Wait!" she commanded. "Use your head. You beat me up and what's going to happen to you? Don't think I won't tell, Icehead – I sure as hell will. I'll tell everybody. You'll be suspended."

To her surprise, Isemonger stopped and seemed to consider the consequences.

How do I get out of this? She watched him cautiously.

"I could hurt you bad. I could make you leave baseball."

Linda shook her head. "Never. You could hurt me, but I could hurt you back. What if I break your pitching hand, or your arm? And if you sent me to the hospital, you wouldn't be playing baseball, either, believe me. The papers would have a field day with the news. I'd take you to court – this is premeditated assault and battery." *Was it? Just keep talking.*

Isemonger stared at the wall. She could rush the door again, but that might provoke him.

"Then you'll have to apologize."

"Apologize?!" Linda guffawed. "For what?"

Looking away from the wall, he concentrated on her. His eyes looked crazed. "For calling me names, you dumb broad! I told you – nobody gets away with that. Nobody." He flexed the fingers of his right hand, looked at them, and then shoved his hand into his pocket.

He's afraid I'll break his fingers . . . I've got to get out of this.

"You can apologize to me tomorrow. In the dugout. Yeah, that's good, in the dugout. You wait until everybody's there, then stand up and walk up to me, see. Then turn and face me, and tell me you have something to say to me. That'll get everybody's attention. Then, when the dugout's quiet, you can tell me you're sorry you called me names."

She was outraged. *Apologize for calling him slime and scum? They were better than he deserved!* "No way, Icehead. No way! If you can't take the heat, get out of the kitchen. Just lay off." She walked by him toward the door.

No go. His arm caught her across the chest, hurling her against Al's desk. Letting herself slide across the desk, she grabbed the edge with her fingertips and kicked out at Isemonger, using the desk as leverage. The blow caught him in the chest, but he pushed her legs aside, pulled her up, punched her in the jaw, and threw her across the room.

The pain was jarring and searing; she was losing control of her head, feeling faint. When she bit down hard on her lips, that pain finally registered, keeping her conscious.

"You're making it with that reporter, aren't you?" he shouted as he approached her. "Harland, too. And Crowder and Griffen," he shouted in disgust.

"It's none of your business!" she screamed at him as she righted herself. "You're *sick*, Icehead, *sick*! Why are you so obsessed with sex? – because you aren't getting any? Do you strike out in bed as often as you do at the plate?" Her hands were clenched at her side in fury.

Isemonger took one step forward and ripped her shirt off. "I'll show you, you bitch! You've been asking for it."

The jolt of fear raced through her again, twice as strong as before, its edges dark and empty. As Isemonger reached out to grab her, she pushed him away, turning to dodge around him. Sticking out a foot, he tripped her, then stood above her.

As he reached down to pull her up, Linda hunched her shoulders together, ducked her head inward, rolled over, and scrambled to her feet, stumbling against a bookcase. All around her she could hear Eagles trophies falling to the floor.

Something wet trickled down one side of her face; the other side felt swollen and numb.

She bent double, away from Isemonger. He grabbed her hair, pulled her up and back, and acted as if he were going to kiss her. But she had picked up a trophy and with all her might she swung it at his head. Icehead saw it coming and put up an arm. Her swing caught him a glancing blow to the jaw. His hand went instantly to his jaw, releasing her.

Looking at the blood on his hand, Isemonger stared at her with cold, chilling eyes. "You're gonna pay for–"

Linda swung the trophy like a bat coming around on a low ball, hitting Icehead in the balls, putting everything she had into the swing.

His scream as he fell was louder than the crash he made against a chair and across the scattered trophies. It was followed by sobbing, whimpering, and screaming. Whatever else, she knew that Isemonger was in deep and genuine pain. *Good, the bastard!* She knelt on one leg beside him and grabbed his hair. Yanking it viciously back, she forced his face in her direction. His eyes, squeezed shut, opened wide. "If you ever try that again, I'll knock your balls over the center-field fence." She stared at him, then pushed his head away forcefully, letting it thunk to the floor.

Standing, she wiped a hand across her face. Blood. A sound behind her made her move away. Isemonger was vomiting. She looked down at him, uncertain what to do. What she wanted to do was walk out and leave him there. He'd probably still be there in the morning when Al came to work. Al! Jesus Christ! Look at Al's office! Across from his desk, her reflection in the window stared back at her. She picked up the remains of her shirt, slipped it on, then picked up the phone and got the number of one of the team physicians. She told him where to come to find Isemonger. Then she turned and walked out the door. She could take care of her own cuts and bruises. It was better than spending another second with the team's star pitcher.

7   Double Play

Driving into town, Timothy Michael Curry felt the thrill of victory in his blood. Last night the Eagles had just taken the third in a row from Philadelphia and in so doing had captured second place. Still four games out of first, it was true, but June had only just begun, and the long, long season stretched ahead. Fly, Eagles, fly. Curry hummed a tune to himself as he negotiated the traffic on I-65. Driving north from Indianapolis (where he had spent a week scouting) in the early morning, he encountered little traffic, which was the way he liked it. He wished he'd been there for the series with Philly – but he couldn't scout young baseball players and attend Eagle games at the same time. That was the only disadvantage in being a scout. Still, he made it a point to get into Chicago at least twice a month, catching a couple of games each time.

Tonight's game and tomorrow's day game were against Texas. Then the team would travel to Atlanta for a series, then back to Chicago to host New York, then to St. Louis. So, thought T. M. Curry, let's take two from Texas. And let's hope that California drops two to New York. They were playing in New York tonight, and it wouldn't be easy. Curry firmly believed that California teams didn't have the guts to take games away from East Coast teams on their own territory. East of the Mississippi, baseball was played hard: a serious business. Out in southern California, baseball was spectators in bikinis and bare chests sipping white wine from plastic cups.

But even if New York beat California, the Eagles would have to beat Texas two in a row. Statistically, that should be easy. But Curry had been around baseball long enough to know that the games that should be easy usually weren't. Either the team wasn't pumped up enough, or it acted too confident, or the lesser team was hungrier. There was a multiplicity of reasons why the easy games turned out to be hard. Unfortunately, in baseball the hard ones also turned out to be hard. There was no easy road to pennants, champagne, trophies, and World Series rings.

Absentmindedly, Curry fingered his World Series ring. How he would love to see the Eagles – today's Eagles – win their own rings. They could, too. A great team. Straightening behind the wheel, he followed the curve of the road as it poured into I-90. Now traffic was picking up. Too many trucks on the roads. Why couldn't freight travel by rail and leave the roads to drivers? A team that he, Timothy Michael Curry, took credit for, yessirree. Scouts were the unsung heroes of baseball. The public knew they existed but never thought of them when praise was due. No – they praised the players, the manager (maybe), the coaches (not as often as they should), the general manager (hardly ever), the owner (that was getting too farfetched). But not the scouts. Yet who had seen these players from the time they were ten years old? Who had followed them, sat behind countless home-plate screens on countless dried-grass fields, evaluating, assessing, recommending? The scout, that's who. He was responsible for the present-day Chicago Eagles. What a team! Curry wanted the Eagles to win. That was the reason for staying in baseball, wasn't it?

Fighting the thickening traffic, Curry observed that Chicago was hemmed in by a heavy fog. Driving became more difficult. He amused himself by comparing today's Eagles to the last Eagle world champions. Today's players seemed different. They were paid more, for one thing, and it showed. They wore gold chains and long hair and used hair spray. There were far more black players, and more Hispanic ones, too. Was Hector Gutierrez ever going to learn to speak English? Curry had first scouted him in Venezuela. A potentially great right fielder. But *were* they really different? Puzzled by his own question, he tapped his fingers on the steering wheel. On the outside, they were different. But on the inside . . . hell, they were still playing the same grand game, in the same grand way (grander, sometimes), to the same fans. Today's team had a woman on it, though. Incredible! Only the Eagles, too. Nobody else was crazy enough to do it. Nobody else had Al Mowerinski's personal reasons for doing it, that's what it was. Nobody else was trying to make up for the past (and how!) the way Al was. Well, he wasn't going to get all worked up about it right now – he came here to see the Eagles take two from Texas.

Pulling into his parking place in Eagle Stadium, Curry looked at his watch. Only 9:30. The team wouldn't start showing up until 11:00 or so. But Al would probably be in his office. Curry was hungry. Maybe he could persuade Al to grab breakfast with him; they could talk about the prospects Curry had filed reports on.

Walking down the long rooftop corridor to Al's office,

Curry saw Neal Vanderlin pacing the floor in front of the office. Vanderlin was kicking at the woodwork. What had Al done – barred him from his office, for chrissake? That made no sense.

Spotting him, Vanderlin stopped his pacing.

"Morning," greeted Curry noncommittally. He wasn't about to take sides in any dispute with the press.

Turning on his heel, Vanderlin resumed his pacing.

What was eating him? Sometimes reporters were as temperamental as ball players. Curry shrugged and opened the door to the outer office.

Al's secretary was on the phone. She looked tense. Curry knocked on the door to Al's office just as she made frantic motions that he shouldn't do so. "Don't go in th–" she started to say, and then the door was wrenched open by Big Al, who looked him over slowly, then motioned with a nod of the head that he should enter the office.

"Morning, Al. What's –" Jesus H. Christ! Al's office was a fucking mess: scattered trophies, a toppled bookcase, and what was . . . Curry stared speechlessly at Sunshine, who was sitting in a chair off to the side of Al's desk. She had a black eye, a swollen lip, a puffed up cheek and nose. And what was . . . what was that smell? His nose wrinkled, trying to place it. Puke. Somebody had puked in Al's office – in addition to taking a baseball bat to the bookcase and trophies.

"Tell her, Curry," commanded Al, striding across the room, turning, and striding right back. "Tell her we can trade Isemonger and still win the pennant."

What?! Was Big Al crazy?! No way. No way was Curry going to tell her that.

"You have to treat everybody the same," she snapped at Al, ignoring Curry.

"I *am* treating everybody the same!" roared Al. "I don't allow rape on my team! *Anybody* who tries it gets traded! I don't understand you, Linda. He lures you in here, he beats you up, he tries to rape you, and you don't want him traded."

Oh shitshitshit. Curry sank into a chair, turning his nose away from the smell behind him, shielding his face behind his hands.

He watched as Sunshine spread her hands, trying to reason with Al. "I told you, there was more to it. Yeah, he wanted to beat me up. Yeah, that's why he sent the note. But he wasn't going to beat me up after all. I told you, he'd have settled for an apology."

"Apology?!" roared Al. "I won't have you apologizing to that turd!"

"That's kinda what I thought, too," Linda mumbled.

Swinging around toward Curry, Al trembled with rage. "Rape. Can you believe it, Curry? Can you believe it? The scum!" Turning toward Linda, he shouted, "And you don't want him traded!"

"I'd *love* it if he were traded!" she shouted, stalking to the window. "There's nothing I'd love better. He never thinks of the team. He's a complete creep. Don't you think my life would be a hell of a lot pleasanter without him?"

"Yes!" roared Al. "So I'm trading him. Curry," he demanded, "who wants him? Who can we get for him? I want to dump him. If I don't, I'll kill him."

Curry cleared his throat. "Um . . . Al. Al, it's almost the trading deadline. Kind of late. I don't think . . . ." Curry didn't know what to say.

Crossing to his desk, Al knocked the lid off his cigar box, pulled out a fistful of cigars, extracted one from the fistful, and dropped the others. Some made it into the box, some didn't. "We can–" Al turned and stared at Curry. "You don't know what happened, do you?"

Curry looked around the office slowly, then looked at Linda, who was standing at the window, staring defiantly at Al. And him. "I can figure it out, Al. But what . . . why . . .?"

"*Why?*" snorted Al, trying to light his cigar. "That bastard doesn't need a reason. He sent her a note last night. Here." Al pulled a paper out of his pocket. Puffing his cigar, Al choked on the smoke. Curry pounded him on the back. Al ground the cigar out in an ashtray and labored to recover his breath. In the silence, Curry read the note. He handed it back to Al, not knowing what to say. Rape. Rape was . . . Curry couldn't think what it was, except that it was horrible. It was worse than bush. It was beyond the pale. And yet . . . trade Isemonger? "You said . . . attempted rape?" he asked Al, not looking at Linda.

As if sensing his equivocation, Al glared at him. "That," he said, pointing to the wiped-up puke spot on the floor, "is where Isemonger ended up. He's in the goddamn hospital now."

The hospital?! You couldn't trade an injured pitcher, for chrissake – not for anybody decent, anyway. Curry still didn't have the complete picture. "You came in last night . . . and stopped it?" he asked.

"No. No," replied Al slowly. "If I'd have been here . . . No, Curry. She hit him in the balls with one of the trophies. He'll be out of the lineup for a week."

Jesus! Curry looked at Linda. Then: "Who else knows about this, Al?"

"Nobody. Except that Vanderlin came down with her. What does he know, Linda? Were you discussing this with him?"

"What do you mean, 'discussing'?" she retaliated. "I told you: he came down to my apartment as I was going out. He wanted to know what happened. I told him I'd tell him later."

Curry shook his head. There was no such thing as "later" to a newsman. They'd hound you until they got the facts. The smell in Al's office was terrible. If Al wasn't going to smoke a cigar, then Curry would. Selecting one of the cigars scattered across the desktop, he unwrapped it and lit it. "Vanderlin's pacing the hall," he said to nobody in particular.

"Good!" snapped Al. "I'll be able to tell him who we traded Isemonger to!"

"Al . . . isn't there . . . another way?" asked Curry.

"Don't do it," pleaded Linda. "It's wrong."

"Wrong!" exploded Al, making Curry felt the conversation had returned to its beginning. "You stand there and tell me it's wrong to trade somebody who tried to rape you?"

"It's wrong to be inconsistent. It's wrong to treat me as special." She walked up to Al and pointed a finger at him. "If you trade him, then you have to trade Harland for punching Isemonger, you have to trade Griffen for punching him, and you have to trade me for punching him, too."

"Those were goddamn *punches*, Linda – rape is different."

"I *know* it's different. I *know* it's worse. But maybe it's just worse in degree. The *principle* is the same: violence."

Al shook his head. "Curry. Tell her. Tell her it's not the same."

Jesus. Did he have to be in the middle of this? Trade Isemonger? Curry puffed on his cigar. "I don't know, Al. Back when we played for the Eagles, we had our share of fights in the clubhouse. People weren't traded for fighting one another. They were traded for not helping the team."

Al decided to try another cigar. "Nobody was traded for fighting, that's true. But fighting was bad for the team – you know that, Curry. And people who were bad for the team were traded."

"Because they couldn't play their position!" interrupted Linda, as if she had been there. "Because they were thinking of themselves, not the team!"

Today's generation, thought Curry. They acted like they knew everything. Still . . . "She's right," reasoned Curry. "Isemonger starts losing games, trade him. Until then – well, . . . Jesus, Al, I don't know."

Al puffed on his cigar. Curry studied the glowing tip of his own cigar.

"I'll have to think about it," conceded Al.

The three of them sat around in silence for a few minutes, then Linda asked, "Can I go now?"

Al stared at her.

"I haven't had breakfast," she explained.

"Have a doctor look at your face. I don't want you playing if he says you can't," ordered Al, pointing a cigar at her.

"I can play," she assured him. "There's nothing wrong with me." She edged toward the door, eager to be gone.

"Linda." The anger gone from his voice, Al walked over to her and placed an arm on her shoulder.

She looked at him, her eyebrows raised.

"Don't fall for anything that stupid again, okay?"

Blushing, she looked down at the carpet. "I won't," she mumbled.

With one of his arms still draped around her shoulder, Al walked her to the door, opened it, and saw her out.

Closing the door, he turned to Curry, shaking his head. "I

don't know, Curry. What do you think?"

"Um. Well." Curry cleared his throat. "I think she's right, Al. We've got to think of the team."

"Yeah." Al stared at him, then broke into a proud grin. "Yeah, I think she's right, too."

"What *happened* to you?" asked Margie, Al's secretary, as Linda closed the door to Al's office behind her.

"Isemonger happened to me."

Margie gasped. "This is the last straw! I've never been able to stand that guy!"

Margie's modest sense of outrage made Linda laugh – her first laugh since the game last night.

"Well, I don't care! You should see your face. You look awful, you poor thing."

Grimacing, Linda touched her fingertips to her swollen cheek. Her nose hurt when she pressed it. It was easier to look at Margie through her right eye than through her left, which was puffy. "I know. I had to look into the mirror this morning."

"You be sure to see one of the team doctors."

"I will." Linda waved goodbye on her way out the door.

Neal grabbed her by the arm as soon as she stepped into the corridor. "What happened?" he demanded.

She frowned at him. "Neal, I said later."

"It's later. It's two hours later. That's as late as later's going to get, Linda. I want to know what happened. Who did this to you?" He shook her arm as he spoke, as if the answer would come rattling out of it and fall to the floor, ready to be picked up and put into the papers.

Removing her arm from his grasp, she gave a weary sigh.

"I'm hungry. I'm tired. I didn't get four hours of decent sleep last night. My nose hurts. My eye is puffy and runny. I've just had a long argument with Al." She stared at Neal, who stared back belligerently. "I need to eat. And I need time to think. Okay?"

He turned around in a circle, kicked the baseboard in the hallway, and turned around in another circle. "We can go eat, then," he said, stopping in front of her. "But later is coming up real soon."

They found a diner nearby, slipped into a booth in the back, and ordered breakfast. Neal stared at her in silence. Every so often he would shake his head, grimace, and look away. "I'm probably going to get fired," he muttered.

"Why?" she asked in surprise.

"Because I could be talking to Al. To Margie. To Curry. I could be hunting down every goddamn Eagle player to see what happened. I'm supposed to hunt down the news, not wait around for it to decide when to speak."

"C'mon, Neal, you aren't going to get fired. You're just saying that." She sensed that there was more to his being upset than what he was saying: it wasn't just that he wanted a story. There was something else. *He really cares about me.* Staring at Neal, she realized that whatever he had been saying hadn't registered. "Huh?"

"When did this happen?" he demanded angrily. "Not in the game. I listened to the game on the radio. They didn't say anything about another fight. Hey!" Neal grabbed the waitress by the arm. "These scrambled eggs aren't cooked. I ordered them firm."

The waitress gave him a weary look, looked at Linda's face, glanced quickly back at Neal, then removed the plate of runny eggs without a word.

Neal hung his head in his hands. "It was Isemonger, wasn't it?" he asked without lifting his head.

"Yes."

He looked up swiftly, his face contorted. "When?"

"Last night. Look, Neal, I need to . . . to think. I just have to sit here and eat breakfast and think things out without your asking me all those W questions – Who, What, When, Where, Why."

"Okay. Okay, think."

"Not if you're going to scowl at me all through breakfast."

Returning with a plate of firm scrambled eggs, the waitress placed it in front of Neal without a word.

Buttering his toast as if it were an enemy, Neal took several deep breaths. "I'll try to be silent and unscowling."

"Don't be silent. Talk. I can think better if I'm listening sometimes." She had eaten half her scrambled eggs, and all of her toast. She signaled to the waitress. "More toast, please."

"Okay. Let's talk," agreed Neal. "Think we'll win tonight?"

Linda couldn't tell whether he was being sarcastic or not. She decided to take him at face value. "I think so. They're in the basement in the standings. But we can't be too confident." She studied Neal to see what he thought, but he seemed to have exhausted his supply of conversation. *Whether* or not to tell him what happened was not the point: she had already crossed that bridge by telling him it was Isemonger. She couldn't tell him that much and then not tell him the rest. But something was making it difficult. Two things. The first was the team. She didn't know what they were going to think about this – Isemonger out for a week. Would they say it proved that women shouldn't be in baseball? Right: with women around, creeps like Icehead couldn't control themselves. *Why don't they get rid of the creeps, then, not the women?* Would it be a setback for her? The team *certainly* would want to keep quiet what had happened. That's what baseball players were like. Not just baseball players. Privileged groups of all kinds. They'd be furious that she had told Neal. What had Neal called their behavior? Ring-around-the- reporter, that was it. There was Al, too. He hadn't *ordered* her not to tell Neal, but maybe he had implied it. Maybe, maybe not. She was going to tell him, that's all there was to it. She trusted him to do whatever he thought right. It would be nice if *somebody* knew what was right: she didn't, that was for sure.

"Immature," muttered Neal. "Fucking immature."

"If you're talking about Isemonger, I agree."

"I said once, in a column, that baseball players had to have emotional maturity as well as physical maturity."

Linda looked up from her food to watch Neal sip his coffee. What was he getting at?

"That wasn't – isn't – an original observation. Emotional maturity is what separates teenagers from adults. Physical maturity, too, of course, but unless death intervenes, they all reach physical maturity. Emotional maturity is another question. Baseball is filled with a lot of boys. You've met them, especially in the minors. They throw their batting helmets around, they pick personal vendettas with umpires, other players, even teammates. They aren't the players who make it, Linda. They aren't the ones who will be around for twenty years. It takes a lot of maturity to go out there and play the best physical and mental game you can, day after day, night after night."

Listening to Neal always made her feel better. Suddenly

she grinned. "Do they kick baseboards in the hallway?"

"That isn't a sign of emotional immaturity," he replied seriously. "There was nobody around but me, then you. We weren't in front of 50,000 people. I was frustrated. And angry. And worried. But my temper was entirely under control. I did nothing that should have embarrassed me."

"It was just a joke, Neal."

"I don't feel like joking. I want to hear what happened between you and Isemonger."

She told him what happened, leaving out nothing, not even the argument in Al's office about trading Icehead. Neal listened without a word, asking no questions, making no comments. When she finished, she noticed that he had bent his fork into a circle. They stood, put down a tip, and pooled money to pay the check. "This is not," said Neal, dropping his twisted pretzel of a fork onto the plate, "a sign of emotional immaturity."

"No, I didn't think so. Looks like a sign of physical maturity to me."

"Damn right."

Curry pulled the crease of his pants at the knee and lowered himself into the chair beside Al. "Evening, Al." He thought Al looked the worse for wear. Well, he could understand that. First the fight on Monday night television nearly two weeks ago. Then Isemonger attacking Sunshine and ending up in the hospital last week. Icehead had no idea how lucky he was – lucky she didn't hit him so hard it ruptured his testicles. Icehead didn't know how lucky he was in another way, either: not a word of the incident in Al's office reached the papers, even though the reporters swarmed around the team, asking them questions about Linda's bruises and Icehead's hospitalization. Curry wondered what Al had said or done to keep Vanderlin from reporting the facts. Maybe nothing. Maybe Vanderlin had decided they shouldn't be reported.

Anyway, Isemonger was lucky. She wasn't anyone to fool around with, nosirree. Curry had been there in the clubhouse that night, when Knuff, stuffing tobacco into his mouth and pacing the clubhouse, had demanded of Linda: "Okay, okay. I know what he did was wrong. But did you have to hit him in the balls and lay him up in the hospital?" She had glared at him, then replied, "No, Bobby, I didn't *have* to – I *wanted* to!" Griffen, lacing up his spikes, had looked up. "Right on!" he had muttered. Knuff had turned several shades of white, then red, and nearly swallowed his tobacco plug. Finally, he had simply returned to his locker and sat there, shaking his head. It's a good thing, thought Curry, that Lenny Black had not been around when she said it. Oh, she'd have said it in front of Black, Curry was convinced of that. Black, a mean, vindictive bastard if there ever was one, would have flown into a rage at the slightest provocation. He'd have probably jumped her. She wouldn't have just sat there, either. Then Frank and Zack and Harland would have intervened and . . . Christ, couldn't they just play baseball? Couldn't they just go about their business and play baseball? They had dropped the first one to Texas, taken the second. Even steven. Then to Atlanta, where they took two and dropped one. But damn it, California had done the same, and the Eagles were still four games out of first.

"You look kind of lousy, Al," sympathized Curry.

Al lifted an eyebrow at him, then went back to studying the team. "Lenny's starting Isemonger tonight," Al told him after a period of comfortable silence.

Shifting uncomfortably, Curry nodded. "Big game tonight." It was, in fact, another Monday night game-of-the-week. The Eagles were getting more Monday night games-of-the-week this year than Curry had ever thought possible. Nothing like national television for increasing the coffers. And increased coffers meant more money to spend on better players when trading time came. Yeah, national television. This was a chance for the Eagles to show their stuff: look good, win more fans. Let them not, thought Curry, repeat the brouhaha of two weeks ago.

The game with New York started, and he and Al concentrated on what they knew best, watching the grace and precision and power that exploded in moments they would cherish forever. As he watched, Curry fidgeted. It was one of the few disadvantages of being tall. His knees stuck out of the stadium chairs at a rakish angle. He could never watch a game sitting down here without fidgeting, trying to arrange his angular frame into one of the wooden seats. He glanced at Al. Al was immobile, sitting like a stone in the tiny chair. Big Al did not fidget.

In the top of the sixth, Jack Doyle, the New York center fielder, hit a homer with one on. 2-0, New York. In the bottom of the seventh Frank Laughing's single drove Harland home. 2-1, New York. Bobby Knuff led off the bottom of the eighth with a long fly ball into the glove of Jack Doyle. One out. Then Sunshine came to the plate. Curry hoped for a homer. Not impossible: she had three already. But he would settle for any hit at all. The Eagles could soar. This season was different: he could feel it in his bones. This season the Eagles would win the pennant.

Sunshine eked out a single, a leg hit for sure. Then Crowder stepped up and walloped the ball. The bat broke, its pieces flying in two different directions as he flung it away. Gouging a path between the pitcher's legs, the ball flew into the outstretched glove of the running second baseman, where it bounced around long enough for Sunshine to take a pop-up slide into second, sight the windmill motion of the third base coach, and run for third while the rookie New York second baseman pulled the boner of throwing the ball over the first baseman's head. When New York finally had the ball under control, Sunshine was on third and Crowder on second. Two on now, one out. Fly, Eagles, fly.

Isemonger stepped up to the plate. "Just avoid hitting into a double, Icehead," muttered Curry. Bring the runner home, he added silently. Just bring the runner home.

Al remained silent.

Then Curry watched the third base coach go through a series of signals. "Holy shit!" he whispered to Al. "The sign is on to steal home." He watched Sunshine acknowledge in another flurry of signals. Steal home? The move was unlike Black, who played an essentially conservative game. If your team is down by one run in the bottom of the eighth and you have one out and *two* runners in scoring position, you don't steal. You wait for somebody to bring you home, that's what you do. Not that home was hard to steal. It was comparatively easy to steal. Something told Curry, however, that neither ease nor wisdom was calling the plays here.

Watching intently, Curry could almost hear Linda counting to herself. Before the pitch was delivered, she was running full tilt toward home. And then Icehead, who was supposed to stand at the plate and take the world's longest swing to protect the runner and hinder the catcher, stepped back from the plate. "Swing at the ball!" shouted Curry, jumping to his feet. "Don't step back! Get in there, damn it! Swing!"

Al's hand grabbed him by the belt and rudely yanked him back into his seat. As he met the seat with a jarring sensation, Curry kept his eyes on the slide. The New York catcher, protecting his team's margin of victory, given all the time and space in the world by Isemonger, blocked Linda, his head colliding with hers as she failed to get under him in time. Curry could hear the crack from where he sat, just as he could see the umpire's signal: Out!

He gripped the arms of his seat with both hands. It seemed to him that Al had stopped breathing, but a cigar glowing fierce red in his mouth testified to the presence of oxygen. Linda did not get up. Neither did the New York catcher. Players crowded around the plate blocked his view; then they stepped back to make way for the trainer and give the injured players air.

Next to him, Big Al emerged from his seat like some ancient monster of long-ago waters, rising slowly to the surface, brushing by Curry as if he weren't even there. Turning to watch him go, Curry saw him snuff out the fire of the cigar with his fingertips, then throw it, almost casually, it seemed, against the concrete steps.

T. M. Curry got up and followed Al Mowerinski.

Al stopped behind the home-plate screen. Curry stopped with him. They saw the catcher and Linda sitting up, holding their heads. Al stood there a moment, then turned left. Curry watched the scoreboard.The Eagles, failing to score in the bottom of the ninth, lost.

Al returned. "Linda's been hospitalized," Al explained as he led the way to the clubhouse. "Possible concussion. The catcher, too. Probably nothing serious."

In the clubhouse, reporters crowded around Black, asking him to explain his reasons for putting the steal of home on. Al marched directly to Isemonger's locker. Icehead was just starting to unbutton his shirt.

"You're gone," said Al.

For three full seconds, Isemonger, standing there with his hands on his shirt buttons, stared at the owner of the Eagles uncomprehendingly. Then, as recognition flooded his face, Al continued. "You handed New York an Eagle loss, just to make a teammate look bad. I traded you for anything I could get. Pack your bags and leave."

Isemonger flushed an angry red. For one wild moment, Curry thought he was going to take a swing at Big Al. Instead, he sneered. "Where?" he asked.

"San Francisco."

That, Curry noted with satisfaction, wiped the sneer off Icehead's face. Frisco wasn't the bottom of the barrel. But it was sitting right on top of the bottom, that's for sure.

Lenny Black must have left the reporters to stand behind Al, because out of seemingly nowhere Curry saw him grab Al's shoulder and try to spin him around. Black succeeded only in looking ridiculous. Excalibur couldn't be moved by a moral midget. Curry looked away in embarrassment.

Al turned. "Stay out of my way, Black," he warned, starting toward the door.

Lenny, grasping at Big Al, managed only to catch pieces of his clothing before they were inexorably drawn out of his path as the immovable object and the irresistible force (both of them embodied in Big Al) continued toward the swinging doors of the clubhouse.

"You'll be sorry! You'll be sorry for this!" screamed Lenny, furiously jumping up and down like a manager accosting an umpire who has flagrantly cheated his team, his shrieks filling the clubhouse and echoing in the corridor.

"You'll be sorry." Those had been the last words Al had ever heard Amanda say. For who-knows-how-many times in the last few weeks he sat in his living room, scotch and ice and glass at hand, and thought about Amanda.

She had not been easy to live with after the Girls' League folded. Nothing possessed her like baseball had. Al urged her to go to college, maybe teach gym in a high school. But Mandy wasn't the teaching kind. Vicarious thrills weren't her style. She wanted to play baseball, not teach softball. She wanted to be in a real game situation, not a play situation that ended when the school bell rang. Looking back on it now, he understood what it must have been like for her, for any person out of her time. Living with him must have been torture: he got to play baseball, she didn't.

But back then, as much as he loved her, he couldn't stop the fights. They started over silly things. "I'm not going out with your friends," she would say. That would start some of the fights.

"Al, would you quit baseball if I asked you to?" That was what started the last one.

Al had stared at her. She was curled into the wing chair, her seemingly resilient curls matted against one of the arms.

He knelt beside her and stroked her hair, a worried look in

his eyes. "Mandy, what made you ask that?"

"I want to know. Would you?"

"I'd do anything for you, Mandy. You know that."

"Would you quit baseball?"

Al jumped up. He was rushed, had to be at the field in thirty minutes. "Jesus, Mandy, what kind of question is that?! That's not like you. Are you really asking me to quit?" he asked, not believing it for a moment as he stared into the mirror to knot his tie.

"Yes."

He looked at her. She stared back defiantly, tears starting in her eyes. "I want you to quit so we can be happy together."

Two steps took him to the chair. He bent down and kissed her, wiping away two tears with one of his thick fingers. "Mandy, we're happy. I love you. You're the only person in the world I love. The only thing that would make me happier is if–"

Amanda clenched her fist and pounded the arm of the chair, startling him. "You aren't answering my question! Will you quit baseball?"

"Come on, Mandy!" Al shouted, angry now himself. "It's a dumb question! I love baseball. Why would you want me to quit it? *You* love baseball! It's not as if you hate the game, you know. I never asked you to quit. No, much as I wanted to, so we could be together, I never asked *you* to quit!" Shrugging on his jacket, Al realized he sounded a bit self-righteous. But her question grated on him. It was so much like the questions he had heard wives ask. Would you do this for me, would you do that, do you love me enough to do this – never expecting the things to be done, just asking the questions.

"I've got to go, Mand," he relented. He opened the door and started out, but he couldn't leave without looking back at her. She was crying. He came back in. "Aw, Mandy, c'mon. What's wrong?"

"You'll be sorry," she said, snuffling. "You'll be sorry."

He couldn't get any more out of her, so he left.

When he came home, Mandy was gone. Packed. Gone.

He tried to find her everywhere, but where could he go? She had no more family, the grandparents who raised her having died not long after she began to play baseball. He called her friends, called everybody in the Girls' League he could think of, walked the streets at night, went to police stations. Nobody had heard from her. He nearly went crazy. His hitting power vanished; his fielding disintegrated. He was pulled out of the game for weeks at a time. There was talk of a trade next season.

Finally, in December, he did what he should have done all along: he hired a private detective. Two months later, the detective had news for him. Final news. News from which there was no return. News that couldn't be rewritten another way. Mandy had been pregnant. Had entered an unwed mother's home. And had died giving birth.

Stumbling out of the detective's office, Al walked the five miles to snow-filled Eagle Stadium. He got one of the keepers to let him in, and then he sat in the empty stadium, not even brushing the snow off the bleacher seat. Why hadn't she told him? Why had she done this to him? He had wanted to get married. Christ, he had made that clear enough! Why? He simply didn't understand.

Al kept things to himself. He went on a drinking binge that lasted from February through April. He couldn't see the ball, let alone hit it. He didn't care. Words buzzed around his head in the locker room. *You're going to be traded, Al. Snap out of it, Al.* He must have fought with and whopped every player on the team, some three or four at a time. He didn't remember.

He did remember Curry calling him Big Al Hasbinski. Didn't have the makings of a big leaguer, Curry said. Al would have killed him with his bare hands, but others managed to hold him back.

He would show Curry. Dumb Irishman. Curry was jealous because Al was a better hitter, anyway. He sobered up. He thought. He told himself it wasn't his fault. If Mandy could have played baseball, none of this would have happened. That was the crux of the matter and nothing else. He would make it up to her someday.

Sitting home alone, Al poured himself the last of still another bottle of scotch. He looked at the picture of Linda on his wall and thought of Amanda. He hadn't cared about other women when Amanda was alive, and he was only occasionally interested in them after she died. He had promised himself more than twenty years ago that he would change things if he could. It had taken him a long time to find her. But he had. She was the one, he told himself, looking at her picture. She was the one.

Harland had just hit into a double play when the nurse walked into the room. Linda turned off the sound but watched the picture. "Hi, Sherry. How much longer?"

"Good morning, Sunshine," responded the nurse, taking Linda's wrist in her hand and checking the pulse. "About an hour. Maybe sooner. How do you feel?"

"Not bad."

The nurse raised an eyebrow skeptically. Reaching into a

pocket of her uniform, she extracted a baseball, handing it to Linda. "For my daughter. She'd like an autograph."

Linda, dressed in a red Hawaiian shirt, white pants, and leather sandals, looking every bit a baseball player, delightedly sat up straight on the bed. "Oh, yeah? I'd love to. Got a pen?"

The nurse produced a pen from still another pocket and, perhaps noting Linda's skeptical look at the odd instrument, pronounced: "It'll write. I use it for charts all the time."

"What's her name?"

"Teri."

"Terry with a y?" asked Linda, rotating the baseball in her left hand, getting it settled.

"No. With an i. And one r."

"How old is she?"

"Eight." The nurse hesitated, watching Linda write. "If you had a daughter," she asked, "what would you want her to grow up to be?"

"A decent human being," answered Linda, returning the ball and pen and gingerly touching her head.

The nurse pursed her lips. "What career, I meant."

"That's easy. Anything she wanted to be."

The nurse sighed. "Teri wants to be a baseball player."

"Wonderful!" laughed Linda.

The nurse read the autograph, glanced up at Linda's head, then smiled. "She's only eight. Maybe she'll outgrow it." Giving the unwrinkled bed a professional pat, the room a glance, she walked to the door, then turned. "Thanks for the autograph. And good luck. Maybe we'll see you at a ball game some day."

"I hope so," replied Linda to the already disappearing figure. Propping her feet on the bed's footboard, she lay on her back, arms clasped behind her head, watching the soundless game on television. The Eagles were in St. Louis. Frank had just drawn a base on balls. At the ball game. It was a good feeling to have young fans. She wondered if her being in baseball would make any difference to the future. It had to, didn't it? She sighed, throwing both arms out to the sides, as if she were being crucified. The future was the future. The present would be a lot better if it looked more like the future. To her, that meant more women out on the baseball diamond. Being the only woman on the team was like being a woman on a construction site, or in the coal mines, or in the "new army." She had read about them. For them, the women, it was hell. Men had a terrible problem of adjustment. They couldn't take women. Forty women with a thousand men. A drop of water in the formerly all-male bucket. But at least they had each other for support. Two hundred women with a thousand men. Better, but still not good enough. The more women there were, though, the more conditions would improve. Jackie Robinson's life probably improved as more blacks made the majors. Two more women out there in the lineup would make a universe of difference.

Frank was thrown out on his way to second, and the top half of the inning ended. Lifting an arm, Linda looked at her watch. Al had said somebody from the team would come to take her home. But the team was in St. Louis, so who was he going to send? The financial manager?

The hair on her arm suddenly tingled, warning her. She rose on an elbow and looked at the door. Neal was standing there, staring at her. "How long have you been there?" she asked accusingly but happily. She was always happy when she saw Neal.

"Just wondering whether you were conscious," he

answered, entering the room. "What were you thinking about so hard?"

"Women." Twisting, she sat up, dangling her feet off the high hospital bed.

"What about them?" he asked, looking around the room.

"We need more of them. On the team. In baseball."

About to pick up her almost-empty suitcase, he stopped, considering it. "Yeah," he answered, picking up the suitcase. "At least it would keep the hospitals busy."

"Yes," she replied, dropping to the floor, "and not all the patients would be women." She paused. "You look as if you're taking me home."

"No head damage, I see."

"Why aren't you in St. Louis?"

"Hey-hey – there's more news than baseball, you know! I cover the horses, football, basketball, soccer, hockey, swimming. My god, the range of my talent sometimes amazes me – I'll have to ask my boss for a raise."

Smiling, Linda kidded him back, "Come on, Neal. Al said somebody from the team would take me home. Since when have you been on the team?"

Neal coughed. "I called Al and, uh, volunteered," he replied hastily. "Since we live in the same building and all." Picking up her suitcase, he put his other arm around her shoulder lightly, ushered her out the door, and insisted on checking her out of the hospital. Standing in the lobby waiting for him, she wondered what she was going to do with her time for the next two weeks. She had fully expected to return to the team to play. She would have even sat on the bench for a day or two. But no, those weren't the orders she got from Al Mowerinski. No, *he* put her on the fifteen-day disabled list and called up a player from the minors to sit on the bench while Zack played short.

"This way," said Neal, tapping her on the shoulder and leading the way to the parking lot.

Linda followed him. What nerve! She wasn't a fifteen-day disabled case. Who did Al Mowerinski think he was, anyway? She kicked at a small piece of gravel. Instead of bouncing off the toe of her sandal, it wedged itself between her foot and the leather. She hobbled after Neal.

Neal steered around the vehicles on Lake Shore Drive. Linda released the bucket-seat lever and leaned back, thinking. The car swerved, and she looked up as Neal passed an Orkin pest exterminator car traveling under twenty miles an hour, obstructing the flow of traffic. Pest control reminded her of Isemonger. *Good riddance.* Isemonger's behavior at the plate had proved for everyone (at least for everyone who understood how baseball was played) that he had been bad for the team, more concerned with himself than with the Eagles.

The ride home was short. Linda hid a smile as she unlocked the door to her apartment and stepped in. Neal had insisted on bringing her to the door before he went up to his apartment to get Homer. He even thrust his head in her doorway and looked around. Did he think Icehead was lurking inside?

Waiting for Neal, she sank into the couch, hands behind her neck, elbows almost touching in front of her. She stared at the toes of her shoes, then pointed her toes toward her shins, feeling the tendons stretch. Al Mowerinski made her feel as if he controlled her life. She didn't like it. Reaching for the handgrips, she squeezed them automatically, thinking about other things. Thirty squeezes up; turn grips upside down; thirty

squeezes down. Switch to left hand. Repeat. Still staring at
nothing, she felt for the dime she kept on the end table, inserted
it between the grips, and squeezed as hard and as long as she
could, keeping the dime from dropping. She put down the
handgrips and grabbed a baseball, gripping it across the
stitching and squeezing. All she wanted to do was play
baseball. She lobbed the baseball into a wicker basket across
the room.

Neal pushed open the door. The kitten wriggled out of his
arms, pranced over to Linda, and pounced on her lap. She
fondled Homer, feeling the purrs.

Neal sat down beside her. His fingers rubbed behind
Homer's ears. Homer's purrs multiplied. She was suddenly
aware of the closeness of Neal. She could feel the warmth of
his thigh barely touching hers. Suddenly she felt hot.

He cleared his throat. "There's something I want to ask
you."

Her face felt as if it were scarlet. "What?" she asked.

"Well, old Thwack-n-Thwart – that's my boss – asked me
to ask you."

Her flush subsided.

"He . . . well, – Thwardz, that's his real name – wants to
know if, since you're on the disabled list, you'd be willing to do
some guest columns for the *Sun Vindicator*."

She sat upright, leaving Homer to purr for attention. "A
guest column?"

"Yeah. On baseball. Maybe on other sports." Neal lifted
Homer off her lap and caressed him. "Thwardz would give you
all the facts. He just asked me to ask you."

"Why? Didn't he want to ask me himself?"

Neal chuckled softly. "I think he's afraid of you."

"Are you serious?" *Afraid?* She looked at Neal. Was he afraid of her, also?

"Sort of. Anyway, what do you think?"

"I don't know." She thought about it a while. "I think I like the idea." She reached over to stroke the errant Homer. "What do you think?"

"Great! I was hoping you'd like it."

They sat in silence that grew awkward. "If you feel well enough," suggested Neal, standing and walking around her apartment, "we can go down to the *Vindicator* and talk to Thwardz now."

Linda thought he seemed nervous. "Neal?"

He looked at her.

"Why didn't you write about me and Isemonger? What happened in Al's office, I mean."

Neal turned his back to her and walked over to the window and looked out at Lake Michigan.

"Don't you want to tell me?" she asked, half-indignant.

"No. It's not that." He turned toward her. "I don't know why. Al asked me not to. I knew he would. There's an unspoken tradition in baseball reporting – you don't report the behind-the-scenes fights, affairs, whatever. I . . . well, Al's asking isn't what stopped me. It . . . it's hard to know sometimes what to tell and what not to tell. There's such a double standard. If Isemonger had tried to beat up, or rape, a reporter, I'd have written about it. He'd have stepped outside the bounds of baseball. He'd have practically been attacking the Constitution! But –" Neal scratched his head. "But attacking another baseball player . . .. It was hard. It didn't start out as attempted rape, even though it escalated into that. And attempted rape is a bigger issue than punching somebody's lights out. But . . . well,

Linda, you're always saying you want to be treated like just another player. Nobody special." He walked over to the couch and looked down at her. "Are you disappointed?"

The question startled her. Disappointed? "No," she answered. "I'm not disappointed." Curious. That's what she was, curious about how Neal thought. What he thought. Why he thought it. "I guess it is tough, deciding what to report. I never thought about it being tough." She shook her head. "Don't tell me I'm going to have to make all these decisions if I decide to write a column. My head hurts enough as it is!"

"Don't worry about it. Thwack-n-Thwart doesn't expect much head work from ball players."

Thwack, as Linda dubbed him to herself, looked like an editor from a black-and-white Hollywood film: short, slightly pudgy, bald (with tufts of hair near his ears), wearing a pair of gray suit pants, a white shirt with rolled-up sleeves, and a gray suit vest. Behind one ear were three grease pencils – red, black, and green, the colors of each evident by the smudges on the gleaming head. He looked her over briefly, then summarized the situation, jabbing a grease pencil in her direction so forcefully that she moved back a step. "Now, here's the scoop. You'll write three columns a week. Say, 800 to 1,000 words each. Don't worry about money. Neal will tell you what we pay. Not that we have many guest columnists in the sports department. Well? What do you say? Deal?"

It was a deal.

Linda practiced with the Eagles when the team was home. "You bucking to be a sportscaster when you retire, Sunshine?" demanded Griffen as he leaned against the dugout reading one of her articles. "Starting kind of young, aren't you? Hey! Say hey! – this is good stuff you wrote about me! Yeah! 'Best third baseman in the majors for the last four years.' I've been best for five years, Sunshine, but that's okay: you were probably still in pigtails five years ago."

"Braids, Lacey, not pigtails. And besides, you've only been in the majors for six years."

"So? It took me a year to reach my peak."

"*Peak?!*" she demanded, throwing a ball at him. "You mean you aren't going to get any better than this?"

At the games, she would sit with Neal in the press box and get ribbed by the sportscasters about being a baseball player. It wasn't a bad life, for fifteen days.

One evening when the team was out of town (and Neal with it), Linda went to see a professional women's softball game. How could they play in shorts and take themselves seriously, she had wondered as she stretched back against the bleachers, finding support for the small of her back, her arms resting behind her, elbows supporting her weight. Her mother had told her that players in the All-American Girls' Baseball League had had to wear skirts to play in, with bloomers that contained "sliding pads." Her mother had said that the women had hated it, looking upon the feminine uniforms as another handicap in their battle to play baseball.

Linda watched the young women play. Some of them had tremendous power. If you took that power and connected it with an eighty-miles-an- hour *baseball* – who knows what they might be doing? She wished they would try out for baseball.

A smack-thud sounded flat and loud. She watched the ball sail upward, arch softly, and fall surely into the center fielder's waiting glove. It was a chartreuse ball. At least there was experimentation going on here. Kitten ball, it used to be called. Sissy ball. Mushball, Jack Doyle had called it. Now it was just softball. Seventeen million softball players in the country. Could seventeen million be wrong? She shook her head, wondering what they saw in it. All she wanted to do was get back to baseball. She turned in two columns on women's professional baseball: one on the game she had watched, the other more analytical. "Good, good," said Thwack, grumbling only a little when he saw the approach she took.

Let Them Play Baseball

When I watch baseball, be it minor league or major, I'm reminded of my childhood, in which I, along with practically everybody else I knew, grew up playing the game. Baseball is the game of unconquered youth, the game even children aspire to play well, the game in which you try to hit that spinning sphere with a rounded stick, the single most difficult feat in all of sports according to Ted Williams. Baseball is for the youth in all of us, for those who won't quit, who won't compromise, who would rather go down swinging than give up and play softball.

Softball. The very word smacks of compromise, of dreams defeated, of smaller playing fields, shorter visions, and shrunken vistas.

Softball. It's all that's given to women. And it's not enough.

Let's remember that softball wasn't invented for women. And even though softball was invented in Chicago (1887), it wasn't even invented to satisfy that gloveless lunatic fringe of softball players, the Chicago 16-inch-softball players. Softball was invented for convenience. George Hancock, its founder, wanted a game like baseball, but one that could also be played in less space and with less equipment. In other words, Hancock adapted the game of baseball by shrinking its horizons. And when Lewis Rober of Minneapolis invented 12-inch softball in 1895, he wanted the same thing: a game like baseball, but one that could be played in a smaller space, with less equipment. In Rober's case, he also wanted a game that could be played with gloves.

In neither case did the founders specify that softball was more suited to women, baseball more suited for men. Yet, because we live with sexist assumptions about everything, it was assumed that women couldn't play baseball. Or it was assumed that women weren't worth the land and equipment expenses involved in baseball, so they could be shunted off to something like baseball, but not quite the real thing.

There's nothing wrong with playing softball. There's nothing wrong with liking softball. There's not even anything wrong (I guess) with preferring softball. But there is something very wrong with settling for softball if what you really want to play is baseball.

I believe that girls as well as boys should be encouraged to play either game they want, so that, when it comes time for them to choose what they want to do, they'll make a free choice. I realize there are those who will say that this is ridiculous, that children can't play softball. Softball is too big, too awkward, for children to play.

Then let them play baseball. Let them all play baseball. It's the game of eternal youth and eternal hope.

Writing about the invention of softball gave her an idea for future columns, an idea that should have been obvious to her from the beginning: why not write about women's professional baseball? Yes – why not? Hardly anybody knew that women had once played professional baseball (well, almost baseball). She would write about it. Eagerly, she hurried down to the public library. Nothing, practically. Six or seven magazine articles, all from the late 1940s. So she hurried back to Neal: didn't the newspaper have old files or something?

It did, and she wrote the column, stressing one fact over and over: as the softball-that-wasn't-a-baseball-and-baseball-that-wasn't-a-softball grew smaller and harder, the women's batting averages rose. Not only that, but as the women's professional "substitute" for baseball more closely approached the rules of the real thing, the women's playing improved. The next step should have been integration. It wasn't.

Down in the newspaper morgue, she explored the files with Neal.

"Look under 'baseball,'" advised Neal, "and under 'sports.' It's not likely you'll find anything under 'women,' but you can try. Look under 'All-American Girls' Baseball League,' too." Instead of leaving, Neal stayed, quietly reading the clippings.

The files revealed some cheesecake poses and some action shots. Reading through the articles, Linda became instantly interested in one of the players: Amanda Quitman. Amanda Quitman had starred in the Girls' League as long as it had existed – eleven years. "Think of the changes she must have gone through!" Linda told Neal. "I wonder if she thought she'd make the majors," she mused aloud. "How can I find out more about her?" she asked, impatient with the scarcity of material.

"Look under 'Quitman,'" Neal replied, finding the Q file. "Sometimes they cross-file under a person's name, if the name is well known at the time."

They looked but found nothing. Their arms touched as they fingered through the files. She was aware of the hair on Neal's arm, so softly brushing against hers, of his body warmth. Suddenly research seemed unimportant. She glanced at him, wondering why she didn't do something: touch him, kiss him. He was talking, but to her his words had no meaning. "Hmm?" she asked. "What did you just say?"

"I said, sometimes they'll file a woman under her married name." He stood there, totally absorbed in the clippings.

Maybe she had simply imagined that he was interested in her. "That's just great," she said angrily. "How are we supposed to know *if* she got married, let alone who she married?"

"Still another reason for liberation."

"One of thousands," she replied.

They found nothing more, and when they returned to their desks, there was a message for Linda from Al. She called him and learned that he was taking her off the disabled list – today. The team needed her at short. A warm feeling flooded through her. Even if only Al said so, it made her feel good. Today. She glanced at her watch. She had to report to practice in an hour! Hurrying over to Thwack, she explained the situation to him. He grumbled something about leaving a hole in today's paper, but Linda knew he was exaggerating. She looked for Neal, wanting to say good-bye, but Thwack said he had gone back to the files. Maybe he planned to write some articles on Amanda Quitman.

The Eagles, who had slipped back to a tied-for-second with Philadelphia, won that night. Linda looked for Neal after the game, but he wasn't there. She went out to dinner with what started out to be Harland and Zack: it ended up including Lacey Griffen, Ulysses, Frank, and Doug Rooks. They had a "grand time," as Zack concluded late in the evening. Coming home, Linda thought of going up to Neal's apartment to see if he was there. But it was late. She dressed for bed in a large gray PROPERTY OF CHICAGO EAGLES T-shirt, pulled back the sheet, and turned off the light. She thought of Neal. As the weeks and months had passed, she found herself thinking of him more and more. When they were together, she kept hoping something would happen that would lead to their making love. A kiss would be a nice beginning. What was wrong with him, anyway? she asked herself, not for the first time. At first she had interpreted the way he looked at her as the interest of a reporter in a story. Later, she thought he was interested in her in another way. But if the interest was there, he wasn't doing anything about it. One kiss. Then nothing. Was there something wrong with her that he wasn't doing anything? Maybe he was waiting for her. Okay, why couldn't she just – well, just kiss him and see what happened? She wriggled uncomfortably against the sheet, one part of her anticipating the pleasure of the kiss, the other drawing back at the possible embarrassment. She didn't like the thought of striking out. He could simply do nothing. Bad. He could kiss her back out of some sense of obligation. Just as bad. Could he possibly think she would do it to get better press coverage? No, Neal knew her better than that. Didn't he? But that's all he had heard from people like Icehead. She sighed. What if there were some sort of reporter's law of not becoming involved? She rolled over on her side. The situation seemed like a hitless game.

Saturday, July 3, was a hot, muggy Chicago day. Only two games to go before the All-Star break, thought Linda, who had been back for nearly two weeks. The Eagles had played seventy-eight games thus far, winning forty-nine of them for a . 628 percentage. They were in solid second, three games ahead of Philadelphia and just three games out of first. But the worst part of the long season was coming up – the long, hot days of July and August, with many doubleheaders to please the fans and make the 162-game schedule.

Today they were playing an at-home doubleheader against San Francisco. The Eagles won the first game in the bottom of the ninth inning. The break between games seemed too short as the players hurried back to the clubhouse and gulped down tacos, burgers, fries, chips, shakes, Cokes, and coffee. An awful meal for anybody.

Merle Isemonger was pitching for Frisco in the nightcap. Stepping into the batter's box, Linda was nervous. Icehead was big. He loomed out there on the mound like Bigfoot with a baseball. *Looks about as civilized, too. Don't step back – that's what he wants you to do.* She knew what Icehead wanted to do, but would he?

He would and did, throwing a fastball at her head. She fell backward to avoid it. Obviously deliberate. Dusting herself off, she looked at the umpire, raising her eyebrows. *Hey, Ump – didn't that pitch ring a bell? Isn't there a rule against beanballs, huh?* The umpire ignored her silent messages and indicated she should step back into the batter's box. She did. Another beanball pitch and she fell backward again, completely unnerved. This time the umpire cautioned Icehead. The third pitch came in tight on her – so tight she barely escaped with her knuckles intact. The fourth came in tighter than that, resulting in a walk to first.

In her second at-bat, Icehead did the same. Again she raised her eyebrows at the ump, and again he did nothing. "I can't wait until we get some women umpires," she informed him sarcastically. "Play ball!" he warned her. Icebrain's next pitch was high and inside, what they called "chin music." Now the umpire warned Icebrain to throw lower. Again Linda walked.

Standing on first base, fuming, she glared into the Eagles' dugout across the diamond. At this point, the manager would have to do something. Protesting to the umpire was the least he could have done. But Black hadn't stepped out of the dugout. Was he now sitting there and contemplating doing what the unspoken rule of baseball said he should do? Was he going to instruct his pitcher to throw some beanballs at the Frisco shortstop – or at Isemonger?

"Think you'll catch California?" the Frisco first baseman asked her.

"We'll catch them," she replied confidently. *I hope I live to catch California.* Ulysses hit the ball down the right-field line; Linda raced for second. The third base coach waved her on, and she took third on a slide. Looking back, she saw Ulysses on first.

They were left dying on third and first. Frank came out of the dugout, tossing Linda her glove. "What's Black going to do about these beanballs?" she asked Frank, not expecting an answer.

"Nothing. But Charlie's fired up about them. He wants the victory."

To her surprise, Charlie Kovacks threw a brushback at the Frisco shortstop. Black came walking out of the dugout and talked to Charlie. Charlie spit tobacco and pounded the ball into his glove. Then Icebrain came to bat, and Charlie threw another beanball. Black came running out of the dugout. Harland walked to the mound. No need for the infield to attend: Charlie was doing great. She watched from short, expecting Black to walk back to the dugout. Instead, he took the ball from Kovacks, sending him to the shower and calling in a relief pitcher. What was with Black? Charlie was doing great!

Linda went hitless during all four at-bats. So, she thought with relief, did Isemonger. When the Eagles won, 6-4, she counted it a personal victory that two of the runs had been scored by her: she had reached first on a walk every time she came to the plate.

Manager Lenny Black ended his career with the Chicago Eagles exactly thirty seconds after he left the dugout. Al Mowerinski had personally packed up the things in Lenny's desk, pulled his mementos off the wall, and cinched them all into a tattered and discarded duffel bag. Al was waiting outside the manager's office as the team came down the corridor.

"You're gone, too. A check's in the bag. Get out."

If shouting was a sign of not taking things well, then Black didn't take it well. Good riddance, thought Linda, walking around him and heading for the shower. She didn't even feel the usual pang of guilt that maybe Al Mowerinski was trying to protect her. All she wondered about was who Al would hire to manage the team.

8   Sinker

Zack. Zachariah Joseph Weiss was named manager of the Chicago Eagles by Al Mowerinski. The morning *Sun Vindicator* reported that Zack was the youngest manager in the National League. Linda was sitting in a chair, her legs crossed and resting at an angle against her locker. She was trying to eat an orange and read the newspaper article at the same time and had succeeded thus far only in getting the paper splotched with orange juice and the orange covered with ink.

Frank Laughing stuck his head in: "Move it, Linda. Zack wants a meeting."

Discarding both the paper and the orange, she followed Frank into the clubhouse. Bobby Knuff gave her a hostile stare as she came in. Damn it, she thought angrily, I'm getting sick of Knuff's ups and downs. Although he hadn't said so, she knew he blamed her for the loss of Isemonger – a big loss from the pitching staff. What was his problem now – was he upset about losing Lenny Black? Or was he still nursing a grudge over Isemonger? *They're upset because of all the changes. They don't feel comfortable with changes – and they probably blame me for each and every one of them.* She pulled up a chair and sat down between Frank and Griffen.

"What're we supposed to call you now, Zack?" asked Harland.

"You call me Zack, Harland. I don't want to hear any of this Captain or Skipper shit – not from any of you."

"I didn't know your name was Zachariah, Zack. What's it mean?" asked Ulysses, slipping into his baseball spikes.

"It's Hebrew for 'kick ass,' which is what the whole lot of you had better start doing. The heat is on you guys now. You're a team from nowhere suddenly challenging the leader, and everyone's out to get you. Everybody, and don't you forget it. You've got to keep your heads down and play ball."

Linda and twenty-four other players listened in silence. This was the same Zack, but a different Zack, too. No longer one of them, he was one of the others – those who sent you down or brought you up, who put you in or took you out, who played you or let you become as wooden as the bench you continued to sit on. How was this Zack going to see her? she wondered. How would the team play under this Zack?

"The heat is on," he repeated, standing in front of them. "That happens to every team in your position. You've got to face it. And you can. But not if you aren't a team."

Some players looked up, some down, some directly at Zack.

"You know what I'm talking about, Bobby?" demanded Zack.

"No."

"I'm talking about playing baseball." Pausing, Zack looked hard at Knuff. "I'm talking about baseball, a game that goes back to 1842. That's a long time in this country. You're supposed to represent the game – all of you. This is the

American pastime, where everybody's equal in the batter's box, regardless of size, creed, race . . . or sex. Everybody's equal in the batter's box and on the field. And everybody's supposed to give his best. Nobody gives less than his best. Nobody shaves points. When they do, you know what happens – you *know* about the Chicago Black Sox scandal, don't you, Bobby?"

"Yeah, I know about it, Zack," Knuff replied angrily.

"Good. You know about players being removed from the game – forever. Nobody loses deliberately. Not for any reason – not for money, not for spite. Nobody hurts his own team just to get even or just to show up a teammate."

Pacing in front of the players, Zack continued. "Your team is down one run in the bottom of the eighth, Bobby. One out. You've got runners at second and third. That's two runners in scoring position, only one out. One run ties the game; two runs move your team ahead. You're at the plate, Bobby. What do you do? What *must* you do? What is it that you're standing up there to fuckin' *do,* Bobby? Tell him, Harland – what's he got to do."

"Bring the runner home."

"Bring the runner home. *Bring . . . the . . . runner . . . home,*" Zack enunciated. "Hit the ball. All you need is a single. Even a long sacrifice fly will bring the runner home and tie the game. You work as a *team.* That runner on third is your future."

"It wasn't like that," challenged Knuff. "You're talking about Ise–"

"I'm talking baseball, Bobby. You want to talk about another play? Okay, same situation: bottom of the eighth, your team has one out, runners on second and third. You're at bat. You see the third base coach signal, telling the runner on third to steal home. The runner acknowledges the signal. You acknowledge the signal. What's your job now, Bobby?"

"Cut it out, Zack. It wasn't me, and you know it."

"We're talking baseball here, Bobby. We're talking truth for all time. *You're* at the plate, Bobby – what do you do?"

Griffen spoke. "He helps the runner home."

Spinning on his heel, Zack walked over to Griffen. "He helps the runner home. Indeed he does, Griff. He helps the runner home. He stands up there, and as that pitch comes in and that runner is racing for home, the batter attacks that ball with his bat. He swings at it, chops at it, tears after it, trying to reach it no matter where the fuck the pitch is because *he has to help that runner get home.*"

Zack wiped the sweat off his brow. "Isemonger didn't do that, Bobby. Isemonger moved out of the way of the pitch, moved out of the way of everything and everybody so that the runner on third would not score. And Isemonger is who you're bitchin' and moanin' and complainin' about. Isemonger is who you want on your team, Bobby?"

Knuff stared at his shoes.

"You want that kind of player on your team, Harland?" demanded Zack.

"No."

"You want that kind of player on your team, Griffen?"

"No way."

"What about you, Bobby?"

Linda heard a muffled sound from Knuff.

"Say it louder – we can't hear you," demanded Zack.

"No."

"Good. As long as we understand that, we don't care if the heat is on. We don't care because we know we can play baseball like a team. Now get out there and practice, all of you. We're going to kick ass tonight."

The end-of-July game against California went 22 innings, leaving even T. M. Curry exhausted. It started early (1:15 to be precise) and ended in the subdued twilight of a midsummer evening. The first of the three games against California (no way was Curry going to miss this series) the Eagles won; the second they lost. That brought the standings back to what they had been: California three games ahead of the Eagles. The third game, then, would be decisive. The third looked as if it might end in a draw – a tie, a stalemate, maybe even equilibrium. Except that it doesn't happen that way in baseball. No, decisions are definitive in baseball. Contests are decisive. When the dust has settled and the shade has fallen, there stand a victor and a vanquished, a winner and a loser, champs and bums. And that, thought Curry, was the way it ought to be.

Forty-four players it took to play the game, and when it was over, the players, the men on the benches, the men in blue, the crowds thinned by exhaustion – all eventually shuffled away from a decisive contest. This one was finally over. Tomorrow another would begin.

In the twelfth inning, Sunshine hit a long ball down the right-field line. The California right fielder lost the ball as it bounced off the wall and fell into the corner. By the time he had recovered it and thrown to the cutoff man, Sunshine was almost to third. As the Eagles' third base coach saw that the throw was going to miss the cutoff man, he waved Sunshine home. Turning wide at third, she corrected her flight and headed for home. Slide! Safe! That was the game!

No.

The umpire called fan interference. As the ball bounced

off the wall, a fan had leaned over and touched it. Sunshine was given an automatic double, and the game was not over. Curry's temper boiled over. He told Al exactly what he thought of fan interference, where the compulsion to touch a live ball overruled common sense. That fan cost the Eagles a victory; if he hadn't touched the ball, the game would now be over and California would be taking the shower of the defeated.

"Everybody wants to be a ball player," Al replied.

"Well, let them go be a ballplayer when California's up at bat! This is the home team, Al. This is the Eagles."

In the fourteenth inning, with the score tied at 7-7, an extra player entered the game. Curry, sitting in the box beside Big Al, saw it. Fatigue. Fatigue entered the game, creeping and oozing its way into the bones and muscles of the players, insidiously conquering their psyches. By the eighteenth inning, with the score 8-8, the players were spent, done, and it was merely a matter of endurance until the long contest would end. But neither side would give up. The victory was critical. It would either move the Eagles to within two games of first or lift California four games ahead of their second-place rival and opponent.

Well, the Eagles endured. They not only endured, they triumphed, emerging with the victory in their talons, the score standing at 9-8 (on a single by Zowski that brought in Hector Gutierrez, who had somehow summoned up the energy to actually run from second to home) when the players finally made their aching way to the clubhouse.

Curry entered the cool locker room, stood there a minute swigging a too-warm beer, then proceeded to pat each player on the back.

"Outstanding game, Hector. *Fantastico!*"

"Si."

"Good work, Griffen."

"We wore 'em out."

"I knew we'd do it, Zowski."

"No sweat."

"Keep 'em coming, Zack, keep 'em coming."

"Will do, Curry."

"Way to go, Frank."

"Ummpphh."

T. M. Curry did not consider his words mere ritual. They were necessary and must be said. Nothing inspired success like praise. And the Eagles were now only two games (just two games, mind you) behind the first-place team. So you see the logic of it, he said to himself, standing there in the locker room, not seeing what was around him, but seeing the past glories of the Eagles somehow meld into the present ones, making the past alive and giving the present more importance. The logic of it is that first place is not so very far off. Two games only. With a little luck, in just three games the Eagles could be perched on top.

Ah, but yes, said T. M. Curry to T. M. Curry, looking into the paper cup empty of beer, holding it up to the light, seeing the waxy pattern of it, feeling the stickiness of it, and ascertaining with one crushing motion of his large, strong hand that it indeed held no more of the golden brew, that is easier said than done. Easier said than done, my golden-haired lads . . . and lassie . . . for there were still four-and-a-half weeks in August and four weeks in September before some team (at least some team in *this* league) could rest easy and call themselves the pennant winners.

Who could say that the Eagles wouldn't do it? Why not?

What was there to stop them? What, hiccupped T. M. Curry – *what?* Nothing but ignorance and superstition. "Bah!" he said aloud, waving aside the imagined argument. "I never did hold with the theory that the team in first place at the beginning of July is the pennant winner. Bah!"

Superstition . . . superstition. Yes, that was it. He hadn't congratulated the whole team. He hadn't said the ritual things that must be said to the whole team. Casually looking around, ascertaining whether anybody was watching him, Curry slipped out the door and strolled down the tunnel.

Should he knock? No. Yes. Okay.

"Door's open," she said wearily.

Curry stepped in. She was sitting on a stool, strapping a pair of sandals on. She looked surprised.

"Hello, Curry."

"Hello, Linda. Good game."

She stared at him a moment, then responded. "Let's play two."

Feeling awkward, Curry glanced around her locker room, then waved good-bye and backed out of the door. He hurried back to the men's locker room. Once inside, he felt himself again. Confident. At home. Let's play two. What a team the Eagles had. What a team.

Poised. Neck arched forward, eyes ahead. Knees bent, toes flexed. Thighs tight, ready to speed forward, arms back. With a sudden thrust of power Neal was in motion, flying over the water, hitting it with a not-unpleasant stinging sensation, achieving unity with the element.

The chlorine stung his eyes. It always did. He swam a few

lengths: three freestyle, two butterfly, one backstroke, one under water. No pattern to any of it, no training, no rules, just sheer enjoyment. The most relaxing exercise in the world, swimming seemed to him totally effortless. He loved the feeling of freedom in the water, the clean feeling. An air-conditioned exercise.

Swimming under water, he watched the lane lines. Mostly he watched the parts of people, trying to form a concept of what the whole person looked like. It was always interesting to come up and see the person's face and shape, to see how the whole matched up with the slightly distorted parts that churned and whirled away in the water. Not that many of the building's residents churned and whirled in the water: most lay in the hot summer sun, accumulating the sun's rays as burn or tan.

Playing in the water, Neal turned somersaults, floating beneath the surface in a fetal ball. Impossible to sink. Finally, he emerged, his hand squeegeeing the water from his face. A quick dab at the rest of his body with a towel, then the delicious sensation of sprawling on one of the lounge chairs.

August 7. Hot, unusually so. A record-breaking eight days of 100-plus degrees in Chicago. And no end in sight. He could swim. Ball players couldn't. Not on the days they had to play ball.

The Eagles were tied with California for first place, each team having played 112 games and having won 71 of them, for a .634 winning percentage. Each team also had 50 more games to play. Neal was going to bet on the Eagles: their winning percentage was slowly but surely climbing: while California's was falling. Brushing away a water drop whose descending rivulet tickled his back, Neal thought baseball. At first the Eagles had just been making noises in the water; you knew they were there not on the basis of their style but because of their noise. Then they had begun an awkward, freestyle swim toward the shore. The waves came at them. Some they met and rode out; some they misjudged and swallowed; some they tried to take on and got slapped down by. They had been plunging, pitching about. But now their strokes were strong and sure. They saw the shore and could make their way to it. Now for them the strong, sure strokes that pull the powerful swimmers to their destination.

These were the dog days, hot and tired. Closing his eyes, he succumbed to the heat that conquered the city. But it wasn't permitted to conquer ball players, he thought lazily, drifting off to sun-induced kaleidoscope colors behind his eyelids. Lazily his eyes opened. Big cottonball clouds sat perfectly still in the sky. He was sitting still, too. Not here on this lounge chair in the lazy summer sun, but with Linda. For the last several weeks, he had been more or less avoiding her – insofar as a sports reporter could avoid a baseball player in a pennant race.

He sat up, eyes squinting against the harsh heat and light. The situation had been bugging him. He felt she was in danger from what she didn't know. He knew, though. His knowledge was a burden he didn't know how to unload . . . or hide . . . or share. If only she hadn't been writing columns. If only he hadn't been interested. If only Curry . . . if, if, if. He wanted to go up to Al Mowerinski and say, "I know. Tell her, for god's sake. Tell her, tell her, tell her."

He wondered what Linda would do in his situation. Strength versus strength, that was the unwritten rule of baseball. Say, for instance, that the pitcher had a good low fastball, his best pitch. Say, for instance, that the batter was a good low ball hitter. Say, for instance, that the game was in the last innings. What was it going to be? Strength versus strength. Somebody someday was going to throw Linda a low fastball that could knock her off her feet. Out of the batter's box. How was she going to take that pitch?

Neal stepped out of the lounge chair, grabbed his towel, and padded away, into the shockingly cool building, up the elevator, into the haven of his apartment. He had decided. Al was out of town, but when he returned, Neal would talk to him. He might get knocked over the outfield fence for his troubles, but he had to do it.

He had just finished showering and drying when the knocker on his door jarred the silence. Pulling on a pair of rugby shorts, he opened the door.

Linda blinked. She had expected Neal to be home, but she hadn't expected him to be half undressed. More than half. Almost all undressed. It was almost as if he had read her mind. She smiled. "Hi."

He was speechless for what seemed a long time – long enough for a hard-hit ball to hop past the pitcher and into the infield dirt.

"Hi," he replied. "What are– come on in." He held the door open.

Great. The ball was in her glove. She stepped into his apartment. Now what?

She stood there awkwardly. Did he always walk around in just shorts? There were tiny drops of moisture on his chest. Sweat? The pool? A shower? Suddenly she was aware that she had been staring at his bare chest for . . . a long time. Her heart began to race. "Uh, you aren't busy, are you?"

"No, no. Not at all." He walked toward the living room. "Have a seat."

She waited until he chose one, hoping he would take the couch, not a chair. He did. She sat beside him. "I just felt like talking to somebody."

"Any time." He stared at her.

"I'll bet you've just been swimming," she said accusingly, aware that she was still holding the ball. Kind of like watching a slow-motion replay, she thought: what is the shortstop going to *do* with that gloved ball now that she's trapped it?

Neal laughed. "Hey, why do you think I became a sports*writer?!* Easiest training rules in the world."

"You're lucky. I just want to sink into a pool of cool water and not come up till September." *I just want to make love with you, but I can't seem to get the ball out of my glove.*

"Would you like something to drink?"

"Ice water, thanks."

She followed him into the kitchen, leaning against the counter while he fumbled for the glass and ice. She stared at his back. It was smooth and strong-looking. What would it feel like to wrap her arms around him?

Neal handed her the water. She tilted her head back and drank thirstily, then touched her lips with the back of her hand.

"More?" he asked.

"Not now." She set the glass on the counter.

They walked back to the couch, silence awkward between them. Linda slipped off her sandals and curled up on one end of the couch, her bare knees touching Neal's thigh. She smiled at him, aware suddenly that she was going to do it. He was staring at her intently. She moved closer by kneeling to face him. This brought her above him. Slowly, she lowered her face until her lips touched his. She kissed him, tentatively at first, gently, her hands pressing lightly on his shoulders. His responding kiss seemed to be simultaneous with hers. Her tongue parted his lips, penetrating his mouth. He tasted delicious. She was aware that he was pulling her against him, one arm around her shoulders, the other around her hips. She thrust herself even harder against him. They seemed to be all hands and arms and feet and bodies. Still above him, she was now astride him, one of her knees on each side of his legs. She was moving against him, closer and harder. The next thing she knew, the couch was tipping over backward. Neal shouted. She felt him try to throw his weight forward to prevent it. But Linda went with the pitch and they ended up on the floor, laughing as they lay on the overturned couch.

"Are you afraid of me?" she asked, lying across his chest.

"Absolutely. I'm afraid you'll break my back!" He pulled her head down and kissed her.

"Just your couch," she murmured, kissing his earlobe.

"I have a bed." He rolled over, taking her with him.

Linda wrapped her arms around Neal and kissed his neck, his shoulder, his chest. "Ummm. Good."

They lay together on Neal's bed. The air conditioner, on high, was just beginning to cool them. Linda felt the sweat on her chest and stomach begin to tickle. Sitting up, she stretched an arm toward the end of the bed and pulled the sheet over them. "Training rules," she grinned, burrowing against him and draping an arm across his chest. He tilted her face toward his and kissed her. Their lips finally parted; his head dropped against the pillow.

"Neal?" She raised herself on an elbow and looked at him.

"What?"

"I didn't . . . make you do something you didn't want to. Did I?"

It must have struck him as humorous. Laughing, he asked: "You mean make love to you?"

"Make love with me. Yes."

"It was that bad, huh?"

She grinned, straddling him and pinning his arms in mock wrestling. "Come on. You know what I mean." She could feel the sheet cling momentarily to her shoulders, then slip slowly down her back.

"Let go," Neal said, "and I'll tell the truth."

"Tell the truth and I'll let go."

"I've wanted to make love to you since we met in the elevator. Maybe before that. Maybe since I met you in Memphis. I met you," he mocked, "but you didn't meet me, apparently."

She could feel herself blushing. Then he took advantage of it, twisting and toppling her. He lay on top of her. She wrapped her arms around his back.

"The more I knew you," he said, "the more I wanted to make love to you. With you."

He was kissing her throat. Once. Twice. Three. Four. "Wait." She was losing count, becoming aroused. "Then why did we wait so long?"

"Aha! 'We.' You first. Why did you wait so long?"

"Because . . . because I thought you didn't want to."

Now he was kissing her ear. "Impossible."

"No. I did. For a while. Then I thought . . . I thought that there was some sort of 'conflict of interest' or something." She looked at him questioningly.

Neal rolled over on his back, pulling her on top of him.

He was silent for a while. "That was it," he said. "I'm not supposed to get involved with the people I'm covering."

"I'm covering you," she replied.

"Not entirely. My feet are exposed."

"What are you going to do now? Did I mess it up for you?"

Neal looked away. She thought he looked concerned. "I don't know. I think about this conflict of interest stuff. The way most people would see it, I now can't write about the Eagles – or you – objectively. I guess they'd say I should now give up writing about the Eagles. Or give up you." He paused. "What about you? People will find out."

Linda nodded. "I don't know either. I think . . . I think, how can it make any difference what the team will think of me. I think sometimes, Neal, that they'll never accept me as one of them."

He laughed.

"Why are you *laughing?* I mean it."

"You. I'm laughing because it's not true. They're beginning to accept you."

"They have a hell of a way of showing it."

"C'mon, Linda, they're getting better." He squeezed her. "Admit it. Admit they're better than they were."

"Better's a long way from good," she grumbled.

"Better's a hell of a long way from where they were in April. You have to understand, you're very strange to them."

"Yeah, I represent 51 percent of the human race."

"But you don't fit their safe little stereotype of that 51 percent. You don't do the everyday things, you don't say the everyday words, you don't act the everyday way that lets them dismiss you. That's what makes you strange to them: they don't know how to relate to you."

"I want them to relate to me as a ball player."

"They're getting there. Some of them are there already. When they pour champagne on you, they'll all be there."

"Champagne. I like it." She kissed his eyebrows. First the left, then the right.

"Um, I've got an idea," Neal said, closing first one eye, then the other.

"What?"

"Why don't you make a few errors tonight so that I can come down hard on you? – just to show I'm objective?"

"Okay. I'll tell Zack I was breaking training by making love just hours before a game. You can write about it."

"Sort of an inside story, you mean?"

Linda grasped both of his hands, intertwining her fingers with his. Sliding her knees forward, she squeezed herself against Neal, kissing his lips. "Inside story," she whispered between kisses. "Good approach. I'm going to give you more details."

In the press box, Neal sat and watched the pregame warm-up, watching Linda and reflecting with a grin that in her case it was probably a cool-down. Gillespy was hitting grounders to the infield. Frank scooped one up, touched second, threw to Knuff. Knuff to Griffen, Griffen to Linda, Linda to Harland. Christ, he wished there was no game tonight. They could be making love again. The remembrance of it flooded over him. He started getting hard. An embarrassing situation in a room full of 120 reporters. Think of something else. Think of something else.

"Hey, Neal." It was Scott, one of the sports columnists for the *Chicago Banner.* "How's your girl gonna do tonight?"

"How's who going to do?"

"*C'mon,* Vanderlin – is there more than one girl in baseball?"

"There aren't any," he replied, but it was lost on Scott.

The Eagles left the field; the grounds crew came out and erased the footsteps of practice and work; the announcer spoke to all in general and none in particular; the players came out one by one as their names were called; the filled-to-capacity stadium echoed with the cheers of the fans; the players took their positions; "The Star Spangled Banner" was played. The game began. The temperature was eighty-nine degrees.

New York was a spoiler. Jumping between fourth and fifth place in the eastern division, it won games from the three leading teams just often enough to seem to decide the fortunes of the team it played. Would New York spoil Chicago's swim for the shore by winning tonight's game?

Hannibal, pitching for the Eagles, retired the first three New Yorkers without difficulty, getting all three to hit into putouts. Neal liked the way Hannibal pitched, getting the batter to hit the ball to one of the eight other players for an out. Crowder, the Eagles' new leadoff man, led off with a single.

"Batting order's not bad," offered Scott, standing behind Neal and chewing on a hot dog. Neal, smelling the raw onions, hoped Scott didn't drop any down his neck.

"Makes a lot of sense," responded Neal. Zack had originally played with Black's lineup, but now he had made a change. To some it looked as if Zack had taken the nine starters' names, tossed them into a cap, jumbled them up, and pulled them out one by one. No matter how Zack may have thought up the order, the lineup came out traditional. Speed and hitting at the front with Crowder, Sunshine, Griffen. They set the table for the power in the middle: Laughing, Abilene, Zowski. Then came more get-on-base hitters: Knuff and Gutierrez. And, of course, the pitcher.

Linda was in the batter's box. Neal watched intently. All her motions, which he could have described in minute detail before tonight, seemed fresh and new to him, as if he had never seen them before. Familiar, yet unfamiliar. He wondered what she was thinking now. He wanted her to get a hit. It was all a myth about athletes and sex before a game. Still, it was a hot night. It would be hard enough for anybody to play on a night like this.

The first pitch came. Low, but good. Linda swung, catching only a piece of it. Strike one.

"Sucker for a low pitch."

Neal, who had forgotten about Scott, turned around to look at him, slightly annoyed. "That was a good pitch."

"No way. Too low."

It wasn't. Part of Herlihy's excellence as a pitcher was that his low pitches were usually strikes. The sinker, which, if it broke, broke down and in to a right-handed batter, and which sank suddenly as it reached the plate, was his specialty. Like the fastball and the curve, the sinker had been around for a long time. But it was more difficult to master and probably a lot harder to hit. Herlihy also threw sliders, which broke down and away from a right-handed batter. A curved ball without a very pronounced break, the slider was faster than the traditional curve and had some spin. Herlihy was leading the league in strikeouts, and with good reason. There were only two ways to make a batter strike out: make him swing in the wrong place or make him swing at the wrong time. Herlihy's sinker and slider combined to make many batters swing in the wrong place, and his change of pace made many more swing at the wrong time.

Following the strike to Linda with a pickoff move to first, Herlihy tried to get Crowder. Crowder raised a dust storm at first, hitting the dirt and hugging the bag. Safe. Herlihy pitched the ball. Not good enough. One and one the count. Another pickoff move. Another small dust storm. Then a pitch. A second ball, 2 and 1 the count, with the batter now ahead of the pitcher. Neal knew she would make the pitch be there. Herlihy took his stretch and hurled the ball toward a hopeful reunion with the well-oiled leather of the catcher's mitt. The sinker was intercepted by a smooth, level swing that lifted it high over the infield and dropped it into short right. The single sent Ulysses to third. Neal wiped the sweat off his forehead, feeling great relief.

Griffen's single brought Crowder home and Linda to third, with the Eagles taking a 1-0 lead. Laughing hit into a double, and he and Griffen retired to the dugout. Harland struck out and the inning was over.

In the top of the second Don Hannibal struck out the New York leadoff man, bringing Jack Doyle to the plate. Doyle hit a double.

"He's sweet on Sunshine," whispered Scott.

Neal tried to ignore the remark. He had been hearing rumors about Jack Doyle and Linda ever since she had played for the Memphis Arrows. Doyle did nothing to dispel those rumors. Neal wondered if they were true. Hannibal walked the third man at bat. The fourth hit a chopping grounder toward second. Frank came at the ball swiftly. It bobbled out of the glove's webbing, but he recovered it with his bare hand, the ball still trying to hop its way toward right center field. Frank threw to Linda, who was covering second. The runner from first slid, trying to upset her throw with a hard, fast slide to second, legs flying and dust whirling. She threw hard to Knuff, then jumped, legs tucked under. Two for one. The Eagles were out of the inning.

In the Eagles' half of the third, Linda was up again. Herlihy's pitches kept coming over the plate. Low, but over. Down and in. Linda kept hitting them: foul, foul, foul. Nothing and two the count. Finally she met one fully. To Neal, it looked as if she had made contact at the sweet spot, the center of percussion on the bat, where the ball seems to jump off the bat in a smooth, true hit. The ball went sailing high and long into left center. Neal and Scott were on their feet, urging it over the fence.

Unsuccessfully. Jack Doyle made a circus catch and robbed her of the hit. The glory went to the fielder.

"Shit! I knew we never shoulda traded Doyle," grumbled Scott, returning to his chair with a loud thump.

"The Eagles don't need a center fielder," replied Neal.

Scott snorted. "Mowerinski probably got rid of Doyle because he was sweet on Sunshine."

"Don't be stupid, Scottie."

"You're the one who's stupid, Vanderlin. Everybody knows Doyle wanted to get into her pants."

Neal shook his head: at Scott, at the gossip that thrived in the tiny world that was big league baseball, at the crudity of the language, at the relationships it revealed. They probably said the same about him. Who was he kidding? There was no "probably" about it. He knew they did. The thought of his feelings being reduced to such a phrase angered him. Tapping his pencil on his scorecard, Neal frowned: the rumors were going to get worse, not better. There was no going back.

Pulling himself out of his slouch, Neal hunched his shoulders over his scorecard and concentrated on looking at the game. The Eagles had gone down without a run. New York was about to do the same in the top of the fourth. Would Al have traded Jack Doyle because of the rumor? Neal dismissed it as unworthy of the big man. The team, stronger than any Eagle team in the last decade, had been built by Al Mowerinski, former Eagle World Series player, former lawn mower salesman, present owner and general manager of the most exciting team in baseball. Al hadn't planned his moves this season, Neal now realized. They'd been in the planning a long, long time.

To Scott (and others) it looked as if Al Mowerinski did what he did because of Linda. It looked as if Al traded Icehead and fired Black in order to protect her. That was one way of looking at it, no doubt about it. But there was another side to the horsehide. It could be that Al was acting to protect baseball players. Yes, all of them, every last one. The players were there to play the game: to hit the hurled ball, to tag the bags and score the runs. To field the hoppers, snag the bloopers, shag the flies. Whenever hatred, greed, envy, or ego interfered with that, then the person who stepped in to set things right – that person was protecting baseball.

Herlihy hurled his sinkers, but the Eagles stayed afloat, 1-0 the final score. Neal took a mouthful of crushed ice from his paper cup, long since drained of Coke. Throwing the cup into the wastebasket, he made his way out of the press box and wandered slowly down to the locker rooms. It seemed to him that an awful lot of games ended 1-0. It seemed to him that an awful lot of those games started with the lone run scored in the beginning. He enjoyed the come-from-behind games as much as anybody did. That kind of playing, that kind of turnaround, was inseparable from the thrill of sports. But he had always liked the 1-0 games, too. The game's not over until the last inning is played, that was the cliché. That was the truth. But somehow Neal found it satisfying to see the beginning count so heavily, too. The beginning was important. Let the endings get their share of star billings, but don't forget the beginnings. Sometimes they made the game.

Linda was enjoying her shower. When you lost, a shower was a necessity, a soothing, healing warmth, something you had to do before you could go out and face the world again. When you won, a shower was a pleasure, a sensual experience. When your team had just captured first place, a shower was something you didn't even notice, because your mind was so full of the future: the division playoffs; the pennant; the Series.

A cold rush of air chilled her. Somebody had opened the swinging door. It couldn't be Neal: he had gone off to write his article. "Who is it?" she called, turning off the water.

There was no reply.

Peering around the corner of the shower stall, she saw nobody. But there was a newspaper on the floor. Wrapping a towel around herself, she padded over to the newspaper, water dripping around her. Standing above it, she stopped. The mammoth headline brought a constriction to her throat. LINDA SUNSHINE: DAUGHTER OF EAGLES' OWNER. Below the headline, a full-page photo (a publicity photo taken more than two years ago) showed her shaking hands with Al. *Plop.*

Another drop of water fell, struck the tabloid, and was absorbed. The water splotches spread quickly and widely, like a stain. They would dry, leaving the newsprint wrinkled but readable.

She stooped to pick up the paper. Her wet hair sent small rivulets of water down her back and the sides of her face. It was a weekly paper of the type sold in grocery stores. Holding the paper at a distance, she walked over to one of the chairs to sit down. Two wet footprints remained at the spot where she had stood.

She stared at the headline and the photo. No, she said silently. It's a junky, trashy paper. It's going to be a pun: they'll mean he's my father symbolically. For a moment she felt lighthearted again, nearly laughing at her fear. She almost smiled. But deeper within, past reasoning, lay a voice that said *It Might Be True.* She looked at the headline again, then at the photo. Two similar faces seemed to stare out at her. She looked for the line that would tell her which page had the story. Finding it, she turned to the page. Dateline: September 2. Two days into the future. Her contempt for this type of journalism was a bilious taste in her mouth. The story was by somebody named Boardstreet Scriber. A phony name for sure. She forced herself to proceed slowly, taking in all the details, every last one.

The story's dateline and byline sat under a headline different from that on the front page. SUNSHINE: DAUGHTER OF BASEBALL GREATS? Here, unlike on the front page, the headline carried a question mark. Her ability to grasp these technical details at such a moment amazed her. When all her thoughts and feelings were confused, her ability to notice details seemed wrong. "Baseball Baron Seeks Revenge," added the headline kicker.

When she started reading, her imposed deliberateness disappeared, swept away before the barrage of unsuspected (and perhaps untrue) information that assaulted her. The paragraphs blurred. So did the photos. She recognized one of Amanda Quitman. Another of a young Al Mowerinski. A third of them together. The article proved nothing but implied everything. She may have been, according to the article, born Linda Quitman, adopted almost immediately. Her parents were not quoted. She knew they would never have granted an interview to any reporter, especially one such as this Boardstreet Scriber, the coward. Couldn't even use his real name.

Linda realized she had to get out. Get out before the reporters came. Hurriedly she dressed. What should she do? Neal. He would know. She leaned against the wall and dialed Neal's number at the newspaper. She hated wall phones. How many desperate conversations took place with at least one of the callers standing up, elbow against a wall, hunched over an uncompromising wall phone? Thwack told her that Neal had just left. She hesitated. Thwack seemed to hesitate also. Maybe he wanted to say something more. After an awkward pause, she thanked him and hung up.

Her parents. *They'll know, won't they? They'll know if it's true.* Quickly, she dialed the number. After twenty rings, she accepted that they weren't home.

Her feelings bouncing around like a badly bobbled grounder, she ran up the stairs to Al's office. Halfway there, she stopped. What would she say to him, ask him? She turned around, walking slowly back down the stairs. Before she reached the bottom, she stopped again, turned, and walked slowly up to his office. Al wasn't there. The office was locked. Where did he live? Was he in the phone book? She thumbed through the remnants of one chained to the nearest public telephone in the stadium. Yes. She memorized the address.

Linda hurried out of the stadium, wanting to avoid the other players, Zack, everybody. Who had thrown the paper into her locker room? One of them? Reaching her car, she realized she still held the tabloid, rolled into a tight tube. Driving slowly out of the parking lot, she headed north, toward the address she had memorized.

The lobby, cool and dark, caused her to blink. She sucked the cool air into her lungs. The doorman smiled at her.

"Al Mowerinski."

"Who's calling?" asked the doorman, picking up the phone and pressing buttons.

"Linda. Just say Linda."

The doorman reported into the silver telephone. She couldn't hear Al's reply, but the doorman stood up, opened the glass door for her, and told her how to get to the apartment.

Her resolution left suddenly. The elevator – cold, impersonal, efficient – seemed too swift. Sighting the stairway, she decided to walk up the four flights. On the fourth floor she emerged from the stairwell, the newspaper still rolled into a tight cylinder. She held it in her right hand, gripping it at one end like a bat. The sudden sunlight, streaming through the arched hallway windows, confused her momentarily. She didn't know which way to turn.

"Linda."

She turned toward the voice. It had a quality, a heavy emotion, that she had never heard from him before. *It's true. It can't be true. But it is. It is true.* Through the late afternoon sunbeams, pouring like golden rays through the windows, bouncing off the highly polished stone-tiled floors, and making visible inconceivably small specks of dust in the air, she walked toward the big man whose shape loomed ahead of her. At the apartment door, she stopped in front of him.

"Linda," he said in a choking voice.

She felt him look hard at her face, at the paper she carried like a weapon, and she thought he wanted to touch her. Her lower lip quivered. She bit it, trying to control it. "Tell me it's not true," she pleaded in a voice she didn't recognize. Then suddenly tears spilled from her eyes.

Al folded her, newspaper and all, into his arms. Muffled, crushed against his chest, the newspaper crushed between them, she couldn't breathe. "Don't cry, Linda. Don't cry. Come inside." He guided her into the apartment.

She stood there after he closed the door, stiff and rigid, angrily brushing away her tears with the back of one hand. "Tell me it's not true!" she demanded in what sounded to her like a high, squeaky voice. But she saw in his face that it was true. Swinging the newspaper tube at him blindly, angrily, she cried, "How could you do this to me?"

"Linda, sit down." He motioned to the couch and chairs.

"No!" Her tears started again. She brushed them away.

"I'm sorry," he said. "I'm sorry. I didn't want it to come out. I – no, that's not true. I did want you to know." One step brought him to her again, and he enveloped her in his arms. She could feel his warm breath as he pressed his head close to hers. Knowing that he wanted to break down her anger and resistance, she held herself rigid against him, shoulders and arms stiff, an unwilling participant.

Al straightened up. He looked down at her. She felt him

pry the bent and shapeless tube from her hand and gently lead her to a chair. She sat down.

"Why didn't you tell me?" she asked. "Why didn't you? You should have . . . have . . . ." Unable to speak, she drew in a ragged breath.

Al brought her a glass of water. She took it.

Sitting down across from her, he pulled his chair up close to her. Their knees almost touched. He ran his fingers through his hair. "I don't know," he said, swallowing. "No. That's not it." Staring at her sorrowfully, he asked, "How could I tell you? When? It didn't seem right to tell you when . . . your parents . . . didn't tell you. Did they?"

She shook her head. "No. No, if they'd have told me . . . if they'd have told me, I would have known you had an .. . . an ulterior motive."

He drew back, staring at her. Then he leaned forward, prodding her knee with a large finger. "A superior motive, Linda – not an ulterior one."

"Superior!" Twisting angrily away from him, she breathed deeply. "It wasn't superior," she mumbled.

"But it was. The motive was to open baseball to anybody who can play it well."

"The motive was to allow your . . . daughter . . . to play baseball."

Al stared at her, rose from his chair, walked to his liquor cabinet, and poured two stiff drinks, handing Linda one.

She pushed the drink away.

"Okay. That was part of the motive, yes. But you couldn't have played if you weren't any good. Better yet, you couldn't have played – couldn't have survived – unless you were *exceptionally* good. Which you are. So my motive resulted in bringing a damn good player to the Eagles."

Staring down at her hands, clenching and unclenching them as if they were gripping a baseball, Linda didn't know what to say. Whatever he said, he did it because she was his daughter. He was treating her special. The only reason she was here was because she was his daughter.

The buzzer sounded. She watched Al walk to the receiver on the wall and press a large hand against it. "No. Send them away, Willie. I don't want to see anybody until I tell you." He replaced the receiver, walked back to his chair, and tried to take one of Linda's hands into his. When she resisted, he placed his hands on her knees.

"You don't want women in baseball," she said suddenly.

"I do, I do! How can you say I don't?"

She shook her head from side to side so vehemently that her hair bounced back and forth. "No! You want *me* in baseball. That's different!"

Al stared at her.

"Don't you understand? Can't you see? You just wanted me, just me. You just wanted your daughter in baseball. It's not fair."

"Of course it's fair, Linda. What are you talking about?" He looked at her in silence for a moment. "Well, maybe it wasn't *smart,* but it was *fair.*"

She felt the squeeze of his hands on her knees. "No. Why aren't there any other women on the team?"

"I haven't found them," he replied quickly. Then, turning the question around, he asked, "Why aren't there any women on the *other* teams?"

Linda had no answer. The phone, which had been ringing endlessly, only to be answered by his automatic machine each time, rang again. He continued to ignore it. "There will be. There *will* be women in baseball. Don't you think I want that?" he implored. "It was what Amanda wanted. It's what I want."

"I don't know," she answered slowly.

Again the phone rang. They ignored it until they were both aware of Neal's voice. "Al, it's Neal. If you're there, please talk to me. I want to know where Linda is. I–"

Al flicked a switch. "She's here," he answered, speaking toward the machine.

"Is she okay?" asked Neal and, in the same breath, "My god, Al, how did that story get in that paper?"

"I don't know. I don't know." He stared at Linda.

"Neal. I'm okay." Her voice quavered.

"Do you want me there?"

"No."

Neal ended the conversation reluctantly. Al switched off the recorder and walked to stand in front of a window. After a while, he turned to look at Linda.

She stood up. "I . . . can't . . . play baseball. It wasn't right."

"It wasn't wrong, Linda. And quitting won't make it right." His voice was quiet, desperately calm. He showed no surprise at her words.

"No." Biting her lip, she started for the door.

"Linda!" His motion was swiftness itself. He stood, not between her and the door, but next to her.

She didn't want him to touch her. The tears would start again. Thrusting out an arm to keep him away, she wrenched open the door and escaped into the corridor. It was cold. She trembled, tears blinding her. Glancing back, she saw Al standing in the doorway, watching her go.

Descending a flight, she dropped down on one of the cold

tiled steps and cried bitterly. Why hadn't he told her? Why hadn't her parents warned her? All she had wanted to do was play baseball. She tried to convince herself there was no point to it now.

9   Turnaround

A grand game it was, the game that put the Chicago Eagles into first place (undisputed and unshared) in the Eastern Division. Timothy Michael Curry sat in the stands, way back, lone as an eagle, away from his customary box seat. He wanted it that way. He'd had the feeling earlier today: this would be it. This would be it, and no backsliding. So he left his family and friends in the box seats and said he would be walking through the crowd, talking to the fans.

He'd had no intention of talking to anybody. He just wanted to sit, back here in the last row of stadium seats, away from the light, away from the crowd. Today he wanted that distance, that separation.

The players looked so tiny, like the little people, sure, as they gracefully waved their magic wands, pivoted and frolicked, cavorted and danced. Sitting this far back, covered by the shade of upper-deck seats, Curry felt some of the magic his ancestors must have felt when telling the stories of the little people. He imagined himself peeking through the gloom of some dense forest, seeing the shafts of sunlight play on the magic circle dance going on down below. This far back, this far away, it seemed to him that the players were at one and the same time both elves and giants. Tiny, they seemed, because they looked so unreachable, so committed to the game and oblivious to what was outside the circle they danced in. Yet they loomed large in his vision at the same time, giants playing the game, seen through the wrong end of a pair of binoculars, doing more than ordinary mortals, and doing it better.

It was a grand game, it was: 10-4, Eagles leading all the way. And it was a grand day, too: the last day of August, the sniff of September already in the air. Four weeks, a little more. All the Eagles had to do was hold on to the lead. Curry was fully confident that they would not only hold on to it, but expand it. His scouting hadn't been for nothing. Laughing, Knuff, Abilene, Crowder, Sunshine, Gutierrez – hadn't he been the one to recommend each? Al had traded for Griffen and Zowski, as well as for Hannibal and Kovacks, but Curry had found the players and helped build the farm system without which no team could ever make the Series. And now the Chicago Eagles would live again. Yessirree, if Timothy Michael Curry had anything to say about it, the Chicago Eagles would live again. The grand old days, they would live again. The pennant would come home, where it belonged.

Time passed. The stadium emptied. But T. M. Curry was still sitting in the stands alone, dreaming of the Series, studying the lengthening rays of sunlight on the infield, when the grounds crew hinted that perhaps he should be joining his friends. Giving them a wave and a friendly grin, he headed toward the clubhouse. There would still be plenty of people there, that he knew.

Something was wrong. He sensed it when he stepped into the clubhouse. It was the atmosphere. Where was the carefree joviality of a team that had just captured first place? Curry stood stark still, puzzled. Had Zack put a moratorium on celebrations? He looked around. The players were in small groups, a few talking, but most silent.

Zack, coming through the swinging doors, saw Curry and stopped.

"Jesus," Curry asked quietly, "what's the matter here, Zack? This isn't what I expected."

Zack focused on Curry for a moment, then motioned with his head toward the manager's office. Back through the swinging doors they went, into Zack's office. Picking up a newspaper, Zack handed it to him.

T. M. Curry looked at the newspaper and turned white. When words failed him, the manager spoke. "That's what's the matter. Who would *do* a thing like that?" Zack demanded, half belligerently, half sorrowfully. "I can't find Linda. Al's got his damned answering machine rigged up. I've had to bar the clubhouse to reporters; they're swarming all over the place . . . . I don't know what's going to come of this, Curry. Just when things were going so well. Now we have this to fight. I want the team concentrating on baseball, damn it, not on this! What are they trying to do – break us apart?"

Curry, still ashen, didn't answer the question because he didn't hear it.

"Well, goddamn it, *say* something!" shouted Zack as he stood behind his desk and leaned toward Curry.

"It's true," he whispered. "God knows, I suspected it, but . . . but I didn't know it, I didn't *know* it."

"What do you mean you suspected it? You thought Al was Linda's *father*? You mean he *is* her father?!" Zack asked incredulously.

Curry rolled the paper in his hand, spun on his heel, and walked away.

"Hey! *Hey!* Curry! Come back here! Where are you going?" Zack ran after him.

Curry ignored him, ignored everything but the long corridor before him. Eventually he sensed that Zack had stopped following him. Curry's footsteps echoed alone in the corridor.

In the cab, he sat with his head in his hands, cursing himself with every name he could think of. He had behaved like a busher. Never, he vowed, would he ever again speak to Lenny Black. Maybe he should give up drinking, too. It was all coming back to him. He cringed at the thought that the Eagles might not win, that Al would be losing Amanda all over again, that Linda . . . he couldn't even imagine what Linda would feel.

When had it been? February? March? Sometime during spring training, something in her face, her movement, something, something, he didn't know what, but he had been sitting in the bleachers watching her play when suddenly he saw not her, but Al; not her, but Amanda. It was then he had known, or felt he had known, what Al was doing. Privately, he had done some scouting around and had found enough to encourage his thoughts. Somehow, some way, she could have been Al's daughter – Al's and Mandy's. What did it matter now, though? Curry thought of Amanda. If things had been different, she might have been his daughter.

The bush thing he had done, which he now feared he might never outlive or correct, was that, after one too many (after many too many, really), he had hinted such to Lenny Black, seeking commiseration and camaraderie against Big Al. Then, as the season had started and the pace of Eagle victories had increased, his speculation had slipped into the back of his mind. Somewhere in the long season (he would never be able to pinpoint where and when) it had come not to matter. That was all – it just slipped away. What mattered was winning. And that's what the Eagles had been doing: winning.

Now what would happen? Curry slammed a shutter in his mind, pushing the thought away. Lenny Black. The bastard! T. M. Curry was convinced that Lenny Black was behind this. Who else could it be? He tried to recall whether he had made veiled hints to anyone else. He couldn't remember. Everything would be okay. Everything would be okay, he repeated to himself. This was just . . . temporary, that's all. These attempts at soothing thoughts fell to the wayside as the cab pulled up to Al's building.

A calm, cool, and collected doorman confronted him. "I'm sorry, sir, but Mr. Mowerinski said he isn't seeing anybody tonight."

"He'll see me. I'm an old friend." Curry choked on the last word. "You pick up that phone and tell him Curry Powder has to see him."

The doorman rolled his eyes and shook his head as if to say Why Do I Bother Trying to Explain? "A Mr. Powder is here and says he has to see you. I tried to tell–"

Curry, whose wrists and arms had met far stronger and far faster obstacles and turned them around, yanked the phone out of the doorman's hands easily. "Al. Curry. I've got to talk to you."

When Curry got off the elevator and turned toward Al's apartment, he saw that the door was open. Stepping inside, he saw Al sitting in a big blockbuster chair. There seemed to be no spirit in him. It reminded Curry of another time. He hurried over and sat on the couch, facing him. "What happened? What . . . was she here?"

"She quit. She quit, Curry."

T. M. Curry turned pale. *"Quit?* No! Why?"

Al shrugged, half angrily, half listlessly. "She says I hired her for the wrong reasons."

It was what he had feared. Kids! They were such . . . such idealists! Why couldn't they see the way things really were? Jesus, they could make you turn gray! Quickly, with just a few questions, Curry got the rest of the story out of Al. He had no time to lose. Leaning over, he placed his hands on Al's shoulders. "Al, listen. Things will be okay. Trust me. I'm going to see her." He got up to go.

He had reached the door when Al spoke. "Curry."

"Yeah?" Curry turned to look at his old baseball buddy.

"What're you going to do?" There was a flicker of hope in the voice.

Curry looked at Big Al Mowerinski and, for the first time in nearly thirty-five years, saw him clearly again, as he had when the kid had first come to the Eagles. For the first time in nearly thirty-five years there was no past floating between them, just a future. And that future would include a pennant-winning team even if Curry had to groom Eagle Stadium on his hands and knees with a pair of manicure scissors. He took a deep breath. "I can't explain, Al. But I'm going to bat for you. For her. For the Eagles."

"Don't call, Curry. Come back here yourself."

"Sure, Al." Curry closed the door behind him. Now all he had to do was deliver.

Linda sat at the kitchen table, trying not to think about Neal and trying to listen to her mother explain why she should play baseball and why they hadn't told her that Al Mowerinski was her father. Her mother, who nearly three years ago had argued against her playing baseball, was now arguing *for* her playing baseball. The world was turning around and around and upside down at the same time.

When Linda had first left Al's apartment, she had gone home, straight to Neal. She had expected – what? Empathy? Agreement that she had done the right thing in quitting?

But Neal, while saying that he understood how badly she felt, had been horrified, then outraged, when she told him she had quit. He had told her that she hadn't done the right thing. "You can't *quit*, Linda – it's wrong for you, and it's wrong for the team."

"That's easy for *you* to say!" she had retorted angrily. What had she wanted – more sympathy? Less analysis?

"It doesn't matter if it's easy to say or hard to say," Neal had replied. "You're hurting yourself, and you're hurting the team. Quitting is swinging at the wrong pitch, in the wrong place, at the wrong time."

Linda had added to all the wrong moves by walking out of Neal's apartment, slamming the door behind her, and driving to the airport, where she had caught the first flight to Pittsburgh. Now, close to one o'clock in the morning, she sat with her parents in the dimly lit kitchen, staring at the dark outside the screen door, listening to the crickets in the soft nighttime silence.

"Did you know her? Did you know Amanda Quitman?

Did you know Al Mowerinski?" Linda's questions tumbled out.

"Yes, I knew Amanda. We corresponded occasionally over the years. Not often, actually. But whenever the Hammond Chicks would get to Ohio, your father and I would drive the ninety miles to see them. So I saw Amanda more than I wrote to her, actually."

"What about Al?" asked Linda.

"No," answered her father. "We didn't know him. Just what Amanda told your mother about him."

"But you knew he was my father." Linda watched her parents look at each other and not answer. "You knew, didn't you?"

"No," answered her mother. "Not for sure. Linda, the way you were adopted was, one day I got a call from Amanda Quitman. She said she had to see me, and she gave me the address where she was. It wasn't far from here, maybe thirty miles. It was an unwed mother's home, although I didn't know that until I got there and saw that Amanda was . . . well, she must have been nine months pregnant. I was so shocked, I didn't say anything. She laughed, to try to make me comfortable, I think, but it was a sad laugh. Then we sat down and she told me . . . well, she told me everything that she wanted me to know, I guess. About the Girls' League folding, which I knew, and about her being pregnant. But not about the father, and, well, she told me that if anything went wrong, she wanted me to have you – to have the baby. I asked her: I asked her who the father was. She said it didn't matter. Then, when I kept asking, she said she didn't want him to know. I asked her if Al Mowerinski knew she was here. We had always thought that Amanda and Al, well, lived together. She said he didn't know and that she didn't want him to know."

Her mother stopped and, after a moment, her father took over the telling. "You see, Linda, Amanda knew about the miscarriages your mother had had – three of them, and then we decided we couldn't . . . that we couldn't have children. We both had wanted children very much. And Amanda knew that."

Her mother wiped at her eyes with a handkerchief. Linda reached over and hugged her. "It was so hard," said her mother through tears. "I know we should have tried to find your father. We should have gotten in touch with Al Mowerinski and asked him if he knew what had happened to Amanda. But we never did."

"But, Mom, you knew he was my father before I signed. You must have known. That's why you acted so . . . so strange. I always wondered why you weren't happy about my signing."

"Yes, we knew," answered her father, taking up the thread of the story. "He came around here; you were maybe eight, nine years old at the time. We were so afraid, weren't we, that he would try to take Linda away?"

Her mother nodded agreement, then added, "He said he didn't know who his daughter was until it was too late to do anything about raising her. I didn't believe him at first. I thought he was trying to trick us."

"But he wasn't," said her father. "It's to his credit. He's a good man. He did the right thing even though doing it was very hard."

Linda watched her father get up from the table and pour himself more coffee. A mere half cup was all that trickled out of the now-empty pot.

"He'd come sometimes to the Little League games. Him and Curry. They'd stand back by the outfield fence."

"You should have told me," argued Linda, burying her

head in her hands, then looking back up. "You didn't want me to sign: why didn't you tell me?"

Her father shrugged. "I don't know. The truth is that I don't know why we didn't tell you. I think we were afraid you wouldn't make it. And it just didn't seem right to tell you that he was signing you because you were his daughter."

"That's why he hired me," Linda said bitterly, her voice cracking.

"His reasons don't count anymore," said her father. "The results count."

Linda started to disagree, but he spoke over her disagreement. "You think Branch Rickey's reasons for hiring Jackie Robinson were pure? They weren't. Concentrate on the results, not the reasons."

"Wait a minute. Let me get this straight. You didn't think I should play at first, but now you think I *should*?" she demanded indignantly.

"People hire their sons," said her mother. "Why not their daughters? You've earned a place on the team."

Linda stood and rubbed her eyes. "I'm too tired. I'm going to bed."

Her mother grabbed her by the arm. "Lindy. You're a good player. You're a better player than we ever thought you'd have the chance to be. When you wake up, decide to go back to the Eagles."

All she decided when she woke up was that she should turn on what remained of the morning news. Watching it, she learned that Al Mowerinski denied that she had quit. He said she was hurt and confused but was still on the team. A lot he knew, thought Linda, clicking off the news angrily.

Her mother served breakfast and refused to let Linda get away without eating it. "And when you're done eating, go upstairs and take a shower. You'll feel a lot better."

Nothing could make her feel a lot better, and she felt like moping around the house to prove it, but her mother practically pushed her up the stairs and into the shower. "All right, all right, I'll *take* a shower!"

"Wash your hair while you're at it. You look terrible. And put on something nice."

Linda stayed under the shower until the hot water gave up. Then she stepped out, toweled off, dried her hair, and, wrapping a towel around herself, walked to her room. What should she wear? It was hot in Freedom, Pennsylvania, too. She decided on a T-shirt, white shorts, and sandals.

Somebody else was in the house. She realized it as she walked down the stairs. And when she turned the corner at the bottom of the stairs, she saw that it was Neal.

"Hello, Linda." He got out of his chair and came toward her.

She backed away a step. "How did you get here?" she demanded.

"He called early this morning," answered her mother, "and asked if you were here. I said you were, and he said he was coming to talk to you."

Linda glared at her mother.

"I picked him up at the airport," said her father cheerfully. "We've been talking about the Eagles the whole time."

Linda glared at her father. "I've quit," she said to Neal. "I told you that."

"I think we should talk about it," answered Neal casually.

"Lots of ball players say they're quitting when they really aren't. They don't want to quit: it's something else that's bothering them."

Walking up to a chair, Linda sat in it angrily.

Neal went back to his chair. "Al announced to the press today that you haven't quit."

"I heard it on television."

Linda's mother and father stood. "I've got lunch to prepare," said her mother, "and your father's got work to do."

"Nice meeting you, Neal." Her father shook hands with Neal, then her mother shook hands with Neal.

They were deliberately leaving her alone with him. And he was going to argue with her. "I don't want to talk about it, Neal."

"There's a game in Pittsburgh today." He glanced at his watch. "I think we can make it if we hurry."

"No."

"You'd rather talk, then?"

"No."

"So it's the game."

Linda stared at him. Were all reporters this persistent?

"We're going to the game," she told her parents as she led Neal out the back door. "Can I borrow the car?"

"Sure, take the car," her father offered.

Neal asked her questions about her hometown while she drove. Then, as she was pulling into one of the baseball parking lots, he told her he had a message for her from Zack.

Linda bit her lip. She would simply ignore Neal. But when she did, he didn't say anything. Finally, she asked, "Okay, what's the message?"

"He told me to tell you you're being fined $1,000 a day for

not showing up."

Parking the car, Linda turned it off angrily, pocketed the keys, and slammed the door.

When she tried to buy the tickets, Neal pushed her aside and paid for them. "You can't afford these," he told her, "until you start playing again."

Her sunglasses were slipping; she angrily jabbed at them, pushing them against her nose. "I thought we weren't going to talk baseball."

"False assumption. What else would we talk about at a baseball game?"

In the top of the third inning, with the home team down by three runs, the Pittsburgh shortstop make an error that gave California a four-run lead. Linda looked at the scoreboard standings. The Eagles were still in first, but were losing to Atlanta today, 2-1. She wondered what inning it was in Atlanta. Who was pitching? Charlie Kovacks, probably.

"The team needs you, Linda."

She ignored him. In the fifth inning, she replied. "They don't want me. They never wanted me in the first place."

"They need you. You're their shortstop. They believe in you."

In the bottom of the seventh, California increased its lead over Pittsburgh by two more runs, making the score 8-2. "I don't know what to believe," Linda said to the empty bleacher seat in front of her. "I don't think I believe in myself anymore. I thought I was signed because I was a good baseball player, but it was all a lie. That isn't why I was signed."

"It wasn't a lie, goddamn it! Look at the results – the results are that you could be rookie of the year. My god, Linda, think of what that means! Think of what it says about you, about women in baseball, about the Eagles' chances."

She turned to him angrily. "I don't care about *results*, Neal, I care about *reasons!*"

"Then you're wrong. Progress is measured in results, not reasons, and thank god it is – historical results are usually better than the reasons that created them. Look at Jackie Ro–"

"Yeah, yeah," she interrupted. "Jackie Robinson. You're going to tell me about Jackie Robinson. Well, I don't want to hear it, Neal. There goes the steal. Safe. It's a lost cause."

Neal bought four hot dogs from the vendor and shoved two into Linda's hands. "If you mean the Eagles without you, you're damn right it's a lost cause. They're trying their best, but they won't make it. Look, Atlanta's leading them 4-1 now." He bit into a hot dog angrily, pointed its remains at the playing field, and said through a mouthful of food, "And California's walking away with this one."

Linda stuffed her hot dogs under the seat. She didn't have the conviction to taste them, let alone chew them. "What do you *want* out of me, Neal? Why are you here?"

Neal threw the remains of his hot dog under an empty chair. "Right now, I want you to play baseball as if your life depended on it, that's what I want!"

"Yeah? Well, it doesn't!"

Pittsburgh rallied in the bottom of the ninth, but not enough, and California won, 8-4. The scoreboard informed whoever was interested that the Eagles lost to Atlanta. So now the standings were even again, Chicago and California tied for first. Neal and Linda both looked at the standings, but neither said anything.

Back at the car, Neal slumped in the passenger seat. "Will you take me to the airport, Linda? I've got a column to get out."

She had wanted to be rid of him all day long, but when it was time to drop him off, she couldn't do it. She parked the car and walked with Neal to the terminal. They sat in miserable silence and then, when it was time for him to board, they stood. Neal turned and pulled her close. "Linda. This is so hard on me. I love you." And then, before she could say anything, he had turned and walked through the boarding gate.

The next day, Linda sat in the backyard with a radio, fiddling with the dial, trying to find the Atlanta-Chicago game. Once she found it, she twisted the dial back and forth, listening to Atlanta-Chicago, then listening to Pittsburgh-California. Through the intense static of the poor reception (what did Pittsburgh care about the Atlanta-Chicago game?), she heard the Eagles lose to Atlanta. Through very clear reception, she heard California lose to Pittsburgh. So it still stood even. Still tied for first. *Why do I care? Why am I listening?*

Stretching, she picked up the radio, turned it off, and wandered back into the house. She leaned against the doorjamb, looking out through the screen, waiting for the evening paper. At four o'clock, it was delivered. Linda turned to the sports section. Neal's column was now carried by the Pittsburgh paper.

Sunshine Not Special

All of Chicago, if not all of the baseball world, is talking about Linda Sunshine, Al Mowerinski, the Chicago Eagles, and the pennant race. They're talking about Mowerinski because it now seems that his motives in signing Linda Sunshine were not historically pure and impersonal. It has come out that Sunshine was the daughter of

Amanda Quitman (the preeminent shortstop and pitcher in the long-since-deceased All-American Girls' Baseball League) and Al Mowerinski. Some of these facts were known to some of the people involved (Mowerinski, Tom and Karen Sunshine), but not all of the facts were known by all of the people until now. And none of the facts were known to Linda Sunshine until she read about them in the press two days ago. People are saying that Al Mowerinski signed Sunshine because she was his daughter and that there is something wrong with such behavior.

Linda Sunshine believes it's wrong, too. That's why she told Al Mowerinski that she was quitting (although the Eagle owner and general manager has said that she has not quit, that he will not accept her quitting). Sunshine has always wanted to be treated as just another baseball player – as nobody special. By this she meant that she didn't want additional or extra help. She didn't want to play baseball as a token, due to some government regulation. She wanted to play on the Eagles because she deserved to play, because she earned her place on the infield dirt.

This is understandable in any walk of life, but especially in a situation where one is the only woman in a male-dominated field. The other players will outright state or not-so-subtly imply that the woman player wouldn't be there if she didn't have special privileges: federal laws, publicity, money, ownership, something. But Sunshine always believed that she never had special privileges. Then, when what appear to have been special privileges are slapped in her face, she reacted by leaving the field of play.

This is understandable, but wrong. All players are special in that they have had special support to get them where they are. Nobody makes it on their own. The special support may have come from a coach, a teacher, a scout, a trainer, a manager, an owner, a father, a mother: someone who believes in them. All baseball players have had special help to get where they are today, and Sunshine is no different from the others. Except that she didn't know it, and it was made public to her and the world in a very bad way.

Linda Sunshine is special to Al Mowerinski because she is his daughter. Because of that, he helped her in a special way. So what?

He did nothing underhanded or dishonest. He did nothing to hurt the Eagles, whose interests he is morally bound to promote. On the contrary, he did everything to help the Eagles. More important, he did everything to help baseball, a game whose interests he (and we, as baseball lovers) is morally bound to protect.

Linda Sunshine is special to people, but she is not special to baseballs. A hard-hit grounder, a whistling line drive, a spiraling pop-up, a pebble in the path of a skimming grounder, a hole in the infield dirt – all of these are totally impersonal things. The baseball, an inanimate object, doesn't single out players and treat them as special. The baseball is impervious to human emotions and aspirations. If baseballs can be said to regard humans in any way (they can't), then they treat Sunshine as totally unspecial – just as they treat the other eight players on the field. And in this environment of baseballs, bats, and gloves, Sunshine stands out. When treated as not special, she has proved her point: she can play baseball with the best of them, and there is no doubt whatsoever that she belongs on the Chicago Eagles.

When treated as not special, Sunshine proves she is special: surpassing what is usual or common, distinct of a kind. She is a rookie on a rookie-of-the-year pace, on a team that is on a pennant-this-year pace. She had better realize this damned quick, because the Eagles need her. Now. She had better stop acting . . . special . . . and get her glove in hand and her feet on the field. Now.

She felt as if she couldn't breathe. Her hand went to her chest and felt a shallow rise and fall. She opened her mouth and inhaled. That resulted only in a coughing fit. When it subsided, she turned from the screen door and walked through the kitchen and out the back door, taking the newssheet that had Neal's article on it with her.

She sat out there, under her favorite tree, until well past dark. Finally, she returned to the house. Everything was quiet and dark. Linda locked the back door, checked the front door, and walked into the kitchen, where the stove light gave off a small yellow glow. She was famished. Opening the refrigerator, she began to take out stacks of food: cold chicken, a few barbecued ribs, two hard-boiled eggs, cottage cheese, pizza. What else? Garlic bread. An orange. And an apple. She heated the garlic bread and ribs and pizza. While she waited for them, she ate the chicken, eggs, cottage cheese, orange, and apple. She felt as if she hadn't eaten in weeks. She washed the dishes and went to bed, setting the alarm for five o'clock.

On the plane back to Chicago, Linda accepted the tray of airline food and ate the scrambled eggs absentmindedly, thinking fleetingly that the food on Eagles' flights was in a different league from this. She thought about baseball. The hardest part of baseball was hitting. The biggest duel in baseball was the duel between the pitcher and the hitter. Between them, it was a struggle to dominate the plate. The batter wanted to stand close enough to the plate to cover its whole width with a swing of the bat. The pitcher wanted the batter to stand so far back that a swing would miss the outside corners. The pitchers believed that the corners of the plate belonged to them: the inside corners, the outside corners. If you stood too close, they'd pitch you tight, trying to shave your knuckles. But you had to stand up against it. Every day. Every day you had to fight to make the plate yours. By rights, the batter could stand anywhere in the batter's box. But the pitchers didn't concede those rights. No way. They were always trying to shave them away, inch by inch. What had Neal said? That she had swung at the wrong pitch, on the wrong plane, at the wrong time. It was worse than that. In the struggle to dominate the plate, she had acted as if she had no right to be at the plate.

Linda knew what she had to do. But it wouldn't be easy. She found her car in the airport parking lot and drove back to her apartment. The closer she got, the more slowly she drove. She pulled the car into Lincoln Park, locked it, and began to walk. *You're avoiding it.*

After what must have been a ten-mile walk, she returned to her car, drove to her apartment, and parked. Maybe she needed groceries. She'd get some. *Avoiding it again. No. Just postponing the inevitable – because I don't know how the inevitable will end.*

Two bags of groceries filled her arms as she walked the two blocks back to her apartment. Another hot, hot day. Probably ninety-five degrees already.

"Hey! Hey, you! Linda Sunshine!"

Linda looked up and saw an old man carrying a cane and wearing an Eagles cap. He was dressed in a suit and tie, which made the baseball cap look incongruous on his head.

"Why aren't you playing baseball?" he demanded. "What's the matter with you?"

His question left her speechless. She was trying to formulate a reply and was conscious of the fact that she was making inarticulate sounds, when he continued.

"You have problems, but they're nothing compared to the problems the Eagles are having."

Raising his cane, he pounded the head of it against one of her grocery bags emphatically. "You get in there and play! Get in there and play!"

Just as Linda realized that the silvery head of his cane had poked a hole in her grocery bag and that its contents were spilling out, the old man turned and walked away, muttering. "Kids today don't know anything about baseball. Back in my day . . . ." She didn't hear anything more because oranges and Gouda cheese and onions were tumbling out of her bag, bouncing on the sidewalk, and rolling into the street. It would have helped if she'd had a glove to field them.

T. M. Curry now knew what a wild goose chase felt like. He had left Al's – what? two days ago? – promising he would see Linda and set things right. She wasn't at the stadium, so, he reasoned, she had to be home. He found her address and went to the building. There was no answer. He was about to give up when he remembered something: hadn't he heard that she and Vanderlin lived in the same building? Yes. And Vanderlin was in. That fact did T. M. Curry little good: all Vanderlin knew was that she had stormed out of his apartment.

Curry had gone back to Eagle Stadium and practically searched under the goddamn bleacher seats. Finally, the day gone and the evening shot to hell along with it, Curry accepted Zack's invitation to accompany the team to Atlanta. Curry had accepted because – well, because he sensed Zack needed to talk things over with somebody; and because he, Curry, needed to sense what was happening to the Eagles; and because, hoping against hope, he thought that Sunshine might show up on the team bus. Or plane. Or maybe even get to Atlanta on her own somehow. There was a snowball's chance in hell of it happening, but if it did, he had to be there to set things right.

What was happening to the Eagles was not good. They were . . . confused. Yes, that was the word: confused. They didn't know how to handle the situation. Curry called Al, told him he thought that Al should come down to Atlanta and talk to the team: explain . . . well, explain that while he was trying to work things out they had to keep playing heads-up ball. Al wasn't ready to do that, yet. Al said that Zack could handle it. Al was giving press conferences telling the newspapers, radios, and television that Linda Sunshine had not quit and that, even if she thought she had, he was not accepting her quitting. And then, when Curry had explained that he couldn't find her, Al had sighed and suggested that he try Freedom, Pennsylvania.

Shit. Why hadn't he thought of that, dummy that he was? So that evening, after spending hours talking to each of the players individually, telling them everything would be okay, Curry had caught a plane from Atlanta to Pittsburgh, arriving late in the evening and checking into a hotel.

Early the next morning he had, for the second time in his life, made the drive from Pittsburgh to Freedom. And when he had found the house and knocked on the door, the woman who answered listened to what he had to say and then said: "You just missed her. Her father's driving her to the airport. She's going back to Chicago. You can catch them if you hurry."

Well, he had hurried, but he hadn't caught them. He had, however, caught the next flight to Chicago, grabbed a cab at O'Hare, and paid the driver extra to take him on the double to her apartment.

All the way there he thought baseball. You had to bring the bat around very fast on a high inside pitch. Get that fat part of the bat, the sweet spot, on the ball. Give it all you had, turn it around. Every baseball player knew that. But every hitter had to tell himself, over and over, the fundamentals of hitting. Hitting was something you could never think about while you were swinging, but something you had to think about for a split second when that ball left the pitcher's hand. You had to bring the bat around very fast on a high inside pitch to get the fat part of the bat on the ball. Had to.

He thought about the Eagles. Curry wanted them to win the pennant as much as he wanted anything. What a team! Zowski, he had the power. He was like Al had been. Maybe not as good, just a little slower than Al. Laughing. There wasn't a player like Laughing anywhere in the world. Indians always did make good athletes. Crowder – just a rookie, but great potential. And then there was Sunshine. Another rookie. But a rookie stuck on base. He would get her over. He would help the Eagles fly again, just like in the old days.

Reaching her building, Curry threw a handful of money at the cab driver, ordered him to wait, and took an elevator to the eighth floor. Stepping out of the elevator, he stopped, straightened his collar and tie, and walked toward her apartment. And, in so doing, he walked past the second elevator, whose doors were just now closing and in which he saw – he swore he saw – Linda Sunshine.

"Hey!" shouted Curry, stunned. "Hey!" He ran forward, ready to pitch himself head-first between the closing doors. But the doors had a head start on Timothy Michael Curry, and he had to stand there and watch her disappear.

No. He looked up at the elevator floor indicator. She was going up. Up. To twelve. Okay. Curry leaned on the elevator button for half an inning, it seemed, until the same elevator that had taken her up came down for him. He punched twelve, smoothed his hair with a hand, straightened his tie, adjusted his collar, and shrugged his shoulders, settling his sport coat around himself authoritatively. When he knocked on the door to Vanderlin's apartment, Curry was as ready as he'd ever be.

As soon as he stepped into the apartment, past a surprised Vanderlin, Curry saw that, while he may have been ready,

Sunshine wasn't. She was walking back and forth across the living room floor as if she were looking for ruts and pebbles on the infield dirt. Then she stopped and stood by the wall and simply stared at him.

"Hello, Linda. How are you?" What a dumb thing to ask.

"I don't know," she replied. "How are you?"

Curry looked around. "Mind if I sit down, Neal?"

Neal gestured toward the couch and chairs. "Can I get you something, Curry?"

"Yeah. Yeah, thanks. A scotch. No water."

As Neal stepped over to the small kitchen to pour a drink, Curry settled into what appeared to be the most comfortable chair in the room. There she was, on base. Now he had to bring her home. "Tell you the truth, Linda, I'm not very well. This stuff that was in the paper. It's a bad business. Bad for everybody. Thanks," he said as Neal handed him the scotch. He needed it.

Neal sat down on the couch and looked at him, probably wondering what he was doing here. Linda continued to stand against the wall, separate.

"I've been to see your . . . ." Here he coughed, swallowed more scotch, and finished, "I've been to see Al."

She just stared at him, not saying a thing.

Neal stared at him, then at Linda, then back at him. Probably wondering what to say in his next column, thought Curry.

He swallowed more scotch. "He's taking it pretty bad. Your quitting, I mean. The rest . . . well, that can't be helped, I guess, and he can get over it. You'll get over it, too," he explained, looking at her. "Someday, not now, I'd like to tell you about Mandy and Al. And me. Just reminiscing, sort of.

Maybe later you'll want to hear it. Not now, though." Still she said nothing.

Curry took another swallow of the ample drink and aimed his next remark at Neal. "I think that eventually Al will come around to see that it's the best thing. Linda's quitting, I mean."

Neal blinked. "What?"

"I think Al will come to see it's best that Linda quit."

"What do you mean?" demanded Neal angrily. "We don't need this, Curry! It's the worst thing that could happen, her quitting!" He jumped up and glared down at Curry. "Goddamn it, Curry, don't you read what I write? You know where I stand on this – you have a hell of a nerve, coming here and . . . and. . . damn it, Curry, you're *wrong*. Al would *never* agree with you!"

Curry slowly shook his head from side to side. "No. No, it's not the worst thing. I think it's the best. Baseball is no place for women. You'll recall," he said to Linda, "I've felt that way all along. I never told you – when I scouted you – because I was sure you knew. I never did agree with Al. I tried to reason with him then. I tried to reason with him now, but he still doesn't see it. He will, though; he'll come to see it the right way." Shaking his head again, he added, "Women just aren't cut out for the majors."

"That's not true," she replied in a surprisingly calm voice. "I play as well as anybody else on the team. I contribute as much. I'm needed as much."

Neal turned to stare at her for a moment, then turned again toward Curry.

"No," argued Timothy Michael Curry, shaking his head. "No. Laughing has a higher average than you. So do Abilene and Griffen. And–"

"Who else?" she demanded. "Nobody else."

"Crowder's catching up. He's just ten points behind you."

"He's been ten points behind all year." She waved her hand against the air, brushing the remark away. "That's all irrelevant anyway. More than twenty players have lower batting averages than me – *they're* good for baseball, but I'm not, huh?"

Neal's head was twisting back and forth, from Curry to Linda, following the pitches.

"None of that will count in the record books," answered Curry, waving away *her* remarks with *his* hand. "I don't want to be an I-told-you-so. No. My point in coming here is to tell you that I think you're making the right decision. You should have made it long ago, but that's not your fault. Everybody's a rookie once."

Out of the corner of his eye, Curry saw the quizzical expression on Neal's face. He avoided looking at Vanderlin. "It would have been better if you'd never signed, of course. But once you signed, it would have been better if you'd quit at the beginning of the season. Still, as it is, you almost made it through one whole season. That's really something. I'll tell you, like I told Al, you've got nothing to be ashamed of. You've held out a hell of a long time – longer than can be expected of a woman trying to do a man's job." Curry held his empty glass up to the light, then up to Neal, and raised his eyebrows.

Neal took the glass and walked backward into the kitchen to pour more scotch, his eyes on Curry.

Accepting the glass with a nod, Curry took a swallow and continued. "There are some people who say you're making the wrong decision. Don't listen to them. Al made a mistake. He should never have hired a woman for baseball. It's his fault, really, not yours."

Curry watched Linda move away from the wall, come up to the couch, and sit down beside Neal, a tight smile on her lips. "You never did want me in baseball, did you?"

"That's right." Curry nodded. "I was against it. Al thinks women can play baseball as well as men. Al has always thought that. Al Mowerinski is wrong. He thinks that you'll change your mind about quitting. He thinks the team needs you. I say you're doing the right thing. Especially now, before the Series. We can bring somebody up from the minors and take the pennant." Curry paused, looking into his scotch, trying to see what she was thinking.

"Nothing I've done all season has made you change your mind, has it?" she asked him.

"Nothing," he answered emphatically. "My mind can't be changed. My mind looks at things the way they are. I see what is. Women were not meant to play baseball."

"You've said that already," Linda told him. "You don't have to keep repeating yourself."

"Sorry. I just want you to know how I feel. I feel it's important to do the best thing for baseball."

Linda stood up and walked to the window. She turned around, her back to the waters of Lake Michigan. "You remind me of Griffen and Knuff," she told him.

He was aware that she was watching him, waiting for a response. But T. M. Curry didn't know how to respond to that remark. He stared into his scotch, looking for an answer.

"I'm glad you came," she said, taking a deep breath. "I've decided that I can't quit. I was wrong to quit on . . . Al . . . like that. Wrong to quit the Eagles."

Curry saw her steal a look at Neal, then continue. "I'm going to call Al and tell him I'll keep playing. If he still wants me to."

"What?!" shouted T. M. Curry loudly. "You can't *do* that! You're wrong, I tell you, wrong!"

Coughing violently, Neal got up, walked into the kitchen, and drank some water. Curry didn't want to look directly at Linda, so he watched Neal who, on his way back from the kitchen, grabbed the scotch bottle, walked over to Curry, and poured the glass full. Then he set the bottle on the glass-topped table beside Curry and sat down again.

"My mind's made up," said Linda. "You can't change it. I want to play baseball. I'm going to play baseball."

Curry sighed and sipped the warming scotch, his third glass since he had entered the apartment. But this was the only one of the three that he really tasted. When he looked up, Linda had turned her back to him. She stood facing the wall, looking at a picture, her hands behind her back. Neal sat hunkered down in the couch, biting his lip.

"This didn't turn out like I expected," said Timothy Michael Curry, slowly shaking his head from side to side, much like an Irish leprechaun. "'Tis a sad state of affairs when a man achieves the opposite of what he intends. Sad, indeed. Sure there's no changing your mind?" He cast a quick glance at Linda.

"None whatsoever," she told the wall.

"Well, then," he said, getting up out of his chair, perhaps not as steadily as he had gotten into it, "it seems I'd better go. I'll have to prepare meself to face Big Al. He'll be telling me that he was right all along. Aye, it's hard to take. Hard to take." He walked toward the door, stumbling once on the rug.

Neal, following him, opened the door and stepped into the hall. "Curry," he said softly, putting an arm around his shoulder, walking him toward the elevator, "someday I'm going to write a column on you. I hope I can make it what you deserve."

Timothy Michael Curry raised an eyebrow at Neal. "Aye? And I imagine this article'll be saying I stood in the way of Baseball Future, as you call it?"

Neal shook his head, laughing. "Curry, you've got all the blarney of Ireland in you."

"Sure 'n' I don't know what you mean," replied Timothy Michael Curry as he stepped into the elevator and disappeared behind its closing doors.

Linda splashed her face with cold water and, cupping the running water into her hand, bent, drank, and rinsed her mouth. She heard Neal return. He came to the open bathroom door, leaned against the doorjamb, and studied her. She vigorously dried her face with a towel, then combed her hair with her fingers and, finally, looked at Neal.

"I'm glad you're going to play," he said.

She gave him a small smile, walked past him into the living room, turned, and asked, "Have you ever heard such blarney in your life?"

"Uh, no."

"Don't go standing there thinking that he fooled me, Neal, because he didn't."

"It was a great story," said Neal with a grin.

"I wouldn't have missed it for the world. That's why . . . uh, that's why I let him go on. But . . . I came here to tell you that I wanted to play. I was going to tell you, only Curry came in right after me. I wanted to tell you first."

Neal walked a few steps toward her. "I'm glad."

"I should never have quit, Neal."

"No. But you got a pitch that knocked you off your feet. Into the backstop."

She shook her head. "When you get a bad pitch – even a pitch that knocks you off your feet and into the backstop – you get up and take the base you earned."

"I'm only trying to say that I understand how you felt." He stepped closer.

Linda looked up at him.

"Linda. Did you read my column?"

"Yes," she said in surprise. "Of course. That's why I came."

Neal wrapped his arms around her and mumbled into her hair. "I thought you might never speak to me again."

She hugged him tightly. "I love you, Neal."

They stood there for what seemed a long time. Then Neal looked at her and asked, "Have you told Al?"

She shook her head. "No. I want to see him. Will you come with me?"

"Sure. But we'd better get a move on if you're going to catch a plane to Atlanta for tonight's game."

Linda smiled at Neal, took his hand, and walked toward the door. "Let's go."

Out on the sidewalk, Timothy Michael Curry walked with a jaunty step toward the waiting cab. Opening the door, he dropped into the seat and, with a flourish of his hand, gave Al's address to the driver.

"Yes, sir," replied the cabbie.

If Al wasn't at his apartment, Curry would take the cab to

Eagle Stadium. If Al wasn't there, Curry and the cabbie would comb the city until they found him. Then Curry would tell Al that he brought the runner home. And then they'd fly down to Atlanta to watch the Eagles step back into first place. And then ... then ....

"Cabbie," asked Timothy Michael Curry, "how would you like to be my personal cabbie for the World Series?"

Barbara Gregorich's works include the novel *She's on First as* well as the nonfiction work, *Women at Play: The Story of Women in Baseball,* which won the SABR-Macmillan Award for Best Baseball Research of the Year. Her works for children include *Waltur Buys a Pig in a Poke* (chosen as a Cooperative Children's Book Center Choice) and *Waltur Paints Himself into a Corner.*

Gregorich studied at Kent State University, the University of Wisconsin, and Harvard. Before becoming a writer, she worked as an English instructor, a typesetter and a letter carrier. She lives in Chicago with her husband, Phil Passen. Her web site is www.barbaragregorich.com